ELVEN
WINTER

ALSO BY BERNHARD HENNEN

The Elven

ELVEN WINTER

THE SAGA OF THE ELVEN

BERNHARD HENNEN

translated by Edwin Miles

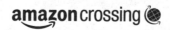

amazoncrossing

Previously published as *Elfenwinter: Elfen 2* by Heyne Verlag in Germany in 2014. Translated from German by Edwin Miles. First published in English by AmazonCrossing in 2018.

Published by AmazonCrossing, Seattle

www.apub.com

Amazon, the Amazon logo, and AmazonCrossing are trademarks of Amazon.com, Inc., or its affiliates.

ISBN-13: 9781503949119
ISBN-10: 1503949117

Cover design by Mike Heath | Magnus Creative

Printed in the United States of America

FOR MENEKSE AND MELIKE,
MY HOME

"Where are we going?"

"Always home."

—*Novalis*

CONTENTS

THE FESTIVAL OF LIGHT

T hey will try to kill the queen."

The tall, young elf woman looked at Ollowain in disbelief. She seemed to think his words were a poor joke. A smile played on her lips but vanished again when he made no sign of returning it.

Ollowain knew well how monstrous his declaration must have sounded. Among the people, Emerelle was the ruler, beloved by all. She was the personification of all that was good, the devoted queen of the Albenkin. Yet there had already been two attempts on her life. "Find a place to hide, somewhere you can observe the crow's nests of the ships around the queen's liburna. The moment you see anything suspicious, shoot! The slightest hesitation could mean Emerelle's death."

The woman stepped to the edge of the terrace and looked down over the city on the harbor. Vahan Calyd lay on a wide, rocky bay at the end of a tongue of land. It was the largest city on the Woodmer, although few of the Albenkin actually lived there. The palace towers, rising proudly above the simple houses, were rarely occupied. Once every twenty-eight years, the princes of Albenmark gathered in Vahan Calyd to celebrate the Festival of Light together. Then, for a few weeks, the city roused itself from its perpetual sleep. Every even halfway important clan maintained at least one house in the town, although most of the time, it stood empty. And while the princes of the Albenkin vied to outdo each other with the splendor of their palace towers, it counted for little more than vain trumpery and mattered only for a few short weeks every twenty-eight years. The rest of the time, the spacious streets were the domain of the stalking fiddler crabs that strayed into Vahan Calyd from the nearby mangrove marshes. The crabs far outnumbered the servants and the holdes who tended Vahan Calyd—and led an even more leisurely life. Then there were the hummingbirds, terns, and troll-finger spiders that built their nests beneath the eaves of the palaces and lived virtually unmolested for generations, until once again the Festival of Light approached. Then thousands of visitors came to the harborside town and filled its streets, and the fiddler crabs were boiled in enormous copper kettles and haggled for on every street corner. Vahan Calyd spilled over with life when, as today, the night of nights grew near and the most imposing ships of Albenmark assembled in the harbor. It was a festival of vanity, a festival at which the princes put their power and wealth on display for one another.

Silwyna turned back to Ollowain. She wore her hair combed back and woven into a long braid, which made her angular face look even more strict. The huntress was esteemed as one of the best archers in all of Albenmark, but what mattered more to the swordmaster was that she was discreet, and even more importantly, he knew that if she were on his side, then she would serve no other master that night. At least, that is what he hoped. Silwyna was one of the Maurawan. Her roots lay with the elvenfolk who lived far in the north, in the inhospitable forests of the Slanga Mountains. The Maurawan elves were seen as unpredictable and sly, and most of them made no secret of their contempt for Emerelle and the pomp and ceremony of her royal court.

"What you are asking me to do is impossible," said Silwyna calmly, and her eyes scanned the wide harbor once again. More than 150 large ships lay at anchor at the quays. A veritable forest of masts jutted skyward above the waters, and the curious were already clambering up the rigging in search of the best viewpoint for the great festival.

"Imagine for a moment that *you* wanted to kill Emerelle just before she received the tribute from the Albenkin princes on the *Moonshadow*'s quarterdeck. How would you go about it?" Ollowain asked.

Silwyna looked around. The sun was just dipping beneath the horizon, and the masts cast long shadows landward. Already the first lights were being lit. The ships had been decorated with garlands of flowers, and more and more of the Albenkin jostled on the decks of the ships and around the harbor. Soon it would be all but impossible to move down there.

Ollowain was running out of time. He had to get down to Magnolia Court, where the queen's entourage was gathering. Perhaps he could still convince Emerelle not to step out on the *Moonshadow*'s decks and become a walking target.

"I would be there." The archer pointed to a turquoise ship with silver fittings on its hull and superstructure. "The *Breath of the Sea*. One would have a good view of Emerelle's grand liburna from there. The ship is far enough away from the *Moonshadow* to avoid too much scrutiny, and the distance between them is enough to give it a good head start when the chase begins."

Ollowain leaned slightly and scrutinized the young elf woman. *She is a Maurawan,* he warned himself. Tracking down prey was her life. A shudder went through him. Even in his dreams, he would never have thought of his queen as *prey*. He straightened up. "Why the *Breath of the Sea*? I've been thinking about the ships down there for the last five hours. What you just said could apply to at least three others."

"How much do you know?"

Ollowain avoided her eye. "Very little." And of the little he knew, he could tell her almost nothing.

"If someone wants to kill the queen with an arrow, then it is because the assassin will want to escape with their life. Or am I mistaken?"

"I hope you are not," Ollowain replied flatly. Everything that had happened so far suggested that Silwyna was right.

"One could flee easily from the *Breath of the Sea*." She pointed toward the galleass, its light turquoise transforming to a pale gray in the twilight. "The other ships are at a distance. They are not anchored close."

"That is to allow the galleass to get its oars down. It needs more room to maneuver," Ollowain explained. Secretly he was annoyed at himself for not thinking of it. He suspected where Silwyna's thought was going.

"It could be towed to open waters as easily as any of the sailing ships. If I wanted to kill the queen, I would position myself in the foremast crow's nest. After the shot, it would be a simple matter to flee across the yard and jump into the harbor. I'd call a dolphin to take me out of the harbor to the mangroves or to a boat waiting out on the open sea."

Ollowain could feel the individual droplets of sweat trickling down his forehead. He looked intently at Silwyna. Had he been mistaken, choosing her? She could think like a murderer only too well. Was that only because she was a huntress? She had prepared herself! To the fleeting glance, she seemed to be dressed for the festival, but he saw more in her than just a harmless guest. She was ready to melt away into the shadows of the night. To lie in wait and to kill. Silwyna was dressed in a dark leather doublet embossed with an elaborate design of flowers. Beneath that she wore a black silk shirt and loose-fitting silk trousers. Her face was painted with bandag, the red-brown juice of the dinko bush. Her pale skin all but disappeared beneath the inky pattern of spirals and stylized wolf heads. Even the leather bracer she wore on her left forearm looked at first like no more than adornment. It was certainly true that dressed as she was for the festival, she made a grim impression, but that would surprise no one, because offending etiquette was just what one would expect of a Maurawan. They were the untamed, raised in the forests. It was rumored that they lived with animals. Ollowain considered that to be just talk, but he knew, too, that many thought the tales to be true.

She suspected something like this, the swordmaster placated himself. *After all, it was* you *who asked her to come with her bow.* On the other hand, on a night like this, it was more usual to meet on a dance floor and not on a concealed terrace high in the queen's palace. At least, not when one was responsible for the security of the queen of Albenmark. Silwyna had suspected that she was being invited to a hunt. And she had dressed accordingly.

"I will go and take a look at the *Breath of the Sea*," she said softly.

Ollowain pursed his lips in exasperation. So naive! "That is the prince of Arkadien's flagship. They won't let you on board. Besides, I don't think the assassin is there."

"I was not planning to ask for permission to board," she replied confidently.

Below, at the harbor, the first lights were being set adrift: hand-sized cork rafts on which oil lamps burned.

Silwyna peered at him; it felt to Ollowain as if she were holding him captive with her eyes. Her irises were a cold light blue ringed by a thin black border. *Wolf's eyes,* he thought with a shiver.

"Tell me what you know! Why would the killer not be aboard the *Breath of the Sea*?" she asked sharply.

"I will not discuss it. Go and hunt for me, and in return I will see to it that you travel to the human world through Atta Aikhjarto's Albenstar."

Silwyna smiled ambiguously. "Why do I always make the mistake of getting involved with you pampered courtiers? I know I am not supposed to follow the human into his world. He will disappoint me. I think I must have fallen from the mother tree as a child and smashed my head on its roots. If the Alben favor me, we will meet one day in a forest, Ollowain, and I promise you that you will be more courteous to me then." She reached for her bow, looked up a final time. "By the way, you have a little sweat on your brow."

"Do I?" Ollowain took a linen handkerchief from behind his belt and dabbed at his eyebrows. "Thank you," he answered tonelessly.

Silwyna did not give him another glance. She swung herself over the railing of the terrace and surefootedly found the narrow kobold steps, half-hidden by creepers, that led down the outer facade of the palace. She trotted easily down the steep stairway. Ollowain could still see her when she climbed away over the thick roots of a mango tree, but then she vanished in the play of light and shadow below.

The swordmaster tucked his sweaty handkerchief back into his belt. He looked down at himself critically and tugged his silk doublet straight—he did not want the steel breastplate concealed beneath the thin fabric to be too obvious. Death had an appointment with Emerelle that night. But he would be there to step between them!

Ollowain's gaze turned to the towers, enveloped now in eerie lights. He did not like Vahan Calyd. It was said that the Alben had created the first of the Albenkin in that enchanted place. There in the south where the forest and the sea merged into one another and formed an enormous mangrove swamp rather than a coastline, there where borders no longer counted, any-thing seemed possible . . . even the seasons of the year had been suspended. All there was in Vahan Calyd was heat and humidity. Nothing ever dried out properly. And the shifting phases of the moon were only differentiated by more or less rain.

Ollowain wiped one hand over his forehead nervously. Most elves learned as children how to arm themselves against heat or cold with a word of power. They could wear a thin silk shirt in the bitter cold of the Snaiwamark without freezing or prance around in magnificent furs there in Vahan Calyd at the Festival of Light without losing so much as a drop of sweat. Ollowain had never mastered that magic. And he perspired—not like the centaurs, whose naked torsos gleamed constantly with sweat in the jungle heat, as if they had oiled their muscles—but occasionally a droplet of perspiration would appear on the swordmaster's forehead, or he might feel his silk shirt clinging to his damp skin. To sweat was unseemly, and it was unbecoming of the commander of the queen's bodyguard.

Soon, at the ceremony, he would be standing at Emerelle's side. Thousands of eyes would be on him. And he knew that there would be whispering. He hated appearing imperfect in any way. Of the races of Albenkin, the elves were the last created and the most perfect of all. They were flawless, and something as apparently insignificant as sweat on one's brows was, for an elf, a stigma, as a face half-consumed by pox scars would be for a kobold.

It had been indelicate of Silwyna to mention the sweat on his brow so directly. But what else would you expect from a Maurawan? Ollowain wished he could have taken any elf but her into his service—would she betray him as she had once betrayed his foster son, Alfadas?

The swordmaster pulled himself together. It was foolish to waste his time in fruitless brooding. He straightened his sword belt and started down the broad marble staircase that led to the inner courtyard. The queen's palace was a towering accumulation of intertwined spires. More than a dozen courtyards and terraces ringed the spires like leaves around a stalk. Most of the palace had been built from the blue-white marble mined in the Iolid Mountains. Over the centuries, the roots of lush trees had infiltrated deep into the stonework. They had taken over the towering palace as if it were no more than an artificial rock. Snake fern grew up the walls, and everywhere one looked, delicate orchids flourished between forking roots or grew on sheltered sills where a little humus had collected.

Emerelle visited Vahan Calyd only once every twenty-eight years. The Festival of Light was celebrated whenever the day of first creation fell on a new-moon night. All the princes of Albenmark celebrated it together. It had once been the custom to elect the king of Albenmark on the night, but Emerelle had now ruled for hundreds of years, and it had not occurred to anyone to question her claim to the throne. To stand for election against Emerelle was hopeless. She was certainly not beloved by everyone, but the princes of Albenkin were so at odds with each other that none could hope to win a majority against Emerelle. But if something were to befall the queen . . . then a new ruler would have to be agreed upon.

For anyone who coveted the throne, the Festival of Light was the best opportunity for an attempt on Emerelle's life. All the princes of Albenmark were already gathered in Vahan Calyd, and they could immediately hold a royal election should anything happen to the queen. An attempt at any other time would make little sense, as it would take more than a year to call the princes together, which would leave plenty of time to weave intrigues and very likely engage in an open power struggle. But if the murder happened during the festival, everyone would be caught unawares—everyone but the one who planned the queen's death. If a prince were to step forward decisively and confidently in the aftermath, he could win the crown in a single night.

Who would voluntarily go after the burden of power? It was a riddle to Ollowain. At court, there were rumors of a secret feud between the queen and Shahondin, the prince of Arkadien, and whisperings that his father's death had been no accident. The queen's spies had reported that the prince's family was pointing the finger at Farodin, the banished. They believed that he had carried out the assassination on the queen's orders. That was absurd, and anyone who knew Farodin could only laugh at such claims. Still, Ollowain had his own spies keeping a sharp eye on the *Breath of the Sea*, Shahondin's flagship.

Were the attacks on Emerelle not about the throne at all? Were they no more than revenge? From that perspective, it made good sense to bring the blood feud to an end during the festival—suspicion would naturally fall on whoever made a subsequent play for power.

Ollowain strode quickly along a bricked tunnel. Blue light seeped from the stones in the ceiling. The fine hairs on the warrior's neck stood on end. The air prickled with magical power.

Thousands of spells were being cast at that moment. Every race and every clan among the Albenkin that had inherited the power was working its magic in that hour. It was a centuries-old competition among the sorcerers, all trying to outdo each other this night. Ollowain thought with horror of the countless opportunities that a skilled sorcerer who was so inclined would have to attack the queen. Three hundred years earlier, his own uncle had died in agony because a spurned lover had snapped her fingers and conjured a swarm of rats in his belly. One word of power was enough to have Emerelle throttled by her own robes or to transform the wine in her chalice into acid. Ollowain had tried many times to persuade Emerelle to confide in a sorceress. The queen needed someone close to her who had no other task than to protect her from magical attacks. But in that particular regard, the queen had proven to be frighteningly obdurate. True, she herself was the preeminent enchantress in Albenmark, and there was probably no one who could match her power. For that reason, she insisted on protecting herself. But at the festival, Emerelle would be distracted by a thousand other things, and a single spell could kill her faster than any arrow.

That very day, Ollowain had argued with Emerelle about her need for extra protection. But the queen had calmly pointed out that none of the failed assassinations had involved magic. Three days earlier, they had found a poisoned thorn embedded in the upholstery of Emerelle's throne. The poison had killed a kobold that had been dusting the royal seat. Then came the block of marble that had crashed into Magnolia Court directly beside Emerelle. An inspection had shown that there was no degradation of the mortar holding the stone in place, but rather a section of the terrace wall had been loosened with a crowbar. Someone had been lurking up there, waiting for the queen to cross the yard.

Ollowain would have given his left hand to know what the murderer was planning next. So far, the assassin had kept his distance from the queen, leading Ollowain to suspect that the next attempt would be with bow and arrow. Emerelle would be departing again in just a few days. Time for the killer was running short. How fanatical was he? If he were prepared to trade his own life for the queen's, he would be virtually impossible to stop—during the festival, hundreds of guests would be close to Emerelle. Or would he perhaps turn to magic after all? Were the two failed attempts a deliberate part of some insidious plan? Was the assassin really a sorcerer?

Ollowain recalled his own mother. At a feast in the Skyhall of Phylangan, she had suddenly smashed the glass in her hand, a flowered goblet fashioned from red quartz. Ollowain, just seven years old, had been sitting opposite her. He still remembered the blood on his mother's white dress and the look in her beautiful green eyes. Full of fear. And then she had plunged the long stem of the crystal glass through her eye and deep into her skull. It could never be ascertained whether she had been caught in the power of a curse or if some alien will had forced her to commit that bloody act. Some said she killed herself in that horrible way to punish Landoran, Ollowain's coldhearted father, but Ollowain had never believed that. She would never have left him behind, alone. Never! She had been murdered.

The swordmaster looked up. He heard the clopping of hooves at the end of the long tunnel, and the light from flaming torches cast dancing shadows on the entrance walls. Centaurs. So the honor guard had decided to appear after all. It puzzled Ollowain that of all her subjects, Emerelle had chosen centaurs to accompany her from the palace to the grand liburna. It seemed to him some-times that the queen had a secret soft spot for creatures that so literally shat all over court etiquette. In the same way, she had liked that rough-hewn human who had come to Albenmark through the Shalyn Falah. Mandred. Mandred the Unbowed, as the courtiers mocked him, referring to how he had insulted the queen at their first meeting by not doing her the proper honor of bowing before her. More than thirty years had passed since that time, but the memories of the Fjordlander were still strong. Where had he gone when he had conspired with his two elven friends against the queen? All trace of the three was lost in the labyrinthine mesh of the Albenpaths.

Ollowain stepped out of the tunnel and looked down on the broad expanse of Magnolia Court. It was the heart of the palace and ruled over by Matha Murganleuk, a magnolia tree so old that its trunk had grown to be as mighty as a stone tower. Emerelle's chambers were perched high among its branches. It was said that Matha Murganleuk gave up some of her own wood so that the queen had a place in which to retreat and spend solitary hours. No one was allowed to follow Emerelle there, not even her maids or kobold servants. It was the only place in Vahan Calyd where the queen could be alone.

She was waiting in the white pavilion. Embedded in the roots of the huge tree, the pavilion was reminiscent of an enormous, half-open magnolia flower. Kobolds and riverbank sprites surrounded the queen. A goat-legged faun handed her a coiled drinking horn, and Emerelle sipped only a little from the heavy gold vessel. Then she said something to the faun, and the bearded fel-low burst out laughing. The centaurs, who had gathered some distance away around a large wine amphora, looked up curiously.

Ollowain let out a silent curse. He was late! They were all waiting for him. It was not good to keep centaurs waiting. They had the uncanny ability to find wine wherever they happened to be. The swordmaster sometimes suspected that remaining sober for more than a day was considered a fault among the manhorses, and he momentarily and with horror envisaged Emerelle being escorted to the grand liburna by a horde of roaring, drunken centaurs. He should not have let himself be delayed!

He took the last three steps up in a single bound and almost trod in a fresh pile of horse dung half-concealed among the roots . . . and that was just another reason why those barbarians were not suited to the royal court!

On the other hand, they were unconditionally loyal. No assassin would ever be among them. When they were involved in a feud, there was nothing secret about it at all. In their eyes, a battle that one could not talk about over a round of drinks wasn't worth the effort.

When Ollowain reached the pavilion, he dropped to one knee before his queen. "I beg forgiveness for having kept you waiting, my queen."

Emerelle smiled. "I know you, Ollowain, and I suspect it was your duties that kept you. Now rise. This is not a day at court. There is no reason to kneel for me any longer."

Was she expecting him to report what had held him up? Or did she already know? Emerelle was able to slice through the veils of the future, and she repeatedly surprised those at court with her knowledge. Is that why she was so calm? Did she know that nothing was going to happen to her that night? Had she made her own preparations without informing even him?

"Let us stand here a moment, Ollowain, and enjoy the loveliness of the evening." She leaned against the pavilion railing and looked up into the branches of Matha Murganleuk. The crown of the magnolia spread across the broad courtyard like an enormous baldachin. The leaves whispered in a light breeze, and here and there, a flower sailed earthward in wide spirals.

The centuries had passed over Emerelle seemingly without effect. She was among the few still alive who had seen the Alben, and yet the queen appeared almost childlike. Emerelle was a delicate figure—Ollowain was more than a head taller. Dark-blond hair tumbled in waves to her bare milk-white shoulders. Tonight she was wearing the Dress of Eyes, shimmering red with a pattern of yellow circles and black points. One had to approach the queen very closely to realize what was so special about the dress—it was alive! Thousands of butterflies had settled onto a plain, green underrobe. With their wings spread, they covered the queen as if to hide her from overly curious looks. When they moved, waves seemed to undulate across the dress. And every wing was marked with a large yellow-black eye.

Without warning, Emerelle turned to him. The butterfly wings rustled softly. The queen held out the golden horn to Ollowain. "Drink, my guardian. You must be thirsty."

Was he sweating again? The queen would never mention his defect openly. But wasn't there a concealed barb in her words? He took the drinking horn.

Emerelle seemed enraptured. She gave him a melancholy smile, and her pale-brown eyes seemed to look right through him. The queen, in her mind, was clearly somewhere far away. The swordmaster took a good swig from the horn. It was cider, perfectly cooled. Fresh and sweet, from late-summer apples.

"Drink it all, down to the dregs," said Emerelle quietly. "This will be a long night." The queen looked up again into the crown of the magnolia tree.

She is saying good-bye, thought Ollowain uneasily. As if she were never going to see Matha Murganleuk again.

His eyes roamed over the walls, which were overgrown with creeping vines. White oriels jutted through the tapestry of plants like rocky outcrops, and lights burned in a few windows. Emerelle had traveled to Vahan Calyd with only a small entourage this year. Master Alvias had remained behind, as had Obilee and many others. Most of the palace there in Vahan Calyd stood empty—which was not unusual, for until the next festival, only a few servants would stay behind to keep the place in order. Too few to control the flourishing wilderness around the Woodmer. In a sense, the condition of the palace reflected Emerelle's rule. She rarely involved herself in the affairs of the elven clans, in the blood feuds of the centaurs or disreputable businesses of the fauns. She left them to their own devices, as long as they did not cross a certain boundary. But when that happened, Emerelle reacted severely. As she had when she banished Noroelle, who had been as close to the queen as a daughter.

Some observers liked to call the palace dilapidated. But for Ollowain, it had an irresistible attraction. The proliferation of plants was cut back only where it threatened the structure of the palace, and over the centuries, a wild beauty had evolved that no builder or gardener could have designed.

Emerelle sighed softly and turned to Ollowain again. With every movement she made, shimmering waves billowed across the Dress of Eyes. And then it settled again, and the large wing eyes seemed to stare at him. "It is time to go."

"I have had a small sailboat prepared, my queen. You do not have to attend the festival. It is a mistake to go there. It is all but impossible for me to keep you from harm in the crowd."

"You cannot run from your fate, Ollowain. It clings to your heels like a shadow. It will catch up with us no matter what we do." She waved to the centaurs, and the exuberant noise of their carousing fell silent. Apart from Orimedes, their leader, there were no warriors of note among them. Until now, Ollowain had considered the queen's choice of honor guard to be no more than a whim, but now he suspected what hidden intention lay behind it.

"You should tell me what you are expecting to happen this evening, my queen," he whispered. "I will be better able to protect you."

"I don't know what will happen. The veils of the future won't show me what they conceal. Something foreign is interfering with my magic, something that can disrupt the spell of the mirror. Its intervention is changing the future almost hourly. I do not know what is waiting for us in the harbor, swordmaster. But one thing is certain: the blood will start to flow tonight. The sword will decide Albenmark's future." Her pupils widened. She stared through him as if she were looking far into the distance, as if she could see the approaching catastrophe in front of her there and then.

The centaurs carried Emerelle's sedan to the pavilion. It had been finished only that day. Servants had decorated it with masses of flowers, and even now, at the start of the evening, dozens of hummingbirds swarmed around the blossoms. Ollowain scrutinized the strange chair doubtfully. A small boat had been used, one of the broad-beamed, flat-bottomed boats the fishermen used among the mangroves. As far as the swordmaster could see, the only change that had been made were a few holes carved in the hull of the boat, where the poles for carrying it had been pushed through. The queen, with her choice of sedan, wanted to express her solidarity with the inhabitants of Vahan Calyd.

Stretching a little, Emerelle stepped from the raised pavilion into the sedan, and Ollowain followed her. The queen braced herself against a crossbar that had been attached unobtrusively to the mast. Every movement she made was accompanied by the soft thrumming of the butterflies' wings. Sometimes, small swarms freed themselves from the dress and fluttered around the queen, never flying more than an arm's length away.

Six padded carrying poles had been pushed through the holes in the hull of the boat. On a command from Orimedes, the centaurs grasped the poles and hoisted the sedan onto their shoulders. Ollowain had to hold tightly to the mast to avoid being thrown off his feet by the sudden jerk. A pack of holdes appeared from beneath the thwarts of the boat. The small green-brown creatures did not even reach Ollowain's knee. They were distant cousins of the kobolds and lived among the mangroves of the Woodmer. Their heads appeared to be far too large for their small, wiry bodies, and each wore nothing but a leather loincloth and a colorful headband.

"Come on, you swamp lice! You're serving the queen!" scolded a gray-haired holde, his headband glimmering with gold thread. He was the only holde to carry a knife at his waist. His yellow eyes gleamed up at the sword-master. "May I offer his most splendid knightship something to drink?" he asked in an unctuous voice. The broad grin on his face bore little correspondence with his oily tone.

Ollowain dabbed the sweat from his forehead.

"Have I already introduced Gondoran, my boatmaster here at the palace?" Emerelle asked casually. "It was his idea to convert this little boat into a sedan."

"Very original," Ollowain replied curtly. "Perhaps it would be better after all to enter the harbor on horseback?"

Gondoran glared malevolently at Ollowain. At the same time, he seemed surprised, for a moment, at least. The suggestion of riding horses instead of using his clever sedan boat had probably ruffled him.

"No," said Emerelle quietly, but her tone of voice made it clear that she would not discuss that particular decision.

The leader of the holdes grinned triumphantly and ordered his men to lower the top of the mast so that the sedan could be carried through the long entrance tunnel and down to the quays.

"March!" the centaur prince commanded. He himself was positioned alongside the mast. Ollowain saw how the weight of the boat pressed into the centaur's shoulders. Orimedes turned his head to Ollowain. The centaur had a broad nose that had clearly been bashed several times. A white scar cut across his left eyebrow, and a poorly groomed blond beard framed his face. Around his chin, the hair was discolored by spilled wine. A wide sword belt fitted with gold stretched across the manhorse's bare chest, and Orimedes also wore a dagger strapped to his upper left arm. All the centaurs stank of wine, sweat, and horsehair.

The column moved off slowly. A troop of riders joined them from another courtyard, magnificently dressed young elves, their horses led by fauns holding the reins. Ollowain knew most of them only fleetingly. They were guests of the palace, and there had been no opportunity to leave them behind.

The tunnel resonated with the sound of hooves. The air was musty and thick and reeked of rotting plants and old stone. In some places, a tangle of fungus, glowing greenly, swelled from the walls. Small lizards sought refuge in the gaps between the stones as the column of riders moved past.

The calls of conch horns greeted them from every tower in the city when they finally exited the tunnel. The street was full of jubilant Albenkin, and a way between them only opened directly in front of the queen's sedan. Cloven-hooved fauns with wild beards carried kobold children—who would otherwise get lost among all the trampling feet—on their shoulders. At the end of the street, Ollowain even saw a frost giant, obviously suffering in the heat, fanning itself with a fan the size of a sail to keep cool. Between the ruined pillars of a crumbling tower stood three of the Oreaden, mountain nymphs who only rarely left the Iolids. Beautiful Apsaras danced on the waters of a large fountain as surely as if they were on parquet. They were slightly more voluptuous than elven women. They had painted their naked bodies with bandag; glyphs twisted like snakes on their skin. It was said that they wrote their most secret desires on their bodies and that they would be true to whoever was able to decipher the arcane script until the way into the moonlight separated the one taken from the one still searching.

A kobold band broke from the ranks of the onlookers. They had all decorated their caps with lotus flowers, which—considering the capriciousness of the small race—was almost the same as wearing a uniform. For a few lively bars, the trumpets, drums, rattles, and triangles followed the bandmaster's stipulations, until his beard suddenly began to twist and writhe and his baton got caught in it. While the bandmaster stumbled and cursed and the merry tune descended into a clanging chaos, Ollowain noticed two Lutins disappear between the legs of an enormous minotaur. The fox-headed kobold clan were notorious for their crude mischief and only ever used their extraordinary magical gifts to play pranks on others.

On the queen's sedan, the holdes were just hoisting the elven flag, a golden horse on a green ground. Ollowain stayed close to the queen. His eyes scanned the crowd restlessly, then swung up to the terraces of the palaces they were passing. In the little boat, they drifted high above the heads of the onlookers around them. It was a nightmare! The queen was a perfect target for the assassin, who was lurking somewhere out there.

Ollowain tried again to put himself into the killer's mind. How would he kill Emerelle if he wanted to? The murderer could hardly have known that Emerelle would appear in this strange sedan chair. Ollowain himself had found out about it just that afternoon. Only the holdes who had prepared the boat had been aware of the queen's intentions in advance. Was it conceivable that one of them had betrayed the secret?

Ollowain balled his fists in helpless fury. It was hopeless. The assassin would always be one step ahead of him. All he could do was react, whereas the killer had a thousand opportunities.

A swarm of tiny riverbank sprites descended from the sky. Hardly bigger than dragonflies, they buzzed around the queen and dusted her hair with perfumed pollen. Hundreds of butterflies ascended from the Dress of Eyes and rose into the air to dance with the sprites in colorful, shimmering circles overhead. Emerelle laughed and waved to the crowd all around.

Petals were thrown from the palace terraces as they passed. The air was filled with pleasant scents. Silk banners flapped and fluttered everywhere, and on the high towers, the elven sorcerers had begun to weave their spells. Crystals broke light into brilliant rainbows. Golden fountains shot into the sky and opened out into brightly colored blooms. Even the simpler houses, which had no sorcerer at their command, radiated a golden light—the people in them had lit hundreds of miniature oil lamps just to take part in this night of the lights.

The warm sound of reed flutes suddenly rang in Ollowain's ear. He caught a glance down an alley, where minotaurs were dancing. They had bound golden censers to their horns and cavorted ecstatically to the music of the flutes, trailing blue-white tendrils of smoke as they danced.

From the corner of his eyes, Ollowain saw something long speeding toward the queen. He pushed Emerelle aside. The flying object hit the breastplate concealed beneath his doublet with a clang. Shocked cries sounded.

The queen was back on her feet instantly and waved to the crowd. "You are too on edge, Ollowain," she whispered, and pointed to the branch, its bark stripped, that lay on the floor of the boat in front of him. Black runes had been burned into the pale wood. A woman's name?

Behind them, two holdes climbed the smooth mast and peered curiously over the queen's shoulder. One had its hair oiled and woven into gleaming braids. It grinned at the swordmaster cheekily and suddenly began to chant, "Oh, Ollowain, the knightly elf, hit by a stick, he pissed himself—"

Emerelle gestured harshly, and Ollowain's taunter fell silent. Then she looked out over the crowd, searching. Finally she pointed to a centaur woman with short-cropped black hair. The womanhorse was rearing and crying out wildly, trying to catch the queen's attention.

Emerelle bent down for the stick, brought it to her lips, and bestowed a kiss on the pale wood. Then she threw it toward the centaur woman in a long arc. "A talisman," she explained. "The centaurs believe that if their women carry a willow branch that I have touched, then they will conceive a son on their next night of love."

Ollowain barely heard the queen's words. A dull thud, almost inaudible over the noise of the festival, had made him turn. The holde that had just been mocking him had been impaled to the mast by an arrow. The shot still vibrated from the force with which it had slammed into the wood. Dark blood swelled from the breast of the dead holde and gathered at the belt that held its leather loincloth in place. The arrow that had killed the taunter was black, its feathers striped in dark gray and white.

Ollowain pulled Emerelle close to him. From the way the arrow had hit the mast, it must have been shot from an elevated position, from one of the ships. Bending down to retrieve the willow had probably saved the queen's life.

"Set us down!" Ollowain ordered the leader of the centaurs.

Orimedes looked up at him in surprise. "Here? In the middle of the crowd? Are you out of your mind?"

Emerelle was trying to twist free of her bodyguard's grasp. The butterflies on her dress had flown up to avoid being crushed between their bodies. They formed a thick cloud around the queen, making it harder for the hidden assassin to find his target. Only a few seconds had passed since the arrow had pierced the holde, but a skilled archer could put three arrows in the air before the first reached its mark.

As if in answer to Ollowain's thought, a second arrow slammed into the thwart directly beside him. The arrow had missed them by little more than a hand's breadth, probably thanks to the swarming butterflies. They fluttered around the queen now in their hundreds.

"My queen, you will die if you insist on staying on this boat," said Ollowain calmly. Now that he could finally do something, all his pent-up tension evaporated.

"Kiss her!" bellowed someone in the crowd, fundamentally misunderstanding Ollowain's actions.

The swordmaster pulled the queen with him to the rail of the boat. He grasped her by the hips and jumped down. Butterfly wings grazed his cheeks. He could hardly see a thing.

"See the mast!" he shouted to the centaur prince. "Someone is shooting at us!" Ollowain pulled Emerelle to safety beneath the hull of the boat. Cries rose all around them now—the first onlookers had probably noticed the dead holde.

"We have to keep what happens concealed." Emerelle freed herself from Ollowain's grip. "If panic breaks out now, hundreds might die in a stampede."

"You can't show yourself!" the swordmaster protested. "You have been lucky so far, my queen, but the next arrow could kill you. There's a killer out there; we cannot give him another chance. You have to return to the palace!"

"What makes you think that a *man* wants to kill me?"

"Whether man or woman is irrelevant right now. The only thing that matters is your safety, my queen! You have to get back to the palace!" Ollowain was all too aware of why he did not want to consider the possibility that a woman had shot at the queen. He should not have taken Silwyna into his confidence!

"Tell the elves behind us to dismount, and make sure the holdes get their dead compatriot from the mast," Ollowain shouted to the centaur prince.

Emerelle stepped out from beneath the boat.

The swordmaster was at her side in an instant. "My queen, please . . ." He saw the glitter of steel close to the queen. A blade! He pushed a young elf back and only then noticed that her polished belt buckle had fooled him. Emerelle placed one hand on his shoulder and pulled him back.

"Remember I was once a warrior myself," she said. "The archer will not be able to hit me among the Albenkin."

"And if there is a second assassin? How am I supposed to protect you from a blade here?"

Emerelle's response was lost in jubilant cries. A swarm of kobolds discovered the queen and pushed toward her. The butterflies from the Dress of Eyes fled, fluttering high in the air above the queen. Emerelle was quickly wedged among sweating bodies. A lamassu—a gigantic, winged oxman from distant Schurabad—ploughed through the crowd and did his best, with his thunderous voice drowning out the noise all around, to engage Emerelle in a philosophical discussion about the transience of all things.

Ollowain finally managed to post the young elves from her retinue in a circle around the queen. Without warning, the crowd gave ground. In that brief moment, a strange change came over the queen. She suddenly seemed as vulnerable as a child.

The clamor on all sides faded, and a kind of passage formed in front of them. Fishermen, merchants, and wise men stood in silent amazement. It was as if they were afraid of overcrowding the frail figure in their midst.

They could move more easily now. Again and again, the queen stopped and reached between the elves of her guard of honor to shake hands or exchange a few words. They crossed a park where sorcerers were making figures formed from flower petals dance through the air.

Ollowain had no time for the beauty of the sorcerers' work. He eyed the dense trees around the park, seeking out any hidden shooter. The way down to the harbor seemed agonizingly long. Emerelle, however, seemed unconcerned. She reveled in the acclaim and bubbled over with a charm that even the steer-headed minotaurs were unable to resist, although they were generally notorious for their cantankerous religiosity, which would tolerate no smile, let alone an outburst of cheering.

Unscathed, the queen reached the quay where the *Moonshadow* was berthed. Even Ollowain, who stood closer to Emerelle every day than practically any other in her inner circle, felt himself caught up in her aura. Was it a spell? Or was it the queen's true face, suddenly revealed? He was not able to say.

The watchmen aboard the grand liburna formed a guard of honor as their mistress came on board. On the main deck, the most important princes of Albenmark stood alongside a festively decorated table. No place was empty. Ollowain scrutinized the proud faces. Most of the princes were elves, representing the peoples of the sea and the plains, the distant islands and the expanses of ice of the Snaiwamark.

All the princes bowed to Emerelle as she stepped aboard the ship, even Shahondin of Arkadien. Some smiled ironically to rob the traditional gesture of some of its solemnity. But none dared challenge Emerelle openly by refusing to bow.

The butterflies had settled onto Emerelle's dress again. Her immersion in the crowds had taken nothing from her majestic appearance. With a measured step, she ascended to the quarterdeck, where all the guests could see her.

A young elf woman came to Ollowain's side. Yilvina. Ollowain had appointed her commander of the elven guards on the *Moonshadow*. "Is everything all right?" she asked quietly.

"No." The swordmaster scowled. "Does it look like it? What precautions have you taken for the queen's safety?"

"Seventy-two armed fighters are aboard. Crossbows in the crow's nests. I have my most reliable fighters on the quarterdeck, all equipped with scuta, as you ordered. And if the worst comes to the worst, three different escape routes have been prepared."

Ollowain relaxed a little. He had fought with Yilvina in many battles. Even during the massacre of Aniscans, when they had been surrounded and outnumbered by barbarians, she had kept a cool head. The swordmaster noted how the guards were posted and nodded his approval. The soldiers on the quarterdeck wore old-fashioned armor with breastplates of polished bronze. Magnificent feathered headdresses swayed atop silver helmets, and they carried large, oval, beautifully emblazoned shields. To an unsuspecting observer, they did not appear threatening at all, but more a part of the colorful backdrop to a feast that was as old as the Albenkin themselves. But in a heartbeat, those shields would form a wooden wall between the queen and any enemy.

Ollowain nodded sharply. "Good work, Yilvina. But send someone up to the foremast. I want the guard up there to keep an eye on the *Breath of the Sea*. There may be an archer hidden on one of her masts."

"I'll take care of it myself." Yilvina turned on her heel and hurried forward.

Emerelle had begun the ceremonial speech in which she declared her renunciation of the throne. She stood at the railing of the quarterdeck and looked down at the princes.

". . . the moon has now completed its long cycle, and the onus of responsibility is heavy on my shoulders." The queen was able to make the traditional clichés sound sincere. But Ollowain knew very well that she would never truly renounce her rule. He positioned himself beside the steps up to the quarterdeck. It was better to stay at Emerelle's side until this night was over.

"You see me here before you without my crown. Now tell me, who among us is to bear the weight of power in the future?"

A moment of silence ensued. Then Hallandan—the prince of Reilimee, the white city by the sea—stepped forward from among the gathered nobles. "I name Emerelle to wear the crown of the swan. Wisdom and benevolence are united in her. She should be the one to rule us."

A sudden gust of wind made the princes' banners along the railing flap. Emerelle opened her mouth, disoriented.

Ollowain bounded up the stairs to the quarterdeck, but the queen had already recovered herself. "Princes of Albenmark . . . is there not one among you who will bear the burden of rule in my place?"

The swordmaster looked at Shahondin, but the ruler of Arkadien remained silent.

"If no other aspires to the throne, then pledge your faithfulness to me," Emerelle went on. "A title is just a word. A crown is just a trifle. But you are the flesh and blood of my rule. Without you, there is no realm at all."

Now the princes approached one at a time, kneeled before Emerelle, and swore their allegiance to her. Ollowain stood behind his queen. He wished he could have read the princes' minds. Their faces were masks, revealing no emotion at all. No doubt most of them truly were loyal to Emerelle, but at least one of them was plotting her death. Perhaps Alathaia, princess of Langollion, who had long been at odds with Emerelle because the princess had supposedly devoted herself to the dark side of magic and strived too much for the treasures hidden at the summit of the Albentop? Or maybe even silent Eleborn, a white-haired waterman, the ruler of the realm beneath the waves? Was it Shahondin after all? Or would it finally prove to be someone with no great name but with a grudge against the queen and a thirst for revenge? Ollowain wished this night would finally be over!

A young elf girl in a pure-white dress ascended to the quarterdeck. On a blue velvet pillow, she carried the crown of Albenmark. It had the stylized shape of a swan just rising into the air from the waters of a lake and was made of white gold and finished with hundreds of slivers of diamond. The head and neck were stretched far forward, while the wings were curved back to form a broad circlet.

Emerelle took the crown. For the space of a heartbeat, she held the precious piece of jewelry above her head so that everyone on board could see it clearly. Then she lowered it onto her head, and a moment of solemn silence followed.

"Take your places at my table, noble princes, and be my guests on this night of wonder." As if at a secret signal, shimmering fountains of light shot into the night sky from atop all the princes' towers in Vahan Calyd. Elated cries rang from the quays and other ships. Albenmark had a queen again.

Aboard the *Moonshadow*, Emerelle sank onto her throne. She seemed utterly exhausted. Ollowain noticed that her right hand was trembling. He moved to the throne and leaned forward slightly. "Are you all right, my queen?"

"The Albenpaths," Emerelle whispered. "Something has moved them. The invisible net between the worlds has been shaken. Someone has used the power of an Albenstone to spin new threads."

"We have a full crew at the oars, my queen. One word, and the lines will be cut." Ollowain pointed out toward the two towers that marked the entrance to the harbor. "We would be on the open sea in less than half an hour—if you so desire."

Emerelle shook her head. "I am the queen. I cannot simply run away, and certainly not when I don't know what I am running from. My responsibility is to protect the races of Albenmark. But it is a relief to know that the *Moonshadow* is ready to sail." She waved over the young elf who had brought her the crown. The girl was standing at the rail above the main deck, looking rather lost. "Keep me company, my dear. What is your name?"

"Sansella, my queen."

"And who appointed you to this task?"

The elf turned toward the guests who had taken their places at the table. "Hallandan, prince of Reilimee. My father," she said proudly.

"I remember seeing you when you were still a small child. And I know you from before, from your previous life. You were always very brave, Sansella. The heart of a heroine beats in your breast."

The young girl reddened. She looked up to the queen, opened her mouth, but then closed it again.

"What do you want to ask?"

"Can you tell me what I was like before?"

Emerelle looked at her intently. "You know that is dangerous! If I tell you who you were, then it may happen that the veil that separates you from your previous life tears open, and in the blink of an eye, all of your memories return. And they will not only be good memories."

Sansella looked downcast. "That's what my father says."

"But I think I can tell you one thing. During the troll wars, you once almost saved my life. But Ollowain, my swordmaster, got in your way. He is very experienced in rescuing me." Emerelle smiled dreamily. "Very experienced."

Ollowain eyed the young girl sharply. Sansella? The name was unfamiliar to him. But he knew her face. He recalled a young warrior woman who had been thrown into the chasm in the trolls' last charge on the Shalyn Falah. Had that warrior been reborn into this girl? He could still see the fear of death in the eyes of the young elf woman when she lost her grip on the bridge. It was good that one was reborn without the old memories!

"My queen!" Shahondin had stood up from the table. "I have prepared a special gift for the entertainment of us all. Will you accept it, Emerelle?"

"Would you accept it if you were in my place?"

The prince of Arkadien pursed his lips. "The evening would be one unforgettable memory poorer if you were to turn it down."

Ollowain's hand sank to the hilt of his sword. What was this now? He glanced instinctively up at the masts of the *Breath of the Sea*.

"Everyone here knows my curiosity," said Emerelle in a merry voice. "Surprise me!"

The swordmaster admired his queen for her courage. She knew the danger, and yet she was putting on as good a face as possible. If she had rejected Shahondin's gift, it would have been obvious to all present that she feared the prince of Arkadien. And that would have been the same as a signal to everyone at all dissatisfied with Emerelle's rule! And maybe it was no more than a gift? Gestures of that kind were not unusual.

"My granddaughter, Lyndwyn, is waiting down on the quay," he said, a lightly remonstrating tone in his voice. "Your guards did not allow her to board the ship. For her age, she has achieved extraordinary mastery of the arts of magic. No one in Arkadien is willing to compete with her."

"Does that speak for the talents of your granddaughter or against the wizards of your clan?" said Hallandan of Reilimee, which earned him approving guffaws.

Shahondin paled slightly but did his best to play down his wrath. "Judge for yourselves when you have seen what Lyndwyn can do."

Emerelle gave Yilvina, who had again taken her post at the entrance to the liburna, a sign, and an elf woman clad in black and silver was escorted on board. She had curly black hair that fell to her shoulders, and her pallid skin was adorned with bandag. Dark snakes decorated her arms and the head of a cobra her forehead. High cheekbones emphasized Lyndwyn's narrow face. Her eyes were as green as limes and shot through with flecks of gold, and her thin lips pointed to single-minded determination. *What sacrifices has she made to master the arts of magic so young?* Ollowain wondered. Was she like him? He thought of the price he had paid to become the swordmaster of Albenmark.

Lyndwyn bowed impeccably before the queen. "I am grateful to you, my queen. It honors me to be permitted to demonstrate my abilities before you."

"Thank me after your showpiece has succeeded, Lyndwyn. I have known the best sorcerers of an entire age, and I will not sully their memory by commending you if your talents do not convince me."

Ollowain's hand still rested on the grip of his sword.

Lyndwyn seemed unruffled by the queen's cool reception. With a self-confidence that bordered on arrogance, she began her work. The sorceress breathed a word of power, and a floating spark appeared in front of her, hardly bigger or brighter than a firefly. She gestured briefly, and the spark began to dance. It drew the outline of a bird against the night sky. Faster and faster it went, hardening certain contours, shading others, making the image more and more solid. Soon, the bird's feathers were complete; a long, curved beak followed. The bird expanded, becoming as big as a horse. It stretched its wings as if to measure their power. And still the spinning spark added more detail to the increasingly lifelike image, deepening the orange of the flame-colored plumage, then adding a point of light to each dark-red eye. Suddenly, a surge of heat radiated from the flame beast. A reverent murmur rose from the seated princes.

With commanding gestures, Lyndwyn made the bird climb higher into the skies, protecting Emerelle's guests from its heat.

Ollowain turned his face upward. The magical form changed once again. It was no longer merely a depiction but seemed awakened to true life and to rear up, rebelling against the will of the young sorceress. The swordmaster had never before seen something living created from a single bright spark. He was entirely captivated by the young elf woman's feat of magic and, for a moment, forgot even his concern for Emerelle.

"Out to sea with you!" Lyndwyn commanded.

The firebird let out a shriek. Then it flew away toward the harbor towers, which were also lit with a pale, blue-white light. To Ollowain, they looked like two lonely sentries at the edge of the darkness. Beyond the towers there were not even any stars to be seen. Clouds had swallowed their light.

The bird had hardly passed the towers when it disappeared.

Lyndwyn seemed confused. She made a hesitant gesture and looked out into the darkness as if spellbound. One of the princes began to clap, then a second and a third joined in, but most of them were looking toward the harbor entrance. They all seemed to be waiting for something. That could not be the end of Lyndwyn's appearance.

And then, in fact, small points of light began to gleam from across the waters. At first only here and there, but within a few moments, there were dozens. And then the first of the points of light rose skyward. Some broke apart as they rose and fell back into the sea, but most climbed higher and higher.

It was an unusual spectacle. Whereas the firebird had amazed the audience with its perfection, now it was the sheer mass that impressed. As the first of the fiery lights began to descend toward the harbor, the swordmaster realized what he was looking at. Fireballs! In the darkness beyond the harbor towers lay a fleet of ships! And they had begun to fire on Vahan Calyd.

With a hissing roar, a fireball burst among the masts of the *Wavedancer*, Hallandan of Reilimee's flagship. The reefed sails caught fire immediately. One of the masts tipped to one side, destroying the rigging. A second fireball burst apart on one of the quays close by.

"Sentries, to me!" Ollowain ordered, but the young warriors stood and stared at the inferno as if paralyzed. In a rage, he wheeled around. "My queen, you have to—" A fireball slammed into the quarterdeck, its scorching heat singeing Ollowain's hair. Some of the flaming charges fell into the water, extinguishing with a loud hissing. Off to starboard, a large sailing ship burned brightly. Flying sparks, acrid smoke, and screams filled the air. As if numb, the swordmaster stared at the place where Emerelle had been sitting a moment before. The throne had disappeared, swept away by the fireball. Ollowain noticed vaguely that the sleeve of his shirt was smoldering. But he felt no pain. It was as if in a dream.

"My queen?" Ollowain walked into the smoke. All over the deck lay chunks of compressed straw. What kinds of shots were these? He stepped on something soft. A hand, torn off. He went down on one knee and tried to drive the smoke away by waving his arms. In front of him lay Sansella. Her head was twisted to a grotesque angle and her face was no more than a bloody mass. He only recognized her from her smoldering dress. Even as he stared at her, the fabric burst into flames.

He saw butterflies, writhing, all over the deck. Their wings burned or crushed, they struggled uselessly to escape the flames, which spread more and more. The shards of a crude clay pot lay around. They were covered in some kind of viscous, sticky mass.

Ollowain beat absently at his shirt to extinguish the smoldering material. He did not feel the sparks burning into his flesh.

"Emerelle?" He stepped over the corpse of one of the queen's guard. And then he saw the queen. She was half-buried beneath smoldering straw. Small burn marks, like pox, covered her face.

With his bare hands, Ollowain heaved the glowing straw aside.

"Sentries!" he bellowed desperately.

Finally, the young soldiers moved. They helped the swordmaster clear away the last of the straw. The queen's undergown was half-burned away, her body gravely wounded, a gaping tear in her chest.

"A shield wall!" Ollowain snarled at the soldiers. "Move! Protect your queen from prying eyes."

Yilvina stepped through the swirling smoke. The elf woman's face was black with soot.

"The princes are abandoning the ship!" she reported. "What should we do? Cast off?"

Ollowain's thoughts came too fast. The air was filled with fireballs. A hundred catapults, maybe more, were firing on the harbor and the city. Many of the ships in the harbor were alight. Was this Shahondin's handiwork?

"Bring me Lyndwyn! She gave the signal to attack the harbor. She knows what's going on here."

Yilvina nodded and disappeared back into the smoke.

Ollowain was certain that Shahondin's granddaughter had guided one of the fireballs onto the quarterdeck. For the princes, it must have looked as if Emerelle were dead. Maybe he could exploit that? He looked down at the queen. One of the soldiers had covered her with a red robe, and only her face was visible. Beside her, on the deck, lay the swan crown, bent and battered. They had to get the queen away from there, but Ollowain did not dare move her. He needed a healer.

"Let me see my daughter. Let me through!"

"Prince, we have strict orders . . ."

"Let him through," Ollowain said. His voice was hoarse. All around him, the air seemed to glow. The guards suddenly ducked behind their shields as a flaming ball of straw hissed past barely an arm's length overhead.

The heat of the glowing ball hit Ollowain like a fist in the face, although the deadly charge had missed the ship.

Hallandan had not even bothered to duck. The tall elf stood as if made of stone and stared down at the small figure at his feet.

The swordmaster laid one hand gently on his arm. "I do not know what pain is tearing at your heart, but I believe your daughter has been destined to save the queen's life, and she will fulfill her destiny. We have to try to get out of the harbor. Emerelle cannot stay in Vahan Calyd any longer. We have an enemy in our midst. Deceit and trickery are his most potent weapons. We can survive only if we turn these weapons against him."

There was a commotion at the steps up to the quarterdeck. "Traitor!" hissed a high male voice.

Yilvina appeared, pushing the young sorceress in front of her. Lyndwyn's artistically arranged hair was in disarray, her left cheek was an ugly blue red, and the eye above swelled almost closed. Her arms were tied behind her back, and a piece of cloth had been stuffed into her mouth as a gag. "We caught her on the quay," Yilvina said. "She was trying to flee the city." The warrior grasped Lyndwyn by the hair and forced her to her kneel in front of Ollowain.

The swordmaster looked at the dying queen, then at Lyndwyn. The traitor squirmed in Yilvina's grip but could not free herself.

"You gave them the signal with your firebird. Who is out there?" Ollowain jerked the gag from her mouth. "Speak!"

The sorceress moistened her lips with her tongue. She held his gaze defiantly.

"I don't know who is attacking us."

Ollowain's hand went to his sword. What did this fool take them for? Everyone on board had witnessed how she had given the signal to attack. And it could be no coincidence that one of the first of the fireballs hit the quarterdeck directly beside the queen. She only dared lie so brazenly because she knew how desperately he needed a healer. "I am not known for my leniency, Lyndwyn." He looked to Emerelle, his queen. A thin line of blood trickled from her lips. Death had reached out his hand for her.

A cold fury took hold of Ollowain. "Who is out there?" he snapped at the sorceress. He drew his sword.

"I don't know," Lyndwyn persisted. She tilted her head slightly to one side, offering him her unprotected throat. "Kill me, Ollowain, and our queen dies within the hour. I am highly skilled in the healing arts." She pointed with her chin toward the city. An indescribable chaos had descended on the quays and the city. Everything with legs was trying to save itself, trying to escape the bedlam by the water. Only Orimedes and his centaurs did not move from their place. They were standing around the queen's sedan, close by the shore. Emerelle had ordered them to wait for her return. And though the world might be coming to an end around them, they waited.

"Where are you going to find a healer, swordmaster?" Lyndwyn asked. "She has maybe a hundred heartbeats left. You can see the life draining from her body! Do you want to go running up and down the quays looking for a healer? The price for your mistrust of me will be the queen's life. Untie me and I will help you! I will do my best, though I fear I will die in the moment my efforts fail. Decide! Your hesitation is killing Emerelle!"

"She's right," said Yilvina, her voice raw.

Ollowain's hand tightened on the grip of his sword. The leather bindings creaked slightly. Lyndwyn was a traitor! And yet he had no choice. "How will you help her?"

"I will cast a cooling spell." Lyndwyn looked down at the queen with disdain. Ollowain did not like the look in her eye at all. There was no mercy in it. Whatever Lyndwyn did she did to get her head out of the noose it was in, and not out of love for her queen.

"My magic will slowly cool Emerelle's body," Lyndwyn continued matter-of-factly. "The blood will then pass through her veins less quickly. I hope, like that, to buy a few hours from death . . . the time I will need, I hope, to close the wound in her chest."

The ship shuddered. A fireball had hit the foredeck. Sparks and thick smoke climbed. Soldiers rushed forward, trying to push the burning straw overboard with their long spears.

Ollowain surrendered to fate. If he wanted to save Emerelle, he had to trust Lyndwyn.

"Untie her," he said to Yilvina. "And stay at her side." He looked down at the sorceress "You're right. If Emerelle dies, you die."

Lyndwyn stretched and massaged the crook of her arm. "I need water," she said.

The swordmaster turned to Hallandan. "Do we have any chance of getting out of the harbor?"

The prince of Reilimee was on his knees beside his daughter. He stroked her blood-caked hair.

"Prince," said Ollowain more insistently. "Can we flee?"

Hallandan was like a man waking from deep sleep. He stared off into the darkness, where flaming balls were still being hurled skyward. "How can I answer you when I don't even know who we are fighting? If we make an attempt with several ships . . . maybe we will make it."

"Listen to me carefully, Hallandan." Ollowain outlined his plan briefly. They needed at least three ships. When he was finished, the prince's expression was stone. Finally, he nodded.

"I will do it, swordmaster. On one condition: that you give me command of the queen's flagship."

"So be it!"

The sea prince hurried away. The swordmaster swept one hand tiredly through his singed hair. Never in his dreams had he imagined he might one day give orders to a prince of Albenmark. And certainly not such orders.

Ollowain went to the steps that led to the quarterdeck and laid one hand on the shoulder of the soldier who had stood back to let Hallandan onto the deck. "Follow me below!"

The young elf seemed surprised. Ollowain avoided meeting the man's eye. He did not want to remember him, did not want to recognize him when he was born into a new life.

Hunting for the Early Lost

We were as wolves,   exiled to foreign lands,
Born like whelps.   Beneath an unknown moon,
We hunted, restive pack,   home far away,
Close the ache for the early lost.

Women it was   who showed the way.
On gilded, glorious trails   through fogs of night,
Galleasses sweeping silent   through surging seas,
Hunting for the early lost.

In wrathful rage, resolute   returned the murdered,
To the Festival of Light,   driven by desire, to find
One alone: Emerelle.   In feverish fire
To ease the hurt for the early lost.

Flames fell from the firmament   where Albenkin caroused.
Ruination rained by fire,   kindling infernos,
And the pride of the butchers of Shalyn Falah   died in ashes,
Seared by the longing for the early lost.

From the "Nightcrags Codex"
Translated by Brother Gundaher
Volume Six of the Temple Library of Luth in Firnstayn, page 112

THE PACK LEADER

Take more time to reload!" The troll had to bawl the order to make himself heard over the din on deck. Orgrim wanted the *Rumbler* to send the last charges flying at the accursed elves. At least in that, he might catch the eye of the king.

The artillery chief below repeated the order, and the arms of the two massive war machines came to a standstill.

"When can we go in and start killing?" came a voice from the deck below. "We shouldn't be burning the elves. I'm here to bash their skulls in personally."

"You'll get plenty of chances for that, Gran," Orgrim replied. "I'm sure you will be happy to get off the sea so you can stop feeding your food to the fishes. I'm starting to worry that you'll be as weak as a fawn when we meet the elves."

Droning laughter sounded from the artillery deck. A hulking figure stepped out of the shadows and looked up at Orgrim. Even among the trolls, Gran was a giant. He towered at least a head taller than every other warrior aboard. "You can talk. But a fighter's worth is not measured in words, but from the number of slain enemies at his feet."

"Then ask Boltan for an abacus, Gran, because your fingers won't do to count the number of elves whose necks I break."

Orgrim had the laughter back on his side. His adversary retreated, muttering into the darkness.

Orgrim had come far. Few trolls made warrior with only thirty summers. Many never made it at all and spent their entire lives in thrall. But Orgrim was already pack leader and commander of his own ship. And there were enough who envied him for it, especially Gran. Orgrim had been hoping that his rival would resort to an insult that would allow him to challenge him to a duel. The long sea journey had weakened Gran. Like most trolls, he could not stand being stuck aboard a ship. The constant swaying and the smell of the sea made them sick, and Orgrim knew that Gran had not eaten anything for days. If there ever were to be a fight, this would be an opportune moment to have it. Orgrim had seen Gran fight—at full strength, he could break the neck of a cave bear with his bare hands.

Basically, he liked the heavily built behemoth, but ever since Orgrim had been pack leader, envy had been eating away at Gran to the point where he could no longer be trusted. He would have to find a way to get rid of Gran, but he knew that single combat with a weakened opponent would not be honorable. Perhaps there would be an opportunity to send him to another pack?

Orgrim leaned against the bulwark of the roughly made aftercastle and looked out over the dark sea. Even out there, there was barely a breath of wind. Over the harbor city, pillars of smoke rose vertically, lit by the red glow of the flames.

With a muffled crack, the arm of a catapult slammed into the thick leather padding of the crossbeam. The force of the impact made the huge ship shudder. A fireball climbed steeply into the night sky. Dozens of the charges were still raining down on the city and harbor, as if the stars themselves were falling from heaven.

Orgrim cursed quietly. As pack leader and commander of a galleass, he had hoped to win renown in this war. He had put so much into mastering his ship in the last two years, to make the sluggish mass of wood do what he wanted it to. Sailing in storms through the floating islands, swallowed by fog in nameless fjords, through winter tempests and the long calms of summer—he went out in every weather, although he feared the sea. He wanted his ship to be the best in the fleet. And now all his efforts had been betrayed. Fame would go to other pack leaders, those who had disembarked in the cypress swamps far to the south of Vahan Calyd. They would attack the city from the rear and break whatever final resistance the elves put up. And they would be the ones to pursue the tyrant queen, the soulless elf woman who was more to blame for the misfortune of the trolls than any other. Emerelle, who had banished them from the world for which the Alben had long ago created them. Sent into exile by the feeble last-created race. But through the centuries of exile in an alien world, the trolls had nurtured their wrath. Now it was their turn. Now they were fighting against the elven rabble and all the worms who squirmed at their feet. The pack leader who first set foot in that dreadful queen's palace would be named as duke of one of the rock fortresses in the Snaiwamark. King Branbeard had promised to establish a new duchy to mark the glory of that act. In all of the other duchies, only a reborn ruler could reign. That was the law among his race. A soul ruled a duchy until that soul was irrevocably destroyed.

This night would be the only opportunity for hundreds of years to win the title of duke by the power of his own deeds. Yet there he stood aboard the *Rumbler*, watching while another pack leader won renown with his fighters while he had to supervise catapults! Orgrim smashed his fist against the bulwark in anger.

A hundred paces to his left, a flame shot up. Screams rang through the night. Yet another of the large galleasses had caught fire. It was not smart to light a fire aboard a huge pile of wood. Most of the oil-drenched balls of straw trailed a broad wake of sparks as they climbed into the sky. Some burst apart the moment they were fired.

Orgrim climbed down from the aftercastle to the artillery deck. "Spread more sand," he shouted to the men by the catapults. Then he silently counted the buckets of sand that stood in long rows along the railing. His ship would not burn! He could live for hundreds of years if he was careful. There would come a second chance for the title of duke. Now what mattered was to survive this night! If one of the large galleasses caught fire and was not extinguished with sand within moments, then it meant death for all on board. No troll could swim. Their bodies were simply too massive to stay on top of the water, and it made no difference how much they paddled or kicked. A troll in the sea was a dead troll.

Two warriors rolled a large ball of straw across the deck. The artillery chief hauled it carefully into the great leather sling at the end of the cata-pult arm. Patiently, he checked that it was sitting as it should before hang-ing the end of the sling into a hook. The arm of the catapult was strained almost to the breaking point. Boltan, the artillery chief, lifted his torch from its holder on the railing. He stayed as far away from the ball of straw as possible, and with his arm outstretched, he held the torch to the gold-shimmering charge.

With a sound like the death rattle of an old dog, the straw caught fire. Boltan jerked back the catapult's locking lever. The arm flew high and slammed into the padded crossbeam. The leather sling opened, and the blazing straw flew away into the darkness.

Orgrim sighed with relief. They had practiced firing the flaming charges so many times, but every time the flames took hold of the straw, he held his breath. He remembered one particular practice shot only too well, when a ball of straw burst apart above the ship and a flaming chunk fell back onto the deck. Boltan had thrown himself onto the burning straw and extinguished it with his own massive body. Even now, in the unsteady light of the only lit torch on board, the flat red scars were visible on his chest. He carried them proudly, as a monument to his courage. No combat could have won him as much renown as that single courageous act. He was known throughout the fleet. The king himself had invited him to his table to tell about his heroic deed and had honored Boltan by bestowing on him the name Fire Eater.

The artillery chief came to Orgrim. Sweat poured in streams from his naked torso. "I've saved the worst of the fireballs for last. For at least two, I'd happily bet that they tear apart before they reach the city."

"Will they at least hold until they are over the water?"

Boltan shrugged. "I wouldn't bet on that." He lowered his voice. "I'd like to throw the rest of them overboard. We've been lucky so far. Who knows how long our luck will hold."

Orgrim looked to the west. Somewhere over there lay Branbeard's flagship. The king would hoist three red lanterns when they were to end their barrage and attack the harbor directly. But all that lit the night were torches and flaming bales. "If not for Gran, I'd agree with you. He'd betray me."

"Then we'll throw him overboard as well," Boltan growled. "He badmouths you to the men. It would be better if he had an accident."

"What about the warriors who might be his friends? And those who are hoping to make pack leader themselves if I fall out of favor?" Orgrim shook his head. "We'd have to throw half the crew overboard, and even then . . ."

"Pack Leader! Ahead to starboard!"

Orgrim charged to the railing. A shadow was sweeping between the pale towers at the harbor entrance. An angular hull split the black mirror of the sea, making it foam. They were coming!

"Throw the rest of the fireballs overboard!" Orgrim commanded. Some of the warriors on the artillery deck looked at him in disbelief, but before any could protest, Boltan bellowed, "Go, go, go! Move your tails, you rat sacks! You heard what your pack leader ordered!" He grabbed hold of one of the large balls himself and, gasping, heaved it over his head. Then he threw it as far out to sea as he could.

The pack leader hurried up the steps to the quarterdeck. He needed to stay close to the helmsman. The elves' ships were faster and more maneuverable than the trolls' galleasses. One mistake and they would be outmaneuvered.

"Man the oars!" he bawled over the noise on deck. "Drummer! A slow rowing beat! Warriors, boarding ramps on deck!"

Orgrim felt his pulse quicken. With a little luck, he could win his duchy after all. Three ships had now made it through the harbor entrance. There was not even a hint of a breeze. The two galleys on the flanks both had their masts down. They were getting ready for battle. The third ship, a huge liburna, lay a little behind the other two.

The pack leader snorted with disdain. The elves made it so obvious. The galleys intended to sacrifice themselves to give the liburna a clear escape route.

The beating of drums sounded from the belly of the *Rumbler*. The oars rattled out through their ports in the massive hull and churned the smooth sea. A jolt ran through the ship, then it began to move. The last bales of straw bobbed in its wake.

"Keep on the white galley!" he ordered the helmsman.

The troll nodded. He leaned against the long tiller with all his weight, and the galleass swung to starboard with agonizing sluggishness.

Orgrim saw the elven galley's bronze ram glinting in the foam, pointing at the hull of the *Rumbler* like a huge arrow.

"Drummer! Ramming speed!" he bawled down to the rowing deck. "Haul on those oars, or they'll send us all to the bottom of the sea!"

More galleasses had broken from the long chain of the trolls' ships and formed in a broad semicircle around the mouth of the Vahan Calyd harbor. Other pack leaders had also sensed fate's beneficence. Orgrim cursed. He would not be the first to reach their precious prey. "Pull, you lazy dogs! Put your backs into it!"

On the main deck, six long boarding ramps lay at the ready. At their front end, sharpened hardwood stakes jutted from the thick planks. They would dig deeply into the deck of the elven ship when the ramp fell.

Orgrim now recognized the crest on the great silk banner wafting languidly from the main mast of the liburna. The night had washed out the colors, but the pack leader could make out a light-colored horse on a dark ground, and he knew what it meant. The tyrant queen's flagship was roiling through the water in front of him!

A shadow moved slowly past the *Rumbler*. The *Stonefist*! The galleass was built a little lighter and had more oars. Orgrim knew he could not win the race against her!

The white elven galley had picked up speed, too, to cut off the new enemy ahead of them. Orgrim reckoned that they would swing around at any moment to direct their deadly ram at the hull of the *Stonefist*. Dull-red points of fire glimmered on board the galley. Small figures gathered around them.

"Keep us away from the *Stonefist*!" Orgrim ordered his helmsman.

A fireball fell into the sea far behind the elven ships. Some of the galleasses had opened fire on the fleeing elves. *Fools*, thought Orgrim. It was not possible to hit even a stationary target with a catapult with any certainty. They were useful when it came to bombarding something the size of a city, not an elven galley.

A second fireball drowned in a column of hissing steam.

Boltan came up to the quarterdeck and brought Orgrim his shield and his massive war hammer.

Suddenly, small flames appeared on the white galley, only to fly high into the sky in the next moment, like tiny copies of the fireballs, and fell toward their target.

Roars of pain sounded from the *Stonefist*. Orgrim saw warriors staggering back from the bulwarks and collapsing on the deck. Flames crept like snakes across the planking. Then, with a dull roar, one of the large straw balls near the catapults caught fire.

A second salvo of flaming arrows descended on the *Stonefist*, and the fire on board spread rapidly. The oarsmen lost their rhythm, and the galleass slewed off course.

"Back to the artillery deck," Orgrim ordered. "We'll be next."

The artillery chief hit his scarred chest with his fist. "But we're prepared." He smiled grimly. "Those elven scum won't take us so easily."

Orgrim pushed his arm through the broad leather loops of his shield. It was made of two-inch-thick oak timbers. No elven arrow would be able to penetrate it.

The liburna had increased its speed and was already moving past the white galley. A wide hole now gaped in the line of troll ships. Only the *Rumbler* lay between the elven ship and the open sea.

In the meantime, the heavy galleass had picked up speed. The distance between them and their prey was decreasing, but flaming arrows now flew from the tyrant's ship, too. Orgrim positioned himself protectively in front of his helmsman and raised his shield. The arrows hammered against the dark wood like puppies' paws, their flames charring smoky tongues into the wood.

The *Rumbler* was washed in the golden light from the arrows that had struck home. The ship looked as if it were lit with dozens of candles. Boltan harried several men across the main deck, smothering the flames with damp felt blankets.

A second rain of arrows pelted onto the deck. One warrior went down gurgling behind the bulwark, a feathered wooden shaft protruding from his neck.

The liburna was less than a hundred steps away. A kind of bed had been set up on its aftercastle, and a figure dressed entirely in black was leaning over it. Was the cowardly tyrant commanding her ship from a daybed of furs and silk? Orgrim grunted with contempt. That fitted with the stories he had heard about Emerelle since his birth.

The *Rumbler* was closing on the elven ship at a sharp angle, but they would miss their quarry by a few paces. The liburna would escape.

"Grappling hooks!" Orgrim screamed.

A fresh hail of arrows descended on the galleass. Now the elves on the white galley were shooting at them, too, just two ship's lengths behind.

Wooden grappling hooks sailed through the air. Orgrim saw one elf caught between the hook and the ship's rail. He was crushed like a rat. A jolt ran through the *Rumbler*. The two ships swung toward one another. The fighters on board the liburna chopped desperately at the tough leather lines. A shrill command sounded. On the port side of the elven ship, the oars were rapidly lifted from the water and pulled inside, to stop them from being smashed between the two hulls.

"Pull the oars—" Orgrim began, but it was too late. The trolls' oaken oars splintered against the elven ship, and from belowdecks came cries of pain as the oarsmen were hurled from their benches and arm-length shards of wood flew all around.

Orgrim stepped to the bulwark. On the artillery deck, the first of the boarding ramps was being run out. But the wooden spikes missed the liburna's railing, and the heavy ramp crashed into the sea. The pack leader saw Gran getting ready to leap onto the elven galley. The huge troll looked down uncertainly at the broad swathe of dark water that still lay between the two ships. In the meantime, the elves prepared themselves to repel the coming attack.

Orgrim cursed quietly. Under no circumstances could he allow his rival to be the first on board. He slid his shield off his arm and lifted it high over his head. Arrows buzzed around him like angry hornets. A shot grazed his temple. With a cry, he hurled the shield into his enemies, and then he leaped after it. For a moment, a gap appeared in the ranks of the elves. The stone head of his war hammer slammed against the enemy shields, the wood bursting apart beneath his furious blows.

The elves fought with silent doggedness while Orgrim bellowed like a raging bear. His enemies dodged back, and a swing went wildly through air. Now the elves threw their shields aside, too. They were different than Orgrim had expected. They eluded his hammer. They neither gave up nor fled. They were like dancing vipers, waiting for the moment to strike. He should not have given up his shield so quickly!

The pack leader swung his heavy hammer in a circle, trying to keep the elves at a distance. Like thunder, the boarding ramps descended onto the ship of the wretched little imps. Wood shattered. The air filled with screams and the insidious whirring of arrows. A numbing blow struck Orgrim on the shoulder. Then a blade shot forward and stabbed him through the heel.

Orgrim went to his knees. He tried to create space for himself, swinging his hammer with all his strength. Then his men were beside him, their large wooden shields covering him.

"Throw them into the sea!" he roared. "Kill them all!" He tried to stand, but his leg collapsed beneath him again. Suddenly, Boltan was there. "This battle is over for you, my friend."

Orgrim supported himself on his war hammer and heaved himself to his feet again. "Your belt!" Glaring light danced before his eyes. "Wrap it around my heel. I have to be able to stand again!"

"There isn't one among us who did not see your courage, Pack Leader. You don't have anything to prove."

"The belt!" Orgrim persisted. "This is not over yet! Wrap my heel with it as tightly as you can."

"They will kill you." Boltan kneeled beside him. He pulled the leather so tight that it creaked.

Orgrim cautiously put his weight on the foot. It was numb, but it did not fold beneath him. With determination, the pack leader picked up his shield and was pushing his way through the crush to the front when an infernal roar erupted behind him. The white galley had reached them. The ram spike bored deep into the *Rumbler*'s hull.

"Abandon ship!" Orgrim bellowed over the noise. "To me, men! We will take the tyrant's ship for our own. To me!"

More galleasses reached the elven ships. They were like wolves attacking an old elk. The elves knew there was no escape, but not one of them yielded. They were not the elves of the songs. Little bastards, slightly built, true, but bastards that knew how to fight. Orgrim would never have thought that their victory would cost them so much blood.

He was among the first to storm the quarterdeck. The last defenders stood between the trolls and the tyrant's bed. Orgrim noticed one elf in particular, in a ragged silk shirt. He fought like a wildcat and mocked the trolls. Nothing seemed able to kill him, and finally he was the last elf standing. A steel breastplate shimmered beneath the tatters of his shirt. Beside him crouched a woman, dressed in black and silver. She seemed to be a shaman. Her face was painted, her hair the color of ripe corn. She held the hand of the figure on the bed. Whoever lay there had a silken sheet pulled over her face.

The victorious trolls stood in a broad circle around the bed. The battle had cooled the warriors' battle lust. No one wanted to die now.

The elf raised his blade, challenging them. "Come on! Where's your courage! A hundred against one, that ought to be enough, even for you."

"Lay down your weapon, and I'll spare your life." The pack leader felt respect for the paltry creature. It would be a shame to kill him. He was wounded, too—he bled from a deep cut to one hip. He would not survive another melee.

The elf laughed and threw back his long blond hair. "Your stink offends my queen. Withdraw from the quarterdeck, and I'll refrain from slaughtering you like the beasts you are. I'll count to three, slowly. That's how much time you have left. Anyone still standing up here after that is dead."

Gran pushed to the front. "The guy's mad. He must have got a knock on the head."

"One!"

Orgrim noted with annoyance that several trolls actually backed away.

"Two!" The elf staggered slightly. He had to hold himself up with one hand on the magnificent bed.

"Thr—"

Orgrim's war hammer flew through the air. The elf tried to duck beneath it, but his wound and the long battle had exhausted him. The massive head of the hammer caught him full in the face. A sharp crack rang out, and bloodied teeth rattled across the deck. Slowly, as if unwilling to concede defeat even in death, the elf sank onto his knees, then fell forward.

Orgrim stepped up and retrieved his war hammer. "That's my meat," he announced in a hoarse voice, and he pointed to the dead elf. "He was stupid, but he was brave. Take an example from his courage!" The troll reached for the silken sheet.

The elf woman fell onto his arm. "Defile me if you want, but let my queen die in peace."

Orgrim looked at her in incomprehension. "What am I supposed to do with a woman who would snap in two if you held her too tight?"

"I beg you, sir. Show mercy!"

"Mercy? Like your queen, who threw our king and the captive dukes into the abyss from the Shalyn Falah and banished my race from Albenmark? No, woman. We have learned a lot from you elves. Mercy turns a victor's strength into weakness."

"I'll do anything for you!"

Orgrim looked at the woman in surprise. Did she want to die? If he chatted with her much longer in front of his warriors, his reputation would suffer. He nodded toward the elf with the smashed face. "Who was that man?"

"Ollowain, swordmaster to the queen."

"Can I have a piece of him?" ask Gran reverently.

Orgrim looked down at the dead figure. His name was almost as well-known among the trolls as that of his queen. Prince of the Bone Bridge, the Dancing Blade, Flenser—his race had many names for this warrior. And if he was there, then it could mean only one thing. Orgrim pulled back the silk sheet and looked into a face disfigured by burns. A diamond-studded diadem encircled the dead woman's forehead. The swan crown of Albenmark!

He lifted the precious piece of jewelry carefully from her head. Then he held it high so that everyone could see it. "The tyrant of Albenmark is dead!"

A QUESTION OF HONOR

Alfadas looked up to the summit of the Hartungscliff on the other side of the fjord. A stone crown graced the top of the steep rock face. It was the gateway to another world. Winter would soon set in in Albenmark, the jarl thought with some melancholy. What would he not give to be able to step through that gate one more time!

Sometimes, when he went off into the woods for days, he climbed up to the stone circle. His father had managed to pass through it on his own. Alfadas thought with deep bitterness about how that same gift had been denied him, although he had lived among the elves for twenty years. It was true that, in the Fjordlands, there was no one to match him as a swordsman. Ollowain, the best sword fighter in Albenmark, had trained him. Over the course of the years, the elf had been many things for him—foster father, teacher, and friend. For most at court, the swordmaster seemed cold and aloof. A living legend, the white knight of the Shalyn Falah. He had devoted himself to one goal—to become the perfect swordsman and warrior. He had traveled so far along that road that no elf could best him.

As absurd as it may have sounded, it was exactly that quality of Ollowain that had made it so easy for Alfadas. He had spent half his life trying to be like an elf, and yet he had always remained the human: to be pitied, to be tolerated. Only around Ollowain were things different. There was no one else like the swordmaster, and for that reason, Alfadas had at times been able to find peace at his side. Of course, he had tried constantly to master all the fine points of fighting and the art of war, but with Ollowain, it was always less bitter to be no more than human.

The sweet, spicy fragrance of fresh cider made the memories of the past fade. Alfadas licked his lips and smiled. He had brought some things back with him from Albenmark. They had not known cider in Firnstayn, and at first the fighters had taunted him, jibing that he was brewing a little juice for beardless boys. But now when Firnstayn celebrated the apple festival, the people came from the neighboring villages for miles around.

He swept his gaze over the small village on the fjord: a few longhouses and huts surrounded by a wooden palisade. Not even a hundred families lived there. Compared with the splendor of Albenmark, it was . . .

No, it was foolish and unfair to compare Firnstayn with Albenmark. *And as long as I think like that, I will never really be one of them,* he chided himself. But deep inside, he knew it was hopeless. He would never truly be one of them! As hard as he tried, he could not understand the people here. How they thought, how they lived . . . he had grown a beard to be more similar to them, but that was just the outward appearance.

When he went away from Firnstayn, there were occasional moments when he could disappear. When he hid his sword, which was too good. When he managed to mimic the harsh, slow timbre of the people . . . but as soon as his name came out, it was over. Everyone in the Fjordlands knew the story of Alfadas Mandredson, and instantly he no longer belonged to those around him. He could never tell if the others feared or admired him. They were simply strange, the people to which he belonged, and his soul could find no way to join them.

One story going around was that his father had conceived him with the elven queen. At the same time, there were people there in the village who had known his mother and who could still remember clearly how Emerelle had come to take him away, who had seen the cavalcade of riders cross the frozen fjord in the eerie faerylight, and who had never forgotten the sight.

"You're dead, giant troll!" Ulric dug the end of a wooden spoon into Alfadas's doublet. "Now fall down, you smelly troll. I've killed you!"

"No honorable warrior fights like that, you know. You should have challenged me."

"But then I wouldn't have won. No one can beat you in a sword fight, Father. Everybody knows that." Ulric had stopped smiling. He looked accusingly at his father, who was clearly unwilling to understand the simplest concepts.

"A true warrior would rather fight a hopeless battle than attack an opponent treacherously and betray his own honor."

Ulric lowered his spoon. "Isn't that sort of dumb?"

Alfadas had to smile. "It is never smart to get mixed up with trolls." He leaned forward, grunted wildly, and threw Ulric over his shoulder. "If you try to talk to them, they'll end the conversation by eating you!"

His son squealed with pleasure and thrashed Alfadas's back with the spoon with all his might. They were already halfway down the hill when someone called out from behind them.

"Blast, I forgot," the boy hissed.

"What?"

"Mother sent me. She said I should go and see if you were standing around somewhere dreaming again." It was clear that the boy found it embarrassing to repeat Asla's words. "She's angry because she's been standing at the apple press the whole afternoon and you haven't helped her."

"Alfadas!" came a shout from atop the hill.

"Hmm. I'm afraid I haven't behaved very honorably at all." He put his son down. "You have to promise me something."

"What is it?"

"Don't take me as a good role model. I'm not a good husband. You mother is always angry at me."

Ulric gave him a gappy grin. "I want to be an honorable man, not a married one." He stabbed wildly with the wooden spoon at some invisible adversary. "When I'm big, I will lead the king's troops. I'll be a hero. I'll be even famouser than you. And . . ." He looked up with his big child's eyes. "Will you give me your magic sword when I'm big? I'll need it if I'm to be a hero."

Alfadas sighed. "I don't have a magic sword. How many times do I have to tell you that?"

Ulric pouted. "I know what's true. Your sword can cut through any shield and any armor. It *is* enchanted! Grandfather says so!"

"It is simply a very good sword." Alfadas kneeled in front of his son to look him in the eye. "My sword was forged by elves. It is an excellent weapon. But there is no magic in it. And when it comes to heroes . . . it is not the weapon that makes the hero. The man who guides the sword must be someone special—like you."

"So will I be a hero when I'm as big as you?"

"You will be, Ulric." He grinned. "At least, if you get out of the habit of sneaking up on trolls. Now let's go to your mother."

They climbed back up the little hill on which the longhouse stood. Everyone in the village had helped to build it after he had married Asla. Alfadas knew that some of the new inhabitants of the village had moved to

Firnstayn only because he lived there. Alfadas the elf-friend, Alfadas, commander of the king's army. They were polite with him, always, but they did not love him. He was something like a particularly dangerous watchdog loose in the yard. Where he was, no fox would go. The villagers felt safer having him around.

Kalf stood by the apple press. The blond giant had been jarl of Firnstayn himself. He was the watchdog before Alfadas came. Alfadas of the magnificent sword belt, Alfadas of the famous father . . .

Asla looked at Alfadas reproachfully. "Where have you been hiding?"

Ulric stepped in front of his father. "He was showing me how to fight honorably."

"I wish you would do me the occasional honor of helping me. What were you doing? Staring up at that accursed mountain again, where your father disappeared with his elven friends?"

"They have names. His friends were Farodin and Nuramon."

"I'll be going, then," said Kalf. He was a big, quiet man. Alfadas knew that he had ruined Kalf's life. If not for him, Kalf would still be jarl and he would have married Asla. There had never been an ill word between them. Alfadas knew that Kalf still loved Asla . . . he had taken no other wife. For all these years, he had lived alone in his little hut down by the river. Alfadas could not look him in the eye for long . . . those sad, sky-blue eyes.

Kalf tapped his forehead fleetingly. "Evenin', Alfadas."

The jarl only nodded. "I'll look after the press," Alfadas said, speaking to his wife.

Asla waved one hand dismissively. "The work's done. I called for you to carry in the barrels of juice, but Kalf has done it instead. All that's left is the pressings." She pointed to the trough beside the press. "You . . . No, Kadlin! Not again!"

Their daughter felt her way along the edge of the trough, then plunged both hands into the golden mash of pressed fruit. She looked up to Alfadas, shook her head with a laugh, and then rubbed the rough apple pulp into her face and hair with both hands.

Asla, exhausted, sat down on the chopping block. "She's just like you, my beautiful, strange man. She knows exactly what she's not supposed to do and does it anyway. And no matter what, I can't stay mad at her for long."

Alfadas sat beside his wife. He placed one hand gently across her shoulders. Her dress was saturated with the scent of apples.

"Why are you so furious?"

Asla wiped her hands on her apron. "Because of the mountain," she said softly. "Sometimes I wish we lived somewhere else, somewhere where I don't have to see it every single day . . . and where you don't have to see it either. I can't stand the way you gaze up to the summit."

"It is just a mountain."

She stared at her red, calloused hands. "No, it is not. From there came the elves who carried you away for twenty years. In the stories, they say their hearts are as cold as winter stars. They—"

"That's nonsense!" Again and again, she talked like that. "You met Farodin and Nuramon yourself. Did they have cold hearts?"

"Farodin was spooky to me. There was nothing human about him—"

"What do you expect? He's an elf!" Alfadas interrupted her. "But they are not coldhearted."

"Did you know many of their women? They say their beauty never fades." She looked again at her damaged hands. "It's been more than eight years since we danced around the stone together. I am scared that they will come and take you away from me. Do elves dance around a stone and promise eternal love, too?"

"No." He reached down for a sliver of wood that lay beside the chopping block and rubbed it between his fingers. "They promise nothing for eternity. They live too long for that. What they promise each other is to separate before the first lie passes between them. They believe that when there is something that they cannot discuss together, then it is time to let the other go."

"Would we still be a couple if we were elves?"

Alfadas could sense her trembling. Why did she torment herself with such questions? Did she not see that he loved her? Alfadas pressed her to him gently. "I have never lied to you."

"Nor I to you."

"All this work is wearing you down, Asla. Should I bring you back a slave woman from Gonthabu next summer?"

She wiped her nose with the back of her hand. "Only if you find one as ugly as the night." She smiled, but her eyes were red with unwept tears.

"Awa!" Kadlin came to them on wobbly legs. Her whole face was smeared with mashed apple. She had her mother's eyes, chestnut brown and full of warmth. "Awa . . ." She stretched her arms up toward Alfadas. He picked her up, and she ran her sticky fingers through his hair, squealing with delight.

He took one of her hands and licked off the sweet bits of apple. Kadlin giggled as his tongue tickled her fingers.

"Da!" She held out her other hand to him.

Asla sighed and stood up. "The first guests will be arriving soon. Can you take care of the fire? The evenings are starting to get cold early now."

Alfadas nodded.

The smile had returned to Asla's eyes as she looked down on the two of them. "It seems no woman can resist you, my beautiful, strange man."

The jarl felt something lukewarm run down his leg. He lifted Kadlin up. A dark patch was spreading across his breeches.

Asla laughed. "Can you take care of our little one? I have to get the bread out of the oven."

BLOOD

Fog crept up the fjord and engulfed the village. Sometimes, from down below, Alfadas heard stifled laughter. All of Firnstayn was celebrating the apple festival. His longhouse lay a little way from the other houses. He no longer remembered if it had been his idea to build there or if Kalf, who was still the jarl at that time, had suggested it. As it was with his house, so it was with Alfadas himself. The house stood on the edge of the village, not at its heart. And while Alfadas was held in high regard, he could not find a way into the hearts of the people. He remained the outsider, even for Asla, who was so fond of calling him her "beautiful, strange man."

Or was he imagining all of it? The hill was the best place, after all. Perhaps they had wanted to honor him? The hard life in the mountains left the people there with little time to be complicated. Normally they would say whatever was on their mind.

The fine hairs on his neck stood on end. Was that a noise? Something moved in the fog. Not a man. A throaty growl came, and Alfadas swung a torch toward it. As if from nowhere, a large black dog appeared. It stalked closer, teeth bared. A deep, bloody weal crossed its snout.

"Heel, Blood!" snarled an imperious voice from the fog.

The dog stopped. It was trembling with tension. Alfadas was expecting the beast to leap at him at any moment. It had a shaggy black coat and a broad leather loop around its neck.

"Greetings, Jarl." A burly man appeared behind the dog and pulled a strap through the leather collar. "Lie!" the man snapped at the dog, which reluctantly lay down.

"Greetings, Ole Erekson." Alfadas did not go to the trouble of faking a sincere tone. He did not like his father-in-law's brother at all. He was an untrustworthy brute who bred dogs and tortured them until they turned into bloodthirsty beasts.

"Aren't you going to ask me in?"

Ole knew exactly what Alfadas thought of him. The two men looked each other up and down. The dog breeder was a squat, solid man with long red hair. His meaty face was framed by an unkempt beard in which broad gray streaks had begun to appear. Ole wore a beautiful deep-red cape held together at his neck by a bronze clasp. He smelled like his dogs: of wet fur, piss, and rotten meat.

"Your dog does not enter my house."

"Not a wise decision, Jarl. Everyone knows how touchy my puppies are." He held his end of the strap high. "How long do you think it would take Blood to chew through this? Do you really want a dog like him straying through the village? You know I raise them to take on wolves and bears. And they're always hungry. I can imagine Blood mistaking a drunkard staggering home for easy prey . . . of course, if you have a chain, we can tie him up out here."

Ole knew very well that there was not a house in the village that possessed a chain. Iron was far too valuable to waste it making chain.

"Why did you bring that monster with you at all?"

The dog breeder smiled broadly. "You've got a few men in from the outlying farms among your guests tonight, no doubt. They can always use a good dog out there in the wilderness. You lock it in a cage, and any stranger who sets foot near your farm will set it off. Something like that is good when you live out in the middle of nowhere. Besides, my dogs are perfect for all kinds of hunting. Could be a bull elk you've cornered or a pack of wolves you want to drive away or an escaped slave you want to get back. My dogs do it all. And they're obedient, too, as long as their master and his whip are close by. Isn't that true, Blood?"

The dog glared up at Ole, full of hate. In the breeder's belt was a whip with balls of lead and sharp thorns woven into it. "When I sell a dog, I hand over the whip I raised it with. That way they know who their new master is. Especially if you give 'em a good hiding with it right after the sale."

"Take the dog away and you'll be welcome as my guest."

Ole stepped so close that Alfadas could smell his reeking breath. "Send me away and I'll go down to the village and tell everyone that you refused me entry to my niece's house for the festival, Jarl. At the next full moon, the village will elect a new jarl. I always thought the title was important to you, Alfadas Mandredson? A man who denies hospitality to a relative will hold a bad hand going into an election. Kalf has many friends. They say that even your wife likes him." He smiled lasciviously. "And maybe even a little more than that."

Alfadas lowered one hand to the grip of the knife he wore at his belt.

Ole laughed. "Your father would have stabbed me dead long ago, but I see no scrap of the great Mandred in you, you elven bastard!"

"You know I'm no half blood! You yourself saw them come for me, or did you already forget about that? Get out of my sight."

"Oh, yes. I saw that coldhearted crew come and take away the son of Mandred and Freya. But do I know who the man is who came back to the village half a lifetime later? Take a look at yourself! Do you have a drop of the hot blood of the Fjordlanders in your veins? A real man would have fought me long ago, half blood! It's your mother's blood, the blood of some elven slut, that holds you back."

"Haven't you heard the stories about the cruelty of the elves, Ole?"

The dog breeder's brow furrowed.

"Stories of humans who encountered them and then disappeared forever," Alfadas continued.

Ole licked his lips nervously. "Heel, Blood!" His voice now sounded hoarse. He drew the whip from his belt and smacked the grip against his thigh.

"If you're right, then you might be in more grave danger than you can imagine." Alfadas reached for the whip and twisted it out of Ole's hand with a jerk.

"Hold, Blood!" the breeder squawked. The beast did not move.

"What were you saying just now? You train them so that they listen to whoever holds the whip. Do you think it would obey me if I ordered it to tear you limb from limb?"

Perspiration gleamed on Ole's forehead. "Sorry. I've been drinking. Makes me say stupid things. You have to—"

"You don't smell like you've been drinking." Alfadas looked down at the dog. "I'm sure no one would be surprised to find that one of your own dogs had ripped your throat out. Do you think that's how elves take revenge? To have a slave driver like you killed by his tormented victims?"

"Yes!" Ole panted. He stared at Alfadas. Waited for a reaction. "I mean, no. I . . ."

The jarl pushed the whip back into the breeder's belt. "Remember this, Ole: I hate being slandered. If I hear one more time—or if I merely suspect—that you've been talking bad about me, then one day they're going to find you among your dogs. The only way they will know it's you lying there is from what's left of your clothes. Until this evening, because you're my wife's only uncle, I have taken pains to overlook the way you've been behaving. But my patience is at an end. Be on your guard against me."

Ole placed one hand on the whip.

Alfadas caught himself wishing that the breeder would try something stupid now.

"I—" Ole began, but then the door of the longhouse opened. Asla's silhouette was framed clearly against the red firelight from inside. The smoke from the fire billowed through the doorway around her.

"So wonderful of you to visit," she greeted her uncle warmly. Then she noticed the dog and hesitated. "Come in," she finally said tonelessly.

Ole glanced at Alfadas, but the jarl revealed no emotion. He waited for the dog breeder to decide for himself.

Asla's uncle wiped his hand nervously across his forehead before he stepped inside the longhouse. The dog stayed close beside him. "Would you have a marrowbone with a bit of meat still on it? Blood is happy as long as he's got something to chew on."

"Blood?" Asla asked in surprise.

Ole nodded down at the black dog. The beast stood almost up to his hip. "I'd used up all the other good names. Killer, Fang, Grinder. They sell much better when they have a dangerous name." Ole raised his voice. "These black bear-hounds from Fargon make ideal watchdogs!"

Alfadas sighed. Ole was a riddle. There were moments when he could have happily strangled him, and the next moment he had to stop himself from laughing out loud. The breeder was the most baffling human he had yet encountered. A heartbeat before, he'd been a downright son of a bitch, but now he managed to play the pitiful clown.

The smoke-heavy air inside the house stung his eyes. The house had a fire pit in the center of its single, large room, but no chimney. The smoke exited only slowly through two small gaps just beneath the gables. It never took long for Alfadas to get used to the smoky air, the burning eyes, and the scratch in his throat. But every time he went inside from being out in the clear air, he found the first moments to be a kind of torture.

His house was fifteen paces long. Half the village had spent five weeks working on it. It was a good house. For elves, it would have been no more impressive than a kobold's cave scratched in the earth, but he was proud of his home. Together, they had built it as well as they possibly could.

Beside the long fire pit were benches where most of the guests were seated. They drank, joked, or simply gazed into the coals in silence. Long wooden tables on heavy trestles groaned under the weight of all the food. Two fat pigs had been slaughtered and roasted on spits. There was cider from the year before, fresh butter, and delicious-smelling bread. Asla had toiled like a slave for three days to prepare for the feast, and even now she did not stand still for a moment. If the king called him back to the south the following year to command his army on its plundering raids, Alfadas swore, then he really would bring a slave woman back who would do the work for her.

She wore her green dress and the amber jewelry that he had given her to mark Kadlin's birth and was the most beautiful woman there. She did not notice how Alfadas sat mutely and observed her. He thought of their argument that afternoon and knew that he ought to tell her how much she meant to him more often. They had been talking together less, recently. There was no ill intent behind it; it was just that they had known each other so long that he understood her without the need for words. *I should change that,* he thought. Talk to her more often, or simply share a joke now and then, like they used to. She did so much for him. The apple festival had been her idea. He had brought the trees to the village, and when, after two years, they bore a few fruit for the first time, Asla had invited all of the important families to join them. Shortly after that, he was elected as jarl for the first time. He knew that he owed the decisive votes to the festival. Since then, there had been an apple festival every year, and now the entire village celebrated when the apple harvest was brought in.

Asla skillfully sliced the bone out of a large ham and gave it to the dog. The huge beast slunk away to a corner by the sleeping compartments, which were hidden from view by heavy woolen drapes beneath the slope of the roof.

Alfadas could hear the bone splintering between Blood's fangs, and he believed in that moment that the creature really could take on a bear. Asla's uncle, meanwhile, had forced himself onto a group of farmers who had come in from the wilderness, gesturing wildly as he talked to them.

The jarl poured himself a cup of cider and crouched beside the fire pit. He listened to the murmur of voices and the quiet melody of the coals. He thought back to his first summer with Asla. She was so different from elven women, so overflowing with life—wild as a summer storm. It was easy to live with her. She carried every thought, every dream on her tongue. And even before the first snows fell, they had danced together around the stone . . . the great snow-white block of stone down below, by the fjord, from which the village took its name—Firnstayn.

"A word, Jarl?" Gundar, the old Luth priest of the village, lowered himself onto the bench beside him without waiting for a reply. The previous year, Alfadas had persuaded him to leave the king's city and move to Firnstayn. He would, in fact, have preferred a Firn priest, but he could not persuade them with either gold or good words to send one of their own to such an insignificant village. Instead, he had to make do with a priest devoted to Luth, the weaver of fate.

When Gundar first arrived, Alfadas feared that the priest was only looking for a place where they would feed him through his declining years. After his first winter in Firnstayn, the priest's appetite had become notorious within a three-days' march of the village. If one visited him in his hut, he always had something bubbling away over the fire. Alfadas had never regretted bringing him to the village. Gundar knew herbs, and he knew souls. Alfadas did not know what strange magic the old man radiated, but since he had been living there, things had become more peaceful. Fewer disputes were brought to court, and many an old grievance was finally settled.

Gundar held a bowl containing hunks of bread and pork on his lap. His white beard gleamed with fat. "Luth is warning us about the winter ahead." The priest had mastered the art of speaking clearly even while chewing. "Early this morning, he sent me the third unfavorable sign in just four days. It was just after breakfast. A portentous time of day! I slit open the pike I planned to fry for lunch, and I found a large black stone inside its body."

"Well, something like that can really spoil an appetite."

"Don't mock the signs sent by the gods, Jarl!" Gundar spat a chunk of gristle into the coals. "A stone like that has no business being in a pike's belly. I am certain that something will be coming here this winter. Something dark, something evil . . . something that does not belong in this land."

Alfadas was surprised at how much the old man could read into a stone that a dumb fish had swallowed, but he refrained from sharing that thought with Gundar. If the priest started voicing his dark presentiments openly there in his house, it would cause unrest. The simple people of the village listened to him. Alfadas hoped he could talk Gundar out of his nonsense the following morning if he went to visit him in his hut with a ham and a basket of fresh cheese.

"You mentioned three signs . . ."

"Oh, yes. Yes." Gundar wiped the juices out of the bowl with a piece of bread. "I don't know if you saw it yourself, but last night there was blood on the moon's crescent. Even as a young priest, I learned that this is a warning from Luth of a coming war."

"Autumn has begun. Soon the first snows will fall. No one wages war at this time of year. Snow and ice would kill more men than any foe."

"And yet Luth is warning us." The old man looked at him searchingly. "Or do you doubt his omens?"

"And what should we do, in your opinion?"

Gundar spread his arms wide, a gesture of helplessness. "I am no more than the vessel of my god. I see his omens. You're the jarl. You have to decide what happens."

"What else have you seen?"

"There is a new stream at the foot of the Hartungscliff. No more than a trickle, but still a sign of impending change. Don't think I'm just some fearful old man, Alfadas. What bothers me is that I've received three very clear harbingers in such a short space of time. For that same reason, I have not said a word to anyone else. The gods are trying to warn us, Alfadas. You have to protect the village, as your father once did when he lured the beast into the mountains and he and his elven friends managed to kill it in Luth's cave. The weaver of fate smiles on your clan, Alfadas. He is sending us these signs so that you can prepare."

"You have no more to eat, Priest." Asla was standing behind them. She had approached without a sound and now set down a bowl of meat on the bench. One had to know her very well to pick up the trace of friendly teasing in her voice. Alfadas was not sure how much of their quiet conversation she might have overheard.

He placed one arm around her hips and pulled her over the bench onto his lap. "Am I going to have to tie you down to make sure you get at least a little rest during our festival?"

"It would be more than enough if you were to give me a helping hand."

"Asla, please. You can see that I am talking with Gundar. I'm attending to our guests in my own way."

"I will leave you two alone, I think," said the priest with a knowing look, and he reached for the new bowl of meat.

"Stay seated, Gundar. You are a wise old man. Don't try to tell me that the squabbles of old married couples are anything new to you." Asla smiled gaily. "I know I've made a good match with my hero. Oh, he's as lazy as the rest of you, but at least he doesn't get drunk and beat me and my children. Sometimes I can even believe that he thinks seriously about how he might be able to help me. It's just a pity that he doesn't turn those thoughts into actions."

Alfadas jabbed her in her side. "If your tongue was a blade, you'd be the swordmistress of the kingdom."

"And if you men had something else in your head besides swords and kingdoms, the world would be far more peaceful than it is. I would love to know what would change if *I* were jarl."

"With all due respect, Asla," the priest said, chewing mightily. "That has never happened. Women are not made for that." He winked slyly. "And do you really think the world would be a better place if Alfadas had prepared all this food today? I fear that in a world like that, men like me would die of hunger."

"How can you know that women would not do a better job if not one has ever led a village as jarl?"

Alfadas felt a sense of satisfaction that the otherwise so eloquent priest was in as much danger of defeat as he himself always was when they argued about this topic.

"There are kingdoms in the south where women reign," Gundar objected. "And you can see what happens to them. Old Horsa Starkshield sends his soldiers every summer to lay waste to their borders and extort protection money from them."

"Oh, yes. I know. And my husband leads Horsa's soldiers from victory to victory, but does that mean the queens there rule badly? Is it their fault that they have a belligerent neighbor who sends his plundering hordes out every spring?"

Alfadas quietly cleared his throat. "Be careful what you say about the king. We are not alone."

"Am I no longer queen in my own house? We ought to—" She broke off in midsentence. Alfadas felt all her limbs stiffen. He instinctively followed her gaze.

Kadlin had crawled out of her sleeping niche and was reaching for Blood's marrowbone.

"Not a sound!" Alfadas hissed. "We cannot afford to alarm that beast in any way." Blood seemed to be asleep. He held the bone between his forepaws.

Kadlin tugged at the fibrous meat and stuffed it into her mouth.

The jarl felt for the knife at his belt. "Talk to Asla as if nothing is the matter at all," he asked the priest. "None of the guests has noticed." He forced himself to stay calm. His heart raced, but he could not let it show. He must not startle Blood. The huge dog could kill Kadlin with a single snap of its jaws. No one in the longhouse would be fast enough to prevent it.

"Please do something," Asla whispered. "We can't just watch."

"Pray for her." Gundar was as pale as death. "Your daughter's life is in Luth's hands."

"I will not . . ."

Alfadas pressed one hand to Asla's lips and forced her to stay seated.

The dog opened its eyes. They were the color of amber. It eyed the small child coldly. Kadlin was half-standing and tore at the large bone. She babbled away in annoyance, because she could not pull it out from under the heavy paws.

Alfadas weighed the knife in his hand. His daughter would survive only if Blood died in a heartbeat. The knife was too light to penetrate the dog's hard skull. Unless he hit its eye. There, where the bone was thinnest. But Kadlin was in the way. If she moved at the wrong moment, the blade would hit her. Alfadas cursed himself for not sending Ole and his dog away.

Blood stretched and lifted one of his paws. With a jerk, Kadlin pulled the bone free and plopped onto her bottom.

"By the gods, the child!" a woman suddenly shrieked. All talk stopped at a stroke. Blood looked up. He bared his teeth and growled.

"Do not move!" Alfadas commanded. "Nobody goes near the dog." From the corner of his eye, he saw Ole push past the farmers and pull the whip from his belt. "Stand still," the jarl hissed furiously. "You are the last person I want near that dog."

Kadlin, too, had noticed the sudden silence. She looked around. Then she reached out her hand, grasped Blood by the nose, and pushed herself back up to her feet. Alfadas held his breath. Kadlin's small fingers stroked the bloody weal on the dog's snout. Blood blinked. He moved his head forward. Then he licked the little girl's face with his great pink tongue.

A sigh went through the room, but the danger had not yet passed. Alfadas reached out with one hand in the direction of his daughter. "Come here, Kadlin. Come to me."

The little girl pressed a kiss to Blood's nose. Then she ran to Alfadas and announced proudly, "Wowow!"

The jarl let go of Asla. She pulled Kadlin to her. "What were you doing, my girl? Never do that again. Please . . ." Her voice choked off in tears. The other women gathered around her.

Ole laid his dog whip on the bench beside Alfadas. "You can keep the mongrel. No one will ever believe he's a bloodthirsty, wolf-killing brute now."

Alfadas had no answer to that. He felt utterly exhausted, and now that the tension had been released, he began to shake all over.

"A bloodhound yields to a child's hand. The fourth omen in as many days," said the priest quietly.

FIRE AND WATER

"Is that you, Ollowain?" Orimedes leaned forward to see his face better. "Why are you dressed up? Do you think a helmet like that will help if a fireball falls on your head?"

"Silence!" Ollowain looked to the rest of the centaurs, who stood farther back on the quay, beside the sedan boat. The swordmaster lowered his head so that the helmet he was now wearing better concealed his face. "Tell your men to bring the skiff to the landing stage. We have wounded who would not survive at sea. We have to get them back to the palace. Are the holdes still on board?"

"Most of the little pests ran off when the barrage started. Only Gondoran and two or three others are still on the boat."

"Either get rid of them now or make sure they can't leave the boat once we get the wounded aboard."

Orimedes looked questioningly at him.

"Go! You have my instructions." Without waiting to see how the centaur prince reacted to his harsh tone, Ollowain turned and hurried along the landing stage. The fewer Albenkin who knew what happened here, the better. They had to make it back to the palace. Even heavily outnumbered, they could defend themselves easily from there.

The swordmaster ducked as a fireball hissed past overhead. Most of the ships in the harbor now stood in flames. A wind had sprung up and blew like hot breath over his face. Fine flakes of ash danced across the quay like black snow.

Emerelle had been carried down to the landing stage. She had been laid on one of the long shields of a soldier, and a silk blanket covered her burned dress. Her face was swollen and so disfigured by her wounds that she was barely recognizable. Deeply worried, Ollowain looked at the patch of blood still spreading on the blanket.

Lyndwyn was kneeling beside the queen. Her eyes were closed, and she held the monarch's hand. Was she helping Emerelle? Or was she fanatical enough to simply sit there and wait for the queen to die, in the knowledge that it would mean her own death as well? Now she, too, wore the plain green tabard of the queen's guard.

The swordmaster looked back toward the city desolately. The quays were emptying, and the streams of fleeing Albenkin choked the streets of the city. There was no other healer; he had no choice but to trust the woman he considered to be a traitor.

Two more wounded lay on their shields on either side of the queen. Young warriors with pale faces . . . Ollowain knew them both. One had been a very promising student of the sword.

He gazed out toward the two towers at the harbor entrance, the border beyond which the *Moonshadow* had disappeared in the darkness. He thought of Sanhardin, the soldier with whom he had exchanged clothes belowdecks. Sanhardin had smeared soot onto his face. There was not much similarity between them, but the soldier was an outstanding sword fighter, and when it came down to it, that would count more than anything else. Sanhardin's sister had donned Lyndwyn's dress. Both knew that Hallandan had been ordered not to escape. The prince would ensure that the queen's liburna was captured and that her enemies would draw the wrong conclusions. Had the *Moonshadow*'s deadly dance already begun?

Ollowain looked around. Several towers in the city still swirled with magical light. Black pillars of smoke rose almost vertically into the night sky. Up there, there was still no wind. A large galley was attempting to escape from the harbor. Its oars were out, and the dark water foamed as the slim ship glided backward away from the quay. Suddenly a strong wind blew from the mangrove swamps toward the city. Several of the burning ships swung on their anchors. Desperately, the helmsman on the galley tried to steer clear. The massive hull of an Arkadienese round ship shattered its port oars. A large cog drifted across the harbor entrance. The first oarsmen were already leaping for their lives from the deck of the galley, their ship hopelessly trapped. In the harbor floated thousands of candles on pieces of cork. Beside them floated the dead, clad in their festive finest.

The wooden landing stage shuddered beneath the centaurs' hooves.

"Set the boat down there," Yilvina ordered. It was her job to assume command, to prevent Ollowain's disguise from being discovered. So far, no one had recognized the injured queen lying among the other wounded, but if

Ollowain were recognized, their subterfuge would soon be uncovered. Every child in Albenmark knew that in times of emergency, the swordmaster stayed infallibly at the side of the queen. But as long as it remained unclear how many traitors—apart from Lyndwyn and the archer that had shot at Emerelle—there still were, it was better for it to be thought that the queen had fled aboard the *Moonshadow*.

The wounded were bedded down with care inside the strange sedan. Gondoran, the leader of the holdes, hopped around between the elves, giving instructions with confidence. Ollowain, with three soldiers of the queen's guard, had disembarked from the liburna before it sailed. So far, none of the three had paid him much attention. As if as an afterthought, he pulled the silk blanket covering the queen a little higher so that it partly covered her face, which was as cold as a corpse's. He shivered—the queen must not die!

He climbed out of the sedan and joined the other guards under Yilvina's command. Only Lyndwyn remained with the wounded. She had now laid one hand on Emerelle's chest. The sorceress's lips moved, but made no sound.

Ollowain glanced covertly at the blood on the silk sheet.

On a sign from Yilvina, the sedan was lifted carefully. One of the wounded groaned a little. The centaurs moved off at a walk, but Ollowain almost had to run to keep up with them.

Many of the warehouses that surrounded the harbor stood in flames, and the swordmaster could see how the flames were spreading deeper into the city. The air was so hot that every breath hurt.

Yilvina led them along the promenade by the quay. The direct route to the palace was blocked. Dead and injured lay where the fireballs had plunged into the crowds of the fleeing. No one tended to them or tried to extinguish the blazing warehouses.

A figure in flaming robes ran screaming from a side alley and plunged into the harbor. They were soon wedged helplessly between kobolds, elves, and a small group of minotaurs, making space for themselves with their horns. Riverbank sprites tumbled from the sky on singed wings and tried to cling to the hair and robes of others seeking to escape, but most of them were trampled underfoot.

The wind grew stronger. Searing hot, it tore at Ollowain's tabard. The swordmaster pulled the helmet off his head. The cheek guards had grown so hot that they were burning his skin. The other three guards did the same. Their faces were red and marked by blisters. Sparks filled the air like red-hot hail. The wind hissed through the narrow alleys of the docks and fanned the flames onward.

Gondoran hopped back and forth aboard the little boat, smothering the sparks falling on the injured.

Yilvina waved and led the party out of the stream of those trying to escape and back down to the quay. "We need water," she panted. Her lips had split, and her eyes were red. "There are buckets. Soak your clothes with water!"

Ollowain obeyed. He hurried down some stone steps leading from the quay to the water and started a chain of buckets. Even the brackish harbor water was uncomfortably warm. The storm wind had now picked up so much that long tongues of flame from the burning ships shot almost horizontally across the water. A short distance away, he saw a riverbank sprite clinging desperately to a bollard. Her delicate wings had melted in the heat to a jellylike mass. She looked at Ollowain, her tiny eyes pleading. Then she was torn away, as if snatched by an invisible fist, and flung onto the pyre of burning ships.

The soldier ahead of Ollowain doused himself with a bucket of water. "You're the last," he called to the swordmaster.

Ollowain did the same, then hurried after the others as they continued along the quay.

The centaurs forged a path more and more mercilessly, pushing aside anyone not fast enough to get out of their way.

Ollowain pressed his way ahead to Orimedes. The prince's steaming, wet hide was covered with burns. Bright sparks danced like flies around his flicking tail. "We have to get away from the quay!" The swordmaster's voice was little more than a croak, almost lost in the infernal din of the flames and the screams of the refugees.

"We will get through," the centaur bawled back. A young elf girl threw her arms around one of his legs. With her face held down, she begged the centaur to help her. Grumbling, he pulled her onto his back. Only then did Ollowain see the injured girl's face. Her eyelashes and eyebrows and the hair above her forehead were burned away. Her nose was no more than a formless hole, and where her eyes should have been gaped bloody hollows. She babbled an endless stream of thanks as she buried her ruined face in the centaur's flowing hair. Her shock at the sudden inferno seemed to have extinguished her sense of pain. At least, for the moment.

"We'll take Lotus Rise!" the swordmaster ordered.

"But that is much steeper! We'll be too slow," Orimedes objected.

"The houses there are built of stone. The flames won't spread as fast up Lotus Rise as they do here in the wooden warehouses."

Ollowain could see the cheek muscles of the centaur tense. Orimedes ground his teeth in anger, but Ollowain's order was to be carried out.

Many of those trying to flee had jumped into the harbor. The water offered a haven from the raging flames, but anyone taking refuge in it would be caught in a trap when their attackers entered the harbor. They would be at the mercy of the conquering forces.

He could not put Emerelle in that position. Who could their enemy be? With whom had Shahondin allied himself?

A deeper sound between the general tumult and the flames made Ollowain prick up his ears. It sounded like a sigh, although it would have been the sigh of a titan.

"The wall—" The scream was lost in the combined roar of a thousand smaller noises. Ollowain instinctively lifted his shield above his head. Heavy blows rained down on him.

The queen! The swordmaster reached over the side of the boat and pulled himself up. All around him, large red shingles came tumbling from above. The warehouse beside them, attacked by the flames, seemed to rise up in a final act of rebellion. It was shedding its roof!

With his large, oval shield, he covered Emerelle's head and upper body. As if by a miracle, the queen had not been hit by any of the falling shingles. Lyndwyn had been less fortunate. She lay unconscious beside Emerelle and was bleeding from a gash on her forehead.

The holdes had sought shelter beneath the low thwarts of the boat. Gondoran was the only one who stayed close to the queen. With desperate courage, he used a broken oar to swat away any shingles that fell in Emerelle's direction. But cursing, he finally had to take cover himself beneath Ollowain's shield.

The centaurs had broken into a gallop. The boat slewed wildly from one side to the other. Suddenly, there was a tremendous jolt. The boat tipped and landed with a cracking noise on stone, as if it had run aground on hidden rocks in a stormy sea. Ollowain was thrown forward and slammed into the mast. His shield arm took the full force of the blow, sending ringing pain shooting through his shoulder. Tears sprang to his eyes. Blinking, he pulled himself together and sat up to see what had happened. Two of the centaurs lay motionless on the ground, their limbs splayed grotesquely. A falling beam had struck both of them. Even as he stared at their dead bodies, a second beam crashed to the ground beside them. One of the centaurs shied and reared up on its hind legs. The boat rocked. Ollowain was just able to grab hold of the mast as the wounded slipped back to the stern. One of the men groaned. The other no longer moved.

"Nessos, you take front left!" Orimedes ordered calmly. "Antafes, stay on the left, beside the sedan. I'll stay right. We take over if anyone else falls. The sedan can't be allowed to fall again. Let's go, we—" A maelstrom of crashing and grinding cut him off. The facade of the warehouse began to lean out in the direction of the quay. Much as Shahondin always bowed with such excessive slowness before Emerelle to mock the very act of submission, the house wall now bowed outward with disdainful sluggishness. A wall of flame twenty paces high, bowing before death.

One of the holdes leaped out of the little boat with a cry and ran for the harbor. The centaurs were straining to make it out of the death zone. All around them, beams and roofing planks pelted down. Ollowain helped Gondoran and his remaining companions toss overboard the burning rubble that fell into the boat. The elf girl who was clinging to Orimedes lost her grip and slipped off his back. Ollowain saw her fall among the hooves of the other manhorses. She was thrown around like a rag doll and finally left behind, lying motionless.

The quay had emptied within moments. Almost everyone still left down there had jumped into the harbor basin. Covered with broken red roofing shingles, the cobblestones looked as if they were bleeding. With their iron-shod hooves, the centaurs had trouble finding a grip and slipped constantly. The boat jolted left and right. Ollowain had crouched low; he kept his back pressed against one of the thwarts and held Emerelle in his arms. Her head rocked with every new jolt.

Nessos went down sprawling. Antafes instantly jumped in and took his place. The blond Nessos tried to get back on his feet, but his legs would not hold him up. Ollowain saw a bloody bone protruding through his hide. The centaur raised his arms defiantly, as if to embrace the wall of flames descending toward him, and then he was engulfed. Like an avalanche of fire, the wall crashed down onto the street, and parts of the roof tumbled into the harbor itself.

The wave of heat hit Ollowain like a punch in the face. He felt his skin draw tight, and his eyes teared again as a wall of sparks showered down on them. Screams rang from the water.

"Up here!" he cried. The centaurs had run past Lotus Rise. "Back!"

A broad marble stairway wound up the fortresslike hillside. After twenty steps and the first bend, they felt as if they had entered another world. Lotus Rise was lined with magnificent structures adorned with columns. Tendrils of ivy wound upward in shaded niches, and on every step, lights had been set out. Only a few of the villas here had caught fire, and kobolds and goat-legged fauns were doing their best to bring the flames under control. They had formed a bucket brigade to a fountain. The towering buildings with their decorative gables blocked the view of the harbor. Only the crimson sky and a few soot-blackened figures who had escaped this far gave any sign of the inferno farther down. Ollowain eyed the few survivors scrambling up Lotus Rise from the flames below mistrustfully. Was someone following them? What had become of the archer who had tried to kill Emerelle? Had he or she seen through their ruse?

Ollowain felt something warm trickle over his hand. The wound in the queen's breast was bleeding again. "We will help you in the palace," he whispered, supporting her head. She could not hear him, his rational mind said, and yet he hoped that in some way he was helping her. As long as he talked to her, he felt less useless.

"It is not much farther. Andorin will heal you. No one casts more powerful healing spells than he."

Only then did Ollowain realize that the centaurs had come to a halt. They had reached the round plaza atop the hill. The villas and palaces had given way to gardens. Up here, the fireballs had hardly done any damage at all. From the hilltop, one could gaze far out to sea, and the hilltop also commanded a view over a large part of the city. The harbor, the warehouses, and the palatial tower of the prince of Reilimee, which stood at the end of a stone pier, had all been consumed by flames.

In the quarters that lay farther from the sea, only a few buildings were burning. But Ollowain could see how the hot wind was driving the fire inland toward a single, gigantic pillar of flame: Emerelle's palace! The swordmaster's breath caught in his throat. The tower lay far beyond the range of the catapults, and the flying sparks could not possibly have carried the fire so deeply into the city yet. Someone must have set fire to the queen's tower! The conspiracy against Emerelle went far deeper than he had feared.

"What now, swordmaster?" asked Orimedes tiredly. The centaur gave his men a signal to set down the sedan. "Where do we go now?"

The elf was still gazing in incomprehension at the burning tower. Was it possible for such a far-reaching conspiracy to remain hidden from Emerelle? Or had she known about everything that would come? He recalled the way she had looked at Matha Murganleuk earlier, the enormous souled tree in Magnolia Court. His intuition had not been mistaken . . . Emerelle had said good-bye. She must have known about the fate of the palace.

"Ollowain!" Orimedes was standing in front of him now. "Where do we go?"

The swordmaster looked around helplessly. "We don't dare take her down there in the sedan. Whoever set fire to the palace is just waiting to get his hands on the queen."

"Nonsense!" the centaur prince grumbled. "That makes no sense. The burning palace is a warning. It would have been much simpler just to lure us into an ambush there."

"Maybe they feel so superior that they just don't care. They know that we can no longer escape them."

"They, they, they!" Orimedes's tail flicked angrily through the air. "Who are 'they' supposed to be? Who is bombarding the city? Who set fire to the palace? Maybe there's a simple explanation for the burning tower. Flying sparks. Or a lamp that got knocked over . . ." His voice trailed off. It must have been clear even to him that no lamp had caused that fire.

Gondoran had climbed out of the boat and joined them. He clambered onto a marble bench and looked down at the palace. "She knew this was going to happen when she called on us to make the sedan."

Ollowain looked up. "Say that again."

"What?"

"The queen instructed you to build this sedan?" What had Emerelle said shortly before they left? *Have I already introduced Gondoran, my boatmaster here at the palace? It was his idea to convert this little boat into a sedan.* "Didn't you make the sedan as a gift to the queen?"

"We did," the boatmaster confirmed. "But she asked for a sedan like this. She asked me to find one of the mussel fishermen's boats from the mangroves."

"But she said—"

"I know what she said at Magnolia Court. And in a certain sense, it was my idea. I chose this boat from a dozen I could have had. But the fundamental idea of converting a boat into a sedan chair was hers. Maybe what she told us at Magnolia Court was a clue of some kind?"

"If you ask me, the whole thing sounds like the whim of a capricious queen," Orimedes objected.

"No!" The swordmaster's voice was determined. "She was not . . . she *is* not capricious! She was worried that there was a traitor very close to her. She wanted to give those who proved true to her a hidden sign. Only those who risked their own lives to carry her through the flames to this hilltop could recognize the hidden meaning of her words."

"You mean, she knew what was happening? But that is . . . that is . . . I don't have words for it! She is almost dead. My tail is half-burned off, half of my men have perished . . . and she knew it all? If that was the case, I should have left her on board her accursed ship." Orimedes stamped his hooves furiously. "That cannot be! She could have stopped all of it!" He pointed back down toward the harbor. "Hundreds, maybe thousands, have died in the last hour. Shame on the queen if she knew that this would happen and did nothing to stop it!"

Ollowain could understand the centaur's straightforward thinking, although his abusive tone was not acceptable. The swordmaster's own belief remained unshaken: Emerelle had done what was right. She had once tried to explain to him what a curse it was to be able to see into the future. When she was still very young, she had saved the life of her brother in arms Mahawan in the first troll war. Ollowain presumed that he had also been the queen's lover, although she had never said so. She had used her knowledge of the future to rescue him, but by doing so, she had fundamentally altered her lover's future. Because he did not die in the hour that fate had determined he should, he could also not be born again. Later, he disappeared during a quest in the Shattered World. He was never reborn, his soul forever erased. Emerelle had explained that Mahawan had been destined to one day wear the crown of Albenmark. She had also said that he would have been a good king. Her selfish actions had robbed Albenmark of that ruler. From then on, Emerelle was extremely careful about using her knowledge of the possible futures.

"She knows what is best for us. We don't need to be able to understand her decisions," Ollowain said.

Orimedes snorted disdainfully. "If her words are full of hidden meanings, then she is still interfering with the course of the future. She could just as easily say, 'Do this, don't do that!'"

Ollowain thought briefly about how he could explain to the pigheaded centaur that a direct order was far from the same as ambiguous insinuations. The latter allowed them the freedom to follow their own instinct. "Hold your tongue. That is an order."

"Don't push too far, elfling!"

Ollowain ignored the threat and turned back to Gondoran. "What else did the queen ask of you? Did she have any specific requests for the construction?"

"She wanted the sedan made in such a way that one could plug the holes and make it float again. We have wooden disks we can fit into the holes that the carrying poles go through. It is not difficult to make the boat watertight again."

Ollowain looked back desperately. A wall of fire separated them from the harbor. Their breathless flight had left him with no time to think. "So she wanted us to escape to sea. And therefore the boat . . . I should have known it sooner!"

"If you think I'm going to carry this blasted sedan back through that fire—" Orimedes began.

Gondoran cleared his throat loudly.

"If I want something from you, I'll let you know," the centaur snarled at the holde.

Gondoran recoiled a little from the manhorse. "With all due respect, noble sirs, you're mistaken. This boat is not built to carry someone on the open sea. A flat-bottomed skiff like this is useful in the mangrove swamps. The water there doesn't move, and there are few spots where it would even rise above your chest, Prince. In many places, it is hardly deeper than a puddle. On the open sea, this boat would fill up with water faster than you could bail it out."

Ollowain gazed off into the darkness, eyes narrowed. About a mile west of the royal palace lay the mussel-fishers' harbor. Was that what Emerelle had wanted? Would they be able to escape from there? All around the palace now, houses were blazing. Ollowain thought he could make out contorted shadows moving among the flames. In the firelight, they seemed unnaturally large. There was fighting going on down there, too. The fires were spreading against the direction of the wind; the rooftops were not falling victim to flying sparks.

Try as he might, Ollowain could not recognize the enemy raging below in the smoke and darkness. The route to the mussel-fishers' harbor was sealed off. Feverishly, Ollowain thought through the choices open to them. A single fighter could no doubt slip through the enemy's ranks easily enough, but getting through with the queen's sedan would be impossible. Unless they went around in a very wide arc. Far to the east, on a tongue of land protruding like a narrow sickle between the sea and the mangrove swamps, was the district of the tanners, a region with such a ghastly reek that no elf would show his face there. With a little luck, they could make it there before their faceless enemy could—and from there find a way out onto the Woodmer.

Ollowain turned to the leader of the holdes. "Which route would you choose to get down to the mangroves?"

Gondoran stared into the darkness and pulled at his pointed chin. "I would go through the cisterns. We would be completely hidden from view down there. And anyone who does not know their way around down there will soon find themselves hopelessly lost."

"And you know how to get through?" Orimedes clearly had no desire to go stumbling around in underground reservoirs.

"My cousin was the master of waters!" Gondoran declared proudly. "When I was still a young lad, he often took me down into the cisterns to help clear the spillway pipes of silt and weed. I know the hidden halls down there as well as I know the mangroves and the Woodmer."

"And we could make it from here to the edge of the city?" asked the centaur prince doubtfully. "That's more than a mile. The cisterns are never that big."

"Do you always talk with such certainty about things you know nothing about, horsefly bait? There certainly are reservoirs almost a mile in length, and many more smaller cisterns, all connected by canals and lock chambers. This city takes a lot of water, and because it is pinned between the sea and the mangroves, drinking water is a valuable commodity. In Vahan Calyd, they've always had to collect the rainwater, which is piped down though filter basins and into the large reservoirs. There's a hidden sea beneath our feet. Even if no rain fell in Vahan Calyd for a year, no one here would go thirsty or have to go without a bath."

"And we could get down there with the skiff?" Ollowain asked doubtfully.

"Oh, yes! There are many boats down there. How else are the master of waters and all his servants supposed to do their jobs? But we have to climb down through one of the lock chambers—there are doors there that are wide enough to get a boat in. Once we get down there, we'll have no more problems." He looked over at the centaur contemptuously. "Unless his four-legged highness here can't swim."

Orimedes replied with a disdainful snort.

"Lead us to the next lock chamber!" Ollowain ordered.

Gondoran looked around for a moment, then pointed westward. "Two hundred paces that way is the Chamber of Roses. That's the nearest way down."

"And we will have to swim?"

The holde nodded. "The boat can't carry all of us. You'll have to hold on to the sides."

The swordmaster stripped off his tunic and ordered Yilvina and the surviving guards to leave behind all unnecessary weight. Nothing was to remain in the cisterns that could give a potential pursuer a clue to their escape route. Ollowain pushed the expendable equipment out of sight beneath an oleander bush. The other elven warriors did the same, following his orders without question—he would be able to rely on them and Yilvina. As for Orimedes and his four centaurs, Ollowain was not so sure.

The manhorses stood a little apart, and their prince was talking insistently to them, gesturing wildly. It was clear what they thought of choosing an escape route that would take them deep underground.

Gondoran and his two remaining companions were examining the hull of the small boat. Ollowain thought about the bad fall they had suffered—if one of the planks was too badly damaged, then all their plans would be for nothing. He went over to the boatmaster.

The holde pointed inside the boat. "One of the guards has kicked the bucket. He's just excess ballast now; best we can do is leave him under the oleander with all that other stuff."

Ollowain tensed. "Watch your tone. Just because I'm dependent on you does not mean you can get away with anything, Boatmaster."

"Oh, no?" The holde sneered. "Let's call a spade a spade. Your comrade here is meat, no more. He was the one who chose to be a fighter, and now he's expired in battle. Among his sort, that's what they call a fulfilled life. My men are fishermen who wanted to go to a party this evening. You can be happy they haven't all taken off."

"You and your men are servants of the queen, as am I, Boatmaster. She knew that she would make her escape in that ridiculous tub. It is your task to get her to safety. The three of you will no more shirk your duty than would my soldiers flee from a battle. If necessary, I will nail your and your companions' feet to the planks of that boat until Emerelle is safe. I do not expect a holde to behave with chivalry, but you will do your duty like everyone else here. Now tell me if the boat has taken any damage."

Gondoran glared furiously but swallowed whatever rebuke he might have been considering. "One plank is cracked. We'll take on a little water, but the boat will float."

The swordmaster leaned over Emerelle. The queen's skin still felt icy. Although Lyndwyn was unconscious, her magic continued to work. The sorceress's dress was pocked with burn marks, her hair singed and her face smeared with blood. And yet there was still something at once uncanny and fearsome about her. Her right hand rested on Emerelle's chest. She really seemed to be trying hard to protect the queen. Had he done her an injustice? No. Anyone could see how she gave the signal to attack. She was a traitor!

Ollowain stroked his dead companion's face and closed his eyes. It was clear that Lyndwyn had done nothing to try to help the two injured guards. Their wounds had not been bandaged, nor was there any sign that she had cast a spell to ease the men's pain. He would have preferred to leave the sorceress behind.

They carried their comrade into the bushes on his shield. There was barely time to say a few words of farewell—honoring the dead meant endangering the living. Without warning, Ollowain had the feeling that they were being watched. He looked around, but in the landscaped gardens surrounding them, there were a hundred hiding places. He could see no one.

When they returned to the boat, Gondoran was standing inside it. The centaurs had hoisted the unusual sedan onto their shoulders again. The holde directed the group down through a garden on the back of the hill until they reached a fountain, behind which a broad stairway led down into the earth. Even there, someone had set a small oil lamp on every step to mark the Festival of Light. It occurred to Ollowain that no one could ever again mark that day without thinking of the terrible fire and all the dead.

The iron-clad hooves of the centaurs clattered on the marble steps. Cautiously, they descended into the depths until they reached a large door; they lowered the skiff gently to the ground. The door had neither handle nor hinges.

Orimedes ran one hand reverently over the door. "That's gold, isn't it?" he breathed. "Pure gold. Enough to pay for a palace. A fortune."

"Every lock down here, every tooth of every gear, every fitting is made of gold. No other metal resists water over the centuries as well as gold can," Gondoran explained condescendingly. "When these cisterns were built, only the very best materials were used."

Gondoran jumped down from the boat and went to the golden portal. He pressed his cheek against the cold metal, stroked the door with circular movements, and whispered something.

"What did you say?" asked Orimedes.

"That's a secret of the guardians of the water. If this was not about the queen, I would never let you in. We don't want to let every stinking barbarian into the cisterns to cool his feet in drinking water." Gondoran dodged a kick from the prince and waved them into a broad hall. Moonstones shimmering silvery blue were set into the arches of the vaulted ceiling, bathing the hall in mysterious light. From somewhere in the distance came a low rumbling, like thunder. Ollowain thought he could feel the floor underfoot tremble slightly.

The entire hall was built of marble. At chest height, a wide frieze of onyx and mother-of-pearl ran around the sides, displaying a pattern of stylized waves. In the cold light of the hall, it seemed as if the waves moved, like the gentle swell of the sea on a full-moon night.

"Bring the boat inside!" the holde ordered. "From now on, we won't be needing the poles. Pull them out and we can seal the boat."

Ollowain was surprised at the natural authority that the little boatman suddenly radiated. He seemed completely changed. Down here was his realm, and no one doubted that. Without a grumbled word, the centaurs did as they were told.

The swordmaster looked around. The cool splendor of the hall had something about it that made one feel utterly insignificant. It had been created for ages and was worthy of any king's palace. And yet hardly any of the city's inhabitants ever came here. All of this beauty lay hidden. Ollowain looked up the long steps they had come down, washed in the glow from the oil lamps. The fires in the harbor made the night sky appear purple. Momentarily lost in thought, he recalled the curtain closing on a theater stage. Down here, in the cool magnificence of the cisterns, he felt himself strangely far removed from everything that had happened this night. One act had come to an end. A new chapter in the history of Albenmark was beginning.

The soft hum of metal jolted him out of his thoughts. Yilvina had drawn both of her short swords. She pointed up the steps with one of the blades. "There's someone up there! An archer. I saw his shadow clearly against the night sky."

Ollowain could see no one, but he did not doubt Yilvina's word for a moment. Since starting their ascent of Lotus Rise, he had sensed that they were being followed. Yilvina's words confirmed it—they were not yet out of danger! "How do we get to the water?" he asked Gondoran.

The holde pointed to the decorative frieze on the wall. "The seventh wave. If you push it, a hidden entry opens."

"And how do you close the golden portal?"

"That closes automatically," Gondoran replied matter-of-factly. "This is the entrance to the hidden lake and not the gatehouse of a fortress. We have no influence on when the entrance to the Chamber of Roses closes. But the door that leads down to the cisterns can be closed from the inside. Anyone who doesn't know how to find it will have a hard time following us."

Ollowain counted the waves in the frieze and pressed on the concealed release. He heard a faint click, then a grating noise. A section of the wall swung open. The distant thundering was now more distinct, and a blast of cold, damp air rose from the depths—Ollowain shivered. Beyond the secret door, a stairway led downward into a dark abyss.

Gondoran passed through first. "There is a supply of torches here."

The centaurs looked uncertainly into the darkness. "Maybe we should stay behind and catch that archer," one of them murmured.

"That's not what matters." Orimedes reached for the stern of the boat. "We have to get the queen out of the city." He pointed his chin toward the dark entrance. "And that is the only way still open to us. Grab hold! We have no time to lose!"

A torch flared to life with a muffled hiss. Gondoran was standing in front of a chest with gold fittings. The holde took out two more torches and pushed them into his belt. The centaurs tentatively started down the steps, with Yilvina and Ollowain bringing up the rear. As the heavy secret door closed, they could see the golden portal also sliding slowly out of the wall. For a moment, Ollowain thought he heard hasty footsteps descending to the blue-lit hall, but the impression quickly faded.

The stairway led past a tiled wall depicting images of a riverscape, the thickets along the shore concealing myriad species of birds. The air was saturated and smelled of wet stone. Their route led them to a stone quay where two boats were tied.

Under Gondoran's watchful eye, the centaurs lowered the boat holding the queen into the water, while his companions retrieved two paddles stowed out of sight beneath the thwarts and slipped them through the rowlocks. Then the boatmaster took over the tiller in the stern. He placed his torch in a holder on the mast, and they extinguished the other lights.

Ollowain had never been afraid of the dark, but the depth of the blackness down there was a trial for him. The light cast by the smoky torch on the mast barely made it beyond the sides of the boat. He felt as if he had stumbled into the nothingness that lay beyond the Albenpaths, a place where no life had a place. A traveler who erred from a path between the worlds was lost forever, it was said. At which point had he strayed from the path this night? When had he taken the first false step? When he had met with Silwyna?

The swordmaster slid from the small dock into the water and reached for the boat. He exhaled in shock: the water in the cistern was ice-cold!

"We should not have climbed into this hole," Orimedes growled. "Something just slithered over my leg. We'll get lost and end up eaten by fish."

"That must be your own shaking tail between your legs, manhorse. There are no fish here!" said Gondoran sharply. "Nor bugs, nor rats. Nothing that could contaminate water lives down here. Just a few ghosts, but you don't have to fear that a ghost will piss in your water supply. This is drinking water, and the master of waters does not suffer the presence of anything here that could pollute it. But these are special circumstances."

The others had also clambered from the dock into the water. Slowly, the little boat set off into the darkness. After a few moments, the stairway and dock had vanished in the blackness behind them. The torchlight did not reach the ceiling of the cistern. Ollowain tried to suppress the feeling nagging at him, the impression of being lost. Not having a visible goal was something unaccustomed. Where were they supposed to go when they reached the mangroves? Their best course would be to escape through an Albenstar, but to do that they needed Lyndwyn's help. Ollowain knew neither the necessary magic to open a portal to the Albenpaths nor where one was even supposed to go looking for them. In Vahan Calyd were two large Albenstars, he knew. One lay beneath Emerelle's burning tower, and the second was close to Shahondin's palace, both routes closed to him. He had heard of more Albenstars farther out on the Woodmer, though . . .

Ollowain looked at the sorceress. Although the gash on her head appeared superficial and he did not believe she was seriously injured, she was still unconscious. Lyndwyn could lead them in the wrong direction among the Albenpaths without him noticing anything. Only when they stepped out through a gate again would they see where the sorceress had taken them.

"See that?" Yilvina pointed back the way they had come. Behind and above them, high up, a small, silvery rectangle seemed punched out of the darkness. A shadow stepped through the light, then the rectangle disappeared and the darkness, apart from the torch on the boat, was once again complete. "Who was that?"

Gondoran had noticed the light, too. He said nothing, but he kept glancing behind them as he guided the skiff through the cistern.

The thundering ahead of them grew louder and louder. The boatmaster helmed them through a golden lock door into a channel. It was so narrow there that the sidewalls were within arm's reach. The water in the channel was not very deep, and they had solid ground underfoot as they felt their way forward. An archer there would be able to stand firmly and could shoot . . . They were safer in the deep water of the cistern.

Ollowain dropped back a little. Was it Silwyna? Had he been mistaken about her? Ahead of them in the tunnel gleamed a light as bright as a summer day, and he sensed the power of old magic. Where had the holde brought them?

Yilvina came back to him. She waved and said something, but her words were drowned out by the deafening thunder of water. The tunnel widened. They reached a large, circular vault, its ceiling studded with glowing barinstones. Gold pipes with artfully formed outflows jutted from the marble walls. Some looked like the stylized heads of birds with broad bills, others like dolphins or even wolves. There must have been hundreds of them. The water shot from the spouts in broad fans, and the bright light made it look like liquid crystal. The air was suffused with a fine mist; shimmering rainbows spanned the cascades.

Ollowain moved forward again to keep up with the boat. The basin in this magnificent domed hall was not deep, and the water flowed so powerfully that the swordmaster struggled to stay on his feet, although the swirling masses barely reached his knees. The centaurs had an even harder job. With their horse-shoes, they found little grip on the smooth stone underfoot and had to hold on to the edge of the boat to prevent themselves from being toppled by the current.

The fountains beat down on Ollowain. Even the floor of the great chamber vibrated under the force of the falling water. And though all of them had to fight the ancient force of the water, Gondoran himself seemed unconcerned. He stood in the stern of the skiff, steadfastly holding the tiller, bellowing a song at the top of his lungs.

Engulfed in the din of the water, Ollowain could not hear all the words; the song seemed to be about a holde woman whose breasts were bountiful springs. The quarrelsome little creature was a puzzle . . . was he singing to hide his fear, or was he truly as joyful as he sounded? The domed hall was incredibly beautiful—the light, the rainbows, the gleaming white stone of the walls. If not for the infernal noise, one could enjoy being in there simply to see it and to open one's soul to the beauty of that hidden wonder.

Gondoran steered the boat through a wall of water. His two companions bailed as fast as they could to stop the boat from filling up. The fountains were like a curtain of crystal, none closer than two paces from the marble walls of the domed hall. But just there, the current was even stronger. Large bricked arches in the walls greedily swallowed the outflowing water. Channels led out of the circular hall in every direction . . . Ollowain could not see that they were marked in any particular way. To him, all the openings looked alike, but Gondoran obviously knew exactly where he was. At the seventh channel they passed, he turned the rudder and steered the boat back into darkness.

The tunnel seemed only to amplify the roar of the falling water. The holdes finally managed to relight the torch, which had been extinguished by the fountains.

"Isn't it wonderful? The Hall of Falling Waters . . . ," the boatmaster said when the noise behind them had finally ebbed. "I've spent entire days in here."

"*Wonderful* is not the word that *I* would use," said Yilvina. "*Spectacular*, perhaps."

"What do you know about the beauty of the water?" Gondoran replied, put out. "You have no idea how much work it takes to tend to the water."

"You talk about water as if you were tending a herd of cows," the centaur prince mocked. "How hard can it be to take care of water?"

"If we did not take care of the water, then all of Vahan Calyd would only have lukewarm, stale broth to drink! It starts with making sure that no rats or unwashed centaurs find their way down here for a bath. Every drop here is filtered through deep filter pits. The Normirga, our queen's people, built Vahan Calyd a long time ago. They devised magical pumps that keep the water in motion, like a giant heart. Water was created to flow, to pulse, to tumble from heights. That's how you keep it alive, manhorse. When it tumbles from the spouts in the Hall of Falling Waters, it breathes. And my people tend this magnificent creation."

"Well, I fear I just evacuated my bowels in your water, Gondoran. I'll wear sackcloth and ashes and do penance, but I could not restrain myself any longer."

The other centaurs burst out laughing, but Gondoran only stared wide-eyed at the prince.

"You . . . what?"

"I'm afraid I overdid things a little at lunch. And then all the excitement. The fire. The escape. It does stimulate one's digestion."

"That's a joke, isn't it?" said the holde pleadingly. "Please tell me you're joking."

"I never joke about my own droppings," Orimedes replied with a grin. "When it's time to go, it's time to go. And I must say, I've had some embarrassing moments at certain elven celebrations. We are as the Alben made us." He shrugged. "But in this huge amount of water, it's bound to spread well."

Gondoran did not reply. He and his two companions fell into silence while the centaurs continued with their crude jokes.

The tunnel led them through a lock chamber into another cistern, and they had to swim again. Ollowain looked back from time to time. It would be a miracle if their pursuers had not lost their trail in the Hall of Falling Waters. Gondoran had not said anything, but the swordmaster was certain that the holde had chosen to pass through the curtain of water at a point a good distance above the tunnel that they had then entered. Whoever was following them had a choice of more than two dozen channels that led out of the domed hall.

Yet Ollowain continued to look back. It had also been improbable that their pursuer would find the secret door so fast . . .

When none of the holdes reacted to the centaurs' provocations, the man-horses also soon fell silent, and the entire party drifted on through the dark without a sound in their little island of light. Now and then they passed one of the enormous columns that carried the cistern ceiling. Ollowain allowed his thoughts to wander. He thought back to the times with Alfadas. The queen, back then, had given him the task of raising Alfadas. At first, he had thought of it as a punishment. What could one expect of a human, after all? He was supposed to teach him how to fight with the sword, knowing full well that he would not live long enough to master even one of the twenty-seven arts of killing. Yilvina, his best student for centuries, had so far achieved mastery in four of the arts and could now best even Ollowain himself when fighting with two swords.

The human had surprised him, though. Despite lacking the time to reach perfection, his burning ambition and his almost uncanny talent balanced out that disadvantage. In the world of humans, there would be no one to equal him. Ollowain wondered what had become of his student. Did he possess the maturity to handle the skill he had? Or had he used it to become a tyrant?

If only Alfadas had never met Silwyna! The Maurawan had awakened a dark side in the human. She had wounded him in a way that had never healed.

It was too bitter to think about that. There was so much that the young man could have achieved, but he chose instead to flee Albenmark.

The swordmaster looked back over his shoulder and listened. Behind him lay only darkness and silence. He'd had no choice—he had to ask for her help. Silwyna was the best archer he was able to find at such short notice. He smiled grimly. If *she* had shot at the queen, she would never have missed her target.

"Swordmaster?" Gondoran's voice shook Ollowain out of his thoughts. The holde pointed ahead, where a tiny red point of light was visible in the darkness. "Something is not right ahead. Both doors to the cistern look to be wide open. That can't happen. What should we do?"

"How far is it to the door?"

The boatmaster shrugged. "Three hundred feet, perhaps."

"Douse the torch!"

Gondoran obeyed. "It won't help now. If someone is there watching the cistern, they would have seen us coming long ago."

"I'll go check. Stay here and wait on a sign from me. Is there a box of torches there?"

"Of course. There's one at every entrance."

Ollowain stripped off his tabard. The sword alone was heavy enough. He had never been an outstanding swimmer, so better to leave everything he didn't absolutely need. He slung the leather sword belt across his chest and back and pulled it tight.

"I'll come with you," said Orimedes. "Waiting here and doing nothing is not for me."

Ollowain sighed inwardly. The last thing he needed at his side now was the volatile centaur prince.

"With no disrespect, my friend, I will attempt to reach the exit as covertly as possible. I appreciate your offer, but I must turn it down."

"I can move silently," the prince persisted.

"And who will protect the queen if I don't come back? You are the born leader. You will find a way! I need you here, Orimedes."

The centaur grunted. "Sometimes I hate being a prince. Good luck."

"If you are able to follow me, I will swing a burning torch in a circle." Ollowain pushed away from the boat. With strong, even strokes, he swam toward the light.

THE CONFESSION

Y ou have broken the seal and foolishly ignored my warning. I ask you a final time, return this letter to its hiding place if you want your conscience to remain clean.

A single, dark act can destroy a life of noble-mindedness. And it is such an act that I must report. I had hoped, for the part I played, to go into the moonlight. I thought it was my destiny. But I was mistaken. I cannot go on living with my knowledge of what happened on this night. And yet it would be a crime to sacrifice the truth to the lies, as it will happen. None among the Albenkin would believe the trolls. And even they are unlikely ever to discover what really happened. I have to write it down, for the truth may not be forgotten for all time.

When this is complete, I will erase my memory of it forever and will never again touch the seal of this letter. Be warned one final time, unknown witness to my disgrace! You do not want to know the truth! Never again will you look at Albenmark with innocent eyes if you read on now.

Emerelle issued an order for the king and the dukes of the trolls to be taken to the Shalyn Falah. It was said that from there, they would be led to their imprisonment in a secret location, but that their folk would forever be banished from Albenmark. We paid too dearly, with too much blood, for our victory. We attacked them from every side, and the trolls imagined they were lost. For that reason, they surrendered their weapons and put themselves at our mercy. They believed that we had surrounded them with far superior numbers, but in truth they were stronger than we, and if they had risen a final time, nothing in Albenmark would have been able to stand in their way. Our victory was tarnished, achieved through deception as it was. All of us, that night, knew that the children of the Alben would need decades to recover from the preceding battles.

But all of that cannot excuse what happened. Still my hope is that you, unknown witness to my disgrace, can at least understand why it happened. Could we allow the reign over Albenmark to pass into the hands of its most terrible children?

The troll king and his dukes were gagged and led out onto the Shalyn Falah with their eyes bound. They probably thought they were to be taken to the dungeon of the fortress on the other side of the bridge. Then Emerelle commanded her swordmaster to push the trolls into the abyss. But honorable Ollowain, who had never before hesitated to follow his queen's command, refused. Then another warrior, by the name of Farodin, offered to carry out her command. Farodin's lover Aileen had been killed by trolls. But Emerelle forbade him—she did not want an act of revenge. She wanted an executioner with a cold heart to commit the bloody deed and thereby to save Albenmark. And so I stepped forward. Gagged and blind, they fell in silence, like stones, into the chasm.

In the belief that their dukes were our prisoners, the trolls would not begin a search for their leaders. And it may be that their souls can no longer clothe themselves in flesh in the human world. No one knows if that is possible. I hope for peace. But I fear that the trolls will one day discover the secret of this night. For then peace will never again be possible, and Albenmark will drown in the blood of its children.

From the estate of Master Alvias

THE VOICE FROM THE LIGHT

The elven ship scraped along the harbor wall, and several trolls jumped from the deck to tie it up. A spear hit one of the warriors.

Orgrim pointed to the tower bathed in cold light that stood at the end of the wall. "Go and smash that door down and kill the elves inside." The pack leader was furious. First, he had had to ask other pack leaders to tow the elven ship, and then it was impossible to actually enter the harbor. Orgrim had pictured himself entering the city in triumph, carrying the queen's body on his shield so that everyone could see her. But fate was threatening to steal away his fame. Entering the harbor would be insane with dozens of burning wrecks still drifting around. The troll fleet was now tying up at the long outer wall, which had been built to protect the inner harbor from the waves of the open sea.

More and more warrior packs were jumping down from the ships and storming toward the city with shrieks and bellows. As far as Orgrim could see, they were met with no serious resistance anywhere. After the fight on board the queen's ship, he was happy about that. The elves were small and weak, that much was true. A single blow from a club would break their bones and make them cough up their lungs, but it was damned hard to hit them in the first place. And their blades were quick and cut deep.

"Pack leader, a visitor!" Boltan had come storming onto the quarterdeck and pointed now out to sea. "The king!"

A huge shadow was emerging from the wall of grim ship silhouettes. The red lanterns lit the mainmast. The *Deathbringer*, the king's own ship! Had he seen who had boarded the elven liburna first? Orgrim mentally cursed himself for a fool. The king was only coming to see the captured ship. How could he have observed the boarding battle from a distance and at night?

Orgrim stepped up to the bed where the tyrant's twisted body lay. His large hands stroked the swan crown. It had really happened. He had killed the queen's swordmaster and captured Emerelle's cadaver. No one could take that from him. He had no need to take part in the fighting in the city.

The *Deathbringer*'s oars were pulled in and lines cast out. Slowly, the huge ship turned alongside the wall. Its decks lay more than eight ells higher.

The elven ship groaned as it became wedged between the *Deathbringer* and the harbor wall. Orgrim heard wood split. The miserable little vermin could not even build a solid boat! It amazed him that their thin-skinned ships managed to survive storms at all.

A boarding ramp crashed onto the deck of the liburna. King Branbeard and his entourage climbed down. The king of the trolls was a stocky figure and somewhat shorter than most of his kind. Bony bulges protruded above his eyes, giving the impression that two horns were beginning to emerge from the base of his forehead. Branbeard's nose was broad and somewhat crooked. Impressive scars adorned his face and scalp—the king had been victorious in single combat many times. A wolfskin cape hung over his shoulders, and he wore a greasy leather kilt. "Hey-ho, Fire Eater!" Branbeard approached Boltan and clapped him on the shoulder. "Congratulations on your catch!" He swept his eyes across the dead elves on deck and smiled with satisfaction. "You really tanned their hides. Tomorrow you shall sit at my table."

"I . . ." Boltan squirmed with embarrassment. "Orgrim is pack leader. I am only the artillery chief."

"I know that." The king sniffed sharply, then blew his nose out on the deck. "But you really gave those elven cockroaches something to think about." Branbeard pointed to a cut on the artillery chief's arm. "And I see you did not shy from those accursed elven blades either. I was talking about you just yesterday, Boltan. Smothering a fire with your own body! By the Alben, I need more men like you! It's as I said: tomorrow evening, I want to see you at my table!"

Orgrim was struggling to contain himself. What was the king doing? Was he trying to insult him in front of all his warriors?

Branbeard turned around. He stank of mead and patted Orgrim's cheek patronizingly. "Well, my whelp. Was it clever of me to give you a pack of your own?" His eyes blazed beneath his bulging brows. "Where is your ship?"

Orgrim ignored the question. Calling someone "whelp"—a helpless creature not yet weaned from its mother's teats—counted as a terrible slur among troll warriors. Only with an effort was Orgrim able to keep his composure. The king was obviously drunk.

"The tyrant is dead. And I struck down her swordmaster." He pointed to the makeshift bed of skins on which Emerelle was laid out. "Our rain of fire destroyed the elven queen."

The king sniffed loudly again. "That's supposed to be her?" He stepped to the body and stared at Emerelle for a long time. "Her face is too burned. And she's wearing the dress of a young maiden. Elven witch! I'd been hoping . . ." He shook his head. "No, I don't remember her anymore." He spat on the swordmaster's body, which was still lying where Orgrim's war hammer had felled him. "She stood and watched when I was led out onto the Shalyn Falah. Mandrag!" He waved over one of the men in his entourage. "Do you remember how she had me sent flying?"

A gray-haired old warrior stepped to the king's side. He bit hard on his bottom lip as he stared at the tyrant queen. Then he reached for the crown. Orgrim saw tears of rage sparkle in the old troll's eyes. "I remember this." He lifted the crown and showed it to all around him. "She wore this on the night of treachery. I recognize it! It has to be her."

Branbeard grunted in annoyance. "*Has to be* isn't good enough! Bring Skanga down here!" The king turned to Orgrim. "You still owe me an answer, whelp!"

Orgrim did not understand.

"Your ship!" the king snarled at him.

"The elves sank it. They rammed the *Rumbler* when we boarded here, but they could not repel us from the queen's ship again."

"*Could not repel us from the queen's ship,*" Branbeard mocked. "I entrusted a ship to you, whelp, because I'd been told you were worthy of being a pack leader. And where is it now? Lying on the bottom of the sea!"

"None of my men went down with it, and I captured this elven ship. If I had not boarded it, the elves would have escaped with the body of their queen."

Branbeard stamped so hard that the wood beneath his foot creaked threateningly. "You call this a ship? It's elven junk, no more! Don't try to talk your way out of it, whelp. The other pack leaders who lost their ships this night were at least smart enough to stay out of my sight." He turned to the old warrior. "How many ships did we lose, Mandrag?"

"Four, my king."

"Four ships! Each with more than two hundred warriors on board—that's an army! And all of them burned?"

"Yes, my king."

"I never again want to see any of those thrice-cursed fireballs on board a troll ship. And you can toss those catapults overboard tomorrow. We're trolls! No one can match our strength. From this day forth and for all time, I decree that stones will be *thrown*, and that fire has no business being on board a troll ship." He sniffed violently and spat at Orgrim's feet. "There is only one thing more stupid, and that is to lose your own ship to an elven tub. You were warned, weren't you? Or did someone forget to mention the iron rams on their ships? You should have paid more attention to the *Rumbler*, whelp!"

A bowed figure appeared at the top of the boarding ramp. With her gout-ridden fingers, she held tightly to the rail. All talk ceased. Orgrim had never seen Skanga, the great shaman of his race, in the flesh. She tottered carefully down the steep wooden bridge. The shaman wore a coarse dress so patched that it was no longer possible to guess its original color. Every step she took was accompanied by a soft rustling and clicking—around her wrinkled neck hung dozens of amulets and charms: small figures carved from bone, stone rings, feathers, the dried head of a bird, and something that looked like half a raven's wing. The stories about her power were countless. It was said that she could kill with a look, and that she had been alive since the days when the Alben still moved among their children.

"I hope you had a good reason to send for me." She spoke softly, her voice slightly hoarse, but every word was very clear.

"Pack Leader Orgrim believes he has stumbled onto the tyrant's body." Branbeard sniffed again, but this time he stepped briefly to the rail instead of spitting on the deck.

Skanga turned to Orgrim. Her eyes were covered with a thin white mucus. She reached out and placed her hand in his. "Lead me to Emerelle, whelp."

It felt to Orgrim as if he were holding a dried branch. The shaman's fingers were hard, and he had the impression they were numb. Her nails were as curved as a bear's. Skanga looked up at him and blinked. "I know you, whelp. Come to me when the fights are done." She giggled quietly. "So Orgrim is your name now."

Orgrim's stomach clenched. He had heard that the shaman sometimes had young, strong warriors brought to her, and that she stole from their life force.

He led her to where the queen lay. Despite her milky eyes, Skanga did not seem really blind at all. She took a long step over the dead body of the swordmaster without him having to warn her. Why had she wanted to hold his hand? To find out if he was the right victim for her blood magic?

The shaman laid her knotty hand on the dead queen's chest and picked at the torn dress. Then she let out a grunt of annoyance and felt Emerelle's forehead, her long nails digging into the burned flesh. Skanga murmured softly to herself, and Orgrim understood not a single word of what she said. She commanded the elf woman to return, and her voice had taken on a dark, unnatural quality. The pack leader shuddered. Suddenly, the air around them had grown cooler. A gust of wind rushed in from the open sea and rattled the rigging. The lips of the dead queen trembled. Her mouth fell open. Light dripped in viscous threads, like honey, from the corners of her mouth and radiated through her closed eyelids. A heartbreaking whimper could be heard.

"Don't resist," Skanga breathed. "I have called back your light, elf. I can hold it as long as I want. You are now reliving the torment of the moment of your death. Your burned flesh. The shattered bones in your body."

The whimpering grew more shrill. The eyelids of the dead woman fluttered. Orgrim took a step back, and in that moment, he was certain that everything he had ever heard about Skanga was true.

"Everyone has always told me what I want to hear. It is useless to struggle; in the end you all talk. Submit. Tell me your name. Just your name, and I will release you."

The dead queen's eyes opened. She had neither eyeballs nor pupils anymore. Only a brilliant light so bright that the pack leader had to avert his eyes.

"Your name!"

"Sa . . . San . . ."

Tears of light trickled from her eyes. Her voice choked into an inarticulate howl, which grew louder and louder and became an agonized shriek. Orgrim had heard the screams of the dying often, but seeing the dead elf tortured beyond death upset him deeply. So there was no peace. Not even in the grave. Never.

"Sansella!" the queen wailed. "My name is Sansella! Sansella!"

Skanga withdrew her hand. The eerie light vanished instantly. The body lay completely still. Orgrim stared at the dead woman in shock. Could the dead tell a lie? Was this the tyrant queen's final deception?

"I can imagine what you are thinking right now." Skanga fixed her milky eyes on him. "The answer is no."

Branbeard spat again at Orgrim's feet. "That's what you sacrificed your ship for, whelp. You are not worthy to be a pack leader. I am taking your pack away from you. From now on, you are a warrior. And I suspect that even that is too much!"

Orgrim looked disbelievingly from the dead body to the king and then to Skanga. The elven bastards had taken everything from him! He was too surprised and shaken to be able get out a single word. For days, all his thoughts had been focused on how he might become a duke, and now he was no longer even a pack leader.

The shaman held the swan crown in her hand and stroked the cold metal. "The bond between them is breaking," she said quietly. "The queen wore this crown for so long that there is a connection between this piece of metal and her, but it is growing weaker and weaker. She seems to be close to death." Skanga had closed her eyes and now pressed the crown firmly to her chest. "She is on the edge of the tree-swamps on the other side of the city."

"Bring her to me!" Branbeard called. "Whoever brings me Emerelle will be a duke! Send ships to stop her from escaping to the open sea. Surround her! Hunt her like wolves hunt a wounded deer. You heard it yourselves—she's dying. Bring her to me! If Emerelle escapes, this victory is worthless!"

BENEATH THE PRICKLY SHROUD

A dead lamassu drifted past Ollowain, its wings spread wide. The strands of its oiled beard surrounded its dark face like dancing water snakes. The enormous pinions and the ox's body had been smashed and broken by numerous heavy blows. Only its sun-browned countenance—with its classical nose, nobly curved brows, and full, sensual lips—remained untouched. The lamassu drifted beneath a broad beam of red light that fell through the gate beneath the cistern's ceiling and onto the water. It was not the only corpse that had been thrown down there.

Ollowain swam to the dock and held on to a gold ring that had been set into the wall, where boats could tie up. Everything was silent. Nothing moved—nothing in the water, nothing on the stairs, nothing on the path leading up to the red light.

Without a sound, the swordmaster pulled himself out of the cistern basin. Ducking low, he ran to the stairs. The white marble floor was smeared with blood. Ollowain drew his sword and, with long paces, strode upward toward the light.

There, too, a secret door led from the cisterns into a magnificent hall. A black frieze with mother-of-pearl trees was the only decoration on the marble walls. Most of the oil lamps on the stairs leading up to the city had been crushed underfoot. There was blood on the walls and floor, and the heavy gold gate had been bashed in. It looked as if an angry giant had hammered it down with his fists. Beyond the gate, the night sky glowed in flickering purple.

The stairs led out into a water garden, where crystalline flowers sprang from golden fountains. In the swirling waters of one of the pools lay two holdes, and blood trailed in fine pink streams toward the drain. Apart from the splashing of the water, there was no sound at all.

Ollowain looked around suspiciously. Whatever had rampaged through here had moved on. From farther up a hill, he heard piercing screams. He had to go back! His duty was to rescue the queen! Vahan Calyd was lost . . . One sword could not turn the tide now, but it might be enough to open a path for Emerelle out of the inferno.

Ollowain slid his sword back into its sheath, then quickly returned to the cistern below to signal his companions. From the water garden, it was only a few hundred steps down to the mangroves. They had almost made it! The centaurs hauled the boat out of the water and carried it out into the night.

As if in greeting, a boulevard of silver columns shot from a pool in the water garden as they stepped out into the open air. A veil of fine mist enveloped them. Gondoran pointed the way they had to go.

"One would truly have to be a horse's ass to think of going for a nighttime stroll carrying a boat," boomed a voice. Shadows surged through the silver veil. A blow from a club shattered Antafes's forelegs. The centaur collapsed to his knees, and Ollowain could only watch as the wet hull of the small boat slipped from the grasp of the remaining centaurs. Orimedes ducked beneath a club and lashed out with his hooves, smashing a troll in the chest.

The skiff skidded across the smooth marble paving. Suddenly, it tipped forward. Gondoran, who had managed to stay upright at the long tiller, let out a shrill cry as the boat accelerated down a stairway as wide as a hillside. The holde tried desperately to steer the boat clear of the statues that rose from the steps on massive pedestals. The rapid slide was taking the boat straight toward the dark waters of the mangroves.

"Guards, spread out!" Ollowain shouted, drawing his sword. Now that the invisible foe finally had a face, the swordmaster felt unbridled rage rise inside him. "Orimedes, make sure the boat gets to safety." He avoided any mention of the queen. "Yilvina, take care of the wounded."

With a leap, Ollowain was on the troll that had knocked Antafes down. A sweep of his sword separated the giant's leg below the knee. Too surprised to cry out, the troll tumbled sideways. Ollowain sidestepped a powerful club swing and ran his sword through his adversary's throat. Orimedes picked up the dying troll's club and positioned himself at the swordmaster's side.

Apparently intimidated by Ollowain's quick kill, the other trolls fell back. One of them raised a horn to his lips and let out a long, wailing signal. The queen's two remaining guards had positioned themselves to Ollowain's left and right. With lowered swords, they waited for the trolls' next assault. While

Yilvina obeyed Ollowain's order, Orimedes still stood at the swordmaster's side.

"Prince, I must ask you to go!" Ollowain glanced over his shoulder. The skiff had disappeared in the darkness. "Protect the wounded. Let me do what I've trained to do for centuries."

"I am no coward who will simply run away!" the centaur protested.

Ollowain kept his voice low. "To flee now so that you might one day return and avenge what has happened tonight takes more courage than to stay here and die." The swordmaster looked around nervously. He did not understand why the trolls had retreated. Between the columns of water pumping from the pool, he could make out the forms of seven of the huge fighters. A signal horn answered from higher up in the city. Reinforcements would arrive soon. He looked down at the dead troll—had he been the leader of the squad?

"There are few escape routes from Vahan Calyd, and our enemies seem to be everywhere. Most of the princes of Albenmark will die tonight, or be taken prisoner, Orimedes. Albenmark needs men like you. Save yourself, you damned mule. And save our injured queen. She is our hope for the future!" From the corner of his eye, Ollowain saw the muscles in Orimedes's cheek tense.

Finally, the manhorse bowed his head. "It was an honor to have known you, swordmaster. For an elf . . ." His voice caught. "If you could drink and curse as well as you fight, you'd have made a very good friend indeed." With that, the centaur turned away and trotted down the steps to Emerelle. If they made it out of the mangrove swamps, Ollowain knew they would certainly be able to find a way back to the safety of the heartland.

He looked to the guards on either side of him. None of them had mastered even one of the arts of killing. It would be a short battle. The swordmaster smiled to give them courage. "Battles are won by those who dare the unexpected. So we'll do what these dumb mountains of meat are counting on the least. We attack!"

Without waiting for an answer from his companions, Ollowain sprinted forward beneath the fountains. In that moment of desperation, he felt utterly free. All his burdens had been lifted from him. All he had to do was what he did best of all. He would not have changed places with the centaur for anything.

Taking the trolls completely by surprise, Ollowain leaped feetfirst at one of them. With his left hand, he grabbed hold of his adversary's tangled beard, and with his right he rammed his sword into the troll's chest. Adroitly, he turned beneath the enemy's flailing hands, pushed himself clear with all his strength, and somersaulted backward, landing lightly in the pool.

"May the rats . . . eat you . . . bastard elf!" the dying troll snarled, both hands pressed to his breast. Dark blood streamed from between his fingers.

The elves had taken the fight to the trolls, but now the trolls charged forward with a howl. Ollowain ducked beneath a mighty swing, and the massive club struck one of the statues and shattered a marble leg. The swordmaster ducked again, rolled between his adversary's legs, and slashed the back of the troll's knee as he returned to his feet.

Screaming, the troll buckled and fell. A strike to his throat turned his cry into a bloody gurgle. Water shot high beside Ollowain. A marble head rumbled across the marble floor of the shallow pool, and a deformed stone knee came flying at him—the swordmaster danced clear of it. One of the trolls had smashed a statue with his war hammer and was now hurling the chunks of stone at Ollowain. "Stand still and fight like a man!" the shaven-headed troll snapped. His deep-set eyes glowed amber. He was more than half as tall again as Ollowain, and at least four times as heavy.

"You surprise me," the swordmaster mocked. "They say the trolls are indomitable fighters, and yet you stand there and throw stones at me like an angry child who's cornered a squirrel."

A piercing scream made Ollowain turn. One of his men had been hit. His adversary leaned down to the dying elf and tore his sword arm off at the shoulder. A fountain of blood sprayed from the horrible wound. The troll licked his own face with a long, wormlike tongue and grunted with satisfaction.

"Well, squirrel, where do we stand now?" the stone thrower called. "Come here and fight me."

"If I count right, I've already cut the throats of two of you already. Do you really think you can beat me?"

The troll picked up its enormous war hammer, which was lying in the pool. "Stand still for a moment and I'll show you."

Ollowain had to smile. A troll with a sense of humor—he had never stumbled across a beast like that before.

"Enough babbling, Urk!"

From the corner of his eye, Ollowain saw the giant that had killed his companion now charge at him. He was swinging the arm of the fallen elf like a club.

The swordmaster dropped to one knee and leaned back. Drops of blood spattered his face as the arm missed him by inches. Ollowain tensed, rose quickly, and kicked the troll hard in the crotch.

Ollowain's blade flew up like a silver bolt of lightning. The troll warrior raised his victim's arm high. The cold steel separated flesh and bone, and with a turn of his wrist, Ollowain transformed the swing into a stab. The sword found its way between the troll's ribs. Ollowain leaned into it, ramming the weapon into the troll's body to the hilt. Blood gushed from the wound, spraying him across his chest and face. The troll tried to raise his club, but the weapon slipped from his powerless fingers—Ollowain's sword had pierced his heart.

Thick strands of muscle twitched beneath the troll's dark-gray skin; with its sprinkle of paler spots, it looked like living granite. The colossus fell backward, and Ollowain used the weight of the falling body to twist his blade free.

A blow struck the elf on the shoulder, spinning him halfway around. Bright points of light danced before his eyes, and the sword fell from his suddenly numb fingers. Ollowain tried to banish the burning pain, but a second blow knocked him off his feet. A marble foot had struck him in the belly.

Urk took a long step over the swordmaster's fallen body and kicked his sword out of reach. "Well, little squirrel. Got you where I want you now, haven't I? And all you had to do was stand still for one second."

Ollowain rolled to one side but was not fast enough to avoid a kick. He skidded through the shallow water and stopped against the pedestal of a statue. Before he could pull himself together, Urk was over him, pressing one massive foot onto his chest.

"I'm going to fry you myself and eat you, elfling." The troll's pale tongue flickered across his dark lips. Slobber ran from the corners of his mouth. "You are truly a great warrior. I—"

The pressure on Ollowain's chest increased, pushing the air out of his body. Urk stared down at him with bulging eyes. A second tongue—this one of steel—jutted from the side of his mouth. An arrow!

A slender foot hit the back of the troll's knee, and he collapsed backward.

Ollowain saw everything in a blur. His entire body seemed to be made of pain. A face leaned close to his, and Ollowain spoke to it in a toneless voice, "We are too late."

"No, we are not." The face smiled.

Ollowain blinked. Silwyna was bending over him.

"Can you walk? We're in a bit of a hurry." The Maurawan helped him to his feet.

Ollowain felt as if he were standing on stilts. His legs had lost all feeling, as if they were no longer part of him. Every breath he took hurt. His ribs seemed to encircle his lungs like bands of iron. "I can stand by myself," he said, panting.

The archer slung his arm across her shoulders. "Of course. I would suggest that we talk while we walk."

A young elven warrior handed him his sword. Ollowain was trembling too much to get the blade back into its sheath on his back alone. "Where are the others?"

"Dead." The elf avoided his eye. "We . . . I . . ."

Ollowain shook his head tiredly. "Say nothing. Anyone who survives a battle with trolls can count himself brave."

Tears brimmed in the young elf's eyes. "They were so . . . I saw how Marwyn tried to stab one of them, and the sword just slipped off his ribs. And then . . . then . . . the troll . . . with his bare hands . . ."

"Silence!" Silwyna snarled at the soldier. "Stop whining. Be happy that you're still alive!" She was carrying Ollowain more than supporting him. As quickly as her burden allowed, they hurried down the steps.

"What are you doing here?" Ollowain's voice was reduced to a whisper. Every movement, even to speak, caused him pain.

"I thought to myself that you are the queen's swordmaster because you have a special talent for staying alive in situations where others would die. So I followed you."

"But how did you . . ."

"Recognize you?" She laughed. "As a hunter, if I were blind, I'd starve. I saw you go belowdecks with the guardsman. And I saw someone emerge wearing Ollowain's clothes, but who did not move like the swordmaster at all. You might have fooled others with your masquerade, but when I saw a *simple* guardsman bring the centaurs and that little boat to the queen, your plan was clear to me."

Ollowain tried to expel the pain from his thoughts. He could breathe more easily now, at least. "So you followed us into the cisterns?"

"A wet centaur has an unmistakable . . . fragrance. I don't need a normal trail to follow my prey. A scent works just as well."

They had reached a dock at the foot of the stairs. Silwyna pointed to fresh scraping on the wood. "The holde actually managed to keep it on course." She leaned down and picked up a fine splinter. "Let's hope the hull is still watertight."

A dark, watery landscape stretched before them. Smooth black surfaces dotted by low islands. On most of the islands, trees grew, and from their branches hung ghostly white beards. Roots jutted from the mud as vertically as the spears in a pit trap. Fogbanks wafted thickly over the water. There were no lights at all. From behind them came the sound of a horn.

"They have found the dead. We have to hurry now." Silwyna pointed to the end of the scrape marks on the dock. "This is where they put the boat back in the water." She raised her head, sniffing the air like a hunting dog. "They don't have much of a lead. We will catch up with them."

Ollowain needed her help. She lowered him down from the dock until he could hold himself on a pylon. The wood was soft, eaten away by water and time. It smelled of rot. The water itself was lukewarm and felt sluggish, nothing like the water in the cisterns or bubbling from a spring. There was something soft and smooth about it, and also something slimy—it was more viscous than water should be. A rank odor drifted with the fog. Ollowain's feet sank in the mud.

Bodies drifted between the pylons of the dock, their faces standing out as pale flecks against the dark water.

Silwyna and the surviving guardsman slipped down from the dock. They held him beneath his arms, one on each side. Ollowain stared at the young man. He knew his face but could no longer remember his name. He ought to remember the names of his men! He at least owed them that.

"We will try to swim as best we can," Silwyna whispered. "Wading in the mud is too loud and too tiring."

Ollowain let the others pull him along. The warm water relaxed his painful limbs. Slowly he began to feel better. The moon had disappeared below the horizon. Dawn was approaching. It was the best possible time to escape through the mangroves. The breath of the dying night brought fog with it.

After a while, the swordmaster was able to swim unassisted. He had been lucky. A few nasty bruises, but that was about all he had suffered. He owed Silwyna his life. Another heartbeat and Urk would have crushed him with his huge stone hammer.

"They are very close. Hear that?" Silwyna asked.

Ollowain listened for sounds in the fog and heard a smacking noise.

"That is the centaurs," Silwyna whispered. "They must be in shallow water. That way." She pointed toward a thick bank of fog and swam ahead. Soon she disappeared among the drifting vapors, and Ollowain was guided only by sound. And then he saw them. He had swum so close behind them that he had almost touched the rearmost centaur. The boat was no more than an indistinct form ahead. Gondoran must have ordered the last torch to be extinguished.

"Orimedes?"

All sounds stopped instantly.

"It is me, Prince. Ollowain."

"It's his ghost," he heard Gondoran whisper.

"Nonsense!" A shadow broke away from the form of the boat and moved in Ollowain's direction with smacking, sucking steps. "Swordmaster?" The centaur grasped him by the shoulders and lifted him up. A broad grin split the manhorse's beard. "Damned good to see you again."

Ollowain could not say a word. Pain shot through every limb, and tears sprang to his eyes.

Orimedes set him down on his feet. "I would never have thought that the joy of our reunion would bring you to tears, my friend!" He clapped Ollowain on the shoulder. "Thank the Alben you made it!"

"I am not alone," the swordmaster said slowly through gritted teeth. "An archer saved my life. And one of my men also made it."

Together, they waded forward to the skiff. "How is the queen?" Ollowain asked.

The centaur shrugged. "No change. She does not move—nor does the traitor."

Behind them sounded the drawn-out blast of a horn.

Orimedes lowered his voice. "They're out here in the marshes, too, the brutes. If not for the fog, they would have found us long ago." He frowned. "It's a miracle that you found us."

Ollowain nodded. "Yes. Lucky." He wanted to say as little as possible about Silwyna. The Maurawan did not have a good reputation.

"We must hurry," Gondoran pressed. "It's good to have you back, sword-master, but the welcome party will have to be postponed. The water is dropping. The ebb tide is on us, and we have to make sure that we get out of the mangrove channels and into the Woodmer. We will only be safe from these accursed trolls out there."

"And what if they are not only here in the swamps?" Orimedes asked. "What if they were the ones bombarding us from the sea?"

The holde let out an incredulous cackle. "Trolls on ships? Who ever heard of something like that? Nonsense, they won't be looking for us on the Woodmer. Every troll is afraid of the water. As soon as it's deeper than their chests, they piss in their breeches and turn back. That's why we have to get out into open waters."

"But what about whoever was firing at us from the sea?" Ollowain objected. "*Someone* is out there who has no fear of the water."

Gondoran swiped one hand as if brushing away a pesky fly. "Piffle, all of it! Who knows that we—" He glanced mistrustfully at Silwyna. "Who knows that we're trying to escape with wounded? By the time the trolls can pass a message to their allies at sea, we'll be long gone. There's a burning city between them and the harbor. We'll make it!"

As if to prove the holde a liar, a signal horn sounded just then, and worryingly close. The trolls were in the mangroves, certainly. The hunt had only just begun.

The small party pushed on in silence through the mangroves and mud. Gondoran did everything he could to keep the skiff in the deeper channels between the small islands. Low-hanging branches caught their hair and scratched their faces, and apart from the sounds they themselves were making, all was still. No creature moved. Everything living had hidden away from an invisible menace.

Suddenly, some distance ahead, Ollowain spied the pale flicker of a flaming torch. For a few heartbeats, it danced in the fog like a far-off will-o'-the-wisp; then it vanished again.

Ollowain now felt the pull of the tidal currents more strongly. The Woodmer could not be much farther, but the water level was falling at a troubling rate. The winding channels they followed were growing narrower; very soon, they would find themselves grounded in the mud.

From away to their left, where the sea had to be, came the sound of a horn. The fog muffled its wail, and it was impossible to say how far off their pursuers might be.

"They're surrounding us," Silwyna whispered. "It won't be long before they have us."

Ollowain stared into the darkness. Was that already the first glow of dawn on the horizon? The fog still lay over the mangroves like an enormous shroud over a dying world, smothering everything. The air was ripe with the stink of decaying plants. Even the brackish water seemed dead, and their motion through it generated torpid ripples. Although the swordmaster hated the fog, he knew it was their ally. He feared it wouldn't be their ally very long, however: the new day would quickly disperse it.

"How do the trolls know where we are?" he asked the Maurawan.

"They don't. They're hunters, led by instinct, and they will have us before the sun rises. They have left hunting parties behind in the mangroves to intercept anyone trying to escape. Now they are being called together. Were you ever part of a battue, a hunt where dogs and kobolds beat through the bush, driving the prey toward the real hunters? They wait with their pig spears and bows where they know the animals will run. That's our position, swordmaster."

"And how do we escape?"

"You don't want to hear it."

"Tell me."

"We leave Emerelle to her fate, and each of us tries to escape on our own. I would make it," she said confidently. "Perhaps you would, too. The centaurs would make too much noise. The holdes might manage to hide among the roots of the mangroves somewhere. The trolls won't search there." She looked at Lyndwyn, who lay slumped beside the mast. "She will die. Even if she regains consciousness in time. She is not able to be one with the land—finding her will take no skill, and as for the other elf woman, your student—"

"Finding me will take no skill either," Ollowain interrupted her sharply. "I will be where the queen is."

"You won't be able to stop them, swordmaster. What sense does it make to die for a hopeless goal? Do you believe this to be your way into the moonlight?"

"This is the way that my honor demands."

"Well said," the centaur prince chimed in. "Send the coldhearted viper away."

"Honor?" Silwyna laughed ironically. "It's easy to see that it was you who taught the human. Alfadas talked as you do." Ollowain believed he heard a tinge of melancholy in her voice. "You are a romantic, swordmaster. One rarely encounters a man like you among the old. Romantics are always the first to die." She took the quiver from her shoulder and flipped back the protective cover. "*My* allegiance to the queen will last as long as this supply of arrows." She closed the quiver again and released the bow that she had tied to its side. "I fight best alone. I will find a dry place and string my bow. If not too many trolls come, we may meet again."

She lifted the quiver and bow high over her head. The water came to her chest. Without turning back, she waded away. For another heartbeat, she remained visible as a vague form in the mist; then she disappeared from view.

"Who was that good-for-nothing witch?" Orimedes asked indignantly.

"A stranger," said Ollowain thoughtfully. Why had Silwyna opened the quiver for him like that? Wasn't it clear to her that he had seen the arrow in the mast? Or was it perhaps a threat? There were six arrows inside it, and two of them had black-and-white striped feathers, just like the arrow someone had shot at Emerelle. The feathers of a strangling owl. Supposedly, they allowed arrows to fly silently. Assassin's arrows . . . and for hunters? He gazed uneasily in the direction in which Silwyna had disappeared.

A pallid morning glow thinned the mist. Three flecks of light moved ahead of them. They looked to be coming up the channel that the small party was following with their boat.

On a sign from Gondoran, the two holdes that had been poling the skiff forward paused. The lights had vanished in the fog again. But there could be no doubt that they had been moving in their direction.

"Where did the huntress go?" the boatmaster asked.

"She's covering our rear." Ollowain scanned all around for an inlet, a side channel, or a tangle of roots, anything that might be suitable for hiding the boat.

"Centaur shit!" Gondoran grumbled. "The trolls won't let a few arrows stop them. What is *your* plan, swordmaster? How do we escape them?" The holde looked at Ollowain expectantly. All eyes were on him! But he was no miracle worker . . .

Again the horn sounded, the same one that had followed them since they had left the water garden. This time it was three short, breathless blasts. Their pursuers had found them, apparently.

"Your plan!" Gondoran pressed.

"I release you from your service to the queen, Gondoran. You and your men know your way around the mangroves. You have a good chance of escaping."

Now came the sound of hunting horns from all sides. The noose was closing. Ollowain loosened his sword in its sheath.

"You want to send us away? Just like that? Like cowards?" Gondoran asked in outrage. "Do you think we're afraid to die? Do you think we're going to run away *now* to crawl into a hole like swamp rats and hope the trolls go away? Among my people, we three call ourselves warriors, swordmaster. We can kill all of the trolls if we want."

"All of 'em!" one of the other holdes agreed. "We'll smother 'em under the prickly shroud!"

Orimedes laughed. "At least you've got your hearts in the right place, boys."

"This is not a joke," Gondoran replied solemnly. He tipped his head back and looked up to the thickly intertwined branches atop the mangroves. "Do you have the courage to protect your queen with your body instead of your sword, Ollowain?"

"What are you planning?"

Gondoran pointed to a thick growth in a fork in the branches overhead. In the low light, it looked as if the wood was suffering from an abscess. Only on second glance did Ollowain realize he was looking at a nest.

"Gardener bees," said the holde quietly, as if afraid the bee swarm above their heads might overhear him. "They tend the flowers in the mangroves.

Every bee-folk has its own garden. They drive away everything that comes too close to it."

"Ooh, I'm shaking all over! Are you fool enough to think they will scare off the trolls?" the centaur prince jeered. Orimedes drew his sword. "This is what we need. Polished steel, nothing else."

"You have never experienced an angry bee-folk, manhorse, or you would not babble on about them so lightly. The gardener bees won't scare the trolls away. They will kill them. And they will kill us, too, once we have called them. But if you manage to keep your mouth shut when they come, you might just survive."

"Why would that be difficult?" asked Yilvina uneasily.

"You will find out! Nothing here in the mangroves is as deadly as the gardener bees. Not the green tree vipers nor the big sea caimans that sometimes come into the swamps on the rising tide. The bees attack all intruders in their thousands, which is why there are no birds or monkeys here. Nothing. Not even water rats anymore. All of them are dead or have moved to safer territory. And we fishermen only risk going into the mangroves at night, while the bee-folk sleep. If we destroy three or four of their nests, all of the bees will rise. Then the dying starts."

"I can't see how a few bees are supposed to kill a troll," said Orimedes. "You're spouting holdeish faery tales."

Again, the three torches appeared through the fog. They were much closer now. A few moments more and the trolls would literally walk right into them.

"How can we protect Emerelle?" Ollowain asked. He was not ready to give up all hope of saving the queen.

"By lying on top of her. But she will protect herself best of all. As I said, you cannot move and under no circumstances can you open your mouth. Only then, perhaps, will you survive."

"Call the bees, Gondoran," Ollowain said as he pulled himself into the boat. He quickly covered the queen's face with a cloth. Lyndwyn's hand still rested on the queen's chest. It was moving to see how, even unconscious, she was still trying to protect Emerelle. But he would not let himself be fooled. She was certainly not doing it out of any feeling for the queen, but to save her own life.

The holdes removed their headbands, and Gondoran took out a small leather sack of pebbles from beneath one of the thwarts.

"Hey-ho, who do we have here?" The trolls had discovered them!

The boatmaster placed a pebble in his scarf and swung it in a circle over his head. With a dull crack, the missile penetrated the skin of the nearest nest. Gondoran's comrades took aim at other nests, their whirling headbands creating a soft hiss.

Ollowain held his breath. A dark mass billowed from the damaged nest, and then the air was filled with a dull buzzing sound. A gray-black cloud separated from the bees' nest.

The holdes calmly fitted new pebbles into their slings.

The swordmaster kneeled and leaned over the queen protectively.

A cry sounded from the direction of the trolls. Ollowain saw how the bees reacted to the noise. Just a second before, they had been no more than a dark cloud darting aimlessly among the branches. Now the cloud stretched out, only to recoil a moment later into a thick mass as the entire swarm flew toward the trolls.

Ollowain exhaled, relieved. In the fog ahead of them, he heard loud curses. Something splashed through the water, but he could see nothing. Two more bee swarms appeared above them in the tangled branches. Suddenly, a huge figure appeared at the side of the boat, flailing its arms helplessly, screaming, stumbling, falling, and rolling in the brackish water. Ollowain recognized the figure as a troll only from its size, for the body of the giant had lost all of its natural contours. Thousands of bees had descended on the troll, transforming him into a formless, twitching mass. The air was filled with their buzzing now, as loud as thundering hooves of massed riders.

Ollowain did his best to remain absolutely still. Individual bees landed on him, and close up he saw that they were unnaturally large, almost as long as the last two joints of his little finger. Their movements tickled him uncomfortably. The swordmaster felt a fat drop of sweat form on his forehead. Bees crawled everywhere on Emerelle's blanket. Gondoran stared at him from the stern. A large bee dangled from the tip of the holde's nose, but he seemed hardly to notice it at all. In the boatmaster's eyes he read a silent plea not to move.

The troll had hauled himself onto a flat bank of black mud. He held both hands to his throat as if trying to break the chokehold of an invisible adversary.

From the corner of his eye, Ollowain saw the bees descend on one of the centaurs. The manhorse reared up, his tail swinging like a whip. Orimedes hurried to his compatriot's aid, only to disappear beneath the prickly shroud himself.

Ollowain pressed his teeth together. There were bees on his face now. Their small legs probed at his burned skin. Bees tumbled down onto Lyndwyn too, who still lay beside the mast. The sorceress blinked. She opened her eyes for a moment and looked at Ollowain. She did not seem at all like someone waking from a deep sleep, unaware of what was going on around her. She smiled almost coquettishly. Then she closed her eyes again. The bees that had settled on her now flew away, and none went near her again.

Sweat was dripping from Ollowain's forehead. Searing pain shot through his chin. One of the little beasts had stung him. Tears came to his eyes and rolled over his cheeks. The buzzing of the bees closest to him changed. It grew deeper, more menacing!

More and more bees landed on him. Especially on his face. His cheeks burned as the bees stung him repeatedly. In the corners of his eyes. On his neck. Ollowain was trembling, straining to keep still. The buzzing was louder now. They were inside his ears. Then he felt a bee push its way into his nose, its feelers patting at the fine hairs inside.

They crawled across his lips, trying to push their way into his mouth. *Think of something else,* he ordered himself. He tried to remember Nomja. More than a hundred years had passed since she had joined the queen's guard. He had loved her from the first moment he saw her, yet he had never dared admit his feelings to her. And now she was dead, long dead, buried on a foreign world. He wanted to call up her face again. Her fine, well-proportioned lines . . . something crawled across his eye! Ollowain flinched. A bee stung his eyelid! *Nomja! Think of her* . . . The pain was maddening. He could not stand it any longer, all the thousands of bees probing at his face, his body, everywhere. He pinched his eyelids together and was immediately punished for it with stings.

High-pitched screams pierced the buzzing. The dying had begun. They should never have called the bees! He felt his left eyelid swelling. The bees' poison itched and burned. To scratch it would be a relief. Oh, to throw himself into the water!

Think of Nomja! What color were her eyes? He tried to imagine her face. Her fine hair. Her large eyes. Large compound eyes. He was looking at a bee!

A bee with a furry gray-brown body. Its large eyes looked at him expressionlessly while its feelers twitched excitedly.

The bee in his nose pushed in farther. And then he felt the tickle of legs in his throat! He screamed, and they were instantly inside his mouth. Stingers bored into his tongue. Bees crawled across his palate, and he crushed them with his teeth.

He pressed one hand to his mouth. His tongue swelled. Something stung him inside his throat. More bees had forced themselves into his nose. Why were they doing this? What drove them to penetrate his body? It meant their own death!

A bitter taste spread in his mouth. Still, the bees came. Crawling over his face, his arms, in his mouth, everywhere. He grew dizzy. His lungs burned. He had to breathe. Were they in his lungs? No, that was nonsense. That was impossible. And yet, there was something there. Something was cutting off his air. Be calm!

Ollowain thought of the troll that seemed to be struggling against an invisible opponent. Was the bees' poison driving him insane?

Was that smoke he smelled? Had the fire caught up with them? The swordmaster did not dare to open his eyes. He did not want to feel them crawling down his neck again. That would drive him completely mad.

Was it his lungs that were burning? A fire blazed inside him. He jerked his mouth open—the bees immediately swarmed in. He panted like a dog and swallowed dozens of them. He had to cough, inhaled frantically, but the air did not want to reach his lungs. His hands rose to his throat.

He collapsed over the queen. His mouth fell open. The buzzing grew quieter. He felt as if he were falling and, indistinctly, saw dark branches passing by overhead. The fire in his lungs would kill him. He had no strength left. Something crawled across his eye. He saw a single bee fly up, then felt nothing more. All the pain was gone.

A pale face moved in front of the blurred branches. Nomja! No. Her hair had not been black. Lyndwyn. No bees troubled her. Her face was without expression. Something silver sparkled. She held a dagger!

"You will die . . ." The blade came down—he felt it slice into his throat. Then the face of the sorceress vanished in brilliant light.

MORNING ON THE FJORD

Y ou will kill it!" Asla's eyes sparkled with ire. A fine vertical crease appeared between her eyebrows. Alfadas knew that look. Trying to talk to her now would be a waste of time. "Yesterday, Luth took it into his head to save Kadlin, but will he protect her from that brute today? Take the mongrel down to the fjord and kill it. Get it out of here. I don't want to see it in my house ever again!"

Blood pricked up his ears, but his massive head did not rise from his front paws. He looked over attentively at Asla and Alfadas.

"Come!" Alfadas flicked his fingers, beckoning the dog. Instead of standing up, Blood let out a growl.

"Wowow!" Kadlin squealed. She let go of Asla's leg and headed back toward the dog. Alfadas picked her up. He could see Blood's muscles tense beneath his crow-black fur. "Easy now. I'm not hurting her."

Kadlin pinched his cheek and babbled something, then began to laugh. Blood snuffled and stretched.

Alfadas went to the door. The dog shook itself reluctantly, then followed them. At the chopping block, the jarl jerked the heavy axe from the wood. He weighed the weapon in his hand, thinking. The dog could not stay in the house, he told himself. It was only a matter of time before something unfortunate happened. Asla was right. They had to kill him. Alfadas strolled down the hill toward the fjord; off in the distance, the last drifts of fog were lifting from the foot of the Hartungscliff.

The smell of something frying wafted past on the breeze. From somewhere came the monotonous plunging of a butter churn. Kadlin pressed her head to Alfadas's cheek. "Wowow," she explained to him, and she pointed at Blood.

Alfadas had pocketed some of the leftover meat from the previous night's festival. He would toss the meat to Blood to distract him. A last meal from his executioner. He felt terrible. Blood had hurt no one. At least, not yet . . . he had to kill him for what Ole had done to him. Alfadas knew that hardly anyone in the village would give a second thought to whether his treatment of a dog had been fair.

The sky stretched clear and cloudless across the fjord and the mountains. It was still cool. Today would be one of the last sunny days of late summer—when the summer faded with such magnificence, it was always a prelude to an early winter. The first traces of red and gold were already showing in the tops of the oak trees on the opposite shore. Alfadas hated winter in the Fjordlands. He was not made for the cold, and the summers there were always far too short. He thought wistfully of Albenmark; unconsciously, his eyes turned again to the stone crown atop the Hartungscliff.

"Dada!" Kadlin babbled away incessantly and pointed to everything that caught her curious eye. A rock by the shore, a gold leaf in the grass, a piece of wood floating on the water. For her, the world was still full of wonder. Blood looked wherever she pointed and occasionally replied with a short bark.

Alfadas made his way along the shore. He did not want to do the deed in a place he liked to spend time. Soon, the first salmon would be coming up the fjord. He looked forward to that, to spending the entire day fishing by the water.

Finally, he reached a bare stretch of shoreline, an area with no rocks where one could camp, with no old fireplaces between soot-blackened stones. It was a place without a history. Random. A place that one could easily forget again.

The jarl set Kadlin down. The little girl immediately tottered across the pebbly shore to the water's edge. She picked up a gray pebble and tried to throw it into the water, but it fell short; grumbling, she searched around for a fresh stone. Blood lay down close to where she played—he seemed tense, and his ears did not droop. Did he suspect what was coming? Alfadas took the chunks of cooked meat out of his pocket and tossed them to Blood. The dog did not move, and instead Kadlin came back up from the water. She picked at the fibrous meat with her fingers and pushed it into her mouth, and only then did Blood eat one of the chunks.

Suddenly, the dog jumped to its feet, knocking Kadlin over. Kadlin just shook herself and laughed, thinking it was a game. Stiff legged, with his head stretched forward, Blood let out a deep, throaty growl. Kadlin grasped a handful of his fur and pulled herself back to her feet. She tried to imitate the dog's growl.

From the forest above the shore stepped a white-haired figure. Gundar, the Luth priest. He wore a gray smock and had slung a grease-stained leather satchel over his shoulder.

Blood stopped growling but did not take his eyes off the new arrival. The priest ran his hand over his forehead. His face was bright red, and he was panting for breath. "You have quite a stride, Jarl," the old man gasped. "I'm afraid I am no longer built for taking walks before first breakfast." The priest sat down on the pebbly shore and took a bottle out of his satchel. He drank in long drafts, then held the bottle out to Alfadas. "A good drop. Best spring water, from the foot of the Hartungscliff. You'll like it."

The jarl took the bottle but did not put it to his lips. "Why did you follow me?"

"Oh . . . I had a dream. I think that dog might be good for something after all. And I had a notion that you might make a mistake."

Alfadas shook his head. "Dreams, notions . . . we both know what Ole has turned Blood into. It is just a question of when the dog attacks someone, not if. And I don't want it to be my wife or my children. He has to go . . ."

"I understand your concerns, Jarl. But trust in the gods! Have you already forgotten what happened last night? Luth gave you a sign. Respect it. You are one of the most important threads in the tapestry he is weaving to decorate his Golden Hall. I believe it would be wrong to kill the dog." The priest winked. "Tell the truth, Jarl—it was not your idea to take an early morning walk by the fjord with a dog, a child, and an axe."

Alfadas could not suppress a smile. Canny old man! Could he see into his heart? But he would not go against Asla's will. Her decision was correct . . . unjust but sensible. "I have seen what lies beyond the world, Priest. The void. An abyss with no end. Darkness inhabited by disembodied horrors hungry for the light of those with living souls. There are no gods there, no golden halls. I hold you in high regard, Gundar. And I know how much you do for the village. But don't expect me to believe in your god, let alone heed him."

"Are you sure that you have seen everything? We are not like the elves that raised you, Jarl. We are no Albenfolk. And the races of men were not created by the Alben. We have something that they lack. Something they envy us for. We *can* enter the golden halls of the gods, when we have earned the right. And we will celebrate there unto all eternity."

Alfadas sighed. He liked the old man and did not want to injure his feelings. How could he make it clear to him that elves could live forever? What he saw as the promise of a marvelous afterlife was their reality. Alfadas knew the stories of his people, but what halls of the gods could compare with Emerelle's palace? The priests talked about enormous longhouses with gold-plated wooden pillars, where the gods and their chosen indulged in a never-ending banquet. Halls full of smoke and the howls of revelers.

How much more marvelous were the banquet halls of the elves! High and spacious, with walls that looked as if they had been created from pure moonlight. The scent of flowers in the air. And when one of their masters played the flute or plucked the lute, the music went straight into one's heart. Alfadas stroked the smooth shaft of the axe. The wood was dark with sweat. The jarl thought of the long travels he had undertaken with his father on their cursed search for the bastard child.

"I have seen the void, old man. And other places that you could not imagine in your most daring dreams. But I don't believe in golden halls."

"I am not saying that the void you speak of does not exist," Gundar conceded. "A place of darkness and despair. I am sure we have all had hours in which we have felt very close to that place. I even fear that most of us will go there when our hour comes. But it is up to us to decide where our destiny lies."

"Is it?" Alfadas asked cynically, although he was happy to be able to put off for a little while what he had to do . . . at least for as long as he talked with the priest. "Your god is the weaver of fate. How can I decide my future if my path has already been determined? Am I not then Luth's slave? A small figure in the game of the gods, with no will of my own?"

Gundar took an apple out of his bag and bit into it heartily. He looked over at Kadlin, who had returned to the water's edge and was playing with pebbles there. "You misunderstand the nature of Luth, Jarl. It is true that he is the weaver of fate, but he knows what you will do because he knows you very well—it was he who spun the threads of your life, after all. Sometimes he tries to help us by giving us signs. He is a hospitable god, and he would like to see all of us find our way to the golden halls, even though he knows that most of us won't make it. His hope is that we will live our lives with our eyes open to the workings of the gods. Those familiar with Luth's works in their lifetime will find their way to him more easily in death. Unfortunately, most of us are blind to his signs. Even I don't always understand them."

Alfadas shook his head. He would never understand this belief in gods. It was difficult for him even to accept it in others. He did not want to taunt

Gundar, but the old man was starting to upset him. "We should give your god the opportunity to give us one of his signs here and now. The water in the fjord is bitter, but Kadlin tries to drink from it all the time. No doubt Blood will also soon be thirsty. If Kadlin drinks first, then I will spare the dog's life." He looked up to the sky. "Hear me, Luth? Can I make it any easier for you? Blood's life is in your hands. Decide!"

The priest remained astonishingly relaxed. Alfadas had expected indignant protest, or at least to be admonished for challenging a god, but Gundar sat serenely and ate his apple. When he was finished and had spat the seeds into the grass, he said, "It may well be true that there is no one among the humans who can match the famed swordsman Alfadas, the king's duke in times of war, the terror of all enemies of the Northlands, but whatever names and titles you are given, to challenge a god is beyond the powers of even the best of men. It is as if Kadlin were to challenge you to single combat." He smiled. "But Luth is wise and forbearing. I am certain that he will answer you appropriately."

The jarl looked up to the sky. "I'm waiting."

In silence, the two men sat side by side and watched the dog and the child. It was not long before Alfadas regretted his behavior. He was being silly! And still, he did not back down.

Gundar, grinning, polished off a second apple while Kadlin returned from the water. The little girl rubbed her eyes tiredly. Blood lay stretched out on the grass, dozing. Kadlin went to him and snuggled against his scraggy black fur. Soon, she fell asleep.

Alfadas watched the dog for a long time. Thick bands of muscle were hidden beneath the dog's fur, making the beast look bulky and ungainly. The scrape on Blood's snout was covered with a dark scab, and in the morning light, the jarl could see many older scars, too. He thought of the whip that Ole had left behind—torture instrument, made to open deep wounds. Bastard! He ought to take all his dogs away from him.

Gundar had leaned his head back and was looking up at a single lonely cloud passing slowly across the radiant blue of the sky. The priest said not a word, but he smiled silently to himself, and his silence was more eloquent than any words.

Alfadas was still not prepared to concede. One of the two would go down to the water! It did not matter to him if it was Blood or Kadlin. The jarl gave himself up to his thoughts. What would he say to Asla if he returned with the dog? Would she accept a judgment from Luth? Perhaps. She certainly would not accept *his* decision not to kill the dog. It was basically good that he had the priest there as his witness; it would make things easier for him.

It was Gundar who finally broke the silence. "We've been here well over an hour, Jarl. I have to admit that I am now so thirsty myself that I am tempted to drink from the fjord. How much longer do you want to wait?"

"Until we have a sign," Alfadas said defiantly.

The priest sighed. "Don't you think that Luth has long since spoken? We could sit here until dusk, and neither child nor dog would drink from the fjord. Until today, I have always held you to be a clever man, Jarl. You must also have recognized what the answer is. The weaver of fate is not prepared to relieve you of your decision."

Alfadas had expected a speech like this. The most important quality one needed to be a priest was the talent to turn everything that happened to your god's favor. Gundar might have his failings, but he did not lack a silver tongue. "Then what, in your opinion, is your god telling me?"

"Listen to your own heart. Forget everyone else for a moment. Forget me, your wife, even Kadlin. Free yourself of all the invisible shackles weighing you down. Give yourself the time you need to think about your life and its duresses, and then do what you think is right. That will also be Luth's will."

Alfadas gathered his axe and went to Blood. Then he pushed the axe into his belt and picked Kadlin up. For a moment, he looked down at the large, ugly dog. "Come. We'll go and have some breakfast."

THE REED

He felt a pleasant warmth on his cheek. From close by came the soft crackling of a fire. Ollowain tried to open his eyes, but his eyelids were swollen and stuck together. Only with an effort was he finally able to open his left eye slightly, just enough to see the fire. It was not dangerous. A ring of fist-sized white stones encircled it. The wood was as bleached as bones. Some of it burned with greenish flames—driftwood! Ollowain tried to sit up, to see better where he was, but his limbs refused to obey. It was as if he consisted of nothing but his head. And . . . why did he not smell the fire? He concentrated entirely on trying to perceive any kind of smell at all, but nothing came. He could not even feel himself inhale. Not in his nose, not in his mouth. And yet his chest rose and fell. And there was a strange, gurgling noise . . . panic overcame him. Was he dead? He tried to turn his head to the side. Impossible!

His throat was burning. And there was that gurgle again. He was breathing, so why did he not feel it? His body breathed, but no longer through his mouth or nose!

His tongue lay in his mouth like a numb, bloated slab of meat. It was huge, he knew, and he could hardly move it at all. With its tip, he felt thin threads between his teeth. A bitter taste filled his mouth. Now he remembered: the bees! There were no threads; those were legs, bees' legs. He had tried to crush with his teeth and tongue the bees that had forced their way into his mouth. He remembered a dagger. Lyndwyn! She had cut his throat. That was the explanation for everything—he was dead!

"Easy," a familiar voice warned him. Something soft stroked his forehead. "He's come around."

From beyond the fire came an answer that he did not understand. All sound was muted.

"You would do best to lie still, swordmaster." A head framed by short blond hair leaned over him, and a face deformed by numerous red swellings smiled down at him. Ollowain was only able to recognize Yilvina from her voice and hair. Her eyes, too, were swollen closed. She looked down at him through slits so narrow it was impossible to tell the color of her eyes.

"We are saved. Lyndwyn brought us here."

Ollowain wanted to ask where they were, but all that came from his throat was a stertorous gurgle. He tried again. Nothing. He tried to sit up. The gurgling grew louder. His body did not belong to him. He felt his heart racing . . . what was going on with him?

Yilvina pressed him back down. "Easy. You almost died. Lyndwyn had to cut into your throat to stop you from suffocating."

Ollowain tried to raise his hands to his neck. Cut into his throat! What had happened to him? Again, he managed no more than a rattling gurgle. Had that accursed sorceress robbed him of his voice?

Yilvina drew her short sword and held it so that he could see his throat in the reflective metal. A reed was attached there with a lace of thin leather straps. It seemed to stick deep into his flesh. Ollowain's chest rose and fell, and again came that unfamiliar gurgle. He was breathing through the reed! How was that possible? What had Lyndwyn done to him?

"Be calm." Yilvina laid her hand on his arm. "She will heal you. It will just take a little while." She lowered her voice. "She is incredibly powerful. Her abilities seem inexhaustible. She created smoke to drive the gardener bees away from the boat, then she drew the bees' poison out of our blood. For most of us, though, her help came too late. Only Silwyna, Orimedes, and Gondoran are still alive. And the queen. The bees did not harm her at all. And yet she still lies there as if she is dead." Yilvina shook her head dispiritedly. "Lyndwyn says we don't need to worry. She has closed the wound in Emerelle's chest."

Where is Lyndwyn now? Ollowain wanted to ask. And he wanted to see the queen. But his body was a prison to him. He closed his eyes and tried to get his thoughts in order. His helplessness was certainly convenient for Lyndwyn. She would take her time healing him. He listened to his rattling breath uneasily. The sound changed. It sounded . . . stickier. Or was he just imagining it? He ought to sleep. His wounds had always healed well, even without the intervention of magic.

Every time he came close to sleep, he abruptly woke again, and his breathing came harder, pitched higher into a whistle. He was afraid that if he gave himself over to his exhaustion, he might never wake again.

Finally, though, he nodded off. It was a comfort to give in and simply allow things to follow whatever their natural course might be. No more obligations to fulfill. The warmth of the fire caressed his cheeks. He heard the murmur of a low conversation but was unable to understand what was said. Then he saw the troll in front of him again, that massive warrior who had compared him to a squirrel. With a broad grin, he moved toward Ollowain.

"Got you where I want you now." He placed his foot on the swordmaster's chest. The troll stank of rancid fat. Ollowain could clearly see his toenails, how they curled forward slightly and were rimmed with grime. Very slowly, Urk increased the pressure.

Ollowain knew it was only a dream. The trolls had been defeated, and he was in a safe place, yet he was unable to breathe. That could not be! Urk could not follow him into his dreams! He had to wake up!

Blinking, the swordmaster looked around as best he could. He could still open only one eye. The fire had almost burned out. He tried to breathe, but an iron fist seemed to press his throat closed. He tried to scream . . . but no sound escaped his lips. He could hear his companions talking. Very clearly. They were just a few steps away; Lyndwyn was telling them about the Albenpaths.

He tried again, desperately, to draw attention to himself, but he could not even gurgle. It felt as if someone was crushing his throat with the strength of a troll. Ollowain could neither inhale nor exhale. He wanted to jump to his feet and scream, but all he could manage was to flick one hand. This was Lyndwyn's work! She had cast some spell to kill him in the night, and when they found him dead, she would tell the others that, sadly, he had succumbed to his injuries!

"Do you hear that?" Gondoran asked. The conversation immediately ceased. "The gurgling has stopped . . . damn it!"

Suddenly the holde was over him. He bent close to Ollowain's throat.

A smacking sound, and then the air came. So wonderfully cool, so fresh in his throat and lungs.

Gondoran spat. "Damned mucus. I'll sit with him."

The holde swept the hair from Ollowain's forehead. Gondoran's face looked like it always had. He seemed not to have suffered a single sting. With yellow eyes, he scrutinized the swordmaster. "You were lucky. At first I thought she wanted to kill you, although it looked to me as if death already had you in its claws. She cut your throat open. It was a small miracle. Lyndwyn says there is a tube that guides the air from the mouth to the lungs. Because your throat was swollen closed from the bee stings, she had to open it with a blade. To stop the wound from closing again by itself, she pushed the reed into it. A miracle." He clucked his tongue. "Almost, at least. Alas, the reed occasionally fills up with mucus. We have to keep an eye on you, swordmaster, and listen to your breathing. Now and then, the muck has to be sucked out of the reed, or you might run out of puff after all."

Ollowain tried to thank the holde with his eyes. Did he understand? A child was never as helpless as he was now, the swordmaster thought with resignation. All he could do was resist the urge to sleep and hope that his companions did not take their eyes off him again.

"A ship!" Orimedes called. "There's a ship on the horizon. It's heading our way. What should we do?"

"The swordmaster will decide," said a woman's voice calmly. "Carry him over there and lay him on the sand."

Ollowain was lifted up. He could see Silwyna's back—she also seemed to have escaped the bees unscathed. Her clothes were stiff with grime, as if she had rolled in swamp mud, but she did not look to have been stung at all.

"Well, Ollowain," the sorceress said, kneeling beside him where he lay on the sand. "I can well imagine what is going on inside your head. You are one of those men who grabs on to an idea and then has a very hard time letting it go." Lyndwyn had washed her face; her makeup was gone, and there was no sign of the wound left where the shingle hit her head. Beyond those external appearances, though, she seemed changed. She wore an air of satisfaction that was utterly not in keeping with the situation they were in.

"I saw you move your hand. Write in the sand, swordmaster. You are giving the orders here. I am a traitor, after all."

You are not deceiving me, Ollowain wanted to say, but from his throat came only a long gurgle. He grasped a handful of sand and let it trickle through his fingers. He had no choice. Could it be that Hallandan had escaped with the grand liburna? He had to know what was approaching. To make the right decision, he needed to form some idea of their situation. His fingers moved through the sand. He hoped he was writing legibly, because he could not move his hand far. And he had to keep it brief, or the letters would run together.

SHOW SHIP

"Orimedes, take him outside!" the sorceress ordered.

"But isn't he still too weak? You said we should move him as little as possible," the centaur objected.

"He knows what's good for him. I will not argue with him about his orders. Do you want to, manhorse?"

Orimedes leaned down to Ollowain. Like Yilvina, the centaur had also been badly stung. His face and upper body were scabbed and raw where he had scratched open the itchy swellings.

The prince picked him up in his arms with care and carried him out of the cave. A light breeze touched Ollowain's face. White rocks jutted from the sand like old bones, rising to form towering cliffs on which mats of green clung and proliferated. In front of them lay a narrow curve of a sandy bay that was surrounded by needles of rock. Ollowain looked out to sea. Individual trees rose from the azure-blue waters, their trunks as thick as towers and crusted with salt. Thirty paces overhead, perhaps higher, where the wildest waves could not reach them, the crowns of the trees spread wide, home to an abundance of fiddler crabs, seagulls, and cormorants. These were the enormous, ancient mertrees that gave the shallow Woodmer its name. Stronger than cliffs, the massive, furrowed trunks defied even the hurricanes of spring. To approach them too closely was dangerous. Spreading rings of spiky aerial roots rose from the sea around them like crowns of thorns, natural ramparts that kept small boats at a respectful distance.

"Over there," said Orimedes, nodding westward. Although a great distance separated any two trees, they confused the eye when one looked to the horizon. It was like looking out through gigantic iron bars. Finally, Ollowain made out something dark, a hull, above which black sails spread. The ship was too far away to make out any details, but it looked unsettlingly foreign and far bulkier than any elven ship. It was definitely not the queen's liburna.

"Do you see it?" the centaur asked.

The swordmaster gurgled and cursed inwardly.

Orimedes carried him back into the cave, holding him close to his chest. A thin, sticky film of perspiration coated the centaur's skin, and for that moment, at least, Ollowain was glad he could not smell anything.

The prince laid him back on the ground with care. The swordmaster tried to sit up, but it was no use.

"Are you also thinking that we ought to leave this island?" Lyndwyn asked.

YES, he wrote in the sand.

"There is a large Albenstar here in the cave. Seven paths come together. I have already scouted it. Something strange is going on with the Albenpaths." The sorceress gestured vaguely in the direction of Vahan Calyd. "Someone is there in the network of paths and is cutting off all of those that lead back to the heartland. We cannot return to Emerelle's castle. Whoever is up to no good in there must command great power if he is able to destroy the work of the Alben. Is it smart to risk entering the Albenpaths? And where would we go?"

Ollowain's finger glided through the sand. There was a place the trolls would not search.

Lyndwyn looked at him in shock. "Are you sure?"

"Where does he want to go?" Silwyna asked sharply.

Ollowain wiped the name away. He thought of the arrows he had seen in the Maurawan's quiver. She could not be allowed to find out where they were going! They had to leave quickly. No one there should have any opportunity to leave a sign for their pursuers. Ollowain was deeply troubled that their enemies were upon them again so quickly. Was there a traitor among them? Or was it, as Silwyna said, simply because they were such good hunters? He would not take any risks. He had to keep all of them busy, and most importantly of all, they had to leave quickly.

NOW, he wrote in the sand.

His fingers erased the word.

ORIMEDES CARRY QUEEN

He hoped he was making the right decision. But what choice did they have? They could not surrender to the trolls now. They had to flee, and only Lyndwyn could open this final path for them. Again he was forced to trust her. They needed time now to treat their wounds and to help the queen. When Emerelle was better, she would know what course they had to take.

"Then let's go," said the sorceress sullenly. Orimedes picked up the queen. Silwyna and Yilvina bore Ollowain. Gondoran walked beside them; he seemed downcast.

The sea had washed out the rocks and cut a deep tunnel back beneath the mountain. Broken shells crunched underfoot, and although the entrance was already far behind them, it was still light. The white rock around them seemed to shine with its own light, like the walls in Emerelle's palace. It looked transparent, shot through with pale, bluish light. Golden veins traced lines through the rock; they were woven into complex patterns. Spirals and knots seemed to be trying to convey a secret message. The swordmaster felt the hairs on the back of his neck rise. He was not at all skilled in sorcery, but even he could feel the power of the ancient magic that suffused the place.

Eventually, the tunnel opened into a large, round chamber, where black veins mixed with the seams of gold inside the walls. Lyndwyn stepped into the center of the rock chamber and kneeled on the floor. She pressed her left hand flat to the stone and laid her right against her breast. She closed her eyes. Her lips moved.

Ollowain was well aware of the degree to which he was at the mercy of the sorceress. He had to follow her when she led the group along the paths of light. But they would only find out where Lyndwyn took them when they emerged from the second door.

An arch of light rose from the chamber floor, and the black and gold veins rose with it; they danced inside the stone like living beings. The blue light grew brighter and brighter. The stone was like glass—one could see through it out to the sea. A large flock of cormorants rose from the mertree at the entrance to the bay and flew seaward. A sign? It was time to go!

Ollowain moved his head in the direction of the arch of light. It was not the first time that Yilvina stepped through an Albenstar. He had been with her in Aniscans, and they had spent years traveling in the human world. And yet, she seemed tense. Her lips were pressed to a thin line. Together with Silwyna, they stepped through the portal. Darkness wrapped itself around them like an all-smothering cloak. Only a narrow, golden pathway at their feet led away into the darkness.

"Do not stray from the path!" they heard the sorceress's voice behind them. "Anyone who loses the way is lost forever."

THE GIFT OF FREEDOM

The body of the false queen was tied to Branbeard's shield, her head hanging slightly to one side. To stop the crown from falling off, they had pinned it to her skull with thin nails. The shield leaned against the soot-blackened column that rose in the middle of the mussel-fishers' market square. Anyone passing would be able to see the swan crown clearly. And if one were to believe Skanga, the crown by itself would be enough to blind every eye. The burned dead girl looked similar enough to Emerelle, even when seen close up. At her feet lay the false Ollowain and others—the real princes of Albenmark.

Orgrim felt such deception to be unworthy of a troll, and he suspected that the old shaman had devised it, but the idea to have him among the guards standing watch must certainly have come from Branbeard. From where he stood, he could see all the dukes and pack leaders swarming around the king at their victory feast. His fall from grace could not have been made any more clear to him. Gran and Boltan were also among the guards set to watch over the corpse. Sweet-smelling odors of decay emanated from the girl's body—as the heat and the countless flies had already taken their toll on it.

A fearful silence hung over the broad square. All of the Albenkin who had survived the conquest of Vahan Calyd had been herded together there, with only their surviving princes held elsewhere. Many were wounded and at the end of their strength. The trolls had started shunting the survivors to the square before daybreak, and some had been waiting in the heat for hours.

At Branbeard's behest, they had brought water barrels and bread. But the king had not managed to quell the fear with that friendly gesture. Hardly any of the survivors dared meet the eye of a troll. *How could these creatures truly once have been capable of vanquishing them?* Orgrim wondered.

The sound of horns broke the silence. Branbeard stepped forward from his gathered commanders and took up position beside the dead body that wore the swan crown. He inhaled noisily through his nose and spat on the ground.

"Albenkin!" he called in a loud voice. "I have come to give you your freedom. The tyrant is dead!" He turned halfway around to Emerelle and, without warning, rammed his fist into the chest of the dead girl. Her thin ribs shattered. Stinking brown fluid oozed from the wound. Branbeard's fingers rummaged inside the chest cavity; then he jerked his arm free and held a putrid hunk of flesh out toward the prisoners. "A rotting heart has poisoned Albenmark!" he screamed, his voice breaking. "I have now torn it out, to let this land return to health once again. The Alben never wanted one of the races of their children to stand above all others. They never wanted one of us to decide what was just and unjust for all the rest. Or that one alone would say how we all should live, and that those who did not obey were hounded out or even murdered. Last night, we trolls avenged an old injustice. But we are not waging war against Albenmark. We fight only against Emerelle and against all who are true to the tyrant. Which is why you are free to go. Come here, look the dead queen in the face, and carry the tidings to every corner of the land. The races of Albenmark are free! I am the king of my people, but the swan crown will never sit atop my head. And no one will ever bow before it again."

Branbeard sniffed and spat. Without that habitual gesture, the end of his speech would have been more moving, certainly, but even Orgrim had to admit that the words of his king had touched him. Branbeard was a true ruler! And he, Orgrim, could learn a lot from him.

The king's dukes and the other trolls greeted the speech with cheers and jubilation. Horns sounded from every corner of the city. But the Albenkin in the market square were so cowed that at first only a few joined in the cheering. Slowly, more joined in, but it was a poor celebration, and its half-heartedness was obvious.

Centuries spent under Emerelle's heel has shackled the races of the Alben, Orgrim thought. *The winds of freedom have blown over them like a storm, and most of them still hardly dare to breathe. Pathetic creatures!*

The troll observed stately centaurs and powerful minotaurs standing with their arms crossed obstinately. Not one of them ventured to defy the victors with a look; they stood and stared shamefacedly at the ground. Pitiful! But Orgrim was confident that they would regain their pride eventually, though it might only be in the next generation of Albenkin, among those born into freedom.

The guards in the square grabbed hold of several elves and dragged them to the cadaver of the queen. "Look at her! Emerelle is no more than a rotting piece of meat. Look closely, and remember!"

Pale maggots tumbled from the gaping wound in the false queen's chest. The reek that issued from the body was far from regal. One elf woman collapsed, sobbing, when she was forced to approach to within inches of the cadaver. Many who were marched past the queen had tears in their eyes. It was incomprehensible to Orgrim why they mourned for the tyrant.

He looked down at the substitute swordmaster. The events of the night had not allowed Orgrim to enjoy his victory banquet. Now the moment had passed. It was a disgrace that he was not allowed to pay this elven hero his last respects by eating his heart. When he thought about how much spoiled meat lay around the city, a cold fury overcame him. What a waste! He was happy that the fleet would soon be leaving Vahan Calyd again for the north.

Branbeard returned to his entourage. They would go off somewhere now to enjoy a banquet of their own, Orgrim thought with envy. And he was certain that they had saved a few juicy roasts for themselves, a few little elves that they would slaughter only now, heroes who had put up a valiant fight and ended as prisoners. Branbeard's army had cheated him of the best of the pickings! It hurt Orgrim's soul to set free the Albenkin gathered there in the market. One could have feasted for weeks on so much meat.

Orgrim watched a minotaur who had stepped up to the queen. How would his flesh taste? Like beef?

Heavy steps made him look up. A troll warrior with his face covered with decorative scars was coming his way. "Are you the one whose ship was sunk by the elves?"

"Depends who's asking," said Orgrim irritably.

"You are ordered to join the guard of honor at the king's table."

Orgrim could not believe it. Would there be no end to his humiliation? Was he now supposed to stand and watch while Branbeard stuffed his belly?

"Who sent you? The king?"

"No, oh glorious ship sinker." The emissary grinned insolently. "It is Skanga who requests your presence. And if you were idiot enough to let those little bastards sink one of our great galleasses with one of their puny punts, then you'd better not make the mistake of picking a fight with Skanga. Now move your greasy tail!" He pointed to a tower overgrown with dog roses. "You'll find the king and his party over there. I'm to take your place here."

Orgrim committed the soldier's face to memory. As pack leader, he could have beaten the impudent soldier on the spot, but single combat was forbidden to the rank-and-file warriors for the duration of the campaign. The war would not last much longer, however—that was clear—and then he would track down this brainless pile of dung and show him what it meant to mock Orgrim.

He stomped off angrily toward the Rose Tower. He looked contemptuously at the trellis on which the plants climbed upward. If he ever possessed a palace of his own, then he would certainly not start decorating it with greenery. What did that say about the owner? That they were a friend of the riverbank sprites? Or someone who enjoyed watering flowers and loved their fragrance? No, he would impale the heads of his defeated enemies on stakes atop his walls. That kind of decoration meant something! Any visitor would know at a glance what kind of troll they were dealing with and that they had better watch their tongue when they spoke to him.

The noise of the banquet led Orgrim to the yard where Branbeard and his court were celebrating. A cloister surrounded a pool from which a small fountain sprayed, and grapevines covered its pillars. Orgrim picked a fat grape and popped it between his teeth. He had not eaten anything that day; at least the greenery here was useful.

The king and several of his favorite lickspittles sat around a heavy wooden table set against the side of the pool. A few paces away, a fire had been set up on the mosaic floor, and kobolds were now feeding it with wood from smashed furniture. A beast of some sort sizzled on a spit over the fire. Something large and four legged, but Orgrim could not tell exactly what it was. The smell of roasting meat made his mouth water.

The troll was uncertain what he was supposed to do. Skanga sat some distance away from the banquet table in a high-backed armchair. The shaman seemed to have dozed off, and Orgrim felt no desire at all to wake her and ask her why she had ordered him to come. Instead, he hovered in the shadows of the cloister, picked grapes from the vines, and looked at Branbeard. The king was in the best of moods and was talking about his plans for the future. He wanted to level the entire city, but he did not have the time for that. Instead, every house in Vahan Calyd would be put to the torch. Everyone who lived there would be forced to flee. And all of the dead were to be flung into the large caves beneath Vahan Calyd to poison the drinking water for a long time.

"Do you really want to let the Albenkin go? Even the elves?" asked Dumgar, the Duke of Mordrock. "These sly little bastards will rise against us again as soon as they get the opportunity."

The king spat onto the stone face of a singing elf woman in the floor mosaic. "No, my friend. I do not seek to rule Albenmark; they will spend years fighting among themselves about who should wear the swan crown in Emerelle's stead. Infighting and intrigue, that's what they live for. We won't have anything to do with the elves for a very long time. Apart, of course, from those with whom we have old accounts to settle. We will exterminate the Normirga. And who was that fellow who commanded the fleeing ship? Halliwan of somewhere or other . . ." The king looked around for help.

Mandrag, the king's old comrade in arms, finally said, "Hallandan of Reilimee." The gray-haired troll had been left for dead by the elves after the battle of Shalyn Falah. At night, he had dragged himself up between the cliffs and had witnessed the murder of the troll dukes by Emerelle. In the first years of their banishment, Mandrag had been the leader of his race, but after Skanga had recognized the soul of the reborn king, he had stepped down. The king had honored him by making him his closest confidant.

"Right. That Halliwan's city will burn, too. His men sunk one of our ships, but worse than that, they take us trolls for fools. The fellow actually thought he only had to show us a body wearing a crown and we'd start whooping for joy and think the tyrant was dead. Well, you might deceive a whelp like the pack leader on the *Rumbler* like that, but not me. Not the king. I am *offended* by such simpleminded games. And Halliwan's city will pay for it. It will serve as an example to the elves of what we do to friends of the tyrant queen. That will cool the heads of the few elven fighters who might be thinking of revenge."

In silent rage, Orgrim pressed his fingernails into the palms of his hands until they bled. The king missed no opportunity to make him look ridiculous. And the worst thing was that Branbeard was right. He had fallen for the elves' deception and had lost his ship.

"We keep the holdes and kobolds here," Branbeard declared, his mouth full. "Most of them were servants for the elves, and now they'll serve us. They need someone to tell them what to do, and none of the other Albenkin will lose any tears over them. They wouldn't know what to do with freedom if they had it. Half of them are to go on board our ships. We'll take them to our castles in the human world; we could use a few more kobold servants there! The rest will go with the army when we move north."

"We should spread them across several ships," Dumgar advised. "Then at least we won't lose all of them if—"

"Silence!" the king snapped at him, rising to his feet. "And woe to anyone who mentions the price of our return to this world." He scowled in Skanga's direction. "Was there ever a troll king who lost as many warriors in defeat as I've lost in victory?"

Orgrim had heard the rumors that morning. The previous night, during the attack, the news had not been able to spread. But now, in the city, it was being passed from mouth to mouth. Seven ships, it was said, disappeared on the passage through the void. Add to them the four that burned and the sunken *Rumbler*, and it was more than a tenth of their fleet. More than two and a half thousand warriors, dead before they even saw the enemy.

No one knew for certain why the ships had disappeared in the void. They must have strayed from the golden path. But how could that have happened? Skanga had drummed into all of the pack leaders that the slightest negligence would mean death. Their journey through the nothingness had not lasted long. Just a few ship's lengths, it seemed to Orgrim.

A troop of guards entered the courtyard, with four of them surrounding one elf. The creature was dressed in blue and, although shackled, moved with a self-assured arrogance as if *he* had been the victor the previous night.

"I welcome you to my house, Branbeard of the trolls," the elf said in a pleasant voice. "I hope my servants have not neglected you in my absence."

Orgrim almost choked on a grape. The elf had guts! But how long he would keep his head on his shoulders was another matter.

Branbeard set down his drinking horn and weighed the elf up with his deep-set eyes. The king was clearly taken by surprise and did not immediately know what to say.

"Who are you?" he finally grunted. Such a simpleminded question made the king look bad, Orgrim thought. Even a bash over the head with a club would have been better than such a weak response.

"The owner of this palace. Shahondin, prince of Arkadien." He stepped up to the long table and poked a finger into the huge spit roast. "I would say that this lamassu is not yet cooked through. Should I send for one of my cooks to serve you as the leader of a great army ought to be served?"

"We like our meat bloody," Branbeard grunted. "What do you want from me, imp?"

The elf leaned against the table and looked around casually before replying. "I wanted to congratulate you on poaching my game from me. I had sent two hunters of my own to take Emerelle's life. And as things have turned out, you almost beat me to it, great leader."

"What is that supposed to mean?"

The arrogant elf managed to look at the king—who stood more than five heads taller than he—as if he were looking at a buffalo cow staring stupidly back at him. "The duchy of Arkadien finds itself in a blood feud with Emerelle. I had already decided that the queen would not survive the night that is now behind us. Thanks to your intervention, she was able to escape. I have had, however, a reliable report that her sedan was carried up Lotus Rise. And with all due respect for your little masquerade out there, commander, the body you have on display in the mussel-fisher's market is not even wearing the dress that Emerelle had on yesterday evening. She is dressed much more like the unfortunate girl who delivered the swan crown to the queen."

Branbeard's drinking horn fell from his hand. A deathly silence fell over the courtyard. Orgrim wondered how many Albenkin had seen through their trickery. Emerelle had paraded in triumph through half the city before her coronation. Thousands must have seen her.

Orgrim realized how little attention he had paid to her dress. How many guards she had and how they were armed—that was what interested him. But elves were different, and Orgrim could imagine easily that some who had got close enough to her might even know what perfume the tyrant had worn.

"I thought I would offer you my assistance in capturing our runaway queen. If we unite our powers, it should be simplicity itself to locate her." Shahondin snapped his fingers casually and pointed to a kobold working at the fire. "Slavak! Bring me a cup of wine, lightly cooled. You know what I prefer at this hour."

"Why should I trust you?" asked the king, wiping his lips with the back of his hand. He sized up the elf with the look of a butcher considering how best to cut up half a buffalo.

Shahondin remained unimpressed. He frowned, wandered across to the pile of firewood, and picked up a small, carved figure. Shaking his head, he wiped the grime from it with his sleeve and put it to one side. "An image of my grandfather. I whittled it when I was very young. It is far from perfect, but you know how it is with things from younger days—hard to part with. It would be most accommodating of you if you were to refrain from including this little statue in the preparation of your lunch. And to answer your question, Branbeard: Neither friendship nor love is as constant as burning hatred. So what better allies could you ask for?" The kobold brought Shahondin a cup of silver and crystal. The elf raised the cup to Branbeard. "To the tyrant's doom, great leader."

Branbeard was so surprised that he actually bent and picked up his drinking horn. *Does the fool not see that he is making himself a lackey to the elf?* thought Orgrim angrily.

The king lowered himself onto one of the solid wooden benches and fanned a little air over his face with one hand. "This heat!" he grumbled, and signaled to the guards who had led Shahondin forward. "Bring me this pompous elf's brain on a plate. Maybe I will understand him better when I've eaten some of it."

"You are making a mistake, troll," said the elf, keeping his composure. "If you don't catch Emerelle quickly, she will not content herself with merely throwing you and your entourage off a bridge. She will make sure you are never reborn."

"Do you think I'm going to let an imp like you threaten me?" the king chided. "On the floor with him, I'll crush his skull like a rotten apple beneath my foot."

The guards grabbed hold of Shahondin, who did not put up the slightest resistance, and pressed him to the mosaic floor. "I am not threatening you, Branbeard. I am simply telling you what will be."

"Stop!" Skanga had risen from her armchair. With tired, dragging steps, she approached the elf. The guards still held him pinned to the floor. "You're a cocksure whoreson, Prince. I like that." She bent down and ran her fingers through his long hair. "Are there more princes as admirably filled with hate for Emerelle as you are?"

"Without wanting to unduly importunate, I think it meet to point out that my present position is not one in which I would normally conduct such a civilized conversation. If it is not too much trouble, I would be much obliged if you were to induce these two bone breakers to let me up."

Skanga waved the two guards away. Free again, Shahondin stood and patted the dust from his clothes. "My thanks for your intervention, dear lady."

"Answer my question, if you value your life."

The elf, piqued at her directness, pursed his lips. "My son, Vahelmin, has also sworn blood vengeance against the queen. He is a famed hunter and archer. I am certain that he will be of great use when we go after Emerelle."

Skanga stroked her broad chin. "Yes, little elf, that may well be. Who did you task with killing the queen?"

"You will understand that I am loath to talk about such delicate affairs. I would therefore like to say only that my clan considers Emerelle's death a family matter."

"Shall I beat it out of him?" asked Dumgar.

"I can assure you that any treatment of that nature would seal my lips forever," the elf replied proudly.

"I wasn't going to beat you that hard," Dumgar replied. "Not at the start, at least. Can you give him to me, my king?"

"I claim him and his son as my spoils of war," said Skanga softly. "And I don't wish to haggle about it."

The elf bowed gallantly to the shaman. "I am charmed to be the spoils of such a . . . delightful lady."

"The pleasure is entirely mine." Skanga looked him up and down with a gap-toothed smile; then she gave the guards a sign. "Put him somewhere safe, and keep a close eye on him. Find his son, Vahelmin. Bring both of them to me in my tent an hour before sundown."

The shaman retreated to the shadows of the cloister, leaving the king and his companions to their feast. Soon, once again looking weak and burned out, she sat down beside Orgrim, who wondered who she really was: the intense fury able to break through all resistance, giving commands even to the king and hiding her power behind a mask of frailty? Or was she really an exhausted old woman who, in her occasional moments of glory, was able to return to her old power? Orgrim hoped that he would never have enough to do with her to find out the truth. Without wanting it to look like he was making his escape, he tried to leave, because whatever the truth about Skanga, there was one thing he was certain of: She scared him!

"Did you learn anything, whelp?" she asked abruptly with her soft, insistent voice. "Did you notice anything about that elf?"

"Well . . ." The question took Orgrim by surprise. What was this now? Had the old witch decided to make him her pupil? The thought made him shudder. "He was arrogant. But he had courage." Orgrim lowered his voice. "The way he was able to get to the king . . . I liked that."

"Branbeard is not the fool he seems to be. Be careful around him, Orgrim. If he is your enemy, you will not grow to be old." Skanga rubbed her milky eyes and moved deeper into the shadows. "Did you notice that bastard of an elf never once spoke to the king by his royal title? He mocked him and insulted him with every sentence he spoke. That's what they are like, the elves. Not a bad word crossed his lips, and yet he did his best to show Branbeard up. But you are right about one thing. He is truly brave. Brave and filled with hate. And he thinks we are stupid. He will be a useful ally."

"You trust an elf?" Orgrim asked, surprised.

Skanga clucked her tongue. "Did you hear me say that? You have to learn to listen closely, whelp. You have what it takes to be a duke." She smiled inscrutably. "I advise you to stay close to me. It's likely that Branbeard has also seen what you are capable of. And if he has, he will try to have you killed. I am sure that he would have become a good ruler if not for that fiendish blow he took to his forehead. The stubborn idiot forbade me from using my powers to heal him back then. He was probably afraid that I would kill him. His nose has been running ever since, and that is why he has to spit all the time. It's destroyed his self-confidence. He's killed loyal warriors because he got it into his head that they looked at him with ridicule. His flow is slowly driving him insane. He fears me because he believes I will kill him one day to let his soul dress itself in a new body." She rubbed her eyes again. "Only a madwoman would dare meddle with the delicate balance of death and rebirth. His hour will come without any assistance from me."

Orgrim, on his guard, said nothing. He had the feeling that whatever he might say could only be wrong. He had already come too close to the royal court. Better to sit with regular warriors at one of the large fires and to celebrate their victory with a feast.

Skanga rose with a sigh. "I will be expecting you one hour before sundown in my tent at the harbor. Something is going to happen this night that you should see." She seemed less fragile now than she had earlier. Perhaps because she was a creature of the shadows? Orgrim did not like the idea of visiting the shaman in her tent at all. And at the same time as the elves . . . What was she planning?

"Incidentally, Orgrim." Skanga had stopped but did not turn around to him. "You really ought to try the lamassu from the spit. Its meat tastes like beef, but there is also a touch of poultry in it . . . very unusual. You won't soon have another chance to sample a delicacy like that. And they say he fought well. In the water garden close to the swamps, he beat a pack of our warriors singlehandedly. A second pack of hunters cornered him in the caves beneath the city and beat him to death. That is good meat, Orgrim. Very good meat."

THE ARROW IN THE THROAT

The frenzied barking of dogs woke Ole with a start. His head buzzed like a beehive. He had fallen asleep beside his bowl of millet gruel, and the table was sticky with spilled mead. "Shut up, you miserable curs!" he bawled, and regretted it instantly. If the barking of the dogs was like a dagger in his skull, his own yelling hit him like an axe. That wretched mead! He had drunk too much too early in the day!

Dazed, he rose to his feet. Little light made it through the tiny window covered with thinly shaved leather. Outside, the yapping grew more frenzied. He'd been through this before, just a few weeks earlier, when a fox had dared to go strutting between the kennels and his dogs had gone almost insane because they could not get at the bushy-tailed beast.

Beside the door hung the broad bandolier equipped with all his whips—one for each dog, seven in all. He threw the belt over his shoulder and picked up a heavy wooden club leaning against the table. Those mongrels would soon learn who they were dealing with! He'd tan their miserable hides. That was the only way to teach a dog anything.

When Ole opened his door, the dogs immediately fell silent. Cowards! They knew what was coming. He'd teach them not to let a mangy fox get to them!

The sun was low over the houses in the west. The light hit him like two glowing arrows shot through his eyes. The goddamned mead! He felt as if his head would burst at any moment. The pain made him nauseous. He leaned against the door frame for support.

Only now did he realize that the birds in the trees were not twittering; the outside world had grown eerily silent. He blinked. Someone was there, a figure! Standing in front of him as if from nowhere. Against the light, all he saw in the first moment was a dark outline. His eyes watered.

"Which house is the one of Alfadas?" asked a woman's voice, somehow strange. Whoever spoke was not from the Fjordlands. The voice was lilting and musical. Even the simple words sounded like a quiet song. "I am not a master of your language. Please excuse me."

Slowly, the silhouette began to take on color. Ole rubbed his teary eyes. A woman, a stranger, was standing in front of him. Her long hair was combed back and woven into a braid. Her clothes were stiff with dried mud. Unusual clothes—a very tight-fitting leather doublet and torn breeches that revealed an indecent amount of leg. Her white thighs looked very nice indeed . . . Ole felt himself becoming aroused. Was she perhaps a traveling whore? And she'd come knocking on his door! Luth was being good to him today. She even held a wanderer's staff in her hand. Long, slender fingers . . . he imagined them closing around *his* staff. She was a little on the skinny side, perhaps, but he wasn't about to haggle with fate.

"Do you understand me? I have not speak your language for a long time." She smiled apologetically.

Unbelievable, thought Ole. She still had all her teeth, and they gleamed white as glacial ice. "I understand you well. Very well." He reached for her arm. "I know what you need now. Come inside." He blinked. Now he could see clearly. Her eyes! By the gods! They looked like the eyes of a wolf. And her ears! Ole released her arm. He had never seen such ears on a human. Long and pointed.

"I need Alfadas," said the stranger, still friendly. "Is he in there?"

Ole had to hold the door frame to stay on his feet. He felt as if his legs might give way under him at any moment. The jarl had sent for the elves! If only he'd kept his mouth shut the night before and not let himself get carried away. If only he had not insulted Alfadas. "I . . . well . . . ," he stammered. "Please don't hurt me!" Now he saw that what the elf held in her hands was no walker's staff. It was an unstrung bow.

"You smell of fear, like your dogs. Why? What reason do you have to fear me?"

Ole's tongue felt nailed to his palate. He could not speak a word, and his whole body trembled.

"Are you sick maybe, human? Come, I will take you to the huts there so your people can take care of you." She slung her arm beneath his and pulled him along with her. She smelled strange. Like the forest. Very different from a human. The only familiar odor about her was a tinge of smoke. She was strong, too. She supported him easily and helped him walk.

The dogs lay flat on the floors of their kennels and did not move. They knew who had come to get them.

When they were halfway around the house, he saw the others. Several elves and a horse with a human torso growing from its chest! Ole felt his bladder desert him. By the gods, if only he'd held his tongue! If he survived this night, would never say a bad word about the jarl again!

The manhorse was holding a girl with a burned face in his arms, and beside him trotted an ugly little fellow who looked slyly at Ole from his yellow eyes. A broken arrow stuck from the throat of one of the elves, but he was alive! The little party looked rather down-and-out in their grimy, torn clothes, and almost all of them were wounded. The manhorse and two others had a strange skin affliction. Not scratches or a rash, but it did not look good. Fat, red swellings disfigured their faces.

The elf woman supporting him showed no reaction when he pissed his trousers, but the little fellow with the yellow eyes gave him an evil leer when he saw the wet patch.

Ole's hut lay almost a mile from Firnstayn. It stood high above the shore of the fjord, and from there one had a good view toward the village. The elf woman pointed to the small settlement and repeated her question about the jarl's house.

Ole pointed to a long wooden structure on the edge of the village, and the elf with the arrow in his throat gurgled and pointed in a wide arc around the village. Apparently, they wanted to draw as little attention as possible. Ole hoped that the watchtower was occupied, but he knew very well that this particular duty was rarely taken seriously. There had been no threat from enemies for many years.

The small group turned to leave. "I am sure they will help you," the elf still supporting him said.

"I'm all right," Ole insisted. "I can see to myself, thank you. You don't have to go to any trouble."

The huntress looked at him doubtfully and said something to the man with the arrow in his throat, who stopped. The little creature answered in his stead, and it sounded disparaging. The manhorse laughed.

"My companions believe that you are not seriously ill and that we can leave you here. I would like to apologize on behalf of all of us if we did frighten you." She helped him to sit down on a rock by the wayside. Then she set off with the others.

Soon they left the path to the village and sought cover in the undergrowth along the edge of the forest. They quickly disappeared from view.

The dog breeder looked up at the Hartungscliff. The mountain looked as it always did. He had expected to see banners flying among the standing stones or even to see more elves. There was nothing.

"Thank you, Luth," Ole murmured. He would soon climb into the mountains and make an offering to the ironbeards. The weaver of fate had shown himself merciful.

But before he set off on his pilgrimage, he urgently had to warn the Firnstayners. They needed to know what kind of mob had arrived to take refuge under the jarl's roof. Manhorses, elves, and kobolds! He had always known that no good would come of accepting that half-blooded Alfadas into the village. Those friends of his meant trouble! He could smell it!

But before he did any of that, he had to change his trousers.

THE RITUAL

The crimson sky of evening colored the harbor waters as red as freshly spilled blood. The burned-out hulks of the elven ships drifted on the incoming tide, and the harbor swarmed with sharks. Greedily, they fought over the carrion. It was oppressively humid, and an unbearable smell of decomposition hung over the water. Sweat ran down Orgrim's naked torso in broad bands. He looked back to the city with mixed feelings. He had left his weapons and his few possessions behind. He hoped that Boltan would look after them. When Orgrim, not half an hour earlier, arrived at the harbor, Skanga had immediately ordered him aboard her ship, the *Wraithwind*. There had been no time to return to the city and collect his things.

The water foamed to starboard. Huge jaws loomed from the water and sliced through one of the floating bodies with a single bite. A severed arm turned slowly in the red tide; it seemed to wave good-bye to Orgrim, and then it sank.

The troll turned away, feeling uneasy. Skanga had not said what she wanted from him or to where they were sailing. The large ship glided between the two towers, lit pale white, at the harbor entrance. The sea lay before them, as smooth as a mirror. There was not the slightest breath of wind, and yet the *Wraithwind*'s sail creaked and filled. Orgrim had heard many stories about the shaman's ship. If he had known that she did not want to meet him in her tent but would order him aboard this cursed ship, he would not have appeared at all.

Skanga stood on the quarterdeck. She had placed one hand solemnly over her heart and gazed eastward.

As if part of some kind of ceremonial procession, wedge-shaped shark fins skimmed toward the harbor. There must have been hundreds of them. For the moment, Orgrim's anger at all the spoiled meat overcame his fear. He had heard rumors of a great feast supposed to take place in the Rose Tower the following day . . . the way things looked, he was not likely to be back in time to enjoy it.

Shahondin and his son stood a little forward, beside the mainmast of the *Wraithwind*. How could Skanga trust those two imps? They were traitors to their own race! Why should they consider for a moment being loyal to the trolls?

The large galleass made good headway. Its bows swung lazily toward the east, toward the Woodmer. Orgrim crouched by the bulwark and observed the crew. It was said that Skanga personally chose every member of her crew. Some of his own men had been ordered aboard the *Wraithwind* before the invasion. The shaman had wanted Boltan, too, and Orgrim had kept his artillery chief only because he had been badly injured in the fireball incident.

Orgrim nervously considered the possibility that Skanga was attracted to him . . . she did have a certain reputation. Orgrim would prefer to never share his bed with a female again than share it with that old gorgon. She should have her fun with the two elves instead. He grinned to think what Skanga would do with the puffed-up bastards! Now it was the elves' turn to learn what it meant to be at the mercy of the victors. His thoughts drifted, and he found himself brooding about his chances of ever again being chosen by a female. The night after he was appointed pack leader was also the first time he was chosen. It was always the women who decided whom they gave themselves to. And they took only the most renowned or the biggest warriors. Gran, despite his lowly rank, was highly regarded among them, thought Orgrim enviously. And he missed no opportunity to boast about his adventures.

For every ten warriors, there was one female, and many trolls waited a lifetime without ever being chosen. That was the curse of his race. Their females were not infertile, as was said of the elves, among whom few children were born. Most of the troll women had new offspring regularly. But they were a race of warriors. The females were kept safely out of harm's way and well guarded inside their rocky fortresses. Each one had three or four bodyguards to order around.

Orgrim thought of the sway Skanga held over the king. Maybe, secretly, they were a race ruled by their womenfolk. He smiled at the thought. Outsiders never set eyes on a troll woman. There was a legend among the other Albenkin that trolls were born from solid rock in dark caves. Let them believe it! It would fan the flames of the troll fear so many of them shared.

The gentle roll of the swell made him doze. It was very agreeable not to have responsibility for the ship one was traveling aboard. Half-asleep, he thought back to the few nights that he had spent with women. He recalled the sex-crazed bouts, the odor of their bodies dripping sweat, the magnificent tattoos on his lovers' shaven heads, their voluptuous breasts and strong, willing hands.

A shout roused Orgrim from his slumber. He sensed the slowing of the ship. Squinting, he looked around. The moon was high in the heavens, and he estimated that three or four hours had passed since they had left Vahan Calyd. Two anchors rattled into the water, and with a block and tackle roped to the mainmast, one of the *Wraithwind*'s large boats was lowered into the water. The sailors carried out their tasks flawlessly, but the mood on board was depressed. No one cursed. No one laughed. The men did their work in grim silence. An aura of fear lay over the *Wraithwind*.

A troop of oarsmen gathered amidships, under the command of a young pack leader. Around them, Orgrim could see enormous mertrees looming from the sea. The *Wraithwind* must have sailed far out onto the Woodmer while he slept. About half a mile distant, an island jutted from the water like a huge fang. On the beach at its base burned several fires.

Dragging footsteps made Orgrim turn. Skanga! She stepped to the bulwark and waved him over, then nodded sharply toward the island. "Our spies picked up the scent of the escapees there at midday, then lost it again," the shaman explained. "There is a large Albenstar there. I suspected that Emerelle and those faithful to her would come to a place like this. They were fast."

"Will we still be able to catch them?"

Skanga looked at him and frowned. "Do you doubt my skill? The elves have bought themselves a little time, no more. In the labyrinth of the Albenpaths, there are thousands of ways they could have taken. I shall need to use some special sorcery tonight . . ." She looked to the two elves. "And our two honored elven princes will help me greatly with it. Come with me, Orgrim. I want you to understand all that happens tonight."

Skanga climbed into a seat made of woven leather strips and had the crew heave her overboard with the block and tackle and lower her to the ship's boat. Supported by two warriors, she climbed out and sat in the smaller boat. Then, without warning, a large group of trolls fell on Shahondin and Vahelmin. The elves were bound and gagged, their protests ignored, then tossed unceremoniously over the side of the ship. They were fished from the sea with long poles by trolls already in the ship's boat. Orgrim stood and watched with mixed feelings. The entire day, Skanga had been asserting how important the two elves were. And then they were thrown overboard just to save the toil of lowering them with the block and tackle.

Orgrim climbed down the rope ladder and dropped into the bow of the boat. The oarsmen pushed the small vessel away from the hull of the *Wraithwind* and began to row with all their strength. They made sure they kept a respectable amount of water between them and the mertrees, with their rings of spiky roots. The moon glazed the sea with metallic light. Every wave and every cliff stood out with unusual clarity against the silvery water. Orgrim could see crabs climbing the deeply grooved trunks of the giant trees. What a strange part of the world they were in! With trees that abandoned the land and put down roots in the open ocean, and crabs that left the sea to climb trees. What did the little creatures do up there among the branches? Were they nesting?

They had approached to within a hundred paces of the island. Two trolls holding torches stood at the entrance to a rocky bay. The waters close to the island were swirling—reefs seemed to protect the bay like a ring wall protected a castle.

The boat began to rock in the surging sea. Spray hit them in the face. The boatman swung the tiller and brought the ship's boat onto a course parallel to the reefs. They were heading now toward one of the mertrees, standing like a watchtower at the northern end of the entrance to the bay.

"We can't get through here!" the boatman cried desperately. "The tide is already on its way out. The water is too shallow to get into the bay. It will rip out a hole in our bottom."

Orgrim saw that the channel was calmer close to the tree. "Try it over there!"

The boatman shook his head. "Root thorns! They're just as dangerous as the coral."

"Maruk, let Orgrim take the helm!" Skanga ordered.

The boatman looked at Orgrim with hate-filled eyes but rose from his place in the stern. As Orgrim pushed past him, the other hissed, "Probably planning to sink a boat every night, aren't you, bigmouth?"

Orgrim tried not to let anything show, but Maruk's words had cut deeply. Why hadn't he just kept his bright ideas to himself? This was not his boat. If the boatman didn't have the guts for a difficult passage, it was none of his business. Now he'd brought the boatman's problem onto his own head. And he could not afford another failure.

He took his place on the helmsman's thwart in the stern and laid his right hand on the tiller. The dark wood nestled comfortably into the palm of his hand. Orgrim closed his eyes and tried to become one with the boat and the restive sea. He felt the way the waves gently lifted the hull.

"Oars flat!" he commanded, his voice resolute.

Two dozen men were staring at him, and the faces of most of them were not friendly. The boatman was obviously popular with the crew. At least, more popular than the stranger who'd come along for the ride, a stranger known for stupidly losing a ship.

Orgrim shifted all of his concentration to the waves. In the cold seas of the north that he had sailed with the *Rumbler*, every seventh wave rolled in with more power than those before it, but they were in another world here. This sea might have a completely different rhythm. Now! The boat was lifted more strongly. He turned it into the wave and began to count.

"What's he waiting for?" muttered one of the oarsmen.

Don't let them shake you, Orgrim thought. *Four.* He looked ahead to the narrow passage. The moon shining like a lantern in the sky made the shadows of the night look so much deeper to Orgrim. He could see individual root thorns, but where their boat would pass, the thorns did not form a closed circle. Someone had breached the mertree's defensive ramparts. The elves had had to get into the bay themselves, after all, and Orgrim could not imagine that the little imps would be content to wait until the tide was at its highest. That did not suit their overbearing ways. They had cut a path for themselves, no doubt about it! "Ready! Row!" he commanded.

And they would have set a trap, too, said a soft voice in the back of his mind. That kind of treachery was among the elves' most characteristic traits. Orgrim peered ahead into the darkness. Was something there?

"You don't care for the passage now that you've got the helm?" Skanga asked.

Orgrim felt his belly squirm. The last thing he needed right now was the shaman's ire. His hand closed more tightly around the tiller. "Power!" he commanded the oarsmen.

The trolls heaved on the oars with so much force that the boat actually seemed to jump forward. Orgrim steered past several root thorns. They were closer to the rocky shore now, the air filled with spray and salt, but the tide tugged at the fragile vessel like a huge hand. They had almost reached the calmer waters of the bay when Orgrim saw what he had been fearing. A last row of thorns. A passage had been cut through the mertree's roots as far as this final obstacle. Orgrim had been counting the rhythm of the waves the entire time. Would the seventh wave lift the boat high enough to clear the thorns?

"Hold water! All back!" he ordered the trolls. They could not make the attempt too soon. The oarsmen put their backs into it, but the tide slowly pulled them backward in the channel. Orgrim looked behind him. There it was—a fine line coming toward them from seaward. Another moment . . . they could not be too far from the barrier of thorns when the wave took them.

"Ready . . . Row! Go!" The oarsmen hauled with all their might, fighting the power of the ebb tide. The boat rose on the swell until it was riding on the crest of the wave. Orgrim knew it could only last for one or two heartbeats. Their boat was too heavy and too long to stay on the crest. He held his breath. They slid across the thorny barrier. A nerve-curdling scraping noise came from below. Orgrim could feel the rear third of the hull settle on the thorns, and for a moment it felt as if the ebb current was trying to pull them back to sea. Then the next wave came through, and the boat creaked and came free. Orgrim thought the hard wooden thorns had slit open the hull along the length of the boat. A dry cracking sound announced a broken plank. They glided into the calm waters of the small bay. A few more oar strokes and they glided up the narrow, sandy beach.

A group of trackers was there to meet them. They raised Skanga onto their shoulders and carried her up the beach.

"You did that nicely, whelp," the shaman praised when she was back on her own feet again.

"Your boatman would not have done it any worse." Orgrim had no desire at all to insinuate himself into Skanga's good graces. "He knows the boat better. He probably could have cleared the roots completely."

"Don't belittle your own actions. Those who envy you will do that for you. Don't play into their hands, whelp. And now, come! You will do exactly what I tell you and not ask any foolish questions."

The leader of the trackers joined them, a beefy fellow. A little shorter than Orgrim, he had a broad chest adorned with thick decorative scars in the form of a falcon. Except for three braids, the tracker had shaved his head smooth. The braids fell over his right shoulder and were decorated with falcon feathers. His skin in the moonlight looked gray green and was sprinkled with light dots. The look in the tracker's eyes was strange. They radiated a benevolent warmth that Orgrim had noticed before only in the eyes of females. No doubt the tracker had had to stomach his share of ridicule for it in his life. Pale scars on his arms and legs showed that he was not one to avoid a fight. On his upper right arm, half-hidden by the braids, four bloodless weals told of a fight with a cave bear. *No*, thought Orgrim, *whatever his eyes may look like, he has little in common with our well-protected womenfolk.* Even if one of them insisted in a moody moment on going hunting, she was always shielded by so many warriors that nothing could happen to her. The tracker was different. Orgrim reckoned him to be the kind of man happy to retreat alone into the wilderness.

Their guide led them to a series of tracks a short distance from where they had landed the ship's boat. "There was a centaur, a kobold or holde, and three elves who could walk alone," the tracker explained. "Their skiff is over there. A strange vessel. There are wooden slats in the hull that can be taken out, but I have no idea what they're for. Perhaps to sink the boat quickly if they were in danger?"

Orgrim recalled what he had heard the day before about the elf queen's peculiar sedan chair. He glanced at Skanga. The old shaman's face had something wolfish about it. Her head stretched forward, she looked like a predator picking up a scent. No doubt she, too, had heard about the queen's sedan.

"When did they get here, Brud?"

"Early afternoon, when the tide was highest." The tracker pointed to the dark entrance to a cave. "They camped over there. The coals were still hot when we arrived. I would say we missed them by an hour at the most."

The shaman stroked her wide chin. "Did you send the ship back immediately?"

"Yes, Skanga. Just as you ordered. There's a tunnel that leads from the back of the cave to a place of power . . . We did not enter it, but you can see it well enough from the tunnel." The tracker made a sign meant to ward off spirits. "The rock glows in there. It is an eerie place. There is only one way in. The iron shoes of the centaur left faint marks on the rocky floor, so at least he went back to the place of power and did not return. It's as if the mountain swallowed him. And the others with him, too—they left no trail on the rocks, but we've searched the entire island while we waited for you to arrive, Skanga. There is no one here. We will take a look at a few coastal caves that you can reach only at low tide, but I am certain our quarry is gone."

Brud led them into a low cave. Orgrim had to duck low not to bang his head on the soot-blackened ceiling. Brud pointed to the fireplace and to two shallow depressions in the sand. "Two of them were lying here. I suspect that they are traveling with two casualties who are not able to walk unaided. That would make seven altogether."

"A magical number," Skanga murmured. "A strong alliance. Not to be divided." The shaman crouched beside the smaller of the two depressions and ran her fingers through the sand. Orgrim wondered if she were able to talk to the grains of sand. The shaman's gaze was unfocused. She seemed to have forgotten everything around her. Were her lips moving? Was she casting a spell?

Suddenly, Skanga started. With her clawlike fingernails, she picked something out of the sand that looked like a small piece of a wilted leaf.

"What is it?" Brud asked.

Skanga smiled and rubbed her discovery between her fingers. "A small piece of burned butterfly wing. Take me to that place of power and have the oarsmen bring in the elves and the chest from the boat." With a long sigh, she straightened up again. "Oh, Brud. This is Orgrim. I am considering making him pack leader on the *Wraithwind*."

The tracker glanced briefly at Orgrim. "I've heard of him" was all he said.

Orgrim cursed silently. Oh, everyone had heard of him! Had heard of the hapless pack leader whose ship had been sunk by the elves. He wished he were lying on the bottom of the sea with the *Rumbler*. The thought of becoming pack leader on the *Wraithwind* did not cheer him. Far from it. That was no command. That was demotion to lickspittle of the moody shaman. He had to put himself out of her reach, and the sooner the better!

"Orgrim?" She waved him to her. "We're going to take a look at this place of power now, where our quarry disappeared into the rocks. You are not afraid, are you?"

The troll straightened his shoulders, knocking his head lightly on the roof of the cave. "I have steered my ship through the void. Why should I fear a cave?"

"Why indeed . . ." Skanga chuckled in a way that sent a shudder through Orgrim. "Just a cave, isn't it? What could happen in a cave?"

Orgrim found reason to regret his words faster than he ever would have dreamed. Brud led them into a tunnel in which they all had to stoop. They were surrounded by white stone. At first, they needed torches to see their way, but the stone soon changed in the most uncanny way—it began to glow from the inside. The boundary between stone and air seemed to blur. The rock turned from white to a translucent blue, the color of the sky on a clear summer's day. But it was still there, as Orgrim painfully discovered when he forgot to keep his head down. He could see far into the rock. Golden veins traced paths in the luminescent stone, all leading toward a point that lay somewhere at the end of the tunnel.

The more Orgrim looked at the veins in the stone, the more he felt that they were softly vibrating. As if they were alive. The hairs on his neck rose. The thought that he was in the middle of something living scared him. It was as if they were being eaten. With every step he took, he could better understand Brud's not wanting to enter whatever cave lay ahead of them at the end of the tunnel. Was it some kind of stone stomach? Would nothing remain of them but a stony belch, echoing back down the tunnel to the beach, the moment they crossed the threshold of the cave?

Orgrim berated himself. Skanga would never risk coming this way if some deadly peril was lying in wait, unless . . . had she protected herself with her sorcery?

All there is at the end is an Albenstar, Orgrim tried to convince himself. A magical place, certainly, but not a place of immediate danger. It was a gateway that led to the paths of the ancients. He knew what that was like! He had sailed his ship safely along an Albenpath! Except that the gate at sea had looked completely different. There had been nothing ahead of them until Skanga had created an arch of steam that shone in all the colors of a rainbow. It had been huge, big enough for even Branbeard's ship to pass through, with many paces' clearance between the top of the masthead and the vertex of the arch.

Orgrim's steps grew more uncertain. He could still vaguely make out the floor of the cave, but even there the stone had become almost transparent, and he had the feeling that he was walking through the sky. Beneath him lay a bottomless abyss, and all around he could see through the rock walls and beyond to the moonlit sea.

Magical tripe, said the troll to himself. *Something the elves came up with to unnerve trolls like me.* But he would not make it so easy for them. Defiantly, he set his jaw and gritted his teeth and promptly knocked his head on the tunnel ceiling again. He locked his eyes onto Skanga, who walked directly ahead of him.

Finally, the narrow tunnel widened, and they stepped out into a large cave, where black veins entwined with the gold like braids inside the transparent rock.

"Put the elves over here," Skanga commanded the oarsmen. "And bring up the chest." Brud and his trackers did not set foot in the cave. *Did they know better?* Orgrim wondered. He looked around curiously, noticed a strange prickling sensation on his skin, the kind he felt just before a summer storm. An unpleasant metallic odor filled the air, mixed with the smell of salt, kelp, and the sea.

"I want Maruk here!" The shaman had opened the wooden chest and taken out a chunk of chalk. She began to draw a large circle on the cave floor, around the two elves. Shahondin and Vahelmin twisted uselessly against their bonds. Blank fear was in their eyes. Did they know what Skanga was planning?

"Make yourself useful, whelp!" Skanga pushed the chalk into Orgrim's hand. "Go over the line one more time. It doesn't have to be pretty or regular. It just can't have any gaps. Do your best!"

Orgrim did as he was told, keeping in mind her instruction not to ask any questions. He carefully traced over the chalk line while Skanga drew a second, smaller circle with red chalk. Then, from the chest, she withdrew jewelry and clothing crafted from some delicate fabric. The items smelled burned, a smell that banished the odors of the sea from the cave.

"You thought you could make fun of Branbeard, didn't you?"

Orgrim looked up in shock, but Skanga was not talking to him. She was talking to the two gagged elves.

"You think we trolls are stupid. You planned to deceive us. It would never occur to you to offer us your help if you were not damned certain that you could swindle us. But I saw through you, Shahondin. This is not, for you, just about killing Emerelle, as you told us. You wanted her crown, too. Even now you have not given up that dream."

The elf managed to rise to his knees. Half-choked noises penetrated his gag.

"No. I heard enough from you earlier. But you know what? You will be a loyal and self-sacrificing servant to Branbeard and me. You will hate us. More than Emerelle. And yet you will do everything to fulfill my wish." The old crone giggled. "Courage failing you? Believe me, in your wildest dreams, you could not imagine what I am planning to do with you and your son. You will find Emerelle for me. I will transform you into perfect hunters."

Skanga leaned forward and sniffed at Shahondin's hair, but her expression was disappointed. "You don't even smell of fear now, elfling. Odors don't stick to your kind, do they . . . that is, unless you ornament yourselves with them. I feared as much. But they like strong smells. They are drawn to them, as the smell of blood attracts sharks from far and wide to the harbor of Vahan Calyd." She turned around. "Ah, Maruk. There you are." The boatman stood indecisively at the cave entrance. Skanga beckoned him inside. "Come here and join the two elves for a moment. Make sure they don't slide around too much and wipe away any part of the circle."

The shaman inspected Orgrim's work and nodded with satisfaction. "Good work, whelp. Now get the candles you find in the chest and set them out here, wherever you think fit. Candles are always good when one is dealing with the darkness, wouldn't you agree?"

"Oh . . . definitely," Orgrim replied hesitantly, wondering if Skanga had gone mad.

The shaman took a small leather flask from one of the folds of her patchwork robe. She emptied its contents in a single draft, puffing out her cheeks as she did so. Then she sprayed a mist of dark-brown juice over the two prisoners from between her pressed-together lips. "Better like this, pretty elves. Cod liver oil and seal blood. Now you smell like something, elfling. All I have to worry about now is how to tell you apart in the future."

Orgrim had fetched the candles, but he found nothing with which to light them. Brud and the seamen with the torches had retreated. "Skanga?"

The shaman silenced him with an impatient gesture. "Just put them out. I'll take care of everything else later. Don't disturb an old woman when she finally has a little joy in her life." She stroked her gnarled fingers over Shahondin's face. "You must be hundreds of years old, elfling. Yet your face is as smooth and flawless as a virgin's tits the first time she bleeds. I have always envied you elves that."

Orgrim did not take his eyes off Skanga as he set up the thick black candles. What was all this with the elves? Suddenly, the shaman pushed one finger sideways into Shahondin's eye, causing the eyeball to pop out. It hung on his cheek by a thin thread. The prince reared up against his bonds, but the gag in his mouth reduced his screaming to a muffled gurgle.

Skanga closed her hand around the eye hanging on his cheek. "I enjoy it very much when I am able to combine the amusing with the utilitarian. I have to be able to tell the difference between you and Vahelmin, after all." With a jerk, she snapped the thin thread from which the eyeball hung and popped the eye into her mouth. Chewing pleasurably, she turned to Orgrim.

"You've put out enough of the candles. Now stand in the other circle and don't move from it until I allow you to."

Skanga placed her left hand over her heart and snapped her fingers. Instantly, all the candles were alight. They gave off a rank, heavy fetor.

Orgrim did as Skanga bade him. The red circle was small. What was she planning to do with him? Why did he have to stand there by himself? And why was Maruk grinning at him like that? Did he know what was about to happen? The boatman was now standing with Skanga beside the large white circle. The shaman had placed one hand amicably on his shoulder.

Orgrim could smell the sour reek of fear emanating from himself. He was no coward! But he fought best when he had his enemy in plain sight in front of him. This business with the elves was unearthly.

Skanga began to sing softly. The dark veins deep in the rock danced to the rhythm of her song. The ground underfoot seemed to vibrate slightly. Close to the white circle, an arch of golden light appeared from the rock. It surrounded an entry to the darkness. The void! Anyone who had seen it once would recognize it again. It was beyond comparison even with the darkness of a clouded, moonless night. The void was more dense . . . and one could sense that no light would ever shine beyond the golden path.

Skanga's song had changed. Her voice no longer formed words. It had become a deep, throaty growl. At the same time, a strange transformation overcame Maruk. His skin shriveled and wrinkled. His eyes were wide open. And from his mouth dripped a thread of sticky golden light. Twisting like a worm, the thread danced to Skanga's song. As if weightless, it drifted in the air, then disappeared through the gate that the shaman had opened.

A panting noise emanated from the void. Something pushed itself through the gate. Hunched, lurking, malicious, a living shadow. The golden thread seemed to have drawn the shadow through the gate . . . But no, Orgrim realized his mistake. The reality was different. The shadow creature was devouring the light.

A second creature emerged from the darkness, and the two began to fight in silence over the light.

Maruk had grown smaller, and his eyes were milk white. His skin was now stretched tight, like the skin spanning an old man's skull, and his bones stood out clearly beneath. It was as if Skanga had melted all the flesh out of his body.

The golden thread broke. Maruk tipped forward, falling on his face. The shadow creatures gulped down the last of the light greedily. Then, with low snarls, they prowled around the cave. They reminded Orgrim of large dogs, except that they had no tails. Their form seemed to vary. They sniffed at the clothes and the jewelry strewn on the cave floor.

"These belong to Emerelle, queen of the elves," said Skanga softly. "A strong light burns in her. I want you to find her for me. You will sense it when she returns. A magic weaver with an Albenstone who enters the network of Albenpaths will always cause a tremor."

Orgrim had the feeling that the shadow beasts understood the shaman's words. They paused in their prowling, and though they had no visible eyes or ears, they seemed to turn their senses toward the white circle.

"I will lift the curse of the Alben from you, and you will be able to pass through their stars without being summoned. And I will lend you two bodies, strong bodies suffused with magic, so that you can feel life. All I ask in return is that you find Emerelle for me before the coming winter is over. I want her alive. I will come to collect her personally. Your reward will be the light of a hundred Albenkin. I will prepare a feast for you beyond compare, and you will become so powerful that, from that time on, you will be able to hunt on your own. All the shackles that bind you will be cast off."

One of the figures abruptly turned and prowled around the red circle. One dark paw darted forward. Dark claws slid across an invisible wall, making a dreadful scraping noise, as if one were dragging the sharp edge of a flint stone across a steel blade.

Orgrim held his breath. The shadow reached out a second paw and pulled itself up against the barrier. Orgrim had to fight down the urge to step backward. If he left the magic circle, he was lost. He stared fearfully at the cave floor. Was the thin red line really unbroken? Beneath him pulsed the black veins in the transparent rock. They were more numerous than before.

The shadow creature gave up on him, and both of them went back to circling the white ring.

"Are we agreed?" Skanga asked, her voice insistent now.

Orgrim heard no answer. But the shaman wiped away part of the enchanted circle with her foot. One of the shadows glided through the gap and sniffed at the two defenseless elves. The second crept around behind Skanga.

"Watch out!" Orgrim shouted.

The shadow beast had straightened itself and lunged at Skanga's neck. White light flared. A smell like burned fur spread. "Children, do you think I would summon you if I did not take precautions?" She reached for the shadow and forced it effortlessly to the floor. "I only created the magic circle so that you would not get at the pretty little elves too quickly. Now take your bodies! You know what I expect of you!"

The shadows crouched over the two prisoners. It took Orgrim some moments to realize what he was seeing. He had imagined the repulsive creatures tearing the elves apart, but nothing of the sort happened. Shahondin and his son breathed the shadows in. In thin wisps, they pushed their way inside the elves through their noses. And slowly, slowly, the shadow creatures paled until they had vanished entirely. The elves lay as if dead. Skanga stepped inside the circle, cut through their bonds, and pulled the gags from their mouths. "You can come to me now, Orgrim. You are no longer in any danger."

Hardly had Skanga spoken when Vahelmin sat up with a scream. His hands grasped at his face—it was deforming, as if something beneath his skin was trying by force to change the way he looked. His jaw became elongated, his hands clawing at convulsing skin and muscle. His forehead grew flatter, receded. Vahelmin's fine silk shirt tore apart. Bands of muscle as thick as snakes twisted beneath the skin of his shoulders. Claws broke from his fingertips. He threw himself around and now crouched on all fours like an animal. His back arched, and his arms and legs grew longer and thinner. Shahondin, too, had begun to change, his body transforming like his son's. A long jaw bordered with white fangs pushed outward from his face. His empty eye socket filled with a blood-red ball.

When the unearthly transformation was complete, two huge beasts crouched side by side inside the chalk circle. The shadow beasts were no longer disembodied outlines, but neither could they be called creatures of flesh and blood. They looked a little like wolves but were as big as horses, and gaunt. They were covered with short white fur and very long snouts, and their ears were somewhat reminiscent of the elven ears they had once been. Blue-white light swirled around them, and one could see through them in the same way as through the walls of the cave.

Orgrim wondered if the magic of the cave had influenced their appearance.

"Neither claw nor tooth can hurt you," intoned Skanga solemnly. "Nor the silver steel of the elves. But avoid the iron of the kobolds, for their weapons can cause you injury." The shaman turned to Orgrim. "Aren't they pretty? My children . . ."

"They look dangerous," Orgrim said evasively.

Skanga laughed. "Dangerous! They are insatiable predatory beasts! They tear the light out of a body, the essence of your being, the part that can be reborn. If they attack you, they leave no wounds. But you end up like poor Maruk there." She pointed at the cadaver, no more than skin and bones, that still lay in the spell circle. "They do not destroy your physical frame like other predators. They destroy you utterly. The elves especially fear them, for the elves are reborn more frequently than any others of the Albenkin. They call these spawn of the void Shi-Handan, which means soul eater. Anyone fool enough to shelter Emerelle will regret it." She laughed heartily, looking at her handiwork. "Kill anyone with her. Only the queen is forbidden to you."

"Shahondin and Vahelmin are their first victims?"

"No!" The shaman shook her head with such resolution that the amulets on her chest rattled. "They can hear us. It is their burning hatred that drives the Shi-Handan. They live on inside them. I can even give them their old form back again." Skanga laughed jauntily. "You hear that? If you think about it, I've done you a favor. You can spread death and mayhem among the followers of the queen and bring Emerelle down without anyone recognizing you at all. No one knows about your pact with me. Go and do what your hearts have always desired. In return I will give you back your bodies. The soul eaters will not need you anymore once I reward them with the sacrifices I have promised.

Look at their eyes, Orgrim. In their eyes you can see that two souls now dwell inside the Shi-Handan." She beckoned the soul eaters to her.

Orgrim had to summon all his courage to stand his ground before the monsters. Icy air streamed around him as the two creatures stalked. One had mismatched eyes, blue and blood red. And from each eye glared two black pupils.

"Go now, my darlings. Good hunting!"

Skanga's creations obeyed her like two well-trained hunting dogs. Without hesitation, they loped away into the darkness beyond the golden gate.

"Will you really be able to change Shahondin and Vahelmin back again?"

The shaman shrugged. "I don't know. I doubt it, frankly. More important was for those two little elves to believe me. Taking his eye was just for show, to scare them. I don't put much store in lukewarm eyeballs between meals. But if you make someone fear you, you make them more willing to believe. Shahondin was tough, and he understood something of magic. In other circumstances, he would never have fallen into line. And he truly does live on inside the Shi-Handan, which is why he has to believe there is a way back. His spirit will hold the beast in check when they find Emerelle. It will be he who is responsible for us capturing her alive. Time to go, Pack Leader. As soon as the tide allows, I want to get back to the *Wraithwind*. A new ship awaits your command."

"It seems to be very easy to fall out of favor with you, Skanga."

"Only if one disappoints me, Orgrim." She turned around and looked intently at him. "I appreciate it when my men have the courage to tell me what they think to my face. At least, as long as they tell me privately. Bring a few of your people from the *Rumbler*." She kicked one foot against Maruk's sagging corpse. "One *does* tend to have occasional sudden losses . . . always good to have a few extra crew on board."

Orgrim decided on the spot not to take with him anyone he held in any regard. That would be poor recompense for his comrades' loyalty. "There is one warrior there, a real giant, that I would like to have at my side very much. His name is Gran. Maybe you have heard of him."

"No." Skanga shuffled off in the direction of the tunnel. "But I know Boltan. His wounds must have healed by now. Bring him along, too, Pack Leader. His exceptional bravery is still the talk of the king's court."

A NIGHT OF LOVE, ALMOST

The entire day, Alfadas had tried to put things right. He had made the children laugh, but Asla glared furiously at the terrible dog. She had talked to Ole at midday, and he had promised that he would consider taking the beast back. To make his decision easier, Asla had given him a jug of mead left over from the feast.

The children were sleeping now. Alfadas sat by the fire pit, carving a new wooden sword for Ulric. Now and then, he looked covertly in her direction, but she would not make it easy for him! Asla pretended that she did not notice him looking. She was stitching a tear in Kadlin's favorite dress.

Blood lay in front of Kadlin's sleeping niche. The dog realized that she was looking at him, and he held her eye defiantly. Mongrel cur! The dog was treating her as if *she* were the stranger in that house! *She* should have been the one to take him to the fjord! She would certainly not have brought him home again. Asla could not suppress a smile—it must have been very difficult for Alfadas to claim in all seriousness that the dog stood under Luth's protection. She knew very well that her husband did not believe in the gods. Everyone in the village knew it. It was the only reason why he was never elected unanimously as jarl. There were some who said openly that having such a godless fellow as jarl would one day bring calamity down on Firnstayn, but there were never enough of those dissenters to keep him from the post.

"He will look after you when I have to travel to the royal court next spring," said Alfadas suddenly.

Asla bit down hard on her lip. She would not laugh! He had been trying the whole day to find reasons why it was good that he had returned with Blood. "If I am actually able to keep myself safe from Blood, then there is nothing else in the world I need to fear."

"It was the priest's wish. I would have been committing a sin against Luth if I'd harmed as much as a hair on the beast. Gundar came to the fjord to protect Blood. I would have had to knock him down just to get to the dog!"

"You're exaggerating. Besides, you *never* care what the gods think of you." The truth was, she had already accepted that she would not soon be seeing the last of the black monster. But Alfadas ought to stew in his bad conscience for a while longer.

"My heart is a desert if I have to spend a day without your smile."

He had that look in his eye again . . . the same look she had fallen in love with back then. He was a famous warrior. The man who had ridden with the elves. A living legend. But when he looked at her like that, he became a sad little boy. And all she could do was take him in her arms and console him.

"Plain flattery will get you nowhere! You won't fool me as quickly as you might think. I'm not an innocent virgin anymore!" Her tone was not half as gruff as she might have wanted it to be. He had done it again.

"How can words so hard come from lips as tender as rose petals?"

She looked up. "And what else about me reminds you of a plant? Maybe my hands, because they're as crooked and knotty as old roots?" She had known him long enough to know that something like that would only spur him on to new compliments. Truth be told, she loved it when he babbled that kind of nonsense just to please her. There was not another man in the village who found such words for his wife. If only that damned stone circle were not there. The way he looked up to the Hartungscliff was what blighted her life. She still loved him. If she did not, then it would make no difference to wake one morning and find him gone. Blond Gunbrid was always happy to see her Sven ride away in spring with Alfadas to the king's court and when he did not show his face again until the end of summer. But for herself, it was different, thought Asla bitterly. Usually, on the morning he departed, they quarreled. But the very first night, sleep would not come to her without the feel of his warm breath on her neck.

He had not been in Firnstayn when Kadlin was born. He had seen his daughter for the first time when she was almost half a year old. And this past summer, too, he had been away for too many long weeks.

Why was it taking so long for his next compliment to come? Apart from Blood's soft snuffling and the occasional murmur or hiss from the coals in the fire pit, the house was silent. Had she finally managed to silence him once and for all with her obstinate manner?

"I am sorry if it is so difficult to live with me, my darling. Sometimes I can hardly live with myself, and I feel torn. Then one part of me seems to be far away from the place I am in." Alfadas stood up from the bench by the fire.

He stepped over behind Asla. His strong hands closed around her hips. He breathed a kiss into the nape of her neck. "But wherever I may be, part of me is also with you and the children. I know that is not anything you can hold in your hands, but I hope it is some consolation to your heart the next time you are angry with me."

His fingers unclasped the belt around her dress. Her head told her no. He had to come up with a better apology than that! Not enough had been said! But her body betrayed her. The way he touched her made her shiver with pleasure. Asla stood up and put her sewing aside. He pushed up her dress and caressed the inside of her thighs. She sighed softly. Something seemed to flutter in her belly, and a delicious warmth spread deep inside her. She heard his breeches crumple to the floor. Warm kisses covered the nape of her neck. She lifted her arms to make it easier for him to lift the dress over her head. His hands smelled of resin and beech wood from his carving. They grazed lightly over her breasts, collarbones, neck. Then they were between her thighs again. Every touch sent waves of hunger through her, made her sigh with desire. If he only knew so well what her heart longed for!

With gentle strength, he pressed her forward onto the tabletop. His hands clasped her hips, and she felt something moist, stiff touch her. She groaned aloud in carnal hunger.

And then someone knocked at the door. A soft knocking, almost shy.

Asla tensed. By the gods! Not now! Blood raised his head, growled softly. He looked toward them inquisitively.

The knock repeated, more energetic now. Alfadas cursed. He could not simply pretend not to be there. He was the jarl. If he was needed in the village, it was his duty to go.

"If that's Svenja again, come to complain about a lost chicken, then I'll . . . be upset," Alfadas grumbled. Wearing only his tunic, he went to the door. Asla gathered up her dress from the floor and hid behind one of the thick columns supporting the roof. Blood was acting strangely. He lay on the floor as if he wanted to sink into the earth, his ears pressed flat on his oversized head. He made quiet, whimpering sounds. Who was there?

The heavy door swung open. She saw Alfadas tense, ready to vent his anger, but then he froze. She heard someone whisper but could not catch what was said. The voice sounded strange and unfamiliar. It seemed to be a woman. Her words came like soft music.

Asla hastily pulled her dress on again, then crouched for her husband's breeches.

Alfadas stepped aside. A tall, slim woman entered. The sight of her caused Asla's breath to catch. The stranger was gaunt, too gaunt, and her dress was torn, and yet she was beautiful. Her movements were proud and confident . . . as if she were a queen.

Blood jumped to his feet. He greeted the newcomer with a deep snarl. He stalked toward her on stiff legs. Every trembling fiber of his muscular body seemed to resist an attack, and yet he wanted to drive this unknown visitor out.

Someone else entered. A woman with short blond hair. Sword belts crossed on her chest. She looked around mistrustfully. When she saw Blood, she made a short, commanding gesture toward him. The dog dropped to the floor but kept growling.

A third woman entered. In disbelief, Asla could only stare at the growing parade of guests. The slim, dark-haired woman who had entered first was still talking to Alfadas. The blond with the two swords grasped his wrist in a warrior's greeting. Both of them seemed to know her husband. Only the third remained in the background. She looked all around, her lips pursed contemptuously.

Asla swallowed. What she had always feared had come to pass. The elves had arrived to take her husband away.

OF STRANGERS AND FRIENDS

Lyndwyn tugged carefully at the reed in his throat. It pinched a little, then slid out of the wound. She laid the palm of her hand on the place it had been. Her fingers radiated a benevolent warmth. Three days. Three days that he'd had to put up with the stick in his throat. The sorceress claimed that the journey along the Albenpaths had exhausted her. Ollowain did not believe a word of it!

Lyndwyn removed her hand and looked expectantly at him. "You should be able to speak again now."

The swordmaster's mouth was as dry as dust. He cleared his throat softly. Everyone was standing around him, watching him as he sat on one of the three rough chairs in Alfadas's house.

Ollowain cautiously lifted his fingers to his throat and felt the place where the reed had been. Lyndwyn had removed the leather strips holding it in place. There was neither hard scar tissue nor a rough scab to remind him of where she had sliced into his throat. It was as if the reed had never been there. "Everything seems to be healed." His voice was hoarse and sounded foreign to him.

"Your throat still has to recover a little," said Lyndwyn confidently. "Any pain will soon pass. Don't go looking for anything still wrong. You will see—everything is sorting itself out."

Ollowain looked to the sleeping niche where they had prepared a bed for the queen. Nothing was sorting itself out! How could she talk this way when Emerelle lay there like that? The queen's wounds were healing, but she lay in a deep sleep from which no one and nothing was able to wake her. To Ollowain, her sleep seemed like a flight from the cruel reality of their situation. Or was it Lyndwyn's handiwork? He no longer knew what to think of the sorceress. Without her help, they would never have made it to safety. And Silwyna? In her quiver were arrows that looked exactly like the two that had been shot at Emerelle. Each of them, Lyndwyn and Silwyna, had saved his life during their escape. But what were they supposed to do now? Everyone was still looking at him—now that he could speak again, they expected decisions.

Ollowain smiled. "I would like to express my gratitude to our two hosts," he said calmly. "I am well aware that our presence is a burden on your family's peace, Asla. We will not overstay our welcome, I assure you."

The human looked at him with no warmth in her eyes. "The laws of hospitality are sacred to us. You are welcome in this house."

Ollowain did not know what he had personally done to upset the young woman, but he had sensed her aversion to them ever since their arrival. Had Alfadas told her about Silwyna? No, he would certainly not do anything that stupid.

But their appearance had caused a deep disruption in the lives of the humans. People came from miles around to gape at the strange guests who had come to visit the jarl of Firnstayn. And Asla had to serve all of them. The family's winter stocks were melting away like snow in spring sunshine. She had every reason to be angry.

"I believe I would like to take a little walk. Would you have anything against accompanying me, Alfadas?"

"No, master. On the contrary."

His face still mirrored what he felt. Ollowain had always appreciated that about the humans. Very few of them were any good at dissembling their emotions.

"Can you take Kadlin and Ulric with you?" Asla's words were more an order than a question. "And ask Svenja to bake three more loaves of bread for me for this evening. And bring back a basket of apples from her, too. That manhorse eats enough for all of us!"

"As always, your wish is my command," Alfadas replied cheerfully as he lifted Kadlin onto his shoulders. He waved to his son to join them, and the big, ugly dog followed them outside.

As long as they were in the village, inquisitive eyes followed them. An entire troop of the curious had set up camp at the foot of the small hill on which Alfadas's house perched. Luckily, just then, they were being entertained by Orimedes, who was raising a barrel to his mouth and drinking deeply. The centaur felt at home among the humans, but Silwyna did not—after that first evening, she had vanished into the forests without saying a word about why or where.

"You're the master swordsman who taught my father sword fighting, aren't you?" asked Ulric reverently.

"Yes. He was still younger than you when they brought him to me. He was a very good pupil."

"Would you give me a sword-fighting lesson, master?"

Ollowain had to smile. For a moment, he once again saw the cheeky young boy, hungry for knowledge, that Alfadas had been back then. Ulric was very like his father, although decidedly more respectful. "It would be my honor to cross swords with the son of my best student. From what I've seen, you have a good selection of beautiful swords at home."

"My father carved all of them for me!" Ulric declared with pride. "Usually when he has a quarrel with my mother, he carves me a sword. And they like to quarrel."

Or perhaps he had been mistaken about the young lad's respectfulness toward adults, thought Ollowain, amused.

They strolled along the path that led from the back of the village into the forest. The swordmaster found the human world uncanny in a way that he found difficult to put into words. Something about the air there was not right. It blurred one's view into the distance, and even the simplest arrangements of things seemed disordered. The positions of the trees in relation to one another, or the way their branches grew. Even the rustling of their leaves in the wind sounded different if one listened closely. Different from Albenmark. Maybe it was because there was so little magic in the human world? And maybe it was completely natural for worlds to distinguish themselves from one another. What did he know about such things, after all? He had other matters to worry about.

They walked for a long way in silence. The only sound was Ulric shouting challenges to invisible opponents beside the path they followed and occasionally slashing at bushes or mushrooms with his wooden sword.

"Are things really as bad as Yilvina said?" Alfadas suddenly asked.

Ollowain had sat in silence as his companion had reported on the fall of Vahan Calyd and on the battle with the trolls. The cut in his throat had not allowed him to speak, and he had not been unhappy to not have to tell that particular story.

"She has not told you half of it."

"What will you do now?"

Ollowain lifted one hand in a gesture of hopelessness. "I don't know. Maybe I should go to the Snaiwamark. The trolls will probably head there next."

"What makes you think so?"

"It is the home of my people, the Normirga, and also Emerelle's clan. The trolls have two reasons to attack there. Presumably, they would search there for Emerelle, and they are very likely inclined to avenge themselves in blood against an entire clan. Even if that were not the case, they would want to retake their old homeland. They were driven out of the Snaiwamark—it is the land the Alben once gave to them."

"But why would they want blood vengeance against an entire clan? What do the rest of them have to do with it? What—" Alfadas broke off.

"You have been living among humans again for a long time, my friend. You think in their terms, on their scale. Though the atrocities of the last troll war happened hundreds of years ago, many elves who took part in them are still alive today. The wounds our races have inflicted on each other run too deep." Ollowain briefly considered telling Alfadas about the massacre on the Shalyn Falah—about the murder of the troll king and his dukes—but he decided to say nothing. What had happened that night was too shameful. "Sometimes, our long lives become a curse. The old wounds won't heal because they cannot be forgotten. You must still remember Farodin. For more than seven hundred years, he has been carrying on a feud with a troll duke. He alone knows how many times he has killed the troll and how many times he has been reborn, only to die again at Farodin's hand."

"You should not take Emerelle back to Albenmark with you. Not in the condition she is in now. Leave her here with me. Asla and I will take care of her."

"And I will, too!" said Ulric very seriously. "I can get her something to drink if she is thirsty, and tell her stories if she gets bored."

Ollowain stroked the boy's hair. "I am certain that my queen would appreciate your offer very much indeed." He glanced at Alfadas. "But in good conscience, I cannot burden you with that."

"No? So you really want to take her with you to the permanent ice of the Snaiwamark? To exactly the place you expect the trolls to attack next? No one would look for her here. Who would even suspect that the mighty Emerelle would go into hiding in the human world? Name one place that would be safer for Emerelle, and I will let you leave with her."

Alfadas's objections were not easily swept aside. And yet Ollowain did not have a good feeling about what the jarl was proposing. Ollowain's own plan had been to hide there for a few days, long enough for Emerelle to regain her strength, but no more. He had not considered at all the possibility that she might not readily recover from her injuries, and now he did not know what was to be done. In his mind, it would always have been up to the queen, there in Firnstayn, to decree how they would proceed. "I will sleep on it one more night," Ollowain finally replied.

Alfadas smiled broadly. "Why? I've never known you to be this hesitant. My words will be the same tomorrow as today. Why wait?"

"Perhaps because despite my age, I have not yet given up hope of attaining wisdom overnight," Ollowain replied, and laughed.

Suddenly, Blood stopped and growled softly. He was glaring at a thicket a short way ahead. Ollowain could see nothing suspicious, but he had the feeling they were being watched. And something had come over Ulric, too. He rubbed his arms. "It's cold here under the trees," he said.

"Then let's go down to the fjord."

"Ata, ata!" Kadlin cried enthusiastically, as if she had understood what her father had said.

"Silwyna?" Alfadas called toward the bushy thicket. But no reply came.

"This is where Grandpa fought the monster," Ulric explained. The boy pointed at the hazel bush. "That's where it was hiding. And this is where they found Grandpa's friends. All dead."

"Who told you that?" Alfadas asked in annoyance.

"Grandfather Erek. He told me everything about the fight with the man-boar. Grandfather says that this place is cursed because it's where his father's friends died. That's why it's always cold here."

"And *I* say you're cold because your good-for-nothing grandfather has been telling you scary stories about this place." Alfadas took his son by the hand. "Now let's go."

Ollowain looked at the dense hazel bush one last time. Something was there. He could sense it. The dog had not become restive for nothing. Something lurked there.

Was it possible that the trolls had followed them through the labyrinth of the Albenpaths? No, that was absurd. You did not leave tracks in the Albenpaths.

Ollowain strode after Alfadas and soon caught up with him and the children. Ulric thrashed at the trunk of a young birch with his sword and rained invective on the tree as he did so—some of his curses would have impressed even Orimedes.

"Silwyna was at the hazel bush," said Alfadas softly. "I can still sense when she is close by. Like I used to . . . Why did you bring her with you?"

Ollowain considered lying to him, but whom could he trust if not Alfadas? Alfadas was certainly not involved in any conspiracy against Emerelle, so he told him why she was there.

They could see the waters of the fjord glinting through the trees long before the swordmaster came to the end of the story of the Maurawan and the opaque role she played in their escape.

"She did not shoot at the queen, I'm certain of that," said Alfadas resolutely. "She would never do that."

He is as trusting as ever, thought Ollowain sadly. It would have been wiser not to tell him anything at all. "And you never thought, back then, that she would leave you, did you?"

Alfadas looked up in surprise. "What does one have to do with the other?"

"You have spent the larger part of your life in Albenmark, my friend, but a human life is short. I've had temporary moods that have lasted longer. You don't really know us. Do you truly know whether she might hold a secret grudge against the queen?"

Alfadas shook his head in disbelief. "You have been Emerelle's bodyguard for too long, master. All you see is intrigue and betrayal but not the reality! Your constant concern for the queen has burned you out. Why should Silwyna have saved your life if she had wanted to murder the queen? And why would she be here? She could easily have killed Emerelle when you were incapacitated by the bees."

"You can't begin to think like a Maurawan, Alfadas. And who can blame you? Even in Albenmark, hardly anyone understands that clan of eccentric loners. For her, it is all about the hunt. And if neither I nor Emerelle herself is in a position to protect her, then the queen is no longer worthwhile prey. Don't try to understand her, Alfadas. All that lies in that direction is pain."

His friend's face hardened. With his short blond hair, Alfadas looked strange. Older, tougher, more human. "Silwyna will have had a good reason to leave me. She has never told me what it was, but that does not mean it doesn't exist."

Alfadas's excessive trustfulness was as charming as it was naive. If only the world were as Alfadas wanted to see it!

"Why did she leave my house again so quickly?" said Alfadas, deep in his private thoughts.

"Perhaps because she prefers a forest to your four smoky walls?" Ollowain joked.

The jarl laughed. "Oh, I'm sure she does that. Besides, I think she understood how things stand between Asla and me immediately."

"I think anyone who saw you walking around without your trousers would understand that."

Alfadas reddened. "Silwyna is still beautiful. When I saw her standing in front of me in the doorway, it was as if she had only been gone a moment, and not ten years. I . . . if not for Asla . . ."

"But as it happens, there is Asla. Be happy that you have her. She—"

"She sensed instantly that I knew Silwyna," the jarl interrupted him. "I have never told her about our love."

"Did she never think to ask what your life was like at Emerelle's court?" Ollowain was surprised. He had another image of humans in his mind. He imagined they were not very sensitive creatures . . . something like centaurs, in fact. He would not have believed that Asla was smart enough not to ask a question whose answer she could not bear to hear.

"She does not like it when I talk about those times. I can feel how it gnaws at her. Every time I look up to the stone circle, it makes her angry. But she does not ask questions. Asla is a wonderful woman." They had reached the edge of the forest. In front of them lay a rocky stretch of shore. Ulric charged ahead to the water's edge, and little Kadlin pulled at her father's hair and wanted to get down from his shoulders. "I fear I am not a good husband to her," Alfadas said softly. "She often calls me her 'beautiful, strange man.' Her words are meant to be a joke, but they say exactly what she feels. We have two children. We have been living together for eight years. And I am a stranger to her."

Ollowain placed one hand on his friend's arm. As a young boy, Alfadas— despondent because the young elves were so very superior to him, and yet wanting to hold his own against them—had gone to Ollowain. Even then, it had been hard for the swordmaster to find the right words to advise him. And today . . . what did he know about the hearts of humans? The best he could do was to be there, to listen.

Kadlin began thumping on her father's head with her little fists. She no longer made any effort to hold on—she wanted down!

"It looks like you have a little warrior woman there," said Ollowain, to steer their conversation in another direction.

Alfadas laughed drily and lifted his daughter down. "Women are not trained to fight here." Kadlin stamped her feet angrily and complained bitterly as he held on to a fold of her dress to stop her from running out onto the deeply cleft rocks. Gusty winds threw the waters of the fjord against the shore, and the waves broke into a labyrinth of caves and fissures. Occasionally, without warning, a geyser of spray shot skyward from among the fractured rocks. Ulric was already soaking wet. He was standing on a rocky promontory projecting far out over the fjord, shouting a challenge to the king of the deeps.

Ollowain looked out over the wide waters. The weather had turned, and the sky was now overcast, the waves carrying small foamy crests as they raced shoreward. Far out he saw a small boat, its sail reefed, struggling against the rising sea. He felt a chill run through him. The landscape radiated a raw beauty . . . it suited the humans, he thought. "Who does your son want to fight now?" he asked. "Who is this 'king of the deeps'?"

Alfadas waved a hand dismissively. "Just one of many stories the Fjordlanders like to tell on long winter nights around their fireplaces."

"Do you think one might also tell it to an elf on a gray autumn day?"

The jarl looked at him in surprise. "It is really nothing special."

"It seems to have impressed at least your son quite deeply."

Ulric still stood on the promontory. He was holding his sword aloft now, as if he had just wrung a victory for the ages.

Alfadas had to smile. "Yes. It is the kind of story that mesmerizes children, old soldiers, and fools. A long time ago, when iron was reserved for the weapons of the gods alone, a proud ruler reigned over the fjords, King Osaberg. Many called him Osaberg the Golden, for he wore a heavy breastplate forged from golden bronze. He wore a winged helmet, a mail shirt that reached to his knees, and a large round shield painted with the image of a sea serpent. He was a noble, rich king. Many wars had filled his treasure chamber and also brought him many enemies. Even his own princes envied him, because next to the king, the renown of even the bravest warrior was as dust. In those distant times, the rulers plied the fjords in boats with hulls of leather, as our own fishermen still do today. One summer, on a military campaign, Osaberg and his men were confronted by an enemy army and heavily outnumbered. They say his own princes betrayed him. Whatever the truth may be, they fled in their boats before a sword was even raised. Osaberg and his last loyal followers were surrounded. They fought desperately, but there were simply too many enemy soldiers. The king was the last still standing. When he saw that defeat was inevitable, he sliced through the leather skin of the hull and sank in the fjord in his heavy bronze armor. Before he went down, he shouted to his enemies that he would return and that he would erect a throne of their bones on the bottom of the fjord. Two days later, most of the ships of the traitors and the victorious enemy sank in a sudden storm. Ever since, it is said, King Osaberg wanders the bottom of the fjord restlessly. And sometimes he climbs from the waters to test the courage of the brave in single combat or to spread terror and death among the enemies of the Fjordlands."

"Maybe you should not allow your son to go shouting at that dark ruler. Aren't you afraid that he might hear him?"

Alfadas laughed softly. "We are not in Albenmark here, my friend. It is only a story. The king only lives in the imagination of boys like Ulric and a few old madmen. In my world, such creatures do not exist."

"And the manboar?" Ollowain objected. He still looked out at the restless waters of the fjord, but saw it now through different eyes. Was the ghost of an ancient warrior king lurking there in the depths? "And what about the trolls? Several of their fortresses are little more than three hundred miles from where we stand. And then there are the outcasts of Albenmark who have found refuge in your world . . . It may be that King Osaberg does not exist, but maybe something else is lying in wait at the bottom of the fjord."

"No, my friend. My father-in-law is a fisherman, and his father before him. The tradition goes back many generations. They know everything that lives in the fjord, and there is no king down there. It is a story, no more, something to terrify children and keep them from going too near the water."

Ollowain observed the boy on his rocky ledge. He was strong. Long, wet strands of blond hair clung to his neck. He kept his footing effortlessly on the slippery rocks. He would no doubt become a good sword fighter if Alfadas found the time to train him properly. "Your son does not seem to have been overly terrified by it."

The jarl's eyes lit up proudly. "He is very courageous, it's true. He will be a better leader than me because he knows where his heart belongs."

Ollowain thought wistfully about how he had never had a child of his own. He had never even had a woman at his side for any length of time. There had always been something else in his life that came first, something that seemed more urgent. For hundreds of years, he had dedicated himself solely to serving Emerelle. His conviction that he had made the right choice ran deep, as strange as some of the queen's decisions appeared to be. She looked hundreds of years into the future—no one was able to say what moved her. She fought covert battles to protect the Albenkin, often employing cunning, intrigue, or intimidation, which helped avoid open warfare. Ollowain knew that Emerelle's only goal was what was best for Albenmark. Now, too . . . and yet, when he thought of the fall of Vahan Calyd, he was plagued by doubts. How much had she known? What horrors of the future justified such extreme sacrifice now? He would find that out only if he continued to be loyal to her. He had to save her now, and he had to have the patience to wait and see what the future brought. For the moment, however, he could do nothing more than hope that Emerelle would soon awake from her magical slumber.

Or . . . no, in fact! As long as Emerelle slept and was not in imminent danger, he had time to devote himself to others. By himself, there was nothing he could do against the trolls. Only the queen had the authority to call all of the Albenkin to war. The races of Albenmark would not follow anyone else.

Ollowain looked from Alfadas to his son. His memories of training the jarl to fight with a sword were still fresh. He had taken great pleasure in the formative role he played in Alfadas's development and in seeing his talent grow. He smiled abashedly, then gave a slight nod.

"It would be an honor for me to be permitted to instruct Ulric a little in sword fighting. Though your own father despised the sword as an unmanly weapon, he had a gift for fighting with one. It seems to me that this legacy lives on in your son."

"What better teacher could Ulric ever have? He will be thrilled when I tell him that. He thinks the world of you, Ollowain. I have told him about you many times."

Blood, who had been loping about aimlessly on Ulric's promontory, suddenly began to bark loudly at something in a cleft in the rocks. Ulric ran to the large dog, then waved to his father. "There's something here . . . a dead rabbit. It looks funny."

Ollowain followed his friend out onto the rocks. Ulric, in the meantime, had pressed himself flat onto the rock and was prodding around in the cleft with his wooden sword. Deep down lay the cadaver of the rabbit. It was as shrunken and shriveled as a dried plum. Its fur betrayed no obvious wound.

"What happened to the rabbit, Papa?"

"It's nothing out of the ordinary," said Alfadas lightly. "It must have fallen down there and could not get out again. The heat of the last few days has dried it out, and ravens and other carrion eaters can't get to it down there. That's why it is so well preserved." The jarl took his son's wooden sword, lay flat on the rock, and, with his outstretched arm, succeeded in turning the rabbit over.

Ollowain noted with surprise that no maggots were to be seen on the cadaver.

"Do you feel how warm the rocks still are?" Alfadas asked his son. Ulric pressed the flat of his hand onto the rock and nodded.

"The midday heat has not faded—down there, the rabbit is in something like an oven. It's completely dried out. All that's left is fur and bones." Blood growled as if the explanation did not please him, and Kadlin, whom Alfadas had finally set free, began to growl with him.

The jarl gave the little girl a small poke with his finger, pulled a face, and growled back. Then Ulric joined in, too, and began to bark. Ollowain watched in amazement. He would never understand humans. The elf felt out of place and withdrew. He did not want to spoil the others' fun. He moved off the rocks and looked back out to the fjord again. The boat he had seen a while earlier was now within a hundred paces of the shore. It was a simple, almost circular fishing boat with a hull of animal skins. The only person on board was an old man, who now raised one arm and waved and shouted, but the gusting wind whipped away part of his message. "Alfadas . . . village . . . soldiers!"

THE CHRONICLE OF FIRNSTAYN

*I*n the fifth year in which Alfadas Mandredson served as jarl of Firnstayn, the elves returned. They sought refuge in his hall, where today the Hall of Kings stands. And no less a figure than the elf queen herself fell under his care. The queen of the Albenlands, perilously injured, driven out by her enemies, recalled her foster son. But when she reached the land of the fjords, she fell into a deep sleep. Neither shouts nor shaking, not even the power of magic were able to waken her.

But her final words before she slept were spoken to Alfadas Mandredson, bold duke to the king of the Fjordlands. And she asked him for help in the war against the thieves who would steal her crown.

Now the last of Emerelle's loyal followers were stranded, and they remained many days in Firnstayn, pondering in their despair on what they should do. Word of their presence spread like the wind. And it was not long before King Horsa Starkshield himself discovered who had descended from the Hartungscliff.

Whereupon the old warrior determined to once again saddle his old warhorse Mjölnak and ride the long road to Firnstayn. He brought with him the most renowned among the healers. Horsa knew well that the king was the soul of the country and that if the king were to fall ill, his country would suffer with him. In the generosity of his heart, he had decided to aid Emerelle with whatever means he commanded. But nobility of mind breeds envy and resentment. And in that autumn, no one suspected the disaster that the king's selfless act would call forth that very winter.

Recorded by Haddu Hjemwal

Volume Two of the Temple Library of Luth in Firnstayn, page 15

ROYAL PLANS

Y ou'll come home tomorrow?" Asla asked.
Alfadas had been preparing for a fight, but Asla had remained surprisingly amenable. And what choice did he have when the king ordered him to come?

"Yes, if all goes well, I can be back tomorrow evening."

"I hope so. I'm used to guests who throw up on tables and benches when they're drunk, but I am not used to them shitting beside the fire . . ." She glanced censoriously in the direction of the centaur. Orimedes was making himself useful, splitting firewood. The rest of their guests had retreated inside the house. "What does the king want?"

Alfadas sighed. She had already asked him that three times. "I really don't know. He has ordered me to come to Honnigsvald. The messenger said no more than that. My guess would be that he has gotten wind of our guests and he would like to know what is going on."

"Don't go off to war for him again. Please. I need you here." She stroked his cheek softly. "All the signs point to a particularly hard winter. Don't leave me alone when the time of storms and darkness begins."

What a silly fear! He took her in his arms and pressed her tightly to his chest. "Don't be anxious. No one is fool enough to go to war in winter. Horsa will not ask me to lead his army before next spring." He kissed her and hoped he had been able to allay her fears. Then he swung into the saddle and walked his horse down the hill. Below, several men who had witnessed his leave-taking grinned at him. He hoped the weather would turn for the worse soon—then these gaping idiots would finally abandon their siege of his longhouse.

He turned back one more time at the foot of the hill. Asla was standing in the doorway. She wore her green dress and the fine red shawl that he had brought home for her the previous summer. Her hair hung loosely over her shoulders. The wind blew a long strand of hair—as gold as ripe grain—across her face.

Alfadas was worried. She had never said farewell so tenderly when he rode off to the royal court, and this time it was only a two-day journey. Was she perhaps pregnant? He should talk with Lyndwyn when he returned. As a healer and sorceress, she could no doubt tell if a new life was growing in Asla.

The jarl steered his gray stallion contentedly onto the road that led southward along the shore of the fjord. This time, he would be with Asla when the child came. Whatever the king demanded of him. *Enough, fool,* he chided himself in his mind. *You don't even know if your wife is with child and you're already planning the coming year.*

His gaze wandered out over the gray-blue waters of the fjord. The clouds hung low in the sky, swallowing the distant summits. With hammering wings, a flock of guinea fowl flew loudly from the undergrowth on the edge of the forest. The gray shied sideways. Alfadas peered into the undergrowth—something was there. But he had no time to get caught up in Silwyna's games. If she had something to say to him, then she should come out and say it. He was not the one constantly running away, after all. And if she did not come out and say whatever she had to, then she could rot. He let the stallion feel his spurs and trotted on.

Alfadas felt her eyes on his back as he rode away. Was Ollowain right in his suspicions? That was no concern of his now, he told himself, and yet he kept looking back. Why was she here? Could she not leave him in peace after all? He eased the gray back to a walk. If she were really there at the edge of the forest, she could easily catch up with him now. He wanted to know what she was doing here. And he had to admit to himself that despite everything that had happened, he was not indifferent. Had Asla and the children been unable to extinguish his love for her? What would happen if she stepped out of the forest now? Would he again be captivated by her? He could not allow that! His life was here, in Firnstayn, at the side of his family! He spurred the stallion on again and dashed away. He could not let the past catch up with him again.

The shore road soon narrowed to a track no wider than a game path. Travelers seldom found their way to Firnstayn. It was the most northerly village on the fjord and too small to be of interest to traveling merchants. Anyone in need of good cloth, a sturdy horse, or iron arrow tips traveled to Honnigsvald, which called itself—ambitiously—a city because some of its buildings were built of stone. Admittedly, it had ten times the population of Firnstayn, but measured against the cities that Alfadas had seen, Honnigsvald was little more than an outhouse. A useful outhouse, though: he would take something back for Asla, time permitting.

It began to rain. Alfadas untied the rolled cape from the saddle and slung it around his shoulders. Through the hazy veils of the rain, the far shore was almost invisible. The world closed in. The distant mountains were lost in the gray of the sky. Soon, despite the cloak, the jarl was soaked to the skin. He thought wistfully of the wonderful clothes that the elves had made, the fabric from which rain pearled away as it did from the petals of flowers. One could learn so much from them, if only the band that linked their worlds were a little tighter. But the way things stood, it was entirely up to the elves to decide, for no human had ever managed to pass through their gates unaided. Only his own father, Mandred, had once miraculously managed to do so, although he had never been able to explain how.

The forest there pushed down almost all the way to the waterline. The black trunks of the fir trees retreated up the hill as if in a hall filled with columns. The lower branches had died off because light no longer reached them, and a thick cushion of brown needles covered the ground, absorbing the sound of the horse's hooves. Rain swished among the branches. Everything smelled of resin, decay, and mushrooms. Alfadas pulled his head down between his shoulders and steered his horse through the dark hall of the forest. At least the thin black trunks offered some protection from the rain. Once the sun disappeared, a distinct chill entered the air.

His hair hung in his face in wet strands. The leather of his sword belt creaked softly when he moved. Like the bones of a dead giant, rocky outcrops jutted skyward from the earth. Where the route he had chosen became too difficult, Alfadas had to sidetrack deeply into the woods. Sometimes, when the fjord swung between the mountains in wide bends, he was able to take shortcuts. Whenever possible, he stayed close to the water. He was keeping an eye out for the silvery backs riding the tides—it would not be long before the salmon came. He would sail out with Erek and spend days fishing the fjord. His father-in-law was slowly losing the power of his younger days. Gout had crept into his bones, as it did with everyone who spent their life on the waters. Too many hours of damp and cold had worn him down, but when the salmon started to run, the old man came back to life and his power returned as if by magic. Once, at night by the fire, he had confided to Alfadas that when his time came, he wanted a huge fish to pull him down to the bottom of the fjord. He did not want to perish miserably, coughing blood, on some bitter autumn day or live so long that his old bones grew as frail as moldering wood. "All my life, I have eaten fish. If they get to eat me in the end, it is only fair. Let them lay their roe between my ribs. I will gladly offer their young a safe place to hide," Erek had said back then.

Alfadas liked the old man. One could sit an entire day in a boat with him and not say a word, and yet they would have gotten on famously.

The hours meandered by. The rain did not stop. At dusk, Alfadas climbed down from his saddle. With darkness approaching, it made more sense to look for a place to spend the night, but Honnigsvald was not much farther. Two miles, or three.

Clouds and rain smothered the crimson of evening and hid the moon and stars. Soon it was so dark that the jarl could barely see where he was putting his feet. He stumbled repeatedly on the broad gravel shore. He would not keep the old king waiting. Horsa Starkshield had grown stranger and stranger in the last few years, and if one disappointed him, his reaction was utterly unpredictable.

Finally, Alfadas saw a tiny point of light. It led to the old ferry house, perched with its steep roof like a large boulder high above the shoreline. Beside the house stood a small, dry stable, where Alfadas led his gray. He loosened the girth but did not remove the saddle—they would not be staying long. The straw on the floor of the stable was black and looked as if it had not been changed for many moons. There were no other horses inside. Alfadas rubbed the stallion dry with an old blanket and attached a feedbag full of oats. The large, black eyes of the horse blinked tiredly. The jarl scratched it just above its small, almost circular blaze, where it like to be scratched most of all, and he spoke softly to it, thanking it for carrying him on the long road to Honnigsvald.

When Alfadas stepped out of the stable, he pushed his cloak back from his left shoulder so that his sword was more visible. Beside the ferry house door burned the lamp that had shown him the way. He knocked heavily on the wet wood and stepped inside, to be met by a pall of musty air. The acrid smoke of a turf fire filled the low, long space. A blond fellow with broad shoulders sat hunched over an earthenware mug at a table beside the fire. The ferry house had a brick chimney with iron skewers for cooking, but the vent seemed to be blocked, and the smoke rolled back into the room.

"Where's the ferryman?" Alfadas asked loudly.

The blond raised his head. He had watery blue eyes. His hanging jowls, unkempt moustache, and receding chin made him surly and self-pitying. "No more ferries today."

"Can I hear that from the ferryman himself?"

The man at the table pulled a face and stabbed one thumb over his shoulder. "He's buried behind the house. He'll be sure to listen patiently if you want to complain. It was apoplexy. Hit him in summer while he stood at the tiller, and overboard he went. Sank like King Osaberg in his gold armor. By the time they fished him out again, it was far too late. The elders in Honnigsvald named me and my brothers as the new ferrymen because our father's farm was in debt and we could not hold on to it any longer. For a miserable copper piece in this filthy weather, I won't be taking you over." He pointed to the sleeping niches along the wall. "You can spend the night here. There's still a bit of soup on the fire. I'll take you over tomorrow."

"The king is expecting me," said Alfadas, trying hard not to sound threatening. "Believe me, I would much rather sit by the fire and wait for this rainy night to end."

A fleeting smile crossed the blond man's face. It was now clear to him that he had no other choice than to ferry this stranger across the fjord, but he also appreciated the friendly gesture. He looked Alfadas up and down curiously. "You're the elvenjarl, aren't you? And that . . . that's the famous magical sword."

He was so sick of this story! "I am simply a jarl that the king has ordered to attend him."

The young ferryman grinned broadly. His top teeth were missing. "No, no. You can't fool me. That splendid sword . . . and you came from the north. You must be the elvenjarl! They say the queen of the elves and everyone in her court are paying a visit to Firnstayn. And that they've brought golden tents and amazing animals with them. And the air is filled with sorcery and the smell of roasting meat." He jumped to his feet and went to the two most distant sleeping niches. "Torad, Mag! Come on, on your feet! We're doing one more crossing. The elvenjarl is here and wants to be taken to the king."

Alfadas sighed. The blond man was probably hoping he would pick up a rock on the other side of the fjord and transmute it into gold to pay him. The ferryman's brothers hastily got dressed, staring at Alfadas all the while as if he were a three-legged chicken or some other wondrous beast. Like their brother, they both had scruffy blond hair. They seemed to be somewhat younger, and one had a red brand shaped like a half-moon seared into his cheek. The sign of a thief. When the young man noticed how Alfadas was looking at him, he turned his head defiantly to give him a better view of the scar.

"Mag stole a loaf of bread. We'd had nothing to eat for three full days," said the ferryman unasked. "He was so weak that he could no longer run away fast enough when they went after him."

Alfadas made an effort not to look in Mag's direction again.

The blond laid one arm around Alfadas's shoulders and took him outside. "Kodran's my name." Rain hit them in the face.

Alfadas brought his horse from the stable while the brothers prepared the ferry. It was a large, flat vessel with enough room for two wagons or an entire troop of riders. The jarl felt a little lost as he boarded the spacious boat. It was not fair to make the three brothers do all that work for one man.

With long poles, they propelled the ferry clear of the landing. Torad and Mag took over two long oars while Kodran remained in the stern. Only when they were well out on the water did a few lights on the far shore become visible.

Alfadas pulled the wet cloak closer around his shoulders. He had not been in the ferry house long enough for even a single thread to dry, but long enough to feel the cold even more now.

The journey across the fjord seemed to take an eternity. Alfadas had a bad conscience for having hounded the three brothers out into the night. He groped for his moneybag—the leather felt oily and slippery from the rain. He fumbled at it with his fingertips until he finally managed to open the straps; then he fished out one of the heavy silver pieces from Aniscans. They were lovely coins, with the head of a horse embossed on one side, part of his booty from the previous summer. Asla would certainly not approve if she found out how magnanimous he was with their money, but jealously hoarding his coins was not something the elves had taught him.

The ferryboat bumped against the rope-wound wooden pylons of the landing stage. Mag jumped from the ferry and tied up the heavy boat. Then he hauled on a block and tackle that lowered a drawbridge onto the flat deck of the ferry.

Thick boards nailed crosswise allowed his gray to find a footing as Alfadas led it up the ramp. The stallion was nervous. The wood of the drawbridge was as slippery from all the hours of rain as if someone had smeared it with fish oil, and the gray's hooves thudded heavily as it disembarked.

Kodran reached for the reins and helped Alfadas lead the horse onto the level landing stage. "Will you be returning tomorrow?" the ferryman asked when they were off the drawbridge.

The jarl nodded.

"Then we will spend the night here. We'll sleep in the boatshed."

Alfadas pressed the silver piece into the ferryman's hand. "I don't have enough money to change that," said Kodran grumpily.

"Then let's just say that I've paid in advance for tomorrow's return."

"Even then . . ."

Alfadas raised both hands as if in surrender. "I insulted your brother by staring at him, and I hounded all three of you out of your warm house. Allow me to do something besides cause you trouble. I think that much silver will cover spirits and meat enough to drive the cold out of your bones again. And for a place to sleep that's more comfortable than a boatshed."

Kodran grinned broadly. "I hope you are called to Honnigsvald more often, Elvenjarl."

Alfadas grasped the ferryman's wrist in a warrior's greeting. Kodran stepped back in surprise, but the jarl held his arm tightly. "For me, this is a greeting among men who do their job well. It does not make a difference if it is on the battlefield or at the oars. I'll see you again tomorrow, Kodran." He reached for the reins of the gray and led it up the landing stage toward the city. The horse's hooves made a sound like thunder.

"Who's there?" called a voice from a shack at the end of the stage. The shade of a wooden lamp was pulled back. A ray of golden light cut the darkness.

"Jarl Alfadas Mandredson!"

"You came after all? We'd all given up on you." An old man stepped out of the shack. "I'm the harbor watchman," he announced proudly. He clearly could not care less that probably no one outside Honnigsvald would call a single wooden landing stage a harbor. "I'll take you up to the banquet hall. Watch your step, Jarl. The rain's made a mess of the roads, so don't step in any puddles. Some of them are knee deep." The night watchman went ahead of him through the wooden harbor gate into the weavers' quarter, and from there they made their way up the hill to the banquet hall of the small town. Even from a great distance, the sounds of an orgy of eating and drinking could be heard.

Alfadas insisted on taking his stallion to the stables himself. Only when he knew the horse was well provided for did he let the old man lead him to the banquet hall.

A large fire burned in the center of the hall, and an ox rotated on an iron spit. On simple benches and at tables all around it sat dozens of carousing men. For the king himself, a long wooden platform had been erected, allowing him and a few selected soldiers in his entourage to sit where they could be seen easily from anywhere in the hall. Alfadas had never enjoyed such occasions, where the men drank themselves blind only to wake the next morning in their own vomit. The first victims were already lying under the benches.

Slave girls with iron rings around their necks hurried busily through the spacious hall. The two women turning the ox on its spit had removed all their clothing save a leather loincloth. Their expressions were apathetic, and they ignored the jokes of the drunks.

Alfadas's wet clothes began to steam in the stuffy heat inside. He unclasped the heavy bronze fibula of his cloak and laid the garment over his arm. Then he made his way through the ranks of drinkers toward the king.

A familiar melody penetrated the din, and a voice sang:

"There comes the jarl of Firnenstayn
with his elven blade so fine.
The lion heart of many a fray
Sent by the gods to win the day."

It grew quieter in the hall. Alfadas hated entrances like this, although he knew that the king's skald, Veleif, meant no ill will with his verses.

Horsa Starkshield rose from his seat. He was a tall, old man, but despite his gray hair, he still looked every inch a warrior. As a young man, he had lost one eye to an arrow, and he wore a black bandage over the socket; with his long nose and narrow face, he had the grim look of a bird of prey. Even there in the banquet hall, Horsa wore a short mail shirt. Broad gold bracelets encircled his arms. "My heart opens with joy to see you, Jarl Alfadas Mandredson. Even when you come in looking like a puppy someone's just tried to drown." The king's voice was loud enough to hear above the noise of any battle, and everyone there in the hall could hear his words.

The king raised his heavy mead horn, encrusted with gold, and held it out to Alfadas. "Come and drink, boy. This'll drive out the chill, and when you've drunk enough of it, you can hear the ghosts of your ancestors whispering."

In all his years among the humans, Alfadas had never gotten used to this rough camaraderie. Every time someone welcomed him like this, he was lost for words and the blood rose in his cheeks as if he were a callow youth. Alfadas climbed up to the wooden platform. Unable to offer a quick-witted quip in reply, he simply took the mead horn and drank, letting a good quantity of the sweet liquid pour down his beard. He knew he needed to keep a clear head that night.

He handed the horn back to the king, who smiled. "You're coming on, boy. You're coming on! The first time you sat at my table, you lapped like a kitten at a bowl of milk." He pushed a slave girl aside roughly, just then leaning to refill his horn. "Make room! Make room at my table. The boy should sit at my right hand. I want to hear about the elves that have set up court in Firnstayn."

The other guests of honor squeezed closer together and another chair was brought up for Alfadas. Most of the men nodded affably at him, but there were some who had already drunk too much to hide their jealousy and hate. They envied the unqualified trust of the king that Alfadas, still so young, enjoyed, and they envied the place he took at the king's table, a place they themselves had perhaps hoped to occupy. But most of them liked him, because the victories he had won had brought gold and slaves to the Fjordlands and had made all of them richer.

Alfadas sat at the king's right hand, as ordained. "It is not as has been reported to you, Horsa. Emerelle has not come with her royal entourage. She—"

"My messenger saw a manhorse," Horsa interrupted him. "He also heard that the queen was wounded in a battle. Is it true that elven women fight in their wars as well?"

All conversation at the king's table fell silent. Throughout the large hall, too, all conversation had ceased, everyone trying to catch as much of what Alfadas said as possible. Presumably everyone there had already heard that the elves had come to Firnstayn.

The jarl did not want to lie to the king, but at the same time tried to reveal as little as possible about the Albenkin. The last thing he needed was a bigger audience camped around his house in Firnstayn.

"Queen Emerelle, it is true, is injured. A sly enemy attacked her while the elves were celebrating an important event. They were taken completely by surprise and overrun. Emerelle had to flee. No doubt she will soon assemble an army to avenge the cowardly attack." Alfadas had deliberately downplayed what had happened at Vahan Calyd and clothed the story in simple words. He knew that everyone there had heard stories of plundering raids and blood vengeance before. Like this, he could save himself long explanations.

"Did you hear that, my friends?" Horsa cried. "That brave woman has been a victim of betrayal, and she has turned to us." The king half rose, supporting himself with his fists on the tabletop. A breathless silence reigned in the hall. "Ever since Jarl Mandred asked the elves to help him defeat the terrible manboar, we have stood in debt to the folk who live beyond the magical gates. They sent us their best warriors to help where human courage and human swords failed." He paused for a moment and let his gaze sweep across the men gathered in front of him. Suddenly, he lifted one hand to his ear. He frowned, and it seemed he was listening to a soft, distant sound.

"Do you hear that?" Horsa said.

It was so quiet in the hall that one could hear the crackle of the burning wood in the long fire pit. No one in the hall dared even breathe. Very softly, Alfadas heard the sound of the rain spattering against the shingles on the roof of the banquet hall.

"Norgrimm in his Golden Hall has set the war horn to his lips. I hear it calling."

"I can hear it, too!" cried one of the men below. "Very clearly!"

Alfadas knew the man. It was Ragni, one of the king's bodyguards. Now others also shouted that they could hear the god's war horn. Fools, the lot of them . . . but then Alfadas started. There was something. It came from the river. Softly, distorted by the wind. A horn. Its blasts deep and solemn. A shudder ran through Alfadas. There were no gods! That was impossible!

Horsa spread his arms wide toward the ceiling. "We hear you, Norgrimm! We hear your call!"

"We hear your call!" repeated a hundred voices. No man still sat. All had reached for their swords and axes and swung them now on outstretched arms above their heads.

The guests of honor around Horsa were all on their feet, too. Alfadas was among the last to stand. He could not believe what was going on around him.

"When the elves came to us in our hour of need, I was still a young man, my beard as soft as a cat's fur. But a Fjordlander forgets no debt!" Horsa raised his head, and he seemed to gaze out beyond the soot-black beams of the ceiling and into the starry sky. "I have heard you, Norgrimm. And from this hour onward, the men of the Fjordlands stand at the elves' side!" Horsa himself now drew his sword and thrust it high in the air. "Norgrimm, we hear you!" the old king cried with all his might. "And we follow your call, to honor you, to bring glory on ourselves!"

Horsa abruptly turned and looked at Alfadas. "Jarl of Firnstayn. It is you who has made our kingdom strong. When I call, you come to be my sword. I hereby relieve you of your jarl's title. From this hour forth, you are once again my duke, commander of my army, and first among my soldiers. Lead my men to Albenmark and do not rest until the last enemy has been defeated. And when—and only when—the swords have returned peace, the hour will have come in which you may again be called jarl. Then we will gather here again and celebrate your victory in the majesty of this hall." The king stepped forward and kissed Alfadas on the forehead, sealing his reappointment to duke.

Alfadas stood as if paralyzed. This was madness! But he could not interrupt the king, not there in front of all his guests. He waited until Horsa picked up his mead horn and drank. Then he leaned close to his king and whispered to him, "My king, we cannot fight Emerelle's enemies. They are trolls, each as strong as a cave bear. And Emerelle would never ask us for something that can only end in blood and death."

"Have you ever seen a troll?" the king asked.

"No," Alfadas admitted.

"Then take it from an old king that soldiers are much the same as hunters. With every passing year, the defeated enemies grow stronger in your mind. Besides, I can assure you that my hunters have brought down cave bears before today." He turned his attention back to the crowd in the hall, who were looking to him as if spellbound. "Are we warriors?" he called to them. "Or gutless milksops?"

"We are warriors!" they bellowed back, and beat their fists against their chests.

"And what does a warrior do when a woman come and asks him for help? Does he fight, or does he think up a clever excuse not to?"

"He fights! We'll fight!"

A tear brimmed in Horsa's remaining eye. "The heart of the land speaks from your throats. A courageous heart, insatiable and wild. I am proud to be your king. I am proud to stand here! This very evening, messengers will ride out in all directions, out to the most remote farms, and call all my soldiers to arms. I will review my army in four weeks, here on the shore by Honnigsvald. And Alfadas, my duke, will select the thousand best among my warriors, who will pass through the magical gateway to fight with the elves and take back the queen's throne." Horsa slung one arm around Alfadas's shoulders and pulled his newly appointed duke to his side. "To our duke!"

The men in the hall roared again and raised their swords and mead horns in salute to Alfadas. The thrill of battle was in their eyes. Damned fools! They could not begin to imagine what it meant to fight trolls. Even the elves feared those monsters.

"Tomorrow, Duke Alfadas will take me to the elven queen," said the king. "I will tell her not to fear, that the thousand strongest axes of the Fjordlands will stand with her. She will have everything from me that she needs to win her war."

Alfadas reached for his mead horn and drank. He was surrounded by madmen, all reason—all common sense—gone. But perhaps tomorrow he could change Horsa's mind when he explained to him what he was getting himself into.

The king resumed his seat while Veleif launched into a militaristic tune. "Many of my warriors are discontented," said Horsa quietly. "You win too easily, Duke. This last summer, all our neighbors chose to pay tribute instead of fighting us. The men have to spill a little blood occasionally, or there will be unrest in the kingdom. The call of their king is just what they need."

Alfadas was about to counter, but when he looked into the king's good eye, he understood that the old man was not drunk in the slightest. To go to war as allies to the elves was no folly that had sprung simply from the mood in that hall. The king had clearly been searching for an occasion to go to war. And he would certainly not be talked out of what he had just announced. He was already starting to twist reality to suit his own ends. Emerelle had not asked him for any help! How could she, when she had been unconscious for days? But everybody in the Fjordlands would believe Horsa's words. They *wanted* to believe, he thought despondently. It was the only way for them to be part of a story like those told by the skalds. Besides, Norgrimm himself had sounded his war horn and called them to arms. It had not occurred to anyone there in the hall to go looking for a man with a horn by the river, a man from the king's own court. Horsa, the old fox, had planned it all from the start. That's why it was so important for his "elvenjarl" to appear tonight. Alfadas sighed resignedly and held his horn up to be refilled. Would none of this have happened if he had not driven the ferrymen out in the rain to take him over the fjord?

Such thinking would get him nowhere! Tomorrow he would have to make his king aware of the enemy he was sending his warriors to fight. If the elves were to open the gates of Albenmark to them, then probably no man who passed through would ever return to the Fjordlands . . . himself included. Because twist and turn it as he may, Alfadas had to go with them. A duke who refused his king's command . . . Horsa would never put up with that. It reeked of betrayal. Alfadas knew that staying behind would not mean his survival. Horsa would probably have Ulric killed as well, to prevent him from carrying on a blood feud against the crown when he became a man. Most likely his entire family would be extinguished.

Horsa laughed at one of the skald's verses and pounded the table with his heavy fist. "Good man, that Veleif! His tongue's as sharp as a war axe!" He pinched Alfadas's cheek. "It's good to have you at my side again, lad. I feel twenty years younger when I plan a campaign with you." He pushed across the chunk of roast meat that lay on a board in front of him. "Eat something, boy. You look like a stripling who's had his first mouthful of liquor."

Alfadas tore off a hunk of the meat and began to chew, so as not to have to talk. The world had gone mad! Horsa liked him like his own son. Yet if he refused this insane command, that same king would have him killed. That was how things were among the humans of the Fjordlands. And Asla? Would she understand that he had no choice?

NOT AN EVERYDAY OFFER

Alfadas looked up to the sky. The sun stood as a milky, pale disk behind gray clouds—not much longer and it would be midday. Horsa had still not appeared, although most of his court had been up for hours, and no one dared wake the king after a night of drinking. More than a dozen messengers had already ridden off in all directions to spread the king's harebrained idea throughout his kingdom. With every hour that passed, it would be more difficult to call a halt to the impending disaster. Alfadas had spent the entire morning racking his brains about how he could get the king to retract his order without losing face.

The jarl paced back and forth in front of the stables. It was enough to drive a man insane! If they did not leave soon, there was no way they would reach Firnstayn that day.

A burly man with ice-gray hair stepped into the courtyard. He wore a colorfully embroidered blue smock. The stranger looked at Alfadas as if he were just the person he had been looking for; at the same time, Alfadas was certain he had never seen the man before.

"Alfadas Mandredson?" His voice sounded apologetic.

"Yes."

The man's green eyes lit up. "Excuse me, I know you only from stories."

"Uh-huh. And I don't look at all like the blond giant with the magic sword that the skalds like to turn me into." Alfadas smiled to take the edge off his words. "What can I do for you?"

"My name is Sigvald." The stranger reached to shake hands. He had a strong grip, and his hands were covered in fine white scars. Sigvald smelled of oil and wood. "I would like to suggest a bit of business to you, Jarl. You have a large apple orchard next to your village. Every winter, hunters come to Honnigsvald from Firnstayn and even deeper in the mountains to sell their meat and hides, am I right?"

"What business are you talking about? Are you suggesting you buy my apple harvest? I'm afraid you're too late for that." The jarl was not in the mood to haggle with this unknown merchant.

"All I would like is to make your life easier, Jarl. I would like to rob you of many, many hours of hard labor." Sigvald winked mischievously. "Your orchards, I warrant, grow on the flanks of the mountains, where they can drink their fill of sunshine and are protected from the bitter northern winds. They say that you planted two new sections this very spring."

Alfadas looked at the man with renewed interest. Sigvald had obviously prepared well for this conversation. "So you are planning to rob me?"

The merchant shook his head. "No, no, Jarl. Forgive me, that was an unfortunate joke. I want to spare you many hours of unnecessary work. No doubt you and your people carry the apples in baskets back to your village, which I imagine must be backbreaking toil. And now that you have planted new orchards, it is quite possible that Firnstayn will soon have more apples than the village can use. One could sell those apples here in Honnigsvald for good money."

"What do you want to sell me? Apple baskets?"

Sigvald lifted his hands defensively. "I'm sure you already have more than enough of those. No, I have in mind something that everyone in your village will find useful. A heavy, horse-drawn wagon."

Alfadas looked at the man in disbelief. This had to be a joke! But Sigvald seemed completely serious.

"What good would a wagon do me? Firnstayn is hard to reach even for a rider on horseback. How am I supposed to haul a wagon through the forests?"

Sigvald had clearly reckoned with this objection. "I will give you a road suitable for a wagon. Admittedly, it will only be passable for four or five months of the year, but for that I will assume all of the costs of maintaining it."

Though he looked normal at first sight, the man was as mad as a rabid dog!

"So you can work miracles," said Alfadas, trying not to sound too contemptuous.

"To call me a miracle worker is flattering, indeed. If you give me a mere half an hour of your time, I will show you all you need to know about this road to Firnstayn. Come with me to my workshop. You can also see my beautiful wagons there for yourself. If you like, I can have one hitched up, and we can go for a short ride."

Alfadas looked up at the sky. The day might as well be over—they would never make it to Firnstayn before nightfall now. And there was still no sign of the king. Which meant he could certainly give this talkative lunatic half an hour of his time. At least the man was more entertaining than Horsa's boozing friends.

"All right, Sigvald. Show me these wonder wagons of yours that you're able to sell complete with street."

"You won't regret it!" the salesman assured him.

Alfadas followed the sturdy man from the banquet hall down into the town proper. Most of the buildings of Honnigsvald were simple wooden huts. Wind and weather had bleached the wood, making them look gray and unprepossessing. Frequently, they were decorated with crossed gable beams that ended in carved horse heads or showed dragons. Planks had been laid on the ground in front of the facades of the houses, allowing one to at least walk through the town with halfway dry feet. Along the main road, which they followed down to the harbor, there was even a small stream, its banks reinforced with wooden boards. The residents there emptied waste of every kind into the water, and although most of it was quickly washed away, an odor of feces and putrefaction hung over the street.

A number of houses along the street had been built with door-sized folding shutters along their fronts, which were open even in that hazy weather, and passersby could look into the handicraft workshops beyond. At one shop, dozens of knife handles made of reindeer antler and whalebone were on show in a frame. A furrier displayed her wonderful array of silver fox furs. Alfadas slowed his step. Asla would certainly love one of those. It had been a very long time since they had both been to Honnigsvald together, and then he had been too poor to give her what she liked. Another merchant offered practically every kind of bead imaginable. White beads with colored patterns, supposedly all the way from far Kandastan, and silver and rose-shimmering beads fashioned from shells, amber beads that shone like petrified sunlight, beads of glass from Iskendria, and bone beads engraved with magical symbols from the impenetrable forests of Drusna.

Alfadas took his time. He stopped to watch a copper worker at his trade and a tooth puller carrying out what looked like a massacre while his victim, tied onto a heavy wooden chair, grinned drunkenly up at him.

Finally, they reached the boatsheds at the shore of the fjord. Sigvald led him along to a large building, the walls of which were covered in hand-sized scars where the paint had peeled away.

"Be prepared to enter the home of a miracle worker," the wainwright announced proudly, and led him around the outside of the building to a large open door, where smoke and steam welcomed them. The place smelled of red-hot iron, fresh hemp, and bone glue. Rhythmic hammering beat the time for an obscene song that the men inside were singing.

"A visitor, men! Here he is, the king's hero, Alfadas the elvenjarl!" The hammering and raucous singing ceased.

Alfadas stepped in through the billowing clouds. Inside stood eight vehicles: sledges, hay carts, small and large. Work was currently under way on half of them. In the center of the hall, steam rose from a large, shallow basin. Two burly figures were hard at work bending planks over the steam, planks that were probably destined for a fragile-looking traveling sleigh.

Sigvald led Alfadas to a high, heavy wagon. Four spoked wheels as tall as a man and with thick oak rims bore the weight of the mighty beast. It was almost twice as big as his father-in-law's fishing boat.

The driver's seat was padded and upholstered in oiled brown leather. Right and left of the seat were two brake levers, while over the cargo area stretched a tarpaulin of waxed linen.

"See the iron fittings on the wheels and the solid axles? My wagons can handle even harsh terrain, never fear. They're solid. Most of it is made of well-seasoned oak." He knocked the low side walls of the tray. "Of course, you can fold down the sides and the back. All of the iron parts are made here in my workshop, and the harness, too. There's nothing on a Sigvald wagon that is not produced in this very establishment. I stake my name on every one of these masterpieces."

"And what about the roads that you throw in with your wagons?" Alfadas asked. "Who will build those?" From the corner of his eye, he saw the craftsmen around him grinning. They obviously knew what was coming.

"If you would please follow me." Sigvald led him to the back wall of the building, where two long, iron-reinforced runners were hanging. "All you need are a few strong arms and about half an hour of your day. You can take the wheels off the wagon and set it on these runners. You turn it into a giant sled. As you well know, the fjord is frozen solid at least four moons of every year. There you have your road. And you get the runners for free if you buy the wagon."

Alfadas had to laugh out loud. "You know your business, Sigvald." He thought about what a difference a vehicle like that could make to the village.

Then, with a smile, he imagined going out for a sleigh ride with Asla and the children in winter. Kadlin would be whooping for joy. He could even let Ulric take over the reins for a little while.

Alfadas stepped over to a sled with two benches. It had a beautifully carved swan's head and neck, and its sides were shaped like wings. If he went home with something like that, everyone in the village would laugh at him.

"A smart man tries always to unite comfort and utility, am I right?" the wagon maker said.

"A miracle worker and a mind reader!"

"No, Jarl. I am an upstanding businessman, no more. And I would prefer you to walk out of my shed here without buying a thing than to buy it and regret it later on. This sled here is built for women and children. A man like yourself should not go out in such a vehicle." He pointed to the heavy wagon. "Buy that one, however, and everyone will see its worth. And if you go out with it just for fun, you won't make a fool of yourself."

"And no doubt that thing costs three or four times what the swan sled does."

"Oh, there are many ways to come to an agreement." Sigvald smoothed his blue smock. "They say you have great influence with the king. And if, perchance, he were in need of a wainwright—"

"Stop! I want no part of any such business! Besides, I have neither horses nor oxen to pull a wagon like that."

Sigvald lifted his hands placatingly. "By the gods, Jarl, what do you take me for? I am an honest man, and I know that you are, too. I would not dream of using dishonest means to worm my way into any advantage. And as for draft animals, I happen to have four wonderful cart horses on hand. All reds, a team fit for a king. Hardy, untiring beasts they are, and their coats are warm enough to survive even the hardest winter."

Alfadas thought about how the cart could help them with the apple harvest. And when the wagon was actually in Firnstayn, other uses would soon present themselves. The draft horses could be used to haul tree trunks from the forest down to the village. In the past, that had always been backbreaking work because the few ponies they had in the village, although reasonable beasts for riding, were entirely unsuited to that kind of labor. His own gray, a horse from Emerelle's own stables, was far too valuable to use for hauling logs. It had already covered four mares, and Alfadas dreamed of building up a stable of his own, over time, unparalleled anywhere in the world.

"All right, Jarl. I'll make you an honest deal. I will show you no favors and expect none in return. Give me the weight of four of a draft horse's shoes in gold and send me a cartload of apples each of the next three years, and the horses and wagon are yours. I won't be making any profit on the deal." He smiled abashedly. "I would, however, ask you to allow me to mention to future customers that you bought one of my vehicles."

Alfadas shook his head. The crafty old crook! "That would make you the duke's wainwright."

Sigvald spread his arms wide. "It's the world we live in, Alfadas. *Who* buys from me is as crucial to my business as the quality of my handiwork. I am sure that you will never regret having purchased this magnificent wagon."

"And how do you plan on delivering it to me in Firnstayn? It will still be weeks before the fjord freezes."

"Let that be my concern, Duke. I promise you, in four days at the most, the wagon will be in your village. With the horses, harness, runners . . . basically, everything we have to offer."

Alfadas stepped over to the heavy wagon and stroked its diligently smoothed timbers. He had never before dreamed of owning such a thing, but now it was firing his imagination, and he pictured himself racing with it across the ice! It would give him a lot of pleasure in the future . . . as long as he managed to talk the king out of his insane plan. "Send me a coachman, too, to teach my wife and me how to drive it."

"Of course, Duke. You'll find it an easy wagon to manage—the horses are well trained."

"Were you in the banquet hall last night, Sigvald?"

The wainwright nodded. "Yes."

"Then you heard that the king is planning to go to war. If this wagon is not in Firnstayn before I have to depart for Albenmark, then our deal is void."

Sigvald held out his hand. "Shake my hand, Duke! So shall it be."

And with a handshake, the deal was done. Alfadas felt a little queasy. Never before had he bought anything so expensive. It was also clear to him that he did not really need the wagon at all. After the first drive, he knew that Asla would also be thrilled, but until then he had a few hard days ahead of him. Perhaps, for the time being, he should not say a word to her about the purchase at all?

Alfadas thought of the bead shop on the road back to the banquet hall. He should get something for her there; it would put her in a more conciliatory mood.

He left the wagon maker's workshop behind him, thinking about the wagon, but also brooding on how he could talk the king out of what he was planning. Only when he was standing in front of the bead shop did it occur to him that he had just bought four horses that he had not even seen! He cursed himself for a fool.

Alfadas took his time as he made his way slowly through the town. He bought a few smaller items, delaying his return to the king's halls. Finally, he went to the stables to see to his gray, but a surprise was waiting for him there.

King Horsa stood in the doorway, massaging his forehead.

"Damned mead! I've sworn to keep away from the stuff so many times, too. My head feels like an anvil with a giant pounding on it." Horsa belched. "Don't gape like that! Pick up your feet! I told you what's to be done!"

The courtiers rushed to get out of the king's sight. Only Alfadas stayed. "You should think again, Horsa. Albenmark is no place for humans."

"What's the matter with you?" the king grumbled. "Afraid you'll no longer be the only man in the Fjordlands who's been among the Albenfolk? My decision is made! And don't start with the stories about cave bears and trolls. A brave warrior can beat any opponent."

"You cannot imagine—"

"Oh, I can, Duke. I can imagine very well indeed. Those who return will come back as warriors that nothing and no one in this world can stand up to. With those men under me, I will occupy the entire north. And because they will be heroes, the elves will give them enchanted weapons. And because we stood by the elves in their hour of greatest need, they will be in our debt forever. I will discuss all of that with Emerelle."

"My king, I—"

"No!" Horsa wiped his forehead nervously. "All this talk is making my head explode. Come down to the harbor. They're already loading the boat. I fear I am not in a fit state to sit a saddle. We will be taking the ferry."

"Which ferry?"

But Horsa only grunted something unintelligible and ambled away. Then he turned back one more time. "Bring that nag of yours with you. We're in a hurry."

So that's it, thought Alfadas angrily. The mask was off. Horsa wanted to found an empire, and he was determined to win the elves as his ally. All the mead had finally fogged his brain for good!

Alfadas saddled his horse. Again, he took his time. He could not stop the old man, and Horsa was beloved among the soldiers. He had to give the king more time to destroy himself. He would not sit back and watch Horsa become a tyrant. And because the aging ruler knew that all too well, he—Alfadas— had to go. But if a handful of men survived the terrors awaiting them in Albenmark, Alfadas thought, then he would have a troop at his command that could topple the king. And maybe the assistance offered by the elves would look very different from what Horsa was expecting.

With reins loose, Alfadas rode slowly down to the harbor. It had begun to rain again. The mountains on the far side of the fjord had disappeared behind banks of cloud, and the open waters of the fjord now looked as wide as the sea. If Horsa were to fall overboard . . . the heavy mail shirt he always wore would drag him down to share King Osaberg's grave.

There was turmoil at the ferry mooring. By the time Alfadas arrived, the king seemed to have just arrived himself. For a moment, Alfadas had to smile. Sigvald had wasted no time: the large wagon with its linen cover and four heavy red horses were already on board, the wagon tied securely in place. So that was how they were going to get it to Firnstayn. Who had the wainwright had to bribe to borrow the only ferry from Honnigsvald for a few days?

"It was never my intention to stand in the way of the king, of course," the jarl heard the voice of his trading partner from earlier in the day. Sigvald was surrounded by three soldiers, one of whom had placed a hand threateningly on his shoulder.

"What's going on here?" Alfadas called, urging his gray forward through the crowd.

"This bastard is stealing the king's ferry!" one of Horsa's bodyguards shouted. "They ought to tie him to a millstone and toss him into the fjord."

"This *bastard*, as you call him, is acting on my orders. If you accuse him, then you are accusing me of collusion in the theft of this boat that allegedly belongs to the king." Alfadas swung out of the saddle. He swept his cloak back from his left shoulder to show his sword. "Do you really think you want to call me a thief? You would force me to defend my honor with your blood. But it was probably just a misunderstanding. We both know, after all, that the king does not own the ferry of the city of Honnigsvald, which means that one cannot steal it from him."

The bodyguard took a step back. "You don't scare me, Elvenjarl," he said defiantly. He drew the heavy axe from his belt. He held on to it so tightly that his knuckles were white. "I won't let you call me a liar."

A quick glance and Alfadas knew that neither of the other two body-guards would interfere. One of them was Ragni, the king's man who had heard the horn the other night and who had accompanied Alfadas on two of his annual campaigns—he had seen Alfadas fight.

"Enough!" Horsa stepped through the crowd of spectators. "Ulf! Put your axe away and get on board. I appreciate your willingness to fight for your king. You're a good man. But you've chosen the wrong opponent here. I still need my duke." Then he went on quietly to Alfadas. "What's all this nonsense about the wagon? Tell them to unload it."

"It's a present for my wife."

Horsa peered at him intently; then he suddenly burst out in raucous laughter and began to cough. "You're giving your wife a wagon?" he blurted. "You're madder than I gave you credit for, my elvenjarl. Women love trinkets. Jewels and pretty cloth. Some like a good copper kettle or an iron pan. But I've never heard of a woman who would thank you for a hay cart and a four-horse team. Come, let them clear the ferry. Our departure's been delayed long enough. We won't all fit on the boat."

"Have you considered the practical side of this particular freight?" asked Alfadas calmly. "Beneath that tarpaulin, you can sit out of the rain for the entire journey, my king." The jarl glanced up at the cloud-covered sky. "The way things look, we will get our share of rain, and we certainly won't make it all the way to Firnstayn tonight, and there isn't a single dry place to spend the night between here and there. Aren't you a little beyond the age when one will happily sleep in the mud, Horsa?" To avoid offending the king, Alfadas spoke so quietly that those standing around could not overhear him. "And why travel with a large entourage anyway? You won't need bodyguards on the fjord.

A few servants, perhaps, and an adviser or two. You don't even need horses. From the shore to my house is hardly three hundred paces. There's enough room on the ferry if you can do without some of your followers for a few days."

Horsa stroked his beard thoughtfully. "I'll need my cupbearer and Dalla." He pointed to a pretty young woman standing some way away from the men and looking out over the fjord. "You know what the worst ailment of getting old is, Duke?" He scratched at his crotch. "Everything gets stiff, except this— but Dalla is an excellent healer. And no doubt, she will also serve the elven queen well."

Alfadas looked at the red-haired girl again. He doubted whether Emerelle needed the assistance of a healer who specialized in stiff body parts. But he decided against sharing his opinion with the king.

"Let's get on board the damned ferry," Horsa ordered. "If I stand around in this cold drizzle any longer, I won't even be able to lift a mead horn by myself tonight. Dalla, take your bags and get under the tarpaulin on that wagon. I'll see to you soon. Bring a few hides to the ferry. At my age, you don't sit on cold planks with a naked ass." The king chose three soldiers to help the ferrymen with the rowing, and then the boat slid out onto the waters clear of the shore. Horsa joined the healer beneath the tarpaulin even before they were out of sight of Honnigsvald.

Alfadas thought again about how no one would be surprised if a drunk old man who climbed out of his bed at night to relieve himself fell overboard. The gunwales of the ferry were not even knee-high. And the loose rope that served as a handrail would hardly save the old man if he lost his balance . . .

IN THE STILL OF THE NIGHT

A lfadas sat up, instantly awake. Something on board the ferry had changed. The jarl lay wrapped in a blanket between the high wheels of the wagon. He listened to the noises of the night. The ferryboat had dropped anchor in a small bay. With the onset of dusk, the three brothers had refused to row on. Horsa had sworn at them and threatened to have them drowned, but finally even he had had to accept the dictates of reason. The ferrymen did not know this part of the fjord. They knew nothing about the currents or about any hidden reefs. Sailing on blindly would have been the height of stupidity.

Veleif had done his best to dispel the irritable mood on board with his songs. The king's followers had been reduced to the skald, Dalla the healer, and Horsa's three bodyguards. After a short supper, they had bedded down for the night . . . at least, as well as they could. Alfadas and the others had sought shelter from the drizzling rain between the wheels of the wagon, while over them on the wagon bed Horsa had his pretty healer provide him with one of her special treatments for stiffness. The snorts and groans of the old king had been their lullaby, and Alfadas had managed to sleep only when the din overhead transformed into a throaty snore. The sounds of lovemaking directly above him had aroused him, which in turn made him angry because he despised the old lecher's behavior.

Alfadas pushed those thoughts aside and tried to concentrate on the night sounds. What had changed? The rain had stopped long before. Little waves rippled around the ferryboat. The hawsers holding the anchors grated against the sides of the boat. Alfadas listened to the breathing of the men beside him. Then he heard the timbers of the wagon creak. The king! The snoring had stopped. Horsa was rising. Now the tarpaulin was thrown back. For an old man, he could move surprisingly quietly. Alfadas could make Horsa out at all. There had been a time when he had openly admired the old man, but now he had to get him to see the folly of his plan! Cautiously, he pushed back his blanket. His hands grasped the wheel beside his head, and he pulled himself out from beneath the wagon. The other men continued to breathe slowly and regularly. Everyone else slept.

Horsa had moved forward to the bow. He was looking eastward. He wore a heavy fur thrown across his shoulders that made his form look more solid, but the thin legs beneath stood in grotesque contrast.

The deck was still wet from the rain. A chill ate into Alfadas's naked feet. This was the opportunity he had thought of when they left Honnigsvald. Except that Horsa was not wearing any mail. Could he swim? Even if he could not, he would stay above water long enough to wake everyone with his shouting.

"You've never been wounded in battle, have you, Alfadas?" asked Horsa quietly.

The jarl was surprised that the old man had heard him. He stepped to the king's side.

"You don't know how it is to lie among the wounded," Horsa continued. "It is never as wonderfully silent as it is here, now. They groan. Some cry or pray to the gods or lie there and curse their fate. They fight through the night because they are afraid of the darkness. They wait for dawn to come before they die. Strange, don't you think?"

"Yes. Strange," Alfadas replied. Did Horsa suspect something?

"I've been injured in battle seventeen times, eight times severely enough that I lay among them. The healer wanted to move me away because I was the king, but I felt more alive when I was surrounded by men who were worse off than me. I imagined that, among them, death would overlook me. It's the same when I lie there with a young woman in my arms. Then it is like things used to be . . . for a while. Every night, I have to get up once or twice to pass water. The only time I sleep through the night is when I have drunk very much. And I wake in a wet bed." He laughed bitterly. "Even you will lose this battle, Alfadas. Age cannot be defeated. Unless you die young."

So that's what this is about, Alfadas thought. "Is that why you are sending me to Albenmark? To save me from old age?"

The king did not answer. He stared out over the water in silence. From somewhere out in the darkness came the sound of a splash. A jumping fish?

"If I did not have Veleif in my court, there would already be songs in circulation about Horsa the bed wetter," the king abruptly said. "My skald appreciates hot food every day and a good coat in winter. And his songs are better than those of the other skalds. He is a good man to listen to . . . it is important to keep hold of such things. I guess I should be glad about your foolishness with that wagon, Alfadas. It is better if only a few have seen the elves. And I have listened to you, Duke. Every word. I will visit the queen alone so that no one will be witness to our conversation. No one but you. I need an interpreter, after all."

"She won't be able . . ."

"I know. I said, I listened. She is bedridden and insensible. But Veleif will sing of how her beauty is so blinding that the mere sight of her drives men mad and that this is the reason she has hidden herself away inside your house since she arrived. That is a much better story than the reality. One expects even an elven queen on the run to be unapproachable and intimidating. You will be my witness to how she asked us for help."

"And if I don't lie?"

"Then I have a skald who will tell my story. By the time we are back in Honnigsvald, he will have composed a few pretty verses about Horsa, Alfadas, and the elven queen. I am certain that they will be most moving."

The jarl stepped closer to Horsa's side. He laid one arm across his shoulders. Alfadas wondered if he was strong enough to strangle Horsa. The king would have to be dead already when he entered the water. He must have no chance to scream!

"I wish I had a son like you, Alfadas. By the gods, I've spread my seed far and wide, and Luth alone knows how many women I've humped! And yet I have only one son. You know Egil, of course. He is not the son that one, as a father, would wish to have. Last summer, he stabbed a girl to death because she did not want to let him have his way with her. He talks big and considers himself a gifted swordsman, but it is his so-called friends who constantly let him win. He is a piece of shit. And still, he is my son. You know, of course, how it is to have a son, Alfadas. Whatever he does, you as his father keep one hand over him protectively."

A mournful cry sounded across the water. In the east, a thin gray-silver line marked the outline of the mountains.

"A kingfisher greeting the dawn." Horsa rubbed his hands on his arms. "Not something I will hear many more times."

Beneath the wagon, someone stretched. Alfadas saw Mag, the ferryman with the brand on his cheek, sit up. The moment had passed! "I will swear my allegiance to your son," Alfadas said.

"Of course you will. And you will mean it. But you are a good man. It is only a matter of time before you rise against him. We both know it. And you are not the only good man in the Fjordlands. I will indeed send my best men to the elves . . . every man who I believe would make a better king than Egil."

"That makes no sense, Horsa. What will happen when our neighbors discover our weakness and attack?"

The king sniffed contemptuously. "Our neighbors . . . countries ruled by women. You have put all of them in their place. Your victories, Alfadas, have bought time for Egil. And who knows, maybe he will grow into his kingdom if he only has a few years to do so."

"And if I return with the warriors?" Alfadas asked, more in defiance than because he actually believed it.

"I have thought about your comparison to the cave bears, Duke. It is certainly possible for men to kill a single one of those beasts. But if dozens were to attack, under the command of a half-competent leader and were armed to boot . . . how can humans possibly withstand such a force, even with the best duke in the world leading them? The trolls were able to beat the elves. How can you possibly succeed?"

Again, the call of the kingfisher sounded over the water, a plaintive rise and fall. More sounds came from the wagon as the men woke, one after another. Mag was on his feet and checking the hawsers. The first red glimmer of morning shone beyond the distant peaks, their snow-covered summits mirrored in the crystal waters of the fjord.

"I fear you have missed your chance, Alfadas," said Horsa suddenly.

"What do you mean?"

The king turned to face him. There was sadness in his eye. "We both know what I mean. I tried to make it easy for you. It would not have been a bad end for me. To disappear, just like that . . . Veleif would surely have turned it into a good saga. One can be too honorable, Alfadas."

THE SAGA OF HORSA STARKSHIELD

So beautiful was the visage of Emelda, queen of all the elves, that she hid her face away from human eyes, for every man who looked upon her fell instantly and eternally in love. And so she commanded that a tent be erected on a boat in the middle of the fjord, and only Horsa should attend her, as he was the sturdiest and strongest willed of all men. And the queen, who ruled over treasures beyond counting and the powers of magic, kneeled before Horsa and bade him send his most courageous soldiers to help them, and Alfadas as well, his duke.

Horsa lifted her up, for to see her kneel like that pained his heart. And her breath like the breath of flowers brushed his face. But when Emelda sensed the strength of the king's arms and read the virtue in his own face, she was seized by a deep affection for Horsa.

And thus they stayed a day and a night in the tent on the fjord, and not a sound was heard from either. Her armed warriors grew restless, for their queen had never spent so long with one man. When a second night passed and the call of the kingfisher carried across the waters, they determined to go out from their encampment to their queen. But Emelda emerged from her tent before them, hurrying on the fog across the waters as if the vapors beneath her feet were solid ground. And within a heartbeat, she and all who had come with her were gone.

When Alfadas rowed out to the tent to see that his monarch was not harmed, he found Horsa in a deep sleep. His hair had turned as white as snow, his skin was withered, and his face was deeply furrowed. He had paid the price for his encounter with an immortal. His power was depleted, bound in an alliance with the elves, now and forever more.

Excerpted from the Saga of Horsa Starkshield,

by Veleif Silberhand, Song 72

THE SKYHALL

Ollowain looked down from the stone circle at the small village that had been his safe harbor for the last week. He had a bad conscience about leaving Emerelle behind, but he could not risk taking her back to Albenmark before he knew what was going on.

He grasped Alfadas's hand in a warrior grip. "In thirty days, I'll return. Then we can bring the king's army to Albenmark." Ollowain searched the face of his foster son for an answer to all the questions that stood between them since the king's visit. Alfadas had to know what it meant to take an army of humans to Albenmark. Something had happened between the jarl and the king. It made no difference how warm and sincere Alfadas was, Ollowain could clearly feel the silent sadness that had engulfed the human.

"What about Silwyna?" Alfadas asked.

"She did not want to go back yet." Ollowain shook his head. "She is just as garrulous as you. Yilvina will watch over the queen. She will not leave Emerelle's side."

"Emerelle is safe here."

Ollowain recalled the human king and the strange audience with the queen. He had insisted on kneeling at Emerelle's bedside and had then whispered in her ear. Only he and Alfadas had witnessed the bizarre scene. Afterward, Horsa had lied to his followers and claimed that he had spoken at length with the queen. Humans! They were like children! Ever since they had seen the centaur Orimedes, they had been prepared to believe anything. They seemed to have an insatiable need to touch the manhorse.

"Ready?" Lyndwyn said urgently. Golden light rose from the rock, and a gate opened. "Come on!"

Alfadas took a step back. "We will meet again soon, my friend!" Ollowain stepped quickly into the light, almost as if he were fleeing.

Lyndwyn led them just a few steps through the void; then they stepped out through a second gate. A broad expanse of snow-covered hills spread before them. The wind howled through the branches of a dead tree that stood close beside the gate. From its bleached boughs hung battered shields and the skulls of horses.

Orimedes welcomed the wintry landscape with a whoop of joy. Then he clapped Lyndwyn so heartily on the shoulder that she almost fell face-first into the snow. "Good job, witch! I've never got back here so fast."

"Where are your men?" Gondoran asked indignantly. The holde's teeth were chattering. He pulled on a fur sack that Asla had sewn for him, a shapeless thing with holes for his arms and head.

The centaur spread his arms out wide, as if to take in the entire countryside around them. "Somewhere out there. I come from a race of wanderers. We never stay long in one place. I'll find them. Believe me, you'll like it here. The wind in your hair as you gallop through the hills is wonderful!"

Gondoran's face twisted into a grimace. "I admit I have never in my life seen snow, but it seems to me to be the only form of water that I don't much care for." He lifted his hands to his lips and blew on his clammy fingers.

"You'll get used to it." The centaur wore neither cape nor vest, and the cold seemed not to bother him in the slightest. His breath puffed from his mouth in small clouds. His hooves trampled the snow. "I will gather my warriors and bring them to the Snaiwamark. It will take me a few weeks, Ollowain. One does not go to war without a decent drink first. And each of the clans will expect me to stay for a feast." The centaur grinned broadly. "Some grueling weeks ahead."

"If you'd told me that in advance, I'd have stayed in the human world," Gondoran grumbled. "Going from one orgy of drinking to the next with a centaur in the middle of a world of frozen water! Fate is testing me . . ."

"Did I mention that we expect guests to drain at least one horn of mead with us? Anything less would be an insult."

"As long as you don't piss in your mead, I'll manage."

Orimedes patted the holde's head. "Good boy. My people will have a lot of fun with you, my friend." Then he turned to Ollowain. "Good luck, swordmaster. Until we meet again in the Snaiwamark!" With a whinnying whoop, the prince stormed down the hill.

"So now we're alone," Lyndwyn said. She still wore the damaged dress she had on when they fled Vahan Calyd and had flatly refused to tolerate anything made of coarse human cloth near her skin. She looked intently at Ollowain. Did she expect an apology for how he had treated her as a traitor?

"Can you find the way to Phylangan?" he asked, his voice cool.

"Can your tongue find its way to admitting my innocence?" she replied archly.

"Do you think I trust you because you were forced to help the queen?"

"Do you know what it means to heal, Ollowain? It means experiencing the pain of the injured person. It was not the shingles that robbed me of consciousness when we fled. It was the queen's pain. She had fifty-three separate burns, seven broken bones, a pierced lung, and a gaping wound in her chest. The chest wound alone was enough to kill her, if not for me. And I saved your life, too. What else do I have to do to convince you that I did not give the signal to bombard Vahan Calyd?"

Ollowain looked at her with disdain. She did not appear cold at all, and it was clear to him that she had cast a spell to keep herself warm . . . one of those damned spells he had never managed to learn. And she did not even have to concentrate. It simply happened, just like that.

"You would have to shed your skin to make me trust you. You belong to Shahondin's clan, and Shahondin is a sworn enemy of the queen. It is the skin in which you were born . . . I will never trust you. Now take us to Phylangan."

"And if I simply walk away? I could go anywhere I like."

The swordmaster brought one hand to his sword belt. "Do you think you could get through the gate faster than my blade could fly, traitor?"

"I am a sorceress. It would be a simple matter to protect myself from your sword." She looked at him intensely.

"Shall we try it?"

"If I die, you're stuck." She pointed to the south. The centaur was no more than a small, dark speck among the snow-covered hills. "Orimedes can't see you anymore. And the cold will kill you if you stay here."

"Do you think that would stop me from doing something?"

Lyndwyn lowered her eyes. "And the queen? Who will bring Emerelle back from the human world if you die?"

"Orimedes knows where Emerelle is. He will rescue her if I no longer can."

"So that is why the queen chose you."

"What are you talking about?"

"About *you*, Ollowain," Lyndwyn snapped at him angrily. "You don't exist. All you know is the destination, and you sacrifice everything to reach it. I could understand that if you were doing it for yourself, but you are no more than an empty shell. There is a kind of wasp that lays its eggs inside other insects. The young eat their host slowly, from the inside. That's you, Ollowain. An empty shell in which Emerelle has laid her eggs. You don't exist anymore. You live only for her to use."

"Are you finished?"

She said nothing, just stood and glared at him in her fury. Or was there something else in her eyes?

"Take me to Phylangan!"

She bowed like a servant. "As you wish, master." Lyndwyn kneeled beside the dead tree. Her left hand moved across the snow, feeling for something. She placed her right hand over her heart, then closed her eyes.

Ollowain stepped up close beside her. She was pretty, but he could not let that blind him! Most importantly, she was Shahondin's granddaughter. She was a traitor.

A gate of warm light rose from the snow, the red of the evening sky after a clear summer's day. "Let's go." He took hold of Lyndwyn's wrist roughly and stepped into the void. After just five steps, they stood before another gate, although this one shone in all the colors of the rainbow.

"The destination," said Lyndwyn.

Ollowain was still holding on to her wrist. He was at her mercy. From where he stood, it was impossible to say whether she had truly brought him to Phylangan. The gate might just as easily open into the prince of Arkadien's palace, the heart of Shahondin's snake pit. There was only one way to find out. His mind made up, he stepped through the light. An abyss opened at his feet—he was standing on a bridge of milk-white stone. It had no railings. The stone beneath his feet was polished so smooth that any water falling on it would trickle away. The Shalyn Falah! But that was impossible! There was no Albenstar on the bridge. And the cliffs around the Shalyn Falah were not forested.

Perplexed, Ollowain looked around. The bridge extended only a short distance out over the valley basin, which would have been two miles or more across. The steep mountainsides all around were terraced. The walls mimicked the structure of rocky outcrops, so that at first glance it was hard to see any difference. But their elegant curves betrayed them. Thin, sheer pillars of rock rose vertically from the bottom of the valley in no discernible pattern. The highest of them seemed almost to reach the sky. Fine white rivulets of water descended from their tops, following twisting striae in the blue-gray granite. The entire valley appeared too harmonious to be natural. Ollowain knew it. Almost five hundred years had passed since the last time he had been here; at that time the Skyhall had been much smaller.

The swordmaster looked up to the sky: an illusion. It was translucent blue stone, like that on the island close to Vahan Calyd. But here they had removed all the metallic veins, and the illusion looked far more real. They had real clouds that floated vaguely beneath the pellucid ceiling, moving like drifts of fog on a wind-still morning. Everything there was a single, enormous cavern. The heart of Phylangan, the stone garden, the mountain fortress that watched over the only pass that led to the high plains of Carandamon. On his last visit, the Albenstar had still been in a grotto far above the Skyhall . . . the builders and sorcerers of the Normirga must have expanded the hall massively in the centuries in between.

"Get me away from here," said Lyndwyn softly. She was trembling all over, staring wide-eyed into the gulf below.

Ollowain sighed. That was all he needed! He reached one hand toward her; she was standing just one pace behind him.

"I . . . I can't." She suddenly crouched, pressed both hands against the stone of the bridge. Her eyes still stared as if mesmerized into the abyss. "It feels as if the depths are calling me," she stammered. "I have to jump, to fly like a bird."

"Close your eyes," said Ollowain. "You must not look down. I will lead you across. Come." He crouched beside her. "Turn your eyes away."

"The . . . the chasm . . . it has me. I—"

He grasped her under her chin and forced her to look at his face. "Do you see my eyes? Lose yourself in their abyss. Tell me what color they are."

She tried to turn her head aside again, but he held on to her chin. Her skin was clammy with sweat. All the color had drained from her face. "What do my eyes look like?" Ollowain asked.

"They are green."

The swordmaster took her by one wrist. The palms of her hands were still pressed flat to the surface of the bridge. Her fingers twisted uselessly, trying to find a grip on the smooth stone.

"You will now stand up. Keep looking into my eyes! Don't you think that 'green' does not do them justice? What kind of green are they? Look more closely." Ollowain rose to his feet again. He held Lyndwyn with his gaze, and she hesitantly stood up with him.

"Your eyes are the color of the moss you find on the stones of the sealed Albenstar close to the Shalyn Falah. Your irises are surrounded by a thin black ring. The green is not even; fine lights and shadows run through it."

Slowly, Ollowain moved backward. Lyndwyn followed him on unsteady legs. He held both her hands now and had to look into her face to prevent her from turning her eyes away. Beneath them, the valley floor fell away more than two hundred paces.

"When the dark chasm of your pupils opens, the green changes. It becomes more dense. Darker. I see my reflection in your eyes. Distorted. A grotesque creature . . . I must see in your eyes an image of what you see in me."

Lyndwyn had moved very close to him. Her breath softly touched his lips. She was beautiful . . . and desirable. Ollowain cleared his throat. Was she feeling so much better that she was trying to enchant him with a love spell? Had she only feigned her fear of heights? "It is the curve of my eye that distorts your image, Lyndwyn. No more and no less."

"The whites of your eyes are flawless," she said, ignoring his words. "There is no trace of yellow, no burst veins to insult the white with an obscene red. Your eyelashes are full and delicately curved. There are elf women who would envy you your eyelashes. They are immaculate, like the reputation of the keeper of the Shalyn Falah. The swordmaster. The queen's confidant, the one who knows only his duty."

Her voice was a little deeper than a woman's voice should be, but it was that depth that made her voice sound all the more sensual in Ollowain's ear. Her voice stood in stark contrast to her thin lips. They looked unkissed. *What rubbish*, he thought! And Lyndwyn's eyes were also green, but of a lighter shade and shot through with golden points.

Ollowain tried to concentrate completely on his steps. He did not lower his eyes, but he closed his heart to what he saw. There was something about Lyndwyn that moved him deeply, that addled his feelings. She knew what it meant to sacrifice yourself to an ideal. To strive for perfection. To outshine all others. But what weaknesses was she trying to conceal behind her ambition?

No! His thoughts were once again far too close to her. She was a renegade! *Focus on your steps,* he reprimanded himself. He felt the hard stone through the soft soles of his boots. It was smooth, slippery. And yet this bridge was not as treacherous as the real Shalyn Falah. There was no spray from a river below to wet the stone, nor gusting winds that tugged at one's clothes.

"Do you believe that the eyes could be the window to the soul?" Lyndwyn asked.

"Would I find gold in your soul?"

"Because you consider me a liar and a traitor, you will probably have to answer that question yourself. What use would my words be to you?"

Ollowain was surprised. She had not spoken with any condemnation in her voice. No, she sounded more sad than accusatory. *Be on your guard,* he warned himself. *She is just playing with you. She wants to capture you, to lull your suspicions with gentle words.*

The ground crunched beneath Ollowain's feet. The stone was no longer polished smooth, but rough, and the soles of his boots found better footing. He glanced over his shoulder—they were off the bridge.

Someone clapped.

"I have been the keeper of the Mahdan Falah for more than a hundred years, and I have never yet seen anyone cross it like that." An elven soldier stepped from behind a rosebush. He wore a pale-gray tunic with thin silver trim along the hems. A long dark-red cape billowed from his shoulders, held at the neck by a ring-shaped clasp depicting a snake biting its own tail. His sword belt and leather sheath were the same shade of red as his cape, as was the crest that decorated the high, pointed helmet the keeper held casually under his arm. The elf had long blond hair that fell in curls to his shoulders. There was something doll-like about his pale skin and the even lines of his face. "You are the high point of this season," the keeper continued in his soft, ingratiating voice. "It is rare for anyone to enter the Skyhall through the Albenstar. Would you be so kind as to introduce yourselves?"

"I am Ollowain, swordmaster to Queen Emerelle, and this is Lyndwyn, sorceress at Emerelle's court."

The keeper pursed his lips. "An answer as forbidding as your appearance is adventurous. Now tell me on what business you have come here." Although the soldier maintained as much distance as possible with his words, Ollowain could read the ill-concealed curiosity in his eyes. He was certain that the soldier had heard his name before. Anyone who kept watch over this macabre copy of the Shalyn Falah must certainly know who, for decades, had been in charge of the original.

"We wish to speak to Landoran, the prince of Snaiwamark and the high plateau of Carandamon. We are here in the service of our ruler, Queen Emerelle. Our business cannot be delayed."

"Allow me to point out that it is up to me to decide on the urgency of the business of uninvited guests. As much as it might please the prince to chat with guests who have, no doubt, traveled far, his duties naturally take up a great deal of his time. I will send a messenger to him. May I ask you to wait in the guest pavilion while we await a reply?" The guard clapped his hands, and a kobold stepped out from behind the rosebush. The little fellow wore gray livery and black boots with silver buttons. The colors matched well with his dark, olive-colored skin. The gray of his uniform was more subdued than that worn by the soldier. "Dolmon, you heard our guests," said the guard. "Apprise the prince of their business. Ah . . ." The keeper turned back to Ollowain. "You don't happen to have a letter of introduction that identifies you as a servant of the queen?"

"No. And to be honest, this is the first time anyone has held me up when I have traveled in the queen's service, but I can see that one has to make allowances for the remoteness of Phylangan. Out here in the wilderness, one naturally does not know who is or is not an intimate of the queen." Ollowain noted the grin that appeared on the face of the kobold behind his master's back.

"You may go, Dolmon," said the soldier. "And no dawdling!"

"May I also inquire after your name?" Ollowain asked. "Just for the sake of the report that I have to present to my queen about my journey. You would be amazed at how fastidious Emerelle can be about certain things."

The guard straightened. "My name is Ronardin."

"Very good, Ronardin. Then lead us to your guest pavilion, and I would appreciate it if you would be discreet enough not to offend my traveling companion with your gaze." The soldier had not glanced in Lyndwyn's direction even once, but still he paled. He hurried ahead of them toward a small marble pavilion, from where they had a marvelous view of the Skyhall and the Mahdan Falah. The bridge was identical to the Shalyn Falah in every detail bar one—midarch, it came to an abrupt halt in empty space. Seen from the pavilion, its broad curves were like windows that dissected the panorama beyond.

Tending that landscape of gardens must have been an endlessly arduous task, work that presumably fell on the shoulders of countless kobolds.

The Skyhall might have grown, but nothing of the main characteristics of Normirga society had changed. Ollowain was shocked at how fast he himself had reverted to the pompous tone of voice of his own race. Or had he never really shaken it off?

Grapes, pears, apples, and nuts were arranged picturesquely on a silver platter on a narrow table. A crystal carafe of red wine and four sumptuous glasses completed the still life.

Ollowain took a large grape and ate it. Ronardin stood at the pavilion entrance and avoided looking at either of them. He had clearly not yet gotten over the slanderous accusation that he had looked salaciously at Lyndwyn and now was scrupulous in keeping his back to her. The swordmaster smiled. Ronardin must still be very young or else he would have been aware that behaving as he was, he opened himself to a charge of not paying proper attention to a guest.

There was something soothing about the view out into the enormous cavern, with its artificially terraced walls. Ollowain enjoyed the sweet grape and the wine, spiced as it was with honey, cinnamon, and cloves. It was easy to feel at home in Phylangan, if one only fell into line with the laws of the Normirga.

Lyndwyn had taken a seat on a bench. She sat in a rather unladylike manner, legs apart, leaning back. She looked bored and tired and had plucked a grape for herself. Lost in thought, she rolled the fruit between her fingers.

The pavilion was a good place to wait. Ollowain's eyes wandered over the forested terraces. He would be able to sit there for hours without tiring of the sight. *A view of nature can heal your soul,* his mother had once told him centuries before. At that time, he had been too impatient to open himself to that truth, and he had also been too young to suffer an injured soul. Only time had convinced him of the wisdom in his mother's words.

"My boy! How lovely to see you!" Landoran had stepped into the pavilion without a sound. He had always loved appearing unexpectedly. And with his very first words, he made it clear to Ollowain that nothing at all had changed in their relationship. For the prince, Ollowain was still a boy. No amount of renown could remove the flaw that clung to him. As far as that was concerned, the laws of the Normirga were clear and unremitting. A man who was unable, with his own power and without effort, to protect himself from the intense cold of the land remained a boy. It made no difference how old he was or what he had achieved. He was prohibited from leaving the fortress unaccompanied, as the freezing cold out there could kill within hours. But what might at first glance look like thoughtfulness had been devised to strengthen the hand of those who could work magic. No other elven race was as proud of their magical prowess as the Normirga. And because those who were not blessed with that gift were essentially unable to find a way to leave the fortress, the rest of the Albenkin only ever met powerful sorcerers from that northern race. The most important of all those weavers of magic, Emerelle, came from the Normirga. That Ollowain had managed to break free of that tyranny had left a bad taste in the mouth of many of his race. Ollowain recalled that he, too, had inherited the gift. But on the day of his mother's death, his magical powers were extinguished. Sometimes, the swordmaster believed that it was perhaps only the will to wield those powers that had died in him. He looked at his father, who embodied more than perhaps any other elf the image of the Normirga held by the Albenkin. He radiated coldness and power, and it was difficult to look him in the eye for long.

"You have not changed," Ollowain replied. He held one hand out to Landoran to keep him at arm's length and avoid an embrace. Landoran's handshake was firm. The prince had silver-gray hair and wore a long, flowing robe of dark-gray silk. His face looked emaciated. A thin silver circlet held his long hair back—his father had aged visibly since the last time they had met. Only in his eyes did the old power still burn. He emanated a scent of fresh greenery, as if he had just been interrupted in the middle of trimming a rosebush.

"It is good to see that you are not among the dead, boy." The prince smiled. "I would have been very disappointed if the news that reached us were true."

"I see that you are well-informed, Prince."

"Bad news travels fast." Landoran pulled off a few grapes. "They say the queen is dead. The trolls put her on display in a public square and forced all the survivors to walk past her."

"I assume the body was not in particularly good condition."

The prince pushed a grape into his mouth. "She wore the swan crown."

"Is it that simple? A crown is enough to turn a dead girl into a queen?"

"You know how things are with Emerelle, boy. She has as many enemies as friends." He glanced fleetingly at Lyndwyn. "For some of the princely clans, it is, in fact, that simple."

"Is that how things stand for your own clan?"

Landoran raised one eyebrow. "What exactly do you want? Why have you come here, Ollowain? I am sure it was not easy for you to get here."

"I came to warn you about the trolls. You know that they will come here. And there will certainly be a few thousand of them."

"Imagine a few thousand more and then double it." Landoran pushed another grape into his mouth. "The word is that there are twenty thousand of them."

Ollowain looked at him in surprise. "Impossible! So many . . ."

"Just believe me. I have it from a refugee. There are almost a hundred troll ships anchored outside the harbor at Vahan Calyd. And every one has more than two hundred of those bloodthirsty monsters on board. Their years in the human world have been good to them, it seems. They've been breeding like kobolds."

"Twenty thousand?" Ollowain repeated in disbelief. He tried to imagine such an immense number of troll warriors. That would not be an army anymore. That would be a force of nature! "They will come here," said Ollowain, to drive home his point. "How will you stop them, Landoran?"

"No one has ever conquered the walls of Phylangan. They will be smashed against the ramparts of this fortress like even the mightiest wave shatters against a coastal cliff. The stone garden will never fall!"

"Are you so sure of that? We have never heard of trolls traveling by ship before and likewise never heard of such an overwhelming army of trolls. The word *never* seems to have lost all meaning for the trolls."

"Don't you think you might be panicking just a little, boy?"

"I could never have imagined that I would one day watch Vahan Calyd burn!" the swordmaster replied harshly. "And yet it happened. Don't make the mistake of closing your eyes in blind optimism to what is coming this way."

"I was, in fact, rather seriously disquieted before the two of you appeared here," Landoran admitted. "But you have been kind enough to bring the solution to all our problems with you." He turned to Lyndwyn with a smile. "This young and, dare I say, somewhat unsuitably attired woman, who has clearly not enjoyed the benefits of a courtly upbringing, will be of immeasurable assistance to us. In particular with what she is carrying —so well hidden from a curious glance—around her neck. When Ronardin asked you for proof that you really are emissaries of the queen, you could easily have admitted that Emerelle had sent you here with her Albenstone. Did you perhaps think that I would not sense the aura of its power? With its might, we will succeed in overcoming all threats."

If not for Landoran's presence, Ollowain could happily have slapped Lyndwyn—she had stolen the most precious artifact of the elven race from the unconscious queen. The stone that had once been given to them by the Alben themselves before the mysterious ancients had disappeared forever. It was said that each of their races had received such a stone, each of which contained almost immeasurable power. Used wisely, one could change the world with such a stone.

Landoran could not be allowed to know that Lyndwyn had stolen the stone. If he did, he would very likely not hesitate to take the valuable relic for himself. "Do you realize the importance of our mission now?" asked Ollowain defiantly. "Emerelle has permitted Lyndwyn to use the Albenstone to defend Phylangan. At all costs, the queen wants to prevent a second massacre like the one at Vahan Calyd."

"Where is Emerelle now?" Landoran asked casually.

"In a place from where she is preparing the defense of Albenmark."

"Would not our fortress here be the best place for that?"

Was that a trace of uncertainty he detected in the prince's voice? His face betrayed no emotion at all, yet he seemed tense. He pressed the last grape between his thumb and forefinger to the point where it might burst at any moment. When Landoran realized what Ollowain was looking at, he popped the grape into his mouth.

"Emerelle is not a warrior," the swordmaster replied with conviction. He did not know where the prince's disquiet came from, but he clearly sensed that he could, this once, win the upper hand. He—the boy who had left Carandamon behind centuries earlier in humiliation after failing to learn the spell that would protect him from the cold—had returned. And now he would impose his will on the prince, his father! "The queen's place is not inside the walls of a fortress soon to be stormed by twenty thousand trolls. She will attempt to unite the peoples of Albenmark in battle against the old foes. She will be able to achieve more elsewhere than she could here. She has sent me here in her place. Her sword! First among her warriors. In Emerelle's name,

I hereby request command of Phylangan and all of the troops that can be brought here from the stone palaces of Carandamon before the trolls lay siege."

A deep crease appeared between the prince's brows, just for a moment. Then his face relaxed again, and he burst out laughing.

"You! By the laws of our people, you are still a child, and you demand command of this fortress? Don't be absurd! My soldiers will not follow you, boy. And you dare call yourself the queen's sword? I know that you had led her private guard, and I never understood that. In my eyes, there is not a fighter in Albenmark who deserves that title less than you. I was there to witness how you betrayed the queen when a sharp blade was called for!" He pointed out to the bridge that came to an abrupt end above the deep valley. "Do you know where the Albenstar lies? Exactly there, where the king and the princes of the trolls were pushed to their deaths in the abyss. There, at the site of your disgrace! The place where you refused the queen's direct order. Do you remember the night when you opposed all the elvenfolk? Anyone who spares the life of a troll robs us of our peace!"

"For me, it is the place of my honor, Landoran. I could not prevent the injustice that took place that night, but at least I took no part in it!"

"Injustice? What injustice? The trolls started this war. Have you forgotten how they drove your own people from the high plateau of Carandamon? When there was no other place for us in Albenmark except the stale, fever-plagued mangroves beside the Woodmer? For me, that night on the Shalyn Falah represented the triumph of justice after centuries."

"You are blind, Landoran. Our people could return to Carandamon, that was the law. But this fortress never belonged to us, just as the Snaiwamark was never ours. It was given to the trolls by the Alben. We stole this land when we had the power to do so. We murdered their princes. That night on the Shalyn Falah, we sowed the wind. And now the time has come for us to reap the storm!"

Landoran had recovered his composure, and the more Ollowain worked himself into a rage, the more relaxed the prince became. He went back to the fruit platter and, with infuriating calm, tugged several grapes from their stem. Then he gestured out into the Skyhall.

"Do you know what this was when we came here, Ollowain? A filthy hole in the ground. A few caves, no more, and no better than the dens of animals. It stank of shit and mangy hides. There was no clean water. And now look. Look what we have turned it into! Oh yes, there were once a few caves here where trolls lived, but Phylangan, as you see it now, the stone garden, is a flower that your own people planted and nurtured, Ollowain."

"What I see when I look out there is the victory of aesthetics over ethics. I see an executioner's block used to decorate a landscape. I see a bridge that leads to nothing. You've created quite a symbol for the road on which you have led our people, Landoran!"

A mocking smile crossed the prince's face. "Prettily formulated for a man of the sword, Ollowain. One can see, still, which of the elven clans you outgrew. Of course, your argumentation is marred by a taint of childish indignation, but what else can one expect from a boy who never became a man? Everything you say about the bridge only shows how blinded by wrath and shame you have become. That is no road to nowhere. At its end is an Albenstar. And anyone adept enough can slip from there into the web of Albenpaths. That road leads everywhere, if one has the courage to follow it."

"And it is a wide-open doorway for the trolls," Lyndwyn suddenly said. "I see no defenses here. What will happen if the trolls decide to risk an attack through the Albenstar?"

"That is unthinkable!" Landoran shot back.

"Unthinkable? How do you think they returned to Albenmark? There is only one way to get here from the human world: the Albenpaths. They have already done it once. Why should they waste weeks attacking Phylangan's outer defenses when there is such an easy way to storm the stone garden?"

"Trolls don't think like that!" the prince insisted.

"You are an aesthete. A man who personifies complete freedom of art and self-invention above all moral or spiritual constraints. You are the creator of the wonder of Vahan Calyd and the Skyhall. Do you really believe you know how trolls think?" said Lyndwyn.

The prince lowered his head as if distracted. The sorceress's objections seemed to have shaken him deeply.

Lyndwyn exploited his moment of weakness. "I can understand that you feel so bound by the laws of your people that you challenge the queen's order and cannot hand over command to Ollowain. I would therefore suggest a compromise. According to the laws of the Normirga, I am deemed an adult because I can easily protect myself from the cold with my own powers. More crucially, Emerelle has vouchsafed me the greatest treasure of the elven race."

From beneath her tattered robe, she withdrew a rough stone deeply cut by five furrows. It looked rather nondescript, like a piece of quarried rock. And yet the five furrows transformed it into a jewel, a masterpiece of plain harmony. In its own way, it was perfect.

"Do you think you could entrust me with the fate of Phylangan, given that Emerelle believed me worthy to be the guardian of the Albenstone?"

The audacity of her words left Ollowain speechless. Did this thief and traitor know no shame at all? He had to stop her!

Lyndwyn looked at the prince. "I will trust the advice given me by the swordmaster in all military matters. Emerelle wanted him to lead the defense of this fortress. I will merely be the voice that carries his orders, so that none of your men must submit to the word of a warrior who, in the eyes of your people, never reached manhood. We would be respecting the laws of the Normirga and also the will of Emerelle. We—"

With a deafening hiss, a fountain of steam shot from one of the columnar springs that rose close to the pavilion. A dense white cloud climbed toward the false sky overhead.

The prince had stepped to one of the pillars supporting the pavilion. His expression was concerned; it seemed almost as if he were more interested in the release of steam than in their altercation.

"Your suggestion shows great wisdom, Lyndwyn. I lay the fate of Phylangan in your hands, sorceress."

Ollowain could barely comprehend what had just happened. Within moments, the pretty schemer had managed to wrest command of an enormous fortress city with a lie. And he had been unable to stop her!

If he spoke up and said that Lyndwyn had stolen the Albenstone, Landoran would probably just take it from her and declare that it was for the greater good of all if the mighty artifact was in his care.

Powerless in his fury, the swordmaster looked up to the cloud of steam as it spread wider and wider. Phylangan had hoisted the white flag and put the fate of the city in the hands of the same elf who had rung in the downfall of Vahan Calyd. And he? He was as helpless as he had been when she sent the firebird into the night sky and signaled the start of the bombardment of the harbor.

No, not entirely. This time he knew where the most dangerous enemy of his people stood!

THE TROLLS' PLIGHT

Fables weave, or twist and turn,   and torture words into a
    form
Of fearless fighters' frays,   of cunning and acclaim,
Of joyous, jaunty feasting   of melancholy keening,
But hear ye now the witness   not the minstrel singing.

Atop the scarred escarpment,   the elven city glistered,
Where stabbing sunlight seared,   where treasure brightly
    boasted,
Where wild white horses heaved,   there lay the city Reilimee,
Named with deliberation   proud and radiant Reilimee.
Bravely bore courageous trolls   the war before its very walls.
Clubs and cudgels bludgeoned,   there was no remorse.

Where black ships surged and fell   the reaper swung his scythe,
There before that sturdy town,   Reilimee of song and myth,
A thousand dead piled high   beneath its ramparts proud
And neither toil nor daring   escaped the shroud.
Where a king's lament sounded,   there the cunning stood as
    first
Upon the walls surrounding   Reilimee, proud and cursed.

From the "Nightcrags Codex"

Translated by Brother Gundaher

Volume Six of the Temple Library of Luth in Firnstayn,
page 139

BOARDING RAMPS AND
BATTERING RAMS

P ull starboard oars!" Orgrim bawled with all his might to overcome the noise of the battle.

"Pull starboard oars!" he heard from below, like an echo from the hull of the *Wraithwind*. Skanga had entrusted him, the ship sinker, with her galleass. She was, indeed, not on board—which could be understood as an expression of a certain mistrust—but she considered him capable of carrying off this daring attack and had given her blessing to all of the necessary rebuilding.

The heavy hull of the *Wraithwind* swung around as only the port oars churned the water. On the starboard side, a net interwoven with thick bundles of rags was lowered. It would cushion the impact with the fortified harbor walls.

The defenders' arrows descended like hail onto the *Wraithwind*. The elves had realized that the large galleass was the most dangerous ship in the attacking formation.

Shield men protected Orgrim from the bombardment. The pack leader peered along the long harbor wall, which extended into the turquoise bay like two embracing arms, protecting the harbor and its ships from the surging sea. And now the surging waves of trolls were also being smashed to pieces against it. Three times they had tried to storm the city, and three times they had been beaten back. No one had known how heavily fortified Reilimee was when Branbeard ordered the attack against the elven city.

By land, Reilimee was protected by a double wall. And to seaward, they had this accursed harbor wall. It rose almost ten paces above the water, with watchtowers a good deal higher spaced along it every two ship's lengths. The entrance to the harbor itself was secured by two small fortresses, between which stretched a chain with links as thick as a troll's arm. None of the galleasses had been able to break through that impenetrable barrier.

A shield beside Orgrim suddenly burst apart. Splinters of wood and bone, blood and brain sprayed across the pack leader's chest and face. The shot had blown off the head of one of his shield bearers, and the warrior's two-inch-thick oak shield now had a large, ragged hole in it.

"You should get off the quarterdeck now," Boltan advised, pulling a finger-long shard of wood out of his own chest. "They've spotted you because of the shield bearers." The artillery chief pointed to the closest watchtower on the harbor wall. Behind the battlements, Orgrim saw elven helmets glint in the sunlight.

"I'm curious to know what those damned elven catapults look like," Boltan grumbled. "We overran Vahan Calyd too quickly. There must have been some of the blasted things there, too. We made a mistake there, smashing everything to matchwood."

"We'll be the first on the wall, and I promise you you'll get a few of those catapults as spoils of war. They're—"

His voice was drowned out by an almighty crash. Splintered wood flew across the quarterdeck, and trolls screamed and bawled. Several warriors writhed in a pool of blood on the deck. A second shot had torn a gaping hole in the bulwark. Those damned elven catapults were able to shoot stones horizontally and were many times more accurate than the catapults that Orgrim had seen in the past. The trolls' slingshots, by comparison, bombarded the enemy with rocks fired high in the air, and even an artillery chief as experienced as Boltan could only estimate roughly where a shot would fall and what damage it would do.

Fist-sized stones rained onto the harbor wall, and Orgrim listened with satisfaction to the screams of wounded elves. King Branbeard had ordered his men to bombard the defenders on the walls with stones—not one of the troll ships was still equipped with fireballs.

"Raise the ramps!" Orgrim ordered. The *Wraithwind* was no more than five paces from the harbor wall. "Pull port oars! All hands on deck."

The pack leader watched with keen interest as the heavy boarding ramps were hauled up the masts by block and tackle. The crow's nests above the first yards had been reinforced. Thick bull-leather loops had been attached to the side of the crow's nests, into which one end of each boarding ramp was to be hooked. But that was only possible when the *Wraithwind* lay directly beside the harbor wall, because the tremendous weight they were heaving into the rigging on one side would otherwise cause the ship to founder.

Dozens of trolls, unruffled by the arrows and catapults of the elves, swarmed into the shrouds and yards to carry out the various maneuvers needed to make the assault work. Now was the moment that Skanga's decision only to have the best of the best on board truly counted. Orgrim would not have been able to carry out this attack with any other crew, not without weeks of advance practice.

Flaming arrows now flew at the *Wraithwind*. The previous night, Orgrim had had all sails removed to make his ship less vulnerable to those treacherous missiles. Driven only by oars, the large galleass was miserably sluggish, but reducing the danger of fire far outweighed that disadvantage. Buckets of water stood at the ready all over the decks, and Orgrim had assembled a special squad whose only task in this battle was to smother flames.

A dull blow shook the *Wraithwind*. The galleass had run broadside against the harbor wall. From the topmost crow's nests, trolls tried to wipe out the archers atop the wall.

More and more missiles rained down on the *Wraithwind*. All the elven archers and catapults in range now seemed to have chosen that one ship as their target.

Orgrim was happy to see that all three boarding ramps were ready. They bore long spikes on their undersides like the teeth of predators—jaws of wood, ready to bite into the wall.

"Hoist the leather guards!" Orgrim yelled. Then he took his own shield and descended from the quarterdeck. He would lead the attack over the mainmast, and he was determined to be the first troll to set foot on the walls of Reilimee.

Columns of door-sized wooden frames spanned with wet animal hides were hauled up until they hung suspended from the yards like a leather curtain. They would stop some of the flaming arrows but were mainly intended to make it difficult to shoot at the trolls climbing the masts.

The pack leader slung his shield onto his back and checked that his war hammer sat securely in his belt. "Onto the walls! Smash in their miserable little heads!" Orgrim pulled himself up into the shrouds, and dozens of warriors followed him. The decks and masts resounded with battle cries. Orgrim watched with satisfaction as the suspended leather guards took the brunt of the elves' arrows. His plan was working! At the top of the shrouds, he clambered into the crow's nest. Powerful hands helped him across. At almost the same moment, Gran had reached the foremast crow's nest. The bastard wasn't thinking that *he* would be the first to stand atop the fortress wall?

"Lower the boarding ramps!" Orgrim cried.

The heavy ramps crashed onto the battlements along the wall. The pack leader pushed his arm through the leather loops of his sturdy shield. Then he lifted the heavy oak boards protectively in front of his chest so that he could just see over the top edge. He sensed the restlessness of the men behind him. A stone ball from one of the lethal elven catapults flew past, just missing his head, and tore splinters from the mainmast.

Orgrim pulled the war hammer from his belt. He was determined to take the section of wall in front of him—he would earn his duchy in the end, even if it meant being duke of an accursed elven town like Reilimee.

The boarding ramp vibrated beneath his feet. A few paces and he was at the wall. Spears rose to meet him, and he pushed them aside effortlessly, as if they were no more than bulrushes. With a leap, he found himself on the parapet. The defenders were too close together and could not avoid his hammer. Roaring, he swung it over his head.

An elven commander screamed to his men to retreat. Arrows buried themselves in Orgrim's shield. The defenders there on the wall were far less skillful than the elven fighters who had fought aboard the false queen's ship. They were no less brave, but they could not hold him at bay.

His heavy war hammer shattered shields, helmets, skulls, everything that got in its way. He swung his shield, sending defenders tumbling from the wall. His own men behind him were enraged, cursing and swearing. They could not get by him. The parapet atop the wall was so narrow that no more than two trolls could fight side by side without hindering each other overmuch.

His progress along the wall gained momentum. Some elves leaped over the parapet rather than fall beneath his war hammer. The pale slabs of stone that topped the wall were slippery with blood. Seagulls circled over the watchtower in front of him. They screeched as if to spur the fighters on.

Orgrim saw the door to the tower close. The elves that had not made it in to safety screamed in panic. Some threw down their weapons and dropped to their knees. Cowards! Pathetic! Orgrim grabbed hold of them and threw them out of his way. Then he was at the door. Broad iron bands ran across the gray wood. Rust traced across it like tracks of spilled blood. It stank of shit and vomit, the smell of the battlefield.

Orgrim beat at the door with all his strength. The gray wood shivered, every blow leaving deep gouges. But the door stood.

"Watch out, Pack Leader!"

Orgrim reflexively jerked his shield over his head. Something like water dripped from above, then a torrent of the stuff came down on his shield. A few droplets spattered his face, finding their way through fine cracks in the oak boards of the shield. They burned on his skin. A heavy, oily odor and the smell of boiling meat hung in the air.

The fighter immediately behind him had been less lucky. He lay on his back. His arms twitched helplessly. His face was swollen and gray red, covered in blisters, his eyes wide open. They gleamed as white as boiled eggs surrounded by the scalded flesh.

"Get the battering rams here!" Orgrim ordered. "The doors are too strong to break down with our weapons."

A flaming torch landed at his feet. He bent down quickly and picked it up. The flames were already licking greedily at the hot oil. Orgrim flung the torch into the sea in a rage, then he slid his shield off his arm and smothered the flames.

"Stone throwers! Target those bastards on the towers." He wished his men had some of those powerful, horizontal-firing catapults. Then they could lay siege to watchtowers like this until no one dared show their nose from behind the battlements.

"What's holding up the ram? Do you want to get cooked here?"

Piercing screams made Orgrim look up. At the other end of that section of wall, where the next watchtower rose, the parapet stood in bright flames. Warriors transformed into living torches stumbled back into the mass of their comrades. Their arms wheeling helplessly, they grasped at anyone in reach, carrying death deeper into the ranks of those who had initially escaped the boiling oil and flames.

Now it was Orgrim's warriors who leaped in horror from the walls. A troll tumbled in flames onto the main deck of the *Wraithwind*. Boltan plunged a harpoon into his neck before he could get to his feet again, and another smothered the fire with sand.

"The ram!" bawled Orgrim furiously. They were so close to victory.

Finally, the men began to move. A solid tree trunk was hefted up onto the wall. Its branches had not been completely removed, leaving plenty of places to hold on to it. One end was sharpened.

Orgrim abandoned his cover beneath the lintel. He stuffed his war hammer back in his belt and raised his shield protectively over his head. "Heave! We avenge our dead comrades!"

He saw the murderous looks in the eyes of his men. Many were marked by burns. One with a shaved head had two broken arrows protruding from his left shoulder, but still he reached for the stump of a branch and roared, "Revenge!"

Brud, Skanga's scout, was among those who formed up for the new assault. Screaming war cries, they charged the door. The crash of the battering ram rolled like thunder over the walls. Orgrim felt as if every sinew in his arm must tear apart as the heavy tree trunk rebounded from the door.

"Again!" The trunk flew forward, and this time they were rewarded with the sound of splintering. One of the planks of the door had split.

Arrows whizzed among them. Up above, on the tower, the defenders were mounting a final, desperate attempt to drive them back from the door.

"Revenge!" the troll warriors shouted. "Revenge!" In time to their furious cries, the battering ram pounded against the door. If one man went down, another immediately took his place.

Another plank splintered. And then one of the hinges gave way and the door half tipped inward. Orgrim let go of the tree trunk. He threw himself into the gap in the door.

A sword blade came at him, and he dropped. Splinters of wood grazed his chest. Beneath his weight, the second hinge broke free of its anchor. The door collapsed into the tower.

The pack leader rolled to one side to avoid a slashing spear. The narrow chamber of the tower was filled with bodies. Heavy feet trampled over him. "Revenge!" The battle cry resounded from the walls.

Somehow, Orgrim managed to get back on his feet. In the crowded space, it was impossible to swing his war hammer. Beside him, the shaven-headed troll dropped to his knees, his belly slit open from top to bottom; the dying troll tried with both hands to hold in the guts spilling from the wound.

Orgrim saw the elven blade slice forward again, this time at his own belly. He turned to one side, but this time he was too slow. A long, shallow cut slashed across his stomach.

Enraged, he grabbed hold of the head of the sword fighter and slammed it into the wall with all his strength. Again and again and again.

Around him, the battle ebbed. Someone tore open the door that led out to the next section of the wall and, in the same moment, was hurled back into the tower chamber. Like a child's fist smashing into a mouse nest, an unseen force tore shields and bodies to shreds. In the blink of an eye, the triumphant trolls were transformed into torn corpses.

Orgrim peered out cautiously through the door. The elves had set up one of their mysterious artillery pieces on the wall. In haste, the elves manning it were attempting to reload. Two soldiers heaved a stone the size of a troll's head onto twin guide rails, while two more soldiers turned the spokes of a double winch. The weapon was less than fifty paces away.

The pack leader broke into a run. "Revenge!" he roared in his fear and fury. Behind him, he heard the sound of heavy feet. The battle cry was taken up by other warriors.

The arms of the catapult jolted back another notch, then locked in lethal tension. A sharp click sounded. Orgrim threw himself forward. He felt the blast of wind as the stone flew past, inches over his back. He heard the sounds of tearing flesh and many voices bellowing in pain. Instantly, he was on his feet again.

Accursed elves! They were already reloading. A new stone was lifted onto the rails. Orgrim ran as fast as his legs could carry him. Close beside him was Brud, the scout. The pack leader pulled his war hammer from his belt.

The arm of the catapult moved back in small jerks. Ten more steps. Arrows flew around them. Something slammed into Orgrim's thigh. He ran on. He felt a burning in his chest. The catapult jerked a final time, then froze. Five steps.

The war machine waited like a viper ready to strike. An elf wearing a feathered helmet leaned forward. Orgrim hurled his war hammer. The helmet turned into a bloodied piece of metal.

Two steps more. The artillery crew jumped back. The elves tried to escape through the open door into the next tower.

"Grab that misbegotten thing. We'll jam the door with it!" he shouted to Brud. In the momentum of their charge, they dragged the catapult with them, and Orgrim snatched up his hammer again.

The tower door began to close. The siege machine slammed into the wood, the long guide rails slipping between the door and the framing wall. Something clicked. The arms of the catapult jolted, and the heavy projectile shot forward, carving a bloody corridor through the warriors behind them.

"No!"

In blind rage, Orgrim kicked the door open and threw himself at the elves. In a frenzy, he swung his war hammer left and right. Something slit his cheek open. A sharp blow struck him in the knee. The chamber filled with bodies and the humid heat of freshly spilled blood. And then, suddenly, it was over. Only the groans of the wounded and dying broke the silence.

Orgrim staggered up a narrow wooden staircase. The second tower was theirs! They had conquered an entire section of the wall. Looking down from the top of the tower, he saw the warriors from other ships swarming onto the walls from the boarding ramps on the *Wraithwind*.

The pack leader supported himself wearily on a battlement. The harbor city was huge. From the sea, he discovered—as from the land—it was protected by a double ring wall. The elves were far from beaten, but they had suffered their first defeat. "You will never drive us from this wall again," he swore, exhausted. "And we will never leave Albenmark again."

THE WRONG BATTLE

O rgrim brought his report to an end. He supported himself heavily on the stump of a shattered column, feeling as weak as a newborn child— he had lost a lot of blood in the battle.

The dukes that Branbeard had gathered around him in the ruins of an elven palace looked gravely at Orgrim. Dumgar of Mordrock nodded to him respectfully. Gray-haired Mandrag chewed at his bottom lip, deep in thought.

Branbeard sniffed and spat, adding to the puddle of slime at his feet. "Once again you've used one of our ships without due care," the king said grimly. "The masts and rigging of the *Wraithwind* are wrecked."

Orgrim could not believe it!

"The *Wraithwind* drew the fire of an entire section of that wall. When the elves realized that we presented the greatest danger, they stopped shooting at the other ships completely. Are you reproaching me for succeeding where other pack leaders failed? Would you have preferred our attack to fail again?"

"Don't bite off what you can't chew, whelp!" Branbeard had jumped to his feet and pointed the thigh bone he'd been gnawing on at Orgrim. "You think too highly of yourself. Other pack leaders have been complaining because you took away their best seamen and warriors. You won because you commanded the best of all the packs, not because you're the hero you obviously think you are."

"Don't be unfair, Branbeard," old Mandrag said. "We all know that it was not Orgrim who poached the best men from the other leaders. And he is a courageous fighter. He and the giant Gran were the first on the wall. Rather than criticize him, you should offer him the place of honor at your table, like the kings of our people have done with brave pack leaders since time began."

"*You* think you can tell me what a king has to do? Just because you led our people for a while, do you think you know what it takes to be a king?" Branbeard said venomously.

"Enough!" Skanga snarled. "You are the king, and no one doubts that." The shaman straightened up and stepped into the circle of dukes. "It was a mistake to attack Reilimee, Branbeard. They were warned. It was clear from the start that we would not overrun Reilimee as easily as we took Vahan Calyd."

"Keep your nose out of the business of warriors!" Branbeard threw the bone aside in anger. "Maybe it was rash to risk this battle, but we can't back down now. If we retreat without a victory, it will send a signal to all the races of Albenmark. It will encourage them to oppose us. Reilimee must fall! And this time we let no one escape. When we move on from here, this city will be a field of corpses!"

As much as Orgrim despised his king, he had to agree with what Branbeard said. They could not afford to lose this battle.

"Besides, we need the supplies the city has to offer. All that meat, the well-stocked storehouses . . . the Snaiwamark is meager country. It can't provide for an army as big as ours in winter." Branbeard smiled patronizingly at Skanga. "Don't tell me how to run a war, woman. You know well enough that my soul is rich with the wisdom of many kings."

"Yes. And the arrogance of many kings lives on in you, too. I see very clearly the benefits that victory here means for us. But think about Phylangan. Landoran is a cunning elf. He will know that we are coming. And with every day we lose here, he grows stronger, while our warriors bleed to death before Reilimee's walls. The entrance to Whale Bay is still ice-free, and we can make it a long way west with our ships. With every day we lose, the ice wanders farther south. When Whale Bay freezes, our march to Phylangan will be hundreds of miles longer. Every mile will wear at the strength of our men, while Landoran grows stronger and stronger."

Branbeard laughed in her face. "This is exactly why women don't wage war. They paint everything in such grim colors that they are defeated before the first battle even begins. What is the point of your carping? What is it you want to say to me?" His eyes locked onto Orgrim. "You're a hero, aren't you? The resourceful one, the one who builds bridges in masts to storm walls. What would you do? I know the ambition in you. Show me now that you have the brains a duke needs, not merely the courage."

Orgrim tried to picture the maps of the northern lands that he had studied before their departure for Albenmark. Phylangan lay at the end of a long, ice-covered pass. From the east, that was the only way to reach the stone garden.

"What is it, whelp? Lost your tongue?" the king goaded. "Is that all you really have inside? Silence?"

214

"Between Whale Bay and the pass that leads to Phylangan lies barren land. The elves believe that we are tied down here. But if four or five ships leave the fleet and sail north to Whale Bay, it should not attract too much attention. I think we could be able to take them by surprise. With a thousand fighters, I could cut off their supply route to the east until you arrive with the main army, Branbeard."

"So you want to cut off their supplies. A thousand warriors would do it?" The king sniffed and spat. "An army like that would have to be led by a duke. Is that what you're thinking, you treacherous dog?"

"You asked me what I would do—"

"Silence, Orgrim! I know you! And you want to get away from here and wage your own war. All right, you've got it! I'll give you *one* ship. Two hundred fighters."

"That is too few, my king!" Mandrag said. "When the elves discover how weak his forces are, they will wipe them out."

"More unasked advice, old man." Branbeard turned to face Mandrag. "You will go with the whelp. He seems to be close to your heart."

"All our men are close to my heart," replied Mandrag icily. "Only a fool wastes the lives of warriors."

"Well then, you'd better stick your clever heads together and come up with a plan to get through. Tying bridges to masts won't do it this time, I'm sorry to say."

Orgrim was churning inside. His feeling swung between ire and pride. The king was demanding the impossible. But hadn't it also seemed impossible, just a few days before, to storm the walls of Reilimee from the ships? Now he had his own command, far away from Branbeard's army. If he completed this task well, then not even Branbeard would be able to deny him the title of duke.

"He will take the *Wraithwind*," Skanga said in a voice that brooked no protest. "And Birga will go with him. She will find out what preparations have been made in Phylangan."

Birga was considered a foster daughter to Skanga, and her reputation was almost as bad as the shaman's. Birga was so ugly that she had, allegedly, never touched a male, though some warriors copulated even with hollow tree trunks to purge their excess broth.

The idea that the hag would always be nearby in the future made Orgrim shudder.

PASSION

Ollowain stepped into blinding white. The fabric-covered door slid closed almost silently behind him. The room he had been allocated in the mountain fortress was deceptive to the eye. Everything in it was white. The walls. The large bed. Even the barinstones set into the rock radiated white light and had been placed so skillfully that he himself cast no shadow.

There wasn't a single sharp edge in the room. The walls blended into the ceiling in a gentle curve. The bed was an elongated oval. Even the door through which Ollowain had just entered was round. The milky-white light contributed to blurring any contours.

The swordmaster heard water pouring. He looked around tiredly. His room was large and manifestly designed to confuse the senses. He unbuckled his sword belt and laid it on the bed before looking around more carefully. It was some time before he discovered a white curtain that concealed a small room beyond, where he found a bath. That room, too, was completely white. The basin had been carved directly into the rock and did not look very deep. Pale vapors rose from the water, caressing Ollowain's face. The bottom of the basin was uneven, inviting a bather to stretch out. Beside it stood a low marble massage table with an oval, padded, leather-rimmed opening for one's head. The warm, moist air in the room was pregnant with the scent of exotic flowers. The fragrance made him feel lethargic and sleepy.

Ollowain returned to the main room. He removed the coarsely woven clothes that Alfadas had given him and stretched out on the blanket, which had been sewn from snow-rabbit pelts. The fur felt wonderfully soft against his skin.

After their encounter in the pavilion, Landoran had insisted on having them appear before the council of elders. The council, like Landoran, had rapidly acquiesced to handing over command of Phylangan to Lyndwyn. Such an excessive display of trust was not like his people at all, Ollowain thought. They had never before subjugated themselves to anyone. For centuries, they had even refused to attend the Festival of Light to pay homage to Emerelle as queen, and now they bowed to her supposed order. Something was not right!

They had not even spent much time debating whether to tolerate a small army from the human world as brothers in arms in their fight against the trolls. The discussion had covered no more than details like what humans ate or how they could come up with enough amulets to protect them from the deadly cold of the Snaiwamark. Landoran, however, had flatly refused to allow the Fjordlanders to enter the Skyhall in Phylangan via the Albenstar. He wanted them to use a gateway that opened in the foothills of the Slanga Mountains, some three hundred miles away. A small troop of elves would wait for them there and lead them up to the ice plain, from where they would sail to Phylangan. Landoran explained that he felt it was smarter if the humans, at first, did not see many elves, to give them time to get used to them. And they should get to know the land in which they would be fighting a war. He also had in mind that they should unite with the centaurs on the ice plain. It all sounded very reasonable, and yet Ollowain had the feeling that the prince was only looking for excuses to keep them as far away from Phylangan as possible.

The entire council had paid court to Lyndwyn. She had to take out the Albenstone again and again and show it to them, and they had her repeat three or four times the lie about how Emerelle had entrusted her with the artifact. Were they all blind? Or did they trust Lyndwyn because she was there with him, the true and honest soldier of the queen? His thoughts kept circling around these questions.

Something pressed gently on his temples. He had fallen asleep. Hands caressed his cheeks, glided over the nape of his neck, and began to massage his taut muscles.

Ollowain opened his eyes. The pale face of a woman was leaning over his own, the irises of her eyes as red as blood. Her hair was pulled back tightly and as white as snow. Even her skin was flawless white but for the thin blue veins beneath the skin. Ollowain had never seen her before. "Who are you?"

"Lysilla, from the people of the Normirga," she said calmly while she continued to massage the muscles of his neck.

Was he still dreaming? Ollowain looked around uncertainly. The white chamber was as if made for him. Was it too perfect to be real? And yet . . . Landoran perhaps still remembered how obsessed he had been with the color white as a child. There had even been a time when all he wanted to eat was white food.

Ollowain stretched his neck to better see Lysilla, who was standing behind him. She wore a tight, pure-white wrap dress. He had to smile—this was a dream!

"So you want to be able to see me. But don't get tense. Just tell me." Lysilla stepped to the side of the bed. She laid her hands on his chest; they were warm and felt pleasant. For a moment, she pressed his nipples between her thumb and forefinger, and a warm shudder ran through him. Her hands slid up to his throat. Was it perhaps not a dream at all?

"Who has sent you?"

"No one. They talked about you, Ollowain. But no one sent me." Her hands brushed over his eyes. "Don't look at me. Don't look at anything. Just feel. As long as you keep your eyes open, you cannot be free."

Ollowain obeyed but hesitantly. Lysilla's hands slid around to the back of his neck again. They were strong. He felt callouses on her right hand, but the skin of her left was soft. He knew what that meant. He knew only one kind of work that caused callouses only on the right hand. He opened his eyes and tried to sit up, but Lysilla pushed him back down.

"You are a fighter, aren't you? A sword fighter."

She laughed. "I would not be so presumptuous to call myself that. I am a student of sword fighting, but I am much better at what I am presently doing, at least if you follow my instructions."

"Why should I close my eyes?" Ollowain asked warily.

"You will be able to relax better. And even polite liars can't really bear to look me in the face for long. My eyes . . . they unsettle others. To say anything else is well-mannered nonsense."

She was right. The red irises of her eyes were uncanny. Her gaze was penetrating, disdainful . . . sensual?

"Why are you doing this?"

Her finger touched his lips. "Don't ask. Do you want to experience something wonderful? One or two perfect hours? Then don't ask."

"But—"

"Trust me. Words destroy the beauty of the moment." She took his hand. "Stand up. Come with me." Lysilla crossed to the bathroom. On the floor stood several small crystal bottles that had not been there before. The strange, intoxicating fragrance still lingered in the moist air.

She pointed at the stone massage table. "Lie down. You will enjoy it."

Ollowain obeyed. He was curious. He had never met anyone like Lysilla before.

The stone of the marble table was astonishingly warm. He bedded his face against the leather padding. Something oily dripped onto his back, and then her hands were on him again, strong and tender. Skillfully, she kneaded the tense muscles at the back of his neck. Then her hands slipped down his back. She leaned forward until he felt her body touch his. She was no longer wearing a dress!

"Turn over," she breathed softly.

A strand of her hair had come loose and fell over her shoulder. Lysilla had the small breasts of a warrior woman. The musculature of her right arm was more pronounced. What was he doing? He was looking at her with the eyes of a sword-fighting teacher.

Lysilla leaned forward again. She picked up the band from her dress. "Let me bind your eyes, or else the magic cannot work." She smiled mysteriously. "Stop thinking. Just feel."

Ollowain let it happen. She wrapped the fabric of the band over his eyes twice and pulled the blindfold tight. "Listen to the rush of the water." Lysilla laid one hand on his chest, the second beneath his neck, and gently pushed him back until he was lying flat again. Oil dripped onto his chest. Her fingers toyed with his nipples, then slid down between his thighs. Then she cupped his testes in one hand. Her grip tightened until a sweet pain made him groan.

Ollowain felt dizzy, although he was lying down. Now her hands were feeling their way over his belly. He bucked, moaned. It was as if she were drawing trails of flame across his skin. He wanted her fingers to go deeper again, and at the same time, he did not want her to stop what she was doing just then. Her skin felt softer . . . It must have been the oil.

"Come into the water. I will lead you." She took one hand in hers.

He sat up obediently. She took his other hand. He slipped from the side of the marble table and felt the cool stone floor underfoot. The dizzy feeling increased. To trust another so completely was a new feeling for him. There had to be some kind of intoxicant among the scents rising from the water, he thought.

"Careful, there's a step."

Abashed, Ollowain laughed. He was no longer the master of his senses. Lysilla's voice sounded like it came from beside him, but she was right in front of him! She still held both his hands in hers.

Deliciously warm water swept around his ankles. Feeling his way forward cautiously with his feet, he stepped deeper into the basin until the water came above his hips.

Lysilla pulled him to her. Her breasts pressed against him. Ollowain sensed her arousal, and he felt her thighs embrace his hips. Their lips met, and he kissed her passionately. Then he dug his teeth into the soft flesh of her neck, caressed her breasts, dived down, and let his tongue explore her most hidden parts.

Lysilla pulled him into shallower water. Their love play grew wilder. They fell on each other like wildcats fighting. Ollowain resisted the urge to remove the blindfold. Although it was soaked through, it still hid all sight of his passionate playmate. He had never done anything like this before, not in all the centuries he had lived! What he had missed! And he had never before given himself to an elf woman he had known not even an hour.

In the past, his love affairs had always been conducted in slow, tentative steps. A shy search for proof that his affection would be returned, and always prepared, at any moment, to retreat into the false safety of loneliness.

Lysilla's body shivered. She let out a long, pleasurable groan. Her breath brushed his face. Then, without warning, she bit his bottom lip. The metallic taste of blood filled his mouth.

Ollowain reared up. Lysilla's hands caressed his chest. She had not said a word since they had stepped into the water. The language of passion alone expressed what no words could say.

Lysilla's bite had scared Ollowain, yet had driven him to greater ecstasy. Now her hands seemed to be everywhere at once. She dictated the rhythm of their lovemaking, and he enjoyed it. He put off the moment . . . the brief instant of release.

Wherever her fingers glided over his skin, he responded with trembling. His body felt as if it belonged completely to her. She made him shout with joy or hunger for the next touch. And then she set him free, ending his sweet torture. He cried out loud, over and over, rose up and embraced her. Wrapped around each other, they sat in the water. Too exhausted to keep going. Her hands stroked his back as if consoling a child.

The magic was gone. Her touch no longer set his skin aflame. It was pleasant. Calming. Slowly, sense and reason returned. A warning voice penetrated the ebbing current of lust. Something was wrong. Something had been wrong the whole time. Lysilla's right hand . . . there were no calluses!

In shock, Ollowain grasped the blindfold and pulled it down. Through the confusion of wet, black hair, he found himself looking into green eyes sprinkled with gold. Lyndwyn's eyes!

"It was the only way," she said softly. "We would never have got closer than we did on the bridge, when we looked into each other's eyes. Your reason would have silenced your heart."

Ollowain still could not believe what had happened. "Lysilla, how . . ."

"She found it . . . interesting. Landoran was the one who decided to send her to you. She was supposed to massage you and . . . cheer you up. His words. He said something about how you were besotted with everything the color of snow. And thus, Lysilla. Landoran seems to know you very well . . . he knows everything about you. I could not bear the thought that Lysilla . . ." She faltered. "For her it would have been no more than a game. She thinks you are interesting. I . . . I persuaded her to . . ."

Ollowain felt as if he were standing naked in the middle of a snowstorm. Although the room was almost oppressively warm, he slung his arms across his chest. He could not believe what had happened. Or that he had not noticed! What was going on with him? "How did you persuade her?" he asked quietly, too hurt to be harsh, let alone to abuse Lyndwyn.

"She wanted something from me. I'm not allowed to speak about it. It is no betrayal. A secret, rather . . ."

"What?"

Lyndwyn swept her wet hair out of her face. "I can't tell you," she said. "I don't regret it, Ollowain. It was the right thing. If you could listen to your heart, then you would know that, too."

"What? That I desire a traitor, a thief? You stole the greatest treasure of our people. And today your lies made you the ruler of Phylangan and made me . . ." He could not find the words. She had simply taken him for herself, just as she had taken the Albenstone.

"Emerelle would have died in Vahan Calyd if I had not used the power of the stone. I was too weak to heal just with my own power. I tried! It almost killed me. Ollowain, you saw that for yourself! Creating the firebird drained my powers. How do you think I was able to heal all of you?"

"You healed me with a knife in my throat. What was that? Were the powers of the Albenstone exhausted when it was my turn?"

She shook her head. Tears brimmed in her eyes. "When I use magical power to heal someone close to death, then I reach deep inside them. I share their pain, and sometimes their soul . . . opens up to me. I longed for that, but it could not be allowed to happen in that way. To know you had to be your gift to me."

"Pretty words," said Ollowain bitterly. "I only wish they had not been spoken by a thief. How am I supposed to believe you after you took me like this?"

Her head sank. "Yes, how are you supposed to believe me, my white knight? My father told me the story about the Shalyn Falah, about how you fought the trolls and how you refused to murder the princes. He had a lot of respect for you."

"Of course," Ollowain sniffed. "Your family respects anyone who opposes the queen."

"That was before the feud with Emerelle began. And as much as I detested her, I admired you. Always. I avoided ever meeting you, just to preserve my girlish dreams of the white knight of the Shalyn Falah. The first time I ever saw you was in Vahan Calyd. I was in the crowd on the street when someone shot at Emerelle. And I saw how you protected the queen with your own body. In that moment, I knew that you were the same man in real life that you were in my dreams. And I could no longer do what my grandfather had asked me to. You never had to worry that I would kidnap you and take you through the Albenpaths to Arkadien. I can never go back there. Emerelle was supposed to die after she had put the crown on her head. My bird of light was to light up the quarterdeck so brightly that my brother could not miss her. And if he did miss after all, then I was supposed to kill her myself. But . . . I could not go through with it anymore after I saw you. I positioned myself in front of the queen so that my body shielded her from my brother's arrow. And I sent the bird out to sea. It was not a signal to the trolls and their ships. Don't get me wrong—I still despised Emerelle. But I could not be party to murdering her, not under your eyes. I . . ." She laughed. "As childish as it is . . . when I discovered that you were exactly as I had always imagined, I wanted you to like me. At any price. I wanted to be yours."

Ollowain looked at her incredulously. Could he believe her now? His mistrust had been right all along. And at the same time, he had been mistaken. "I should not leave you anywhere near Emerelle again."

"That is your decision. When I healed her, I was very close to her soul. And it is terrible, Ollowain." She shuddered, and for a moment, the swordmaster had the feeling that a shadow had touched Lyndwyn's own soul. She was a schemer, and he did not trust her all-too-childish declarations of love, but the encounter with Emerelle's soul seemed truly to have frightened her.

"You do not know the queen you serve," Lyndwyn said. "She is every inch a Normirga. Every sense of ethics or morality is subjugated to one single thought: She wants to protect Albenmark. Somewhere beyond the Albenpaths, a terrible enemy is hiding, one of whom even Emerelle is afraid. She is so intent on defeating him that she is willing to sacrifice anything for that goal. She knew that Vahan Calyd would be attacked. And she knew that she would be severely injured. She accepted all of that to prevent the paths that lead into the future from falling into disarray. Because whether we one day defeat the old enemy or whether Albenmark is completely destroyed is dependent on the lives of only a few. And as far as the war with the trolls, Emerelle wanted the trolls to win at Vahan Calyd." She paused and peered into his eyes. Ollowain swallowed. "She sacrificed the city and thousands of Albenkin with it! I healed her. Her body no longer shows any wounds, but her soul is a bottomless pit of agony. There is only one reason why she won't wake up: she is fleeing from what she has done!"

Now Ollowain shook his head resolutely. "Lies! The lies of a thief and murderess!"

Lyndwyn looked at him for a long time. Her eyes were beautiful. They looked so innocent.

"I know you have to see me as a traitor to go on being the white knight of the Shalyn Falah." She stood up and waded through the shallow basin.

The sight of her standing, naked, aroused him. "Where are you going?" he asked angrily.

"I will now pay my price for the one time I truly deceived you. You know what they say: Passion is one side of the coin, suffering the other. Farewell, my white knight." She stepped out through the door and was gone.

Ollowain looked at the blindfold floating on the water in front of him. He felt as if he were still unable to see. He was incapable of telling deception from truth. Had she lied to him? Had Emerelle known about the trolls' attack on Vahan Calyd before it happened? The strange sedan chair seemed to bear out Lyndwyn's claims. At the very least, Emerelle seemed to know that she would have to flee that night and that she would need a boat. And though he could not then understand her motives, he was certain that Emerelle would only ever act in the best interests of Albenmark.

"Lyndwyn?"

No answer. She was probably right. With eyes that could see, he would never have found himself there with her. And yet everything had felt so right, so perfect. He had never loved another woman with such passion. Her own passion, too, had not seemed feigned. Was she telling the truth? Again and again, her words returned: *Passion is one side of the coin, suffering the other.*

A TALK IN THE NIGHT

K nowing what was coming, Alfadas could find no peace. He had even considered taking Asla and the children with him to Albenmark and trying to escape the trolls there. But as a human, where was he supposed to go among the Albenkin? Too many knew him. Who would take in the queen's foster son if the trolls were pursuing her? However he turned things in his mind, his position was hopeless. If Asla stayed in Firnstayn, then she was at least among friends. In the village in which she grew up, she would most easily get through if he did not return.

It was dark when Alfadas made his way down the narrow path that led to the fjord. An unassuming hut close to the water was his goal. Behind the thinly shaved leather that kept the wind out of the only hole to admit any sunlight, a yellow light burned.

Alfadas hesitated for a moment in front of the hut. Was he doing the right thing? He turned his head back and looked up at the stars, as if the answer lay up there. The ghostly green faerylight swept in wide billows across the night sky. Alfadas thought wistfully of the stories his father had told him on such nights, when they had been traveling together. On nights like this, the elves and trolls came to the world of humans, it was said. And this autumn, those stories had come true. His fellowship with the elves had not brought him any luck.

Alfadas made up his mind and stepped to the door of the small hut. He had to get the things in order in this world before he went to Albenmark. Beyond the door, he heard Kalf humming and banging about busily. When Alfadas knocked, the tune fell silent. The door swung open. Kalf looked at him in surprise. The solidly built fisherman was slowly getting older. At his temples, his long blond hair had receded quite a way. Small creases had appeared around his eyes and at the corners of his mouth. Alfadas knew that he was not exactly the fisherman's most welcome guest, but he was asked to come in amiably enough. Somewhat embarrassed, Kalf cleared away a few items of clothing that were strewn around the floor.

The small hut was heavy with the intense smell of fish. On the table lay three lithe silver bodies. Their bellies were slit open, and Kalf had already begun to scale them.

"The first salmon," said Alfadas, surprised.

Kalf grinned like a young boy who had just pulled off a prank. "They got past you this year, Jarl. They came up the fjord with the dusk. It's still only a few . . . the first scouts of the big migration."

Alfadas looked enviously at the salmon. The silver harvest had begun, and he had to go away. In the next two weeks, countless thousands of salmon would move up the fjord and then on into the small rivers and streams, all the way up to the mountains. They brought a second harvest to the village. Their delicate pink flesh would get Firnstayn through the winter. Tomorrow, the fires would be kindled in the dark smokehouses.

Alfadas sat down on a stool. Traditionally, whoever caught the first salmon had a good year ahead, so he had come to the right house.

"Kids are well?" Kalf asked awkwardly.

"Yes . . . no." Alfadas straightened his sword belt. The pommel of the sword was pressing into his side uncomfortably. "Yes, they're well, but I'm not. I try not to let it show in front of them. I will take Ulric with me tomorrow when I ride to Honnigsvald to assemble the army. I would like to have the boy around me. Kadlin is too young . . . and Asla can't leave here. The salmon, you know. For the next two weeks, the village will need every pair of hands it can get." He stared gloomily into the half-burned fire. "I wish I could be here myself."

Kalf took his knife and sliced one of the large salmon into pieces. He pushed the chunks onto a spit, which he hung over the fire. Both men fell silent. Salmon fat hissed as it dripped into the coals.

Alfadas was grateful that Kalf did not plague him with questions. The fisherman took a hunk of bread out of a linen sack and set it on the table. Then he filled a plain wooden mug from a pitcher.

"I'm here because of Asla," said Alfadas, breaking the silence.

Kalf's clear, blue eyes narrowed. "Ah." That was all he had to say to that.

Alfadas knew that if he had not come to Firnstayn that late-summer day eight years earlier, then Asla would have married Kalf. The fisherman was jarl himself back then. And Kalf was popular in the village, although—or perhaps for that reason—he was a man who generally said little.

When Alfadas had come to Firnstayn with his father and the elves, Asla had fallen under the stranger's spell. Night after night, she had hung on every word he spoke as he sat by the shore or the fire and told all the curious listeners about the adventures he'd had with Mandred and the elves.

But since then, the stranger's spell had turned into a curse. That was what stood between him and his wife, more than the king's long military campaigns, which often took him far away for many moons at a time.

"Will you keep an eye on Asla?" Alfadas spoke very softly. He had to overcome a great deal just to get the words out.

Kalf still loved Asla. He could have had any young woman in the village. Even today, older though he was. His popularity was undimmed, though they no longer elected him to be jarl.

But the fisherman had preferred to stay unmarried. Alfadas was certain that if not for Asla, he and Kalf would be friends. He had a lot of respect for the big man, even if he did not like to see him at his house.

Kalf peered at him. "Asla is a woman who can look after herself very well, Jarl. You know that."

"I have never been away in winter." Alfadas thought of how, in recent winters, he had sat by the fire through the dark days and whittled wood. Or how he and Ulric had leaped over tables and benches in wild duels with the wooden swords he carved. Winter had always healed the wounds of summer. He had lain entire nights with Asla in his arms and listened to the howling of the storm winds. And they had loved each other. Almost every night. In winter, he could be for her the man she wished him to be.

"It will be hard for Ulric." Alfadas's voice sounded as raw as it sometimes did in the mornings, when he had drunk too much mead the night before. "He had been looking forward to the winter with me. I promised him that I would take him hunting in the mountains. Will you teach him how to hunt, Kalf?"

The fisherman smiled amiably. "You don't learn to hunt in a single winter. I'll be happy to take him stalking with me. But don't worry. You'll still have plenty to teach him when you come back." Kalf took the spit from the fire and laid it on the table in front of Alfadas. "You did not catch the first salmon of the season this time, but it would be my pleasure if you were the first to taste the fruits of the silver harvest."

Alfadas appreciated the gesture. He cautiously bit off a piece of the hot fish. It was deliciously juicy. Fat ran from the corners of his mouth.

Kalf ate, too. "It'll be a good year for the fish," he announced, both cheeks full.

Alfadas nodded. Had Kalf not understood what he was hinting at when he mentioned hunting? No man on the fjord would ever ask another to teach his son the art of hunting, unless . . .

He could not avoid speaking candidly. Hints were out of place here. He would find no peace if he could not know for certain that Kalf had understood him.

"Every victory is paid for with the dead," he said abruptly.

Kalf simply looked at him and kept eating.

"If something happens to me, I would like you to look after the welfare of my family! I know that if you raise my son, he will become a good and decent man. I am sure Asla thinks the same."

Kalf pushed the fish on the spit aside. "You are the best sword fighter in the Fjordlands. Who do you think can beat you?"

"Where we are going, I was never more than a talented student. Marching to war against the trolls is as insane as if I ordered you to catch a falling oak. It does not matter how skillful or strong you are, the trunk of the tree will crush you to pulp if you get in its way. That's how it will be if we stand in the path of the trolls."

Kalf frowned. "You should tell that to the king."

"He knows it."

The fisherman shook his head. "That makes no sense."

"He wants to get rid of me, Kalf. Me and many more of his fighters."

"You have never been beaten, Jarl. Why should he send you to your death? He would only be hurting himself if he sacrifices you. I am certain you will return."

Alfadas sighed. Kalf had every reason not to be unhappy if he did not come back. It was he, after all, who had knocked the fisherman's life sideways. And now here was Kalf, trying to encourage him. He had come to the right man!

"I know you still love Asla."

"What's that got to do with your war?"

"If she needs help, be there for her and the children. That's all I want to ask."

"I always have been," said Kalf gently, and his tone made Alfadas wince inwardly.

"And you're right. I am damned hard to kill. Don't forget that."

The fisherman smiled disarmingly. "I'm not the one you have to convince of that."

Alfadas had a lump in his throat. The goddamned son of a bitch! He had every reason to wish the jarl dead. Alfadas opened the leather pouch on his belt. He took out the shriveled foot of a bird, as big as a child's hand, and laid it on the table.

"What is that?" Kalf asked in surprise.

"The secret of why the fish always bite better for me than for you. It comes from Albenmark. My father gave it to me. He won it from a manhorse in a bet. I don't know what kind of bird it comes from, but it attracts fish. You only have to hang it in the water, stand still, and wait a little while."

Kalf took the foot, turned it in his fingers, and looked at it from every side. "And there I was railing against the gods because you were even a better fisherman than me. Don't expect me to return it when you come back next spring."

There was something infectious about Kalf's confidence. "I'll just bring a new bird's foot with me from Albenmark. Don't think I'm going to let you become king of the fishermen without a fight." Alfadas laughed. But the fear suddenly returned. It sat in his belly like a heavy block of ice.

REBELS, FARMERS, AND
A FEW GOOD MEN

There's that woman again," said Ulric quietly. The boy was sitting on the saddle in front of Alfadas and pointed to a slim figure standing some distance ahead of them in the shadow of a birch tree. Alfadas and Ulric had almost reached Honnigsvald. Silwyna had followed them the entire way.

"How can she be as fast as us on a horse?"

"Silwyna is Maurawan," Alfadas explained. "She is one of an elven folk that lives in the forests. She is very skilled in finding shortcuts, and we haven't exactly been racing along."

"She isn't running ahead of us this time, Father. What does she want from us?"

"We will ask her." The elf woman waited for them, leaning against the pale birch trunk. Her heavy braid was wrapped around her neck like a snake. She was now wearing trousers and a shirt made of light-colored leather. The torn clothes she had been wearing when she came to the Fjordlands were gone. Alfadas recalled ruefully that she had once given him a leather shirt. It had special fringes that stopped water from penetrating through the seams. It seemed such an endlessly long time since they had roamed together through the forests of Albenmark.

"You sit a saddle well, young man," said the woman pleasantly as they rode up.

"My father is going to give me a pony when we get to Honnigsvald," Ulric declared proudly. "Why are you following us? And why aren't you with your queen, like Yilvina?"

"I'm going to help your father when he chooses the fighters who are going to go with him. Besides, they should get to see an elf woman at least once before they enter my land. When it comes to the queen, one bodyguard is more than enough for someone resting in the house of a friend. We would be insulting your parents if the queen was constantly surrounded by armed guards. We are not among enemies here, after all."

Ulric nodded. "Why do the elven women fight? They don't do that here."

For a moment, Silwyna seemed insulted. "Among elves, there are so few men that they couldn't win without the help of the women," she finally answered archly.

"Does that mean you have a lot of wars?"

"That's enough, Ulric," said Alfadas. "It isn't polite to interrogate someone like that."

"It's all right. Your son just wants to get to know me." Silwyna strode along beside them as they followed a narrow game path through the woods. The trees were bright with autumn leaves, and every breath of the breeze made thousands fall. Red, purple, and gold rained down around them. The forest was celebrating a final time before the long months of darkness and storms began.

Alfadas was surprised at how patiently Silwyna answered all his son's questions. She had changed. From the outside, there was nothing different . . . or was he the one who had changed? Was he looking at her with different eyes? There was a time in which he had hated her. She had taught him what it meant to suffer. And despite everything, she was still close to his heart. Just seeing her was enough to revive all the long-buried feelings.

"Grandfather says there are elves who can run through the trees like squirrels," said Ulric. "Is that true?"

"My father-in-law is a talkative old man," Alfadas apologized.

"It seems to me that the boy knows more about Albenmark than you do, although he has never seen the wonders of my world."

"Oh yes. Grandfather knows so many stories!" Ulric cried enthusiastically. "When Papa isn't home, he comes every evening and tells us all about the queen and the elves, about my grandpa Mandred and the manhorses and the trolls."

I have to have a word with Erek, thought Alfadas angrily. There was a reason he did not tell the children about Albenmark, regardless of how much Ulric pestered him about it. He did not want to plant any longing for that distant world in their hearts. Unlike him, it was not their lot to spend half their days gazing up at the stone circle on top of the Hartungscliff, dreaming about a world that they could not reach by themselves.

"Would you like to find out for yourself what it's like to run through the treetops, Ulric?" Silwyna asked.

"Would you take me with you?"

"If you trust yourself to ride on my back. And only with your father's permission, of course."

Alfadas sighed. How could he refuse now? The Maurawan looked at him with her wolf's eyes, and he had the feeling that it would mean a lot to her to climb through the trees with his son. Did she perhaps envy Asla her children? The jarl recalled some of the less pleasant stories that were told about the elves. About how they stole children . . . would Silwyna ever do something like that? There had been a time when he believed that he could read her eyes, that he knew her. Now he knew better.

"Please, Papa! Say yes," Ulric pleaded.

"I'll see you down by the fjord," he finally grumbled. Back then, the elves had not come for him without a reason. His own father, Mandred, had sold him to Emerelle. Silwyna would take good care of Ulric.

She handed Alfadas her bow, quiver, and hunting bag, which she had slung over her shoulder. Ulric clambered excitedly onto her back. He slung his legs around her hips and his arms around her neck.

"Don't tell your mother a word about this little excursion," Alfadas warned him.

Ulric grinned conspiratorially.

"Don't worry, nothing will happen," said Silwyna in the language of her people. "I will bring him back in one piece."

It was a strange feeling to see Ulric depart with the elf woman . . . the same woman that Alfadas had once been in love with to the point of madness. She ran into the forest with the boy and had vanished in seconds.

Slowly, the jarl turned his gray down the slope toward the fjord. It took him almost half an hour to reach the water, and Ulric and Silwyna were already waiting for him. His son came running toward him, beaming broadly, although he also looked a little pale. "We passed a squirrel," he shouted. "And we saw tons of nests. Silwyna talked to a raven."

Alfadas pulled his son up onto the saddle again and returned Silwyna's weapons. Something seemed to be weighing on her. "You have raised a good boy," she said, but nothing more.

An hour later, they reached the ferry and crossed the fjord to Honnigsvald. The three brothers that Alfadas had met the last time were nowhere in sight.

Instead, a garrulous old man rowed them across in a small skiff. Surreptitiously, Alfadas glanced down into the dark waters. Deep beneath their keel, he saw a silver shimmer: hundreds of fish swimming north.

A large crowd had gathered on the other shore, and a tall, thickset soldier with his hair cut very short was standing on a block of stone, addressing those who had answered the king's summons. Alfadas knew the man. It was Ragni, one of the king's bodyguards. The soldier waved to him.

"Here comes the duke. Look at him! That is what a champion looks like!"

Everyone turned. Alfadas recognized a few old hands in the crowd, companions from past campaigns. But there were also men among them who carried scythes, hammers, or axes that had been forged into makeshift weapons. Impoverished farmers, day laborers, messengers, craftsman who had lost their businesses. Young men, too, in search of adventure. The three brothers from the ferry were also there. This was no army. It was a gathering of the hopeless, those who no longer had anything to gain in the Fjordlands under aging King Horsa.

"Will they all listen to you, Papa?"

"I certainly hope so." Alfadas swung out of the saddle, handed the reins to Silwyna, and said in her language, "Take the boy over there to the forest. I don't want him to hear what I have to tell the men."

Silwyna nodded. Alfadas looked at his "army," hardly more than seven hundred men, he estimated. One group of warriors was particularly conspicuous because they stood there in chains. A black-haired man, his nose slashed deeply and recently by a sword, was the most unmistakable among them. *Another familiar face,* thought the jarl. "Well, Lambi. More trouble with the women?" All around, the men grinned.

"If the king had sent women to ask me to come here, then this would not have been necessary." He raised his hands so that the others could see the heavy iron rings with which he had been chained up. "Release me, Alfadas. Let me go, and I won't tell the greenhorns here what a winter campaign means."

"If I let you go, I'll be losing half the fighting strength of my army," Alfadas replied airily. "And we don't want this splendid squad to go the same way as your nose. Want to tell me how that happened?"

"The king's bastards caught me in my sleep!" He pointed to Ragni. "And that gutless bastard was in charge of 'em."

"He resisted the king's order," Ragni shot back. "He provoked us. His goods have been confiscated, and if he stays here, he'll be hanged. He should be grateful to Horsa that he's even allowed to go with you."

"And why are you here, Ragni?"

"Horsa has made me a war jarl. When I return, he's promised me a farm of my own. I'm here to be your second in command."

"So be it!" *The crafty old devil got you cheaply,* Alfadas thought. He climbed up onto the rock beside Ragni so that all the men could see him.

"All those who have fought in battle, raise your sword arm." The result was a crushing blow. Not even one in ten raised his hand, and a large proportion of the experienced warriors had been taken there in chains. Those men would never take orders from Ragni, and the paupers would only halfheartedly follow a man who had been won over with a title and a promise of land. He needed more lieutenants, and he had to set an example to give his troops more reason to stick together.

"Think you can climb up on this rock with half a nose, Lambi?"

"Yeah. And I'll even kick you in the ass up there if you say another word about my nose, Duke!"

Alfadas reached out his hand and pulled Lambi up onto the rock. "I'd like to introduce all of you to Lambi, about whose nose one does not speak, as one of your war jarls! I know him to be a good fighter and a wise leader. Listen to what he says when he is not swearing—it could save your life one day."

"I would not say that I'm a good choice," Lambi said, with no effort to speak any softer than usual. "You're all welcome to hear it: I promise our duke that I will clear off the first chance I get. Anyone who voluntarily goes to Albenmark to fight gigantic trolls must be out of his mind!"

Alfadas clapped him on the shoulder. "As you can all see, our new war jarl is a man who likes to speak frankly. And he has earned a frank answer. You will go down in history as the first war jarl in the Fjordlands to train his men in chains and to be led to the battlefield in chains. But putting that aside, you can take my word for it that Lambi is a man you can trust, as long as you don't lend him money, leave him alone with a woman he likes the look of, or stupidly turn your back to him."

Some of the men below them laughed, presumably those who did not yet know Lambi and thought he was joking. "Mag of Honnigsvald, come up here and join us. You, too, will be one of my war jarls."

The young ferryman was clearly unimpressed at his promotion, but his two brothers pushed him forward. When he finally stood on the rock beside Alfadas, Mag's face was bright red. He stared out at the crowd like a mouse staring at a cat.

"As you can see, Mag is a man of few words. Some of you may be asking yourselves what it is about this young man that will make you listen to him. The answer to that is simple. Look at his face. See the half-moon he carries!"

Mag swung around and glared at Alfadas. Unbridled fury filled his eyes. "I will—"

Alfadas ignored him. "All of us have to learn to be men like Mag. For me, the half-moon he bears is not the mark of a thief's shame; it is a badge of honor! He was branded because he stole bread for himself and for his brothers. He knew the risk he was taking. He knew he did not have the strength to escape if he was caught in the act. And still he did it. I want you to be like him! I want you not to shy from any peril to help your brothers in arms. If every man in this army can find that courage, then some of us might even manage to return from Albenmark in one piece." He let his eyes scan the motley crowd before him. "I will not try to deceive you. Apart from a few outstanding soldiers like Lambi, you are all here as volunteers. When you follow me to Albenmark, perhaps one in ten will survive. Maybe all of us will perish there. I cannot even promise you that you will get rich there. We will be fighting trolls, and those monsters do not hoard treasure, but they will eat you alive if they get their hands on you. No doubt all of you have heard stories about the elves, about their unearthly skills, about how no man can defeat them in battle. That is true. Tomorrow, I will show you an elf woman. Among her people, she is considered an incomparable archer and a poor swordswoman. And yet I can guarantee that standing in front of me today, there is not more than one or two fighters who can match her with the sword."

"I bet I could beat her black-and-blue if you took my pretty bracelets off!" Lambi shouted.

Some of the men laughed. Alfadas was satisfied. Men like Lambi always found followers quickly. "All right, my friend, I'll take that bet. If you can defeat the elf Silwyna in a practice fight, then I will take away your chains and you can take to your heels. But remember that the king has promised you a hemp necklace if you don't go to Albenmark."

"I know Horsa as a man who promises much and delivers very little. If I am stupid enough to let his bailiffs catch me a second time, then I've deserved no better than the noose. But if your dainty elf manages to beat me—because I lose myself in her beautiful eyes and forget to fight, who knows?—then I promise you I will not try to flee as long as we are in Honnigsvald." Lambi reached down and grabbed his crotch with both hands, swinging his hips in a circle. "Where are the skalds? The story of Lambi and the elf girl will be better than any hero's saga! What do you say, Duke, do we have a bet? Or would you rather hide your delicate elf maid away from a real Fjordlander?"

Alfadas reached out and grasped Lambi's proffered hand. "I hope that you are an honorable man, at least when it comes to a bet."

Lambi grinned broadly. "I promise you this: you will find out."

Rebels, farmers, and a few good men—what an army, Alfadas thought. What an army. They had a right to know what they were facing. That much, at least . . . "Tomorrow, you will see how elves fight. You will be impressed. But these same elves, whom hardly any of us can match, have already lost many battles with the trolls. They fear them as a terrible enemy. One troll has the strength of four or five men, and anyone who makes the mistake of trying to parry one of their blows will be smashed to pieces. They know no fear. If five of you are able to fight in a group and protect one another, then you might just be the equal of the troll. The brutes are almost twice as big as us. Winter's bitter cold does not bother them at all, and they are fighting to get back their old homeland. Sending us to Albenmark is like throwing a child into a bear cage, turning your back, and coming back the next day to see what has happened."

None of the men were laughing now. They were upset, scared. Some stared at Alfadas with gaping mouths. None had expected a speech like that.

"For today, you are dismissed," said Alfadas. "Think about what I have said. I will not be disappointed in those who do not return here tomorrow. You are not cowards, but rather have proven your wisdom. But for those who do return, think tonight about how we puny humans can kill the trolls. Keep this in mind: once a troll is standing in front of you, you are dead. Now go."

"You will be waiting on an empty beach tomorrow," said Ragni angrily. "What the hell was that? The king will be angry when he hears about it."

"I don't believe the duke will get rid of those men so easily, Ragni," said Mag. "I know these men. They know what miserable lives they lead in the Fjordlands. Even a tiny chance of getting rich is more than what they have here."

If Mag was right, thought Alfadas, then it was very possible that even more men might be standing on the shore next morning, ready to decamp to a new world. He had to find a more drastic way to show them what would happen. Finally, he turned to the young ferryman.

"Do you think you can come up with a dozen steers in the next few days? I would gladly buy them. We ought to provide at least part of the provisions we will need ourselves and not leave everything up to the elves."

THE SMALL COUNCIL

"Where is Lyndwyn?"

No one replied. The Small Council of Phylangan had gathered in the pavilion by the Mahdan Falah. None seemed to feel personally addressed by Ollowain.

As the silence dragged on, Landoran finally took mercy on him and answered. "She is otherwise engaged. She wishes you a pleasant trip."

"How am I supposed to go without her?" the swordmaster asked in annoyance. Lyndwyn had not shown her face for ten days. Not since she had made love to him. That memory awoke a sweet torment in Ollowain. Had she really loved him? Or was that, too, only part of a sophisticated plan? She actually seemed to be recognized as the ruler of Phylangan. Ollowain had discovered that on her orders, every other Normirga settlement in the Snaiwamark had been abandoned. All elves who could contribute to their defense remained in Phylangan. The rest were sent to the stone palaces on the Carandamon plateau. It was a wise decision to give up settlements they could never properly defend and to gather their forces in one place. Ollowain had expected her to ask for his advice—he was her military adviser, after all. Supposedly . . .

But he had not seen her at all.

Ollowain again looked into the expressionless faces. The council enjoyed demeaning him, throwing his flaw back in his face! "I cannot open the gateway. Without Lyndwyn, I cannot enter the Albenpaths. Tell me how I am supposed to bring the army of humans here if she does not help me?"

"You are not meant to bring the humans here, but to take them to the Slanga Mountains," Landoran corrected him in his most infuriating tone. "In twenty days, Lyndwyn will open a gateway to the Albenstar close to Firnstayn. She will accompany you and the humans safely back here. Until then, you will have to make do with Lysilla's services. She is an experienced sorceress. Together with Ronardin, she will assist you in preparing the humans for their arrival in Albenmark and for the war."

"It is not in Emerelle's interests for the Albenstone to stay here. I demand its return!"

Landoran raised his eyebrows disapprovingly. Even as a child, Ollowain had hated that disparaging gesture.

"I don't think you can decide what is or is not in Emerelle's interest, especially as the queen has not been informed about the specific circumstances. If she were here, she would endorse what we are doing."

Ollowain was stunned. Landoran's reply, as spokesman of the council, far exceeded even his usual arrogance. The swordmaster knew his father well enough to know that resistance just then was pointless. Landoran would not hesitate to have him arrested if he rebelled against his decision.

"I submit to the wisdom of the council," Ollowain lied unctuously. When he returned, he would have an army behind him. Even if it was only an army of humans, they represented a force that Landoran could not simply override.

For a moment, Landoran seemed surprised. Then he regained his composure. "I will see to it that your departure can take place as soon as possible. You will have a horse and armor from us so that you can properly represent the Normirga people."

Ollowain nodded. During their escape, he'd had to give up his armor. As a warrior, he ought to wear more than just a shirt, even if all the armor signified was vanity—against a troll's mighty blow, no armor could protect him.

"We have sent messengers to most of the Albenkin. If elves, centaurs, lamassu, and all our other brother races support us in our fight, we will easily defeat the trolls." Landoran smiled thinly. "The human offer, militarily speaking, is doubtful, but it is priceless from a diplomatic standpoint. By supporting us, they shame the other races of the Alben, which means that they might conceivably form the core of a major alliance."

Ollowain was growing increasingly warm. He felt droplets of sweat forming on his forehead. The air in the Skyhall seemed strangely oppressive, although that seemed to make little difference to the members of the council. Or was he the only one who felt it? Blasted sorcery! He would not put it past his father to make the pavilion hotter just to humiliate him. Standing there covered in sweat before the most ancient elves of the Normirga was almost as embarrassing as if he could not stop himself from wetting his trousers. They were turning him into a child!

"Do you have any more suggestions? Or perhaps objections?" Landoran asked innocently.

"No!" Ollowain wanted nothing but to get out of the pavilion as fast as possible.

The council brought its meeting to an end. Saying nothing, the council members departed from the pavilion. Unusually few, Ollowain thought. Where were the others? And what had happened to Lyndwyn?

The swordmaster went out to the bridge, but even outside the pavilion, it felt humid. He swept his eyes across the valley. The trees were suffering as much as he was, their leaves drooping on the branches. About half a mile away, a white cloud of water vapor rose from one of the pillars.

Ollowain wiped his forehead with his sleeve. When he returned from the human world, he would find out what was going on here!

POLEAXES AND PIKES

Alfadas pulled the shield brace over his shoulder and nodded to Lambi. The mutilated warrior lifted his club high. "Are you ready, you god-damned whoresons?"

Instead of answering, the warriors beat their shields with their clubs. Their numbers had now swelled to more than fifty. Veteran campaigners who had been through many battles joined their ranks, though most of them were not there voluntarily! Alfadas had had their chains removed so that they could acquit themselves better during the long training hours, but they still wore the iron shackles around their ankles. Every night, they were chained inside their billets.

"Put the fear of Luth into 'em," Lambi shouted. The war jarl had taken his defeat by Silwyna in their sword fight surprisingly easily. But Alfadas was even more surprised that Lambi had not yet tried to escape. As long as Alfadas could keep him under control, the other warriors would fall into line. At least, those who were not there as volunteers.

"More noise!" Lambi bawled, and thrashed at his shield. "And don't stand so close together. Remember, we're huge beasties with nothing better to do than smash in a few farm boys' heads. We're not here to rub our asses together. You can do that tonight when they chain us up in the stables!"

The warriors liked Lambi's coarse humor. They laughed and followed his orders, fanning out wider. All of them were clad in leather armor or chain-mail shirts and armed with shields and helmets as they would be in battle. In place of axes and swords, all they carried were heavy cudgels. They moved across the stony shore toward the formation of farmers, where Silwyna, Mag, and a half-dozen others were in command. Cursing, they did their best to keep the farmers in position. The first four rows were armed with pikes five paces long, almost five hundred men altogether. Behind them stood two rows of men holding poleaxes. Isleif, a smith from a local village that Alfadas had never heard of, had devised the new weapon—an axe head attached to a two-pace-long pole, the tip of which was outfitted with an iron spike. The weapon allowed the wielder to strike before they came in range of the trolls' clubs.

All of the smiths in Honnigsvald were at that moment busy producing more such poleaxes.

The third block in the farmers' formation consisted of archers who were supposed to shoot from behind over the heads of their comrades in arms.

"Fire!" came Silwyna's voice. A hum filled the air. Alfadas reflexively raised his shield over his head, but he could have saved himself the trouble. The arrows, their tips wrapped in rags, fell among the gravel on the shore, far short of their targets.

Only twenty steps to the pikemen in the first row.

"Charge!" Lambi bellowed.

At the same moment, the long pikes descended. Although Mag and his men had been practicing the maneuver for days, their formation quickly fell into disarray.

A second salvo of arrows missed the attackers. This time, the archers had fired too far. With an earsplitting crash, the warriors slammed into the pikemen's formation. The defenders were actually supposed to aim several spearheads at each individual attacker, but their general disarray turned into complete confusion in an instant.

Alfadas pushed two pikes aside with his shield, but with the farmers standing four rows deep, many iron pike tips still threatened. He thrashed furiously at one pike. Several warriors to his left and right fell to the ground. The farmers in the fourth row had attached long hooks to the spearheads and were angling for the attackers' heels.

Lambi had worked his way forward to the first row of farmers. In the best of moods, he jabbed his club at their chests. "You're dead!" he shouted. "And you're dead, too! And one more dead farm boy for my banquet!"

Many of the pikemen dropped their weapons, which were of little use once the attackers had got past the sharp tip. They ran into the men with the poleaxes, who were supposed to advance as soon as the pike formations threatened to break.

Mag yelled furiously at his men to hold their positions. Lambi's warriors roared with laughter as they bashed a path through the helpless confusion of farmers. At least Silwyna still had her archers under control as they beat an orderly retreat.

Alfadas shoved two men aside and reached for the horn at his belt. A long blast signaled the end of the battle. Those still fighting separated. Several of the men were bleeding—in the thrill of the skirmish, some had been unable to restrain themselves. Alfadas considered a few minor injuries acceptable. A man who had suffered a blow to the head from a cudgel might hold his position better next time. Or at least would run away faster.

Groaning, the fighters on both sides settled onto the stones along the shore. It was a sunny day, and the fjord was dotted with boats. Closer to Honnigsvald, too, the salmon catch was in full swing. The entire town breathed the spicy aroma that emanated from the smokehouses, and hardly anyone had time to stop and watch Alfadas and his men training.

Alfadas went to the rocks from where Ulric had watched the battle. His son ran to meet him, wearing a proud smile.

"You won again, Father! No one can stop you and your fighters."

"So it seems." The duke set down his shield and released the chin strap of his helmet. He reached wearily for the water bottle that Ulric had been looking after. With each "victory" he wrung, his hopes of returning alive from Albenmark faded.

"Is something wrong, Father?" Ulric asked, suddenly concerned.

How was he supposed to answer a question like that for the boy? Everything was wrong! "We will have to practice much more before I can say that my army fights well."

Ulric nodded. "Best if you stay close to Lambi and the other soldiers. They fight better."

"I thank you for the advice, my son," he said seriously. He had spent far too little time with Ulric. It would have been smarter not to have brought him along at all. But the boy enjoyed being among the warriors. For him, all of this was a great adventure. "Who do you think is the best sword fighter?"

Ulric pointed to the archers. "Silwyna. No one will watch out for you like she will!"

His words caused Alfadas to flinch inwardly. Did his son suspect something? "Is she really so good?"

Ulric nodded. "I watched her. And you were also there when she beat Lambi. First, she pretended that it was hard for her to parry his sword. He wore himself out. And then, without warning, she . . . she disarmed him faster than I could see! It was like she peeled off a false skin and turned into a completely different person. Like a cat playing with a mouse before she suddenly kills it. I think she has spooky eyes. And I'm glad she's your friend, or else I'd be afraid of her."

Alfadas was relieved to hear his son's argument and was proud at the same time. The comparison with a cat pleased him. That's how Silwyna really was. Elegant, unpredictable, lethal. Something wild lived inside her, something he had never managed to get close to. And many times, he had thought that it was this raw power, this animalistic part of her that had called her back to the forest. She could not have done so otherwise.

He looked up in sudden alarm—a silence had fallen. The murmurings of the exhausted men had ceased. Three figures on horseback were riding toward them along the shore of the fjord. And although Alfadas had grown up in Emerelle's court, even he caught his breath. It was as if three characters from the ancient sagas had stepped without warning into the human world. Two of the riders were dressed in flawless white. They sat astride white horses that were at once slender and strong and faster than the wind. The third rode a gray, the colors of his robes gray and wine red.

All three wore breastplates that sparkled as if fashioned from silver and gold. The light gleamed off their helmets. Sweeping cloaks billowed behind them, and horsehair crests fluttered from their helmets in the wind. Every movement they made was majestic. No human would ever sit so perfectly in a saddle, would ever be so completely one with the movements of the horse they rode.

The army of men watched breathlessly as the mysterious riders drew nearer, holding course for Alfadas. He recognized his old mentor, although the helmet with its nose protection and cheek guards that extended well below the chin almost completely concealed Ollowain's face.

The three reined in their horses a pace and a half in front of him. Ulric pressed close at Alfadas's side.

The lead rider dismounted and, to Alfadas's surprise, kneeled before him. "Greetings, Alfadas Mandredson. My people have sent me to be of service to you. We have come to help train your soldiers and to lead them to Albenmark when the time comes."

It made Alfadas uncomfortable to see his swordmaster and guardian like that. He took Ollowain by the shoulders. "You should not kneel before me," he said softly. "A master does not kneel before his pupils."

The elf did not reply but rose to his feet. It was clear to Alfadas that the gesture was intended to strengthen his position among his men. Everyone was supposed to see that even the fearsome elven warriors respected Commander Alfadas Mandredson.

"It is good to see you, Alfadas," said Ollowain quietly, and squeezed his arm. Then he turned to the two elves accompanying him. "Allow me to introduce Lysilla and Ronardin."

The two elves had, by now, also dismounted and removed their helmets. The elf woman reached out her hand to Alfadas. When he looked into her eyes, he recoiled a little automatically. She smiled with amusement—clearly it was not only humans who reacted to her like that. There was something guarded and mysterious about Lysilla. The pressure of her hand was firm and cool. Ronardin was very different, radiating warmth and curiosity. His eyes darted restlessly back and forth hungrily, not wanting to miss anything of the world of humans.

Alfadas reported the present state of the men's training. Lysilla and Ronardin remained unmoved when he told them that the majority of his fighters were not soldiers at all and that their value in a battle was doubtful, to say the least. But Ollowain's dismay was clear.

In the days that followed, it was the swordmaster especially who put all his ability and ingenuity into training the humans as well as he possibly could. He had hollow models as big as trolls woven from wicker but light enough for one man to carry easily. Then the experienced soldiers slipped inside these willow-wood costumes and charged the formations of pikemen. His goal was to prevent the mere sight of the trolls from completely demoralizing the men. He did not tire of explaining to each and every man where their huge enemies were most vulnerable.

Ronardin and Lysilla were kept busy training the experienced soldiers. They managed to convince almost all of them to put aside their armor and shields, because the best protection against the trolls was agility.

Alfadas dedicated himself to the pikemen, drumming into them how important it was not to think of themselves as an unyielding wall of long spears. They had to direct their pikes with care and target individual attackers so that they could injure them with as many spears as possible. And they had to plant their pikes against the ground and hold them in place with one foot, because no man in the world had the strength to withstand the force of a charging troll.

Evenings, when the volunteers could recover from the day's strains, the field commanders were called together in the banquet hall in Honnigsvald and given extra briefings. Silwyna reported on the various races of Albenmark and on which of them they would soon meet. Lysilla and Ronardin tried to prepare them for the hard winter in the Snaiwamark and how, miraculously, they would soon be able to protect themselves from the cold. They explained the ice gliders and the perils of the crevasses in the glaciers, and on large wooden boards, they drew maps of the Snaiwamark and the regions that bordered it. They also sketched plans of the fortress of Phylangan, marking the quarters intended for the humans and the positions that the men of the Fjordlands were supposed to defend.

Alfadas was glad when he could snatch four or five hours of sleep. Ulric, although he had got his pony, was almost always at his side. Every evening, he listened eagerly to what he heard about Albenmark, and sometimes went as far as to interrupt the war council with questions.

And every day, new volunteers kept arriving. Alfadas could hardly believe it: despite all the frightening rumors he had started, the stream of desperate men willing to risk everything did not abate. Because they could no longer be properly trained, the newcomers were assigned to the ranks of the archers and poleax wielders. Alfadas did not want anyone among the pikemen who had not proved his courage in the exhausting hours of training of the last two weeks. A single man in the front row who dropped his weapon and ran could open up a gap that would mean the downfall of all of them.

The last training day finally arrived, and War Jarl Mag had actually managed to muster ten steers, but even he did not know what Alfadas had in store for them.

It was cold that morning. Fog rose from the fjord and hung like white beards in the forests on the nearby hillsides. The troops had marched out at first light. Alfadas once again stood on his rocky outcrop, holding Ulric at his side. The others all took up their positions along the fjord. The different units acquitted themselves surprisingly well in their maneuvers that morning. Then the pikemen, poleaxers, and archers arranged themselves with their backs to the fjord. On each flank, Alfadas positioned a guard of fifty experienced warriors, with Ragni and Lambi commanding; their job was to shield the men from attacks from the side.

Everybody along the shore knew that Alfadas had planned some kind of final test for them that morning. After that, there would be a feast, and the next day the small army would march off to Firnstayn. Alfadas had banned curious onlookers from the shore; anyone who wanted to watch would have to do so from a boat. For the first time, the men were issued sharp weapons.

It was good to have a block of nine hundred men between the units under Lambi's and Ragni's command. In recent days, a deadly rivalry had developed between the two fighters. Ragni had gathered those loyal to the crown around him, and Lambi all those who had been brought to Honnigsvald in chains. So far, Alfadas had been able to exploit that rivalry to spur the two groups of warriors on and get the best out of them. But the alliance between the two bands had become so bad that Alfadas now feared they would be at each others' throats the moment they had the chance.

"Men!" Alfadas cried. His breath puffed from his mouth in white clouds. "This morning we will see what you have learned. Behind you are the days of fighting wicker men and amiably inclined club swingers. Here, now, you will meet an enemy of flesh and blood. An adversary as fierce and merciless as the trolls. It lurks in the forest, waiting to spill your blood. Now is your final opportunity to leave the troop." Alfadas untied a signal horn fitted with silver from his belt and held it high over his head. Then he pointed with it toward the dark strip of forest behind the shore.

"When I sound this horn three times, our enemies will come from those dark woods. And just as you will not be facing human enemies in Albenmark, today you will need to stand against an enemy that is not of your kind. And you will need to win."

As if to underscore his words, a long howl rose from the forest, almost like the howling of wolves, yet somehow different. Alfadas had to stop himself from smiling. Silwyna was playing her part very well indeed!

Ulric had his hands clenched in his father's tunic. "Nothing can happen to us up here," Alfadas told him quietly.

A deathly silence had fallen over the men along the shore. Apart from the elves, no one knew what would take place in this final test. The long banks of fog along the shore had thickened.

From the side where Lambi's fighters stood came defiant laughter. The rebel had his men well under control. Their laughter spread through the remaining ranks, and the tension eased a little.

"So there are none who would like to leave?" asked Alfadas again. "This is your last opportunity. After this morning, I will personally track down anyone leaving my army, and I will not be merciful. Everyone here should be able to rely on the man beside him. Cowardice and betrayal can have no place among us; if they do, Albenmark will spell our doom. Those whose hearts are too weak should leave now! Not everyone is made to be a warrior. And leaving now demands hardly less courage than looking the enemy in the eye. So do not mock those who want to leave us."

"Can I go, too?" came the unmistakable voice of Lambi. "I'm brave enough to call myself a coward, though I would not advise anyone else to talk about me like that."

"You gave up your chance to leave when you were defeated by a woman in a sword fight, Lambi, about whose nose one does not speak."

Alfadas's words were met with laughter.

"An elven woman, I'd like to remind you!" Lambi shouted, offended. "A woman who had to train for a thousand years to be able to beat the great Lambi!"

Alfadas ignored his war jarl's words. "Is there anyone who would like to go?" The laughter faded. And in fact, around thirty men laid down their weapons and returned to the town. Alfadas was surprised to see Kodran, the oldest of the three brothers from the ferryboat, among them.

When those whose courage had failed them disappeared into the morning mists, Alfadas raised his horn to his lips. Three short, blaring notes sounded as a challenge to the hidden enemy in the forest. In reply came the same long, drawn-out howl, this time accompanied by the sound of breaking branches. Something big was charging through the underbrush.

"Pikes ready!" Ollowain ordered, his voice steady. Together with Ronardin, he stood in the frontmost row, while Lysilla oversaw Lambi and his men.

"Archers ready!" cried Mag to his bowmen. The tension in his voice was clear.

A thick band of fog lay between the forest and the shoreline. Suddenly, the ground began to quake. Gravel crunched beneath heavy feet, thundering just ahead of the men.

The faces of the men close to him were ashen. Despite the cold, sweat beaded on their foreheads. Then a large, horned skull broke through the wall of fog. The snapping of pikes and the cries of falling men rang along the shore. Arrows flew toward the still-invisible enemies. Loud bellows sounded in reply.

A massive black figure had crashed through the formation of pikemen. Men with poleaxes charged forward. Their heavy blades hacked into the steer's withers and skull. Dark blood foamed across the gray stones, and wounds gaped in the beast's flesh.

The next bulls were already coming. Lambi's men roared and charged in counterattack. A gust of wind split the fog, and suddenly only three steers were still standing, all with arrows in their backs. They shied away from the war cries of Lambi's men.

Seven steers lay impaled on pikes in the gravel. When the men realized what they were fighting against, they surged forward. The formation broke, and the last of the steers were ruthlessly dispatched.

Alfadas was satisfied. His army had done better than he expected. None of the steers had made it through to the waters of the fjord, and all men had held their positions. Next, however, they would have to learn not to allow their battle lines to break so quickly when victory seemed assured.

Silwyna waved from the edge of the forest. Alfadas set the horn to his lips and again let out three short, sharp blasts. The yells and laughter of the men died away.

"Today, we will do as our future enemies do and eat our defeated foes," he shouted to the men. "You have fought well! Now feast and enjoy. Tomorrow at sunrise, we march for Firnstayn."

HOME

Orgrim peered into the haze. He heard the rumbling of the glaciers. Huge chunks of ice drifted past the hull of the *Wraithwind*. They had pushed far into Whale Bay, but his charts were not accurate. He could not say for certain where they were.

Not much longer and the morning sun would break through the fog. They were very close to the coast. The *Wraithwind* made only slow headway. Orgrim had spent half the night listening to the song of the glaciers, the dull roar as the ice broke free and plunged into the water. No one on board had closed an eye that night. All his warriors and seamen had found a reason to be on deck. And just this once, he had let them. He felt no different than they did. Very close, beyond the fog, lay the land from which his people had been driven more than seven hundred years before. Mandrag was the only one on board who had ever actually seen their homeland. Even Birga, the shaman, had been born in the human world. And now they were the first to return! Branbeard had intended this assignment as punishment, but everyone aboard the *Wraithwind* saw themselves as the chosen. They would be the first to eat of the Normirga! Orgrim was certain that he could deal the elves some serious defeats if Branbeard was not held up too long at Reilimee.

Loud shouts startled the pack leader out of his daydreams. Beside the ship, large black fins sliced through the gray water. Orcas! Hunters, like they themselves. Killers that could finish even a troll with a single bite. With their black-and-white markings, they were beautiful to look at as they gave the galleass a guard of honor. That was a good omen! Orgrim looked over at Birga, who stood off to one side, alone, as usual. The shaman supported herself heavily on her bone staff. She seemed to have been waiting for him to look in her direction, and she nodded as if she already knew what he wanted to ask.

"A good sign! The spirits of our ancestors await us." Birga had a smoky, pleasant voice. Like Skanga, she moved with a slight stoop. Orgrim did not know how old the shaman was, but she must have been much younger than her mistress. Among all the trolls, only a handful were as old as Mandrag. Only rarely, in fact, did one survive beyond a hundred winters. None at all were like Skanga; his folk whispered that she was as old as time and one of the first creations of the Alben.

Birga wore a robe fashioned from overlapping strips of leather and fur, hundreds of them sewn into a dress. Every strip came from a different beast, some even made from the skin of trolls and humans. She wore a hood pulled forward over her head. Her hands were concealed beneath filthy bandages, and her countenance was hidden behind the facial skin of one of the king's former favorite women—Birga had torn it off personally after the whore had tried to foist a bastard on Branbeard.

The shaman, clothed entirely in the skins of others, showed not the slightest piece of her own skin. Countless rumors made the rounds: that she had thick fur like a dog, scales like a fish, or that she was tattooed from head to foot with magical runes that gave her the power to read thoughts as long as the runes could be kept out of anyone else's sight. Orgrim knew with certainty that he would never attempt to get to the bottom of Birga's secret. There was something about her that chilled him to the bone when he looked into her cold gray eyes. Birga took pleasure in torturing others. And she had a very special way of making others talk . . . even the king's whore had admitted everything in the end.

"There!" cried a lookout, and he pointed to the west. "I see mountains!"

The pack leader turned abruptly as the veils of fog parted. In a moment, they were swept apart as if by a magical hand. Orgrim saw a blue-white glacier pushing out into Whale Bay across a broad face. The ice was lined with deep furrows, dark, horizontal bands dividing the cliff-like wall of ice, which loomed eighty or ninety paces high and was lost on both sides in the fog.

As Orgrim watched, a piece of ice the size of a tower broke from the glacier and tumbled with a boom into the sea. The *Wraithwind* rose and fell, causing several crewmen to lose their footing and slide across the planking. The ship veered dangerously, and breakers crashed over the deck. Orgrim realized how foolish it had been to sail so close to the coastline. A calving glacier could sink their ship. He signaled to the helmsman to put more distance between them and the face of the glacier.

"The Dragontongue," Mandrag murmured. Then he pointed away into the mist. "The Bone Crags must be ahead. There used to be a village below them.

The huts had been built from the jawbones of whales. From there, I went out on the ice with my father in winter to hunt polar bears. We found them close to the holes in the ice where the seals came up to breathe. The ice was red with blood wherever a bear had had a successful hunt. And the seals had no choice but to appear at the holes, even when they knew that a hunter was waiting for them. They would have suffocated beneath the ice otherwise." Tears stood in the old troll's eyes. "Fresh bear meat is delicious."

A large gray mountain appeared through the mist, jutting far out into the bay. There was a good anchorage on its lee side, where the *Wraithwind* would be protected from the winter storms.

"Should we set up our camp here?" the pack leader asked.

Mandrag chewed on his lip thoughtfully for a while. Finally, he shook his head. "No. We still have to sail a good way north; there are broad gravel beaches there. We need to pull the *Wraithwind* onto the beach for the winter. It can't stay in the water, or the ice would crush its hull. My father told me about an elven ship that perished like that. In winter, they mount their ships on giant skids and can sail across the ice as fast as the wind."

Orgrim thought about whether it made sense to put the *Wraithwind* on skids. Perhaps, if one were to take the ship up to the high plateau, but they would need hundreds of trolls to transport the galleass over the coastal mountains. Maybe he ought to talk to Boltan about it. The artillery chief was a constant wellspring of unconventional ideas. He was the one who had come up with the cargo sleds securely tied in the ship's hold, waiting to be put to use. With their help, they would give the elves a deadly surprise.

"Bring the ship another fifty miles up the coast," Mandrag advised. "We should make camp near the entrance to the Swelm Valley. From there, the Wolfpit is only a day's march away. In the past, it was just a small mountain fortress. I don't think there will be many elves living there. With a bit of luck, we'll catch them unawares."

Orgrim's eyes wandered over the coastline, which was showing more and more clearly as the fog melted away. It was a wonderfully wild landscape of rock. The distant homeland that for generations had lived on only in stories. A fresh breeze came off the sea and drove away the last drifts of fog. The pack leader rubbed his bare arms—he loved the bite of the wind on his skin.

The colors of the rocks were now clear to see in the morning light. They were the same shade of gray as his skin. He smiled to recall a story from his childhood, in which the most rebellious of the Alben, the greatest hero in the war against the Devanthar, had carved the first trolls out of the rocks of these mountains and breathed life into them.

Orgrim ran his hands over his raw skin. The story was easy to believe when one saw this stretch of coast.

They had come home!

THE CURSED ARROW

The king's tent was brightly lit. The cold autumn wind tore at the red fabric, making the flames on the torches dance. It was the middle of the night, and Alfadas was in a rage—Horsa had torn him out of Asla's arms and ordered him to come to his tent.

The king, his courtiers, and the vast escort accompanying him had set up camp outside the village. Most of the army from Honnigsvald also had to spend the night outside. Firnstayn did not have nearly enough quarters to accommodate so many guests. Dozens of campfires were dotted along the fjord. Alfadas could well imagine how his men, huddled in their thin blankets, were waiting for the night to finally be over, how they stared into the coals of their fires and imagined what the following day would bring.

A wide circle of guards surrounded the king's tent. The sentries were just far enough away to be unable to hear what was said inside. Horsa had brought more than two hundred soldiers with him—far too many for an escort. He had announced that he had spared no pains to come to Firnstayn to say farewell to his bravest warriors when they departed for Albenmark. And his skald, Veleif, had found plenty of pretty words to lull any suspicions the men might harbor. It was the farmers and craftsmen—those men who owed their lost livelihoods to the injustices in Horsa's realm—who were particularly moved by the king's gesture. For one night, they could feel that they mattered. They truly believed that the king had come only for their sake. *Rotten old fox,* thought Alfadas. *You still know your business too damn well.* He had brought Ollowain with him because he feared he might not be a match for Horsa's flattery and intrigues by himself.

The sentries waved them through without asking questions. Inside his tent, Horsa was alone. He stood beside a pan of glowing coals, holding his hands over it, stretching them and balling them into fists. "I hate this cold, wet weather. Everything hurts on nights like this." He nodded to them to take a place at the table that filled the middle of the tent. A plate of bread and cold chicken meat still lay on it, almost untouched.

Opposite the entrance stood a heavy bed with a beautifully carved wooden frame and a mountain of pelts on top of the mattress.

"Why did you send for me?" Alfadas asked, his tone chilly. He wanted to get this unwelcome discussion over with as quickly as possible.

"Ragni told me about the training your men have been through." It was not clear from Horsa's voice if that was meant as praise or criticism.

"They will hold their own," the duke replied.

"I could still give you some of my knights."

What was the old man up to? Alfadas had no time for these games, but he had to keep his impatience in check, if only for the sake of Asla and the children.

"We won't be able to feed your knights' horses," Ollowain spoke up. "We have to cross a wide ice plain. The animals would drop dead out there."

"But you can feed a herd of sheep?" The king curled his hands into fists again.

"They will feed us," Ollowain said, and smiled. "We don't need to provide anything for them."

Horsa nodded. "I can see the campaign has been planned carefully. You will be a thorn in the trolls' side, Alfadas." The king rubbed his empty eye socket, then joined them at the table. Horsa's breath stank of sour wine.

The king studiously ignored Ollowain. *Perhaps because he's afraid of him,* thought Alfadas. Was Horsa really so naive that he believed the swordmaster did not know what intrigues had already been spun? Or was he counting on the elf's indifference, as long as he got his fighters for the battles ahead?

"Although I admit, I am also worried," Horsa continued. "Who is supposed to protect Emerelle? Who will look after her? There is no healer here in the village, only an old, fat priest."

"Your concern for Emerelle does you credit, King," said Ollowain smoothly. "But in my friend Alfadas's house, Emerelle enjoys all the help we can give. I see no reason to inflict the strains of a long trip to your court on her."

"Time to call things by their proper names!" Horsa suddenly blurted. "I know you plan to deceive me, Alfadas! If I were not here, you might not even go through that portal on top of the cliff. You've got your eye on my throne. And your army of have-nothings and traitors like Lambi is devoted to you.

Even if you do leave tomorrow, who's to say that you won't come back the day after?"

Alfadas looked at Horsa incredulously. The old man had truly gone mad! "Forgive me, but it was your idea to put together an army of malcontents and to send me to Albenmark with them to fight the trolls."

"It was not!" the king rumbled. "You and your elf friends, you took advantage of my good nature and inveigled me into it. But now I see through your plan. There is no war with the trolls in Albenmark! What proof do I have, apart from your word? You knew that I would offer my help as soon as I heard about the elven queen driven out of her own land. You *made* me give you the army that you will use to steal the throne from my son."

"That's not how it is at all!" Alfadas insisted. "Listen to your heart. You will see you have nothing to fear from me."

"Oh, I know, I really don't, not if you go to Albenmark. And just to make sure you don't come back, I'll take Asla and your children with me to Gonthabu. And that sleeping elf woman, too. I can see very clearly that she is someone important. I recognize a princess when I see one. If I never hear from you again, Alfadas, then you can be sure they will come to no harm."

Alfadas's hand dropped to the grip of his sword. "You don't think it was unwise to call we traitors into your tent?"

Horsa glowered at him. "If one expects treason, one prepares. Your house is surrounded, Alfadas. If anything happens to me, your family dies. And your farmer soldiers will die in their sleep tonight." Then the king's wrath vanished as abruptly as it had appeared, and he seemed suddenly tired. "Go, Alfadas. Go and don't come back. That is all I want from you. And don't think I don't know that I am the villain in this piece. You know as well as I that the sagas of our heroes always end in blood and tragedy. That is how things are in the Fjordlands. And that is why you should not hope I would hesitate to have your family murdered if you oppose me."

"Do you know the story of Nazirluma and Aileen?" asked Ollowain in the kind of voice a storyteller would use with children.

Alfadas looked at his friend. Did he not understand how serious their situation was?

Horsa gestured dismissively. "This is neither the time nor the place for childishness. I will take your family with me tomorrow, Alfadas. Make sure no one here in the village puts up any resistance. I would not like to see a bloodbath here." He turned to Ollowain. "And you. Make it clear to your queen's bodyguard that against two hundred soldiers, even the most skillful sword fighter can only lose."

"If you are interested in your son's life, Horsa, then you would do well to listen to my story." The swordmaster spoke politely, but firmly. "Is there anything worse than to stand at the grave of your own child?"

"My son is not even here!" Horsa puffed. "And I will not tell you and your mob where he is. He is beyond your reach!" Despite his words, the old man seemed unsettled. Alfadas would have bet that the king was lying and that Egil was somewhere very close by.

"Are you sure of that? Can you afford to be mistaken, Horsa?" Ollowain asked. "As far as I know, you have only one son."

From the corner of his eye, Alfadas saw something move beneath the pelts covering the king's bed. He was about to draw his sword when he realized that it was Dalla, the healer, who lay there. She seemed to have rolled in her sleep.

Ollowain's calm frightened the king more than did the anger of his duke. "Then tell your blasted story, elf! But don't think it will change a thing. I've thought of everything!"

"Of course!" The swordmaster leaned back in his chair. "Nazirluma was one of the greatest wizards of his day. He was the king of that secretive race the lamassu, and the stories that are told about him are beyond counting. His powerful wings were said to have carried him across the white sea in a single night, although even the fastest ships took three weeks for the journey. He was famous for his cryptic riddles, and some of the spells he cast continue to work to this day, although Nazirluma has been dead more than two thousand years. No doubt people would still talk about that extraordinary, wise man in the highest of terms today if, in his old age, he had not met the elf Aileen, who was one of the Maurawan. She traveled to his royal court in Kandastan to take part in a great archery tournament. Although Aileen did not win the competition, she did attract the attention of the old king because she was exceptionally beautiful. When Nazirluma saw her, he was blinded with love for her. He devised marvelous metaphors for her beauty, and even wrote a poem of over one hundred cantos that he personally presented to her. He courted her like a raw youth who has fallen in love for the very first time.

"At first, Aileen accepted his gifts, for she did not believe the king's wooing was serious. To understand how she could be so mistaken, you should know that a lamassu has the body of a large steer. But from his flanks grow sweeping eagle's wings strong enough to carry him to the summit of the highest of all mountains. Only his head is like that of an elf . . . or rather, more like that of a human, for the faces of the lamassu are always heavily bearded. Some time passed before Aileen understood that the king was actually serious in courting her. Now, the Maurawan are well-known for wearing their heart on their tongue and for expressing themselves especially . . . vividly. And so it happened that Aileen told Nazirluma—to his face, before his entire court— that she would rather mate with a wolf than with a decrepit old ox like him.

"They say that love and hate are two sides of the same coin. And as blinded by love as Nazirluma was, the injury to his pride was beyond measure. Aileen had hardly left the king's high hall when he ordered his bodyguards to attack the elf and teach her the pleasure of being loved by a lamassu until she drew her last breath. And to their eternal shame, the soldiers did as they were ordered.

"Aileen was able to shoot three arrows before she was attacked. With two, she killed two of the huge lamassu. But the third was a Gry-na-Lah, a curse arrow, and she shot it straight up into the sky, because she knew perfectly well who had sent the soldiers. She had written Nazirluma's name on the shaft of an arrow and cast a spell on the missile. The arrow would fly onward, through the sky, unseen, until it found its target.

"When Nazirluma came to his senses, it was too late to recall his assassins. As a learned man, the king knew the Maurawan, their magic, and their weapons well. And he hid himself away in a chamber with no window, no chimney, no shaft for air. One had to pass through three doors to get into the chamber, and the king ordered that never more than one of the doors was to be opened at one time. Nazirluma spent eighty-five days in his self-imposed prison, and in time his confidence grew that the Gry-na-Lah had lost its power. His servants also became careless, because they sensed how their master's fear was abating. On the eighty-fifth day, Nazirluma ordered a bath to be prepared for him. His servants carried pitcher after pitcher of water into the king's magnificent dungeon, and with all their toing and froing, it happened that they kept only the outermost of the three doors closed. That door, however, was less well made than the other two, and there was a knothole in it, a hole so small that I could only just squeeze my little finger through it. But the arrow found it and buried itself in Nazirluma's heart. And the king died in his bath, in his own blood."

Sweat had broken out on Horsa's brow by the time Ollowain finished his story. "What are you trying to tell me with this story, elf?"

The swordmaster spread his hands wide. "Is that so hard to understand? Yilvina, our queen's bodyguard, never puts her bow and arrows aside. And on one of her arrows is the name of your son, Egil."

Horsa sprang to his feet and lunged at Ollowain, but the elf easily dodged the attack. A kick to the back of the old man's knee brought him down. Then Ollowain pressed one foot onto the king's chest, pushing him into the dust. It all happened so fast that Alfadas found no opportunity to intervene—though he didn't mind at all seeing Horsa lying in the dust.

"I am sorry that this was necessary," said Ollowain dejectedly. "We are allies in the war against the trolls, after all. Now listen to me, King. I see your threat against Emerelle and against the family of my friend Alfadas as an aberration, a moment of delusion, the kind of thing that can come over one in the darkest hours of the night, when one has partaken of too much wine. I know Alfadas as well as I know my own heart. And I promise you that your duke would never commit treason against you."

His foster father's words made Alfadas feel ashamed. He thought back to the night on the ferry. Had his years in the human world changed him so much?

"I am prepared to forget everything that has been said tonight," Ollowain went on. "I entered your tent as your ally, King Horsa. Whether I leave it as an ally is now in your hands." The swordmaster removed his foot from the king's chest and took a step back.

Horsa gasped for air, then sat up with some difficulty. His remaining eye was bloodshot. "I think I must have drunk too much," he said, his voice strained.

"I can see how your concern for your son consumes you. I would not like to judge whether your fears are justified." Ollowain offered Horsa his hand, and to Alfadas's surprise, the old man took it and allowed the elf to help him to his feet.

"There is only one power in the Fjordlands capable of damaging the duke's loyalty to your throne," said Ollowain earnestly. "And that power is you, Horsa. Remember that in everything you do."

The solidly built old man and the tall, slim elf stood facing each other. For Alfadas, Ollowain embodied everything that Horsa had lost. Youth, self-confidence, and wisdom. Was the king also aware of that? Tears welled in his eyes, and there was a longing there now, as if he could see the gleam of the halls of the gods on the horizon.

"I believe I have also understood the deeper meaning of the story of the steer king. Thank you for opening my eye," the king said, his voice breaking. Then he turned and looked at Alfadas. "I wish you luck in your campaign, Alfadas. And I hope we meet again. Do you need any more men? I could leave some of my escort for you."

Alfadas was on his guard. The king's change of heart seemed too sudden. Or had Ollowain perhaps cast a spell on the king?

"I am only taking volunteers," he said decisively. "Men who have not yet started a family."

"They are good fighters." Horsa wiped a hand across his eye. "You know many of them already."

And I thought I knew you once, too, Alfadas thought. "We will ask them tomorrow at the gateway. If you would allow us to retire now . . . ?"

Obviously deep in thought, the king nodded.

When they were out of earshot of the sentries, Alfadas decided to be certain.

"Did you use magic on him, Ollowain?"

"No. All I did was try to remind him of the man he used to be."

"I think it was the Gry-na-Lah that has made him think. The curse arrows are a secret of the Maurawan, aren't they?"

Ollowain laughed gently. "Oh yes. So secret that not even the Maurawan know about them. Do you think Emerelle would still be alive today if arrows like that really existed? We'd have no princes or kings at all. The noble houses would have wiped each other out long ago. I made up the story of Nazirluma and Aileen to frighten Horsa, but the old man surprised me. If you ask me, he understood it very differently than I intended. He cannot escape his own death. Life is a battle that we all, ultimately, lose. But to some extent, how people remember us is in our own hands. At the bottom of his heart, Horsa is a good man. He does not want people to remember him as a despot, and if he leaves a burden like that, then Egil will only have a harder time as king. Who wants to be ruled over by the scion of a tyrant? Everyone with a grudge against his father, but who fears the old man, will rise against Egil."

"I only hope that Horsa's wisdom survives longer than one night," Alfadas replied doubtfully. "I think I'd prefer it if Yilvina really had a Gry-na-Lah."

"Don't underestimate Yilvina," the swordmaster warned. "I don't believe there is a human alive who could kill her, and she will also watch over your family. She does not need a curse arrow for that."

The two men had reached Alfadas's longhouse. "I don't think I will sleep tonight," Ollowain suddenly said, and took his leave. Alfadas watched him go until he was swallowed by the darkness.

Determined not to waste the last hours with his family in mute brooding, Alfadas stepped inside his house and was met by the familiar smell of smoke. Soon, his eyes began to water. He cursed softly. The coals in the fire pit were not enough to drive out the darkness, but they gave enough light to cross the large room without stepping on the guests billeting with them, who lay everywhere, rolled in blankets on the floor.

A chain clinked, and Alfadas froze. It was only Lambi or one of his men moving in his sleep. As a precaution, Alfadas had invited the most rebellious of his fighters into his own house, not least to protect them from the king's men.

Alfadas waited for his eyes to adjust to the red twilight. Then he crept between the sleeping men to the niches along the wall. Blood kept guard in front of Kadlin's bed—Alfadas saw the light from the coals reflected in the large dog's black eyes. Blood did not move and made no sound, but he missed nothing that happened in the house, and woe to anyone who dared step too close to Kadlin!

Alfadas patted Blood's massive head. The dog did not react, neither with a friendly snuffle nor, like other dogs, by rolling onto his side so that Alfadas could scratch his belly. He lay there tensely and watched the sleepers; once, he twitched when someone in the darkness murmured to himself in his sleep. Only when Alfadas stood up to check on Kadlin did Blood briefly press his damp snout into Alfadas's hand.

The duke thought back on the events of the evening. Almost every man sleeping there on the floor had killed. They were hard-bitten men, and under normal circumstances, he would not have wanted them under his roof. They had nothing but scorn for the rules of honor that he tried to teach his son. For them, honor meant winning. How they won made no difference. In times of peace, they were bad company, but they were exactly the right men with whom to march into a hopeless battle. Maybe Horsa was right in wanting to be rid of them. The Fjordlands had peaceful times ahead. There were no true enemies, and these men were troublemakers. Even Blood had realized that. Since they had been in the house, the dog had neither eaten nor drunk anything. He had not let the men out of his sight, not for a heartbeat. The men had realized the danger the massive black dog presented. They had sensed that he would attack without warning if they made the slightest mistake, and that the beast could rip out a man's throat with a single bite. Lambi and his cronies had been placid, had avoided getting drunk, and had stayed a respectful distance away from Blood.

Alfadas scratched the dog's ears—it was good to know that Blood was in the house. He would look out for Asla and the children.

Carefully, he pushed aside the curtain covering Kadlin's sleeping niche and looked inside. The little girl had kicked off her blanket and lay with her bottom up in the air and her head pressed into the moss-filled pillow. She wore a serious expression on her face, as she sometimes did when she tried to explain something important. Alfadas smiled. It puzzled him how anyone could sleep like that, but Kadlin's breathing was deep and regular. He pulled her blanket up gently, then watched her as she slept. He wanted to burn that image deep into his memory. It would be his secret treasure in the dark hours yet to come.

Finally, he tore himself away to check on Ulric. His son also lay in a deep sleep, the dagger that Ollowain had given him pressed close by his side. It was a long, slim weapon, almost a short sword. Small pieces of turquoise had been embedded in its silver sheath. Ulric had counted them: eighty-three. The grip had been carved from whalebone and engraved with two lions standing on their hind legs, caught in a deadly embrace. Both had their fangs sunk in the other's neck. The dagger was a gift fit for a king, and since Ulric had received it, it had been his constant companion. Considering their guests that night, it was certainly smarter not to leave such a precious piece lying around. One day, Alfadas thought, his son would make a good warrior. And no doubt he would get annoyed whenever anyone claimed that he owed his strength and his skill to an enchanted elven dagger.

He stroked the boy's mussed hair gently. Ulric squirmed restlessly in his sleep. Cautiously, Alfadas retreated. Then he undressed and slipped into the sleeping niche he shared with Asla.

"What did the old goat want you for this time?" she asked quietly, once he had pulled the wool curtain closed.

"He is worried that I could cheat him when it comes to dividing up the spoils of war. Horsa is convinced that we are all going to come back loaded down with treasure," Alfadas lied as he pushed beneath the blanket. The night was bitterly cold. The first snows would soon arrive. He thought of the men freezing by their fires along the shore. In Albenmark, at least, they would not be cold.

"And what are you going to bring me? Another wagon?"

"Is there something wrong with the one you have?" He slung one arm around her and pulled her to him. Her body was pleasantly warm.

Asla shivered. "It's like winter just crawled into my bed." She turned around to him and kissed his forehead. "Come back to me from Albenmark. That is the only gift I want from you."

The feeling that his stomach was full of ice returned. Did she suspect something? "The elves build very beautiful coaches," he said, to change the subject.

Asla slapped his face playfully. "Are you trying to turn me into a coach driver? Have I uncovered one of your secrets? Do you like elves who take the reins?"

Alfadas pulled her to him. "Actually, I prefer wild riders." Asla's long hair touched his face. Her hands clasped his shoulders.

"There is something else I'd like to have. That smug, dark-haired elf cow who you wanted to poke around my belly . . . Lindone, or whatever her name was. She had a small glass bottle with a kind of water in it that had a wonderful smell. I watched her once as she dabbed a little of it on her neck, and afterward she smelled like a flower garden. The perfume made me feel quite wonderful, and I would like to have something like that, too."

Alfadas buried his face between her breasts. "I like the smell of your skin. No perfume could intoxicate me like that."

She pushed herself up on top of him. "You are a terrible liar. I don't know any man who washes as often as you do. Why would you like my smell if you can't even stand your own?"

"Sometimes, after we've made love, I don't wash for days." He pulled her down and kissed her. When they made love, everything was like it was in that wonderful first year . . . at least, as long as Asla didn't tease him. Back then, she had admired him too much to laugh at his expense. What was behind her wish? Perfume! He really did like the smell of her! It was too dark there in their bed to see anything, but he was certain she was grinning at that moment.

Asla rubbed against him lightly. A pleasant shudder ran through Alfadas's body. The ice in his belly vanished.

"Will you grant my wish?" She raised herself a little.

"I will bring you an entire collection of perfume!"

She rubbed against him again. "One small bottle will do. Then I will forgive you if you come back with another wagon." Her warmth encircled him. Alfadas bit his lips. He did not want the men outside to hear him groan in his lust.

Asla began to move with a slow rhythm. Her warmth flowed over him and carried him away. Away from Horsa and all his cares. They made love more passionately than they had in a long time, and later, as she slept with her head on his chest, he swore that he would return. Whatever happened. That was his last thought before he, too, fell asleep.

Ole plagued him in his dreams. He had brought a dog with him as big as a horse and wanted to sell it to Asla.

GOOD-BYE

Ollowain reached for the hand of the sleeping queen.

"She is still cold," said Yilvina. "Ever since Lyndwyn worked her magic, the warmth refuses to return. I can give her nothing to eat and barely a drop to drink. Her breathing is so shallow that I sometimes think she is like one of the little lizards that stiffens and sleeps in winter and wakes again at the start of spring."

The burns on the queen's face had completely healed and had left no scars. The swordmaster had to think of Lyndwyn's words. Was the queen fleeing from her deeds? Was it that she did not want to wake up? He had known Emerelle a very long time. To run from fate was not like her.

"How are you holding up?" Ollowain said, glancing up at Yilvina.

She looked back at him tiredly. "Life here is not exactly thrilling. I never leave this house. At night, I sleep by the queen's bed. I am always close to her, in case she suddenly awakens."

"You should not lock yourself in," Ollowain urged her.

"I promised to watch over Emerelle," Yilvina replied stubbornly.

"But there are no enemies here."

"And that king?" she said. "I don't trust him. His offer to take Emerelle to his court in Gonthabu sounded to me like he'd been thinking of holding her hostage."

"He won't bother you anymore." Ollowain thought of the night before. He had stayed and watched the king for a long time. The old man had lit more fires inside his tent, and his outline was clearly visible through the canvas walls. Horsa had sat at his table the entire night without moving. Then he had called in his guards and delivered a moving speech on the transience of youth and the eternal glory of valiant deeds. Horsa was a boozer and a whoremonger, a man of power little plagued by scruples. Despite those failings, he had charisma, and he knew his Fjordlanders. Every word he spoke had struck home with them, had lodged in their hearts. In the end, all of them wanted to depart with Alfadas, but he had allowed only one hundred to join his duke's forces.

The army had broken camp hours earlier, but Ollowain had stayed behind to say his farewells to his queen undisturbed. He was also at least a little driven by the hope that Emerelle would perhaps awaken if he kneeled by her bed and talked to her softly. But the queen still lay there as if dead in the bed that Asla had prepared for her.

Ollowain took his leave from Yilvina with a warrior's salute. Even there in the house, she had not removed her twin swords. The belt that held the two blades crossed over her chest, and although she too now wore human clothes, Ollowain had brought her back a mail shirt and vambraces from Phylangan so that she could again look like a warrior of repute. With her cropped hair and high cheekbones, Yilvina's face emanated something forbidding. She seemed cold and unapproachable, and Ollowain hoped that her inhospitable nature would not provoke Asla. Getting on with Yilvina was not the easiest thing in the world. Perhaps she was too much a warrior? Her eyes alone were filled with defiance.

"May your road lead you back to Albenmark," said Ollowain.

"Only at the side of my queen," Yilvina replied curtly.

The swordmaster knew that Yilvina had little time for polite clichés. He left the house silently and mounted his waiting stallion; the magnificent white horse carried him around the fjord until close to the summit of the Hartungscliff. When he reached the swath of scree, he dismounted and led the stallion by the reins.

His route led him past children and old men. Everyone from miles around was on the way to see the magical gateway open. Kalf carried an old woman, too weak to climb the mountain herself, on his back. Ollowain saw a woman carrying in her arms a girl with beautiful brown eyes. The child must have been five or six years old, and her mother spoke to her incessantly, describing the blue of the fjord and how tiny the huts below looked from up so high. Then Ollowain understood: the girl's eyes did not move. They stared into nothingness—the little girl was blind.

He would never understand humans. The scene touched him, though his reason rejected it. It was nonsense to believe that she could describe any more than a fraction of the wonders of this world to her daughter, but the way she rebelled against her daughter's fate, the way she refused to accept that her daughter was excluded, that was worthy of respect!

For a while, he walked beside the woman and listened to her awkward words. She described him, too. She called him a thin, white man with golden hair. Ollowain allowed the girl to touch his hair and his face. He also let her stroke his stallion and then tried to tell her something himself. He was amazed at how helpless his words sounded when he tried to explain what lay ahead of them: the bare dome of the summit, from which a circle of standing stones rose like the points of a crown.

Alfadas stood in the center of the stone circle. The wind tugged at his woolen cloak. Everyone was watching him—including Ulric, who held his brown pony by its reins, and Asla, whose face was very pale.

Kadlin twisted her fingers in Blood's fur. The old Luth priest Gundar was chewing on something but trying to do so without anyone noticing.

Horsa had his hands on his hips, trying to look as kingly as possible, but his impatience was clear. All around, on the slopes and summit, stood the men who would go with Alfadas. Lambi and his companions were still in chains. Ollowain saw the two brothers from the ferry and also Ole, who was talking insistently to someone who obviously did not want to talk to Ole.

Alfadas's fighters were a ragged-looking mob. They carried rolled blankets tied like large sausages across their chests and backs, and each man was loaded down with bags and bottles, emergency provisions for Albenmark, in case something unforeseen happened. Their eyes were bright—they expected no less than a miracle.

Ollowain looked up to the sky restlessly. It was past midday. The gateway that would take them to the Slanga Mountains should already have opened.

Wind swept across the fjord, shattering the mirror of its waters. A single seagull soared above them, looking down curiously at all the people below it. It seemed to Ollowain that the bird was afraid to approach too close to the circle of standing stones: it glided around the top of the mountain in a broad arc.

Suddenly, a column of purple light shot out of the ground at the duke's feet. It grew taller and wider until it was large enough for a wagon to drive through it with ease.

Alfadas raised both arms. The murmurings of the crowd fell silent. Only the rush of the wind and the far cry of the seagull disturbed the silence.

"This is the gateway that will lead us into a world of wonder and horror. Step through the purple light and your past will fall away like a snake's old skin, if that is what you want. Maybe darkness awaits us beyond the gate. Maybe we will reach the Slanga Mountains in a single step. If you see a golden path before you, then follow it. Do not deviate from it even a hair's breadth, or you will be lost in the darkness forever. And if your courage fades now and you are afraid to take the last step, do not worry. Everyone standing on these rocks with me now is a hero. Think of the skald's stories, think of the fabled warriors of the past. You have all followed me to the edge of the world. And of even the most valiant and daring warriors in the Fjordlands, only a handful before you have ever come this far. Are you a fisherman, a trader, a ferryman? It does not matter: you are in no way inferior to the heroes of old. You already have your place in the songs that will one day be sung in the halls of kings. I bow my head before you, and I am proud to be at your side." And Alfadas, in fact, did bow. A gust of wind blew his long hair in his face when he straightened up again. Fierce determination shone in his eyes. "Asla, I love you, and I will return to you, whatever may come." He spoke those words calmly, solemnly, as if swearing an oath. Then he turned and with one step vanished into the gleaming light.

Lysilla came to Ollowain's side. She smiled derisively and spoke to him in the language of her people. "A little melodramatic, these humans."

"Don't great emotions demand great gestures?" The swordmaster held her eye for a moment. He did not smile. Then he looked across to Silwyna. Ollowain knew that the duke's last words applied to her as much as to Asla, but the huntress's face showed nothing.

AT THE THRESHOLD

Vahelmin did not know how much time had passed since Skanga's blood magic had transformed him into a servile beast. Days, weeks . . . or maybe only hours? In the void, there was no way to measure the passing of time.

Sometimes, Vahelmin hoped he might suddenly awaken, that all of this was no more than a terrible dream. But there was that other creature . . . the source of all the grim meanderings in his mind. That being was deep in him. It had its share in everything he thought. Whenever he hoped he might soon wake, he could feel the beast inside him stir, recalling itself to his mind, turning all his dreams to dust again.

The dark creature thought of nothing but light. And yet it shied away from the golden paths that crossed the void, far between. Vahelmin had struggled to teach the beast that these ways were now open to them, that the spell that kept the other creatures of the darkness away from the Albenpaths no longer applied to them.

In return, the beast taught him how to move through the void, where there was no up or down, no solid ground beneath one's feet. From the first moment on, Vahelmin had had the feeling that he was falling through the nothingness. An endless plunge into a bottomless pit . . .

The creature in him had reveled at his fear. The void was a world of no light, no smells, no wind that one could feel against the skin. It was more terrible than any dungeon because you were locked inside it with only yourself and what you could feel inside, but with no sensory impression that might offer even a moment of distraction. In this place, devouring the fear of another was a feast without compare. The creature drove him to the very edge of sanity . . . and perhaps he had even crossed that boundary, for only now did his dark brother teach him how to move. First of all, it tried to make him understand that he was not falling. In a world with no horizon, no landmarks by which he could orient himself, a world with no mountains or valleys, there was also no bottom of the abyss to finally break against. He was falling into nothing more than his own imagining, because there was nothing with which he could fix his place in the world.

Once Vahelmin comprehended that, he had been able to overcome his fear. He learned to move with the power of his thoughts. The network of Albenpaths gave the void a structure, creating waypoints in the trackless abyss.

The creature that Skanga had melded him with feared the Albenpaths like a disobedient dog feared its master's whip. The beast did not dare to tread the paths, and yet it prowled the magical ways constantly. It sensed an intruder the way a spider senses something touching its web. Within a moment—at least, that is what it seemed to Vahelmin—they were at the place where something moved in the web. Lurking, skulking, they besieged the Albenpath with other creatures of the darkness, waiting for one of the interlopers to make the mistake of abandoning the safe path.

If one left the path, the light that marked the pathway faded immediately. From the void, the golden web was invisible. One sensed it when one drew close, but it did not help to find one's bearings in the darkness. The beast inside Vahelmin feared the power with which the Alben had once attired their ways. But now that they were both one, they could break through the protective spell with ease. Now it was Vahelmin who grazed on his dark soul brother's fears as he led him along the path of light.

The moment they passed into the net of Albenpaths, Vahelmin remembered that they were searching for someone. An elf woman . . . the queen! But he could sense no trace of Emerelle. And his memory of Shahondin also returned. Had they not entered the web together? Why had his father abandoned him? Had he picked up the queen's trail?

Driven by a desire not to lag behind Shahondin in any respect, Vahelmin learned that he could also leave the void. In those places where the Albenpaths crossed in a star, it was simple to escape the darkness. When he broke out the first time, he found himself in a place of light and sand, standing in the center of a wide black basalt circle. Curious, he loped through the sea of sand but found nothing he could take as quarry. The land was dead, and so he returned to the void.

After that, he ventured a number of smaller forays, testing his abilities. He passed through Albenstars at random but did not stay out long. Here he killed a rabbit, there a deer. Only when he stepped out into a wintry, steppe-like landscape did he feel an urge to stay longer. His white, translucent form, there, blended perfectly with the snowy backdrop. In contrast to predatory animals, he seemed to emit no scent. He was easily able to approach a herd of yaks and prey among them. His jaws met with no resistance when he bit into the flank of a bull, and he tore the light out of the animals easily. The throes of death were delicious, and to watch the weakening of life and see the panic in the eyes of the other beasts, which did not understand what was happening, was an act he reveled in. The light did not really satisfy him, but murder filled him with joy. Or was that sensation simply his dark brother rejoicing?

One evening, he slipped into a camp of centaurs and murdered a mare that was just then giving birth. As a hunter in that distant time when he had still been an elf, he would never have killed a pregnant animal. It went against every law of the hunt. Now it gave him deep satisfaction to transgress those laws. He killed the defenseless baby boy while he was still connected to his mother by the umbilical cord, and the centaur mare had perished with her child in her arms. Being present to see the frenzy of the enraged father as, drunken, he entered the tent had been almost as arousing as the murder itself. He had just been celebrating the birth of his son with his friends, and in his derangement, he had tried to take his own life.

After hunting, Vahelmin always returned to the void. For him, it was an enormous, unbounded cave. The predator's refuge. And he hoped constantly to find some trace of the queen. Skanga had been so certain that they would pick up Emerelle's trail. Perhaps he only had to wait for the queen to once again enter the network of Albenpaths? He would know if she did, and then he would rob her of her light! A searing pain shot through him. The queen was not his quarry. His limbs seemed about to tear from his body, and he experienced again the night of the transformation, the moment in which Skanga had stolen his body. He was her dog! And he was forbidden from harming the queen. She was Skanga's spoils! And if he was a good dog, then perhaps he might become an elf again one day.

A distant tremor startled him from his memories. Something big was moving through the web of Albenpaths. In a thought, he was beside the path that an opened gate had caused to tremble. Hundreds of humans were on their way through the void. They emanated the smell of fear. Vahelmin spent some time delighting just in their fear before breaking through the spell protecting the path, and began marauding among the humans themselves. He proceeded with care. Some of the men wore mail shirts, and the iron burned when he touched it. Most wore no substantial armor and were armed with only an axe or spear. Killing them was easy.

The beast within him feasted, and he abandoned himself willingly to its cravings. A dozen or more bodies shriveled as he stole their light. Their horror sweetened the killings. But however many he killed, they barely quelled his hunger. It was like eating mussels. One slurped one down but enjoyed the pleasure of eating it for only a fleeting moment before tossing the empty shell aside.

The stream of humans seemed endless, and it soon pleased Vahelmin to only nibble at them, to steal only a portion of their life force. Fear could taste so deliciously diverse! Some of the men who saw him fell into panic and fled the Albenpath, only to become a meal for the shadow creatures that lurked beyond the protective spell.

Where were the men coming from? His curiosity overcame the hunger of the beast. Vahelmin followed the stream of humans back to its source. They were entering the void at a large Albenstar. He abandoned the path and lay watching and waiting. The beast sensed that there were still many humans outside. It wanted to go out, to spread panic and feast on their terror, but Vahelmin thought of the iron weapons. Beyond the gate, the humans would be fighting on known territory. Once they had overcome their initial fear, they could possibly cause him serious injury. He had to take them by surprise, lie in wait for them when the gathering broke up into smaller groups. He imagined how he would bring dread to their villages. Just a little patience, then he could cross the threshold to the human world in safety. It would be a most enjoyable hunt!

A NEW WORLD

Alfadas went from man to man. Most had not noticed at all that something had happened on their passage through the nothingness. They looked around uncertainly in the new world. They were in a clearing in a heavily snowed-in valley. All around them rose gently sloping, forested hills. The elves had pitched a number of silk tents, and colorful banners flapped in the wind, while overhead stretched a clear, blue sky. The sun stood at its zenith, but it gave no warmth. An icy wind blasted across the clearing, carrying ice crystals with it, fine as dust. Alfadas rubbed his hands together. The cold was already creeping into his bones, but the horror of what had happened on the Albenpath went deeper. He looked up at the large, gray menhir that marked the place where the Albenpaths crossed. Intertwined circles had been carved in the stone. If you looked at them for a long time, the lines began to dance before your eyes. He turned away. What had happened? With his father and Ollowain, he had passed through such gates many times when they had been on the search for Noroelle's son. And each time they had been afraid that the structure of time might shift. But he had never heard of anyone being attacked on the paths.

Close by, Mag crouched in the snow. He was talking insistently to his younger brother, Torad, and had placed one hand on his shoulder. The boy had his face buried in his hands.

"Something as cold as ice grabbed at my chest. I only saw it for a moment," Torad sobbed. "I . . . it was something big, white. It was just suddenly there. The man in front of me jumped to the side and disappeared in the darkness. It was . . ." He raised his head. His blond hair had become thinner and his face was deeply creased. He looked like a man who had seen forty summers, but Alfadas knew that Torad was only sixteen.

He turned away. No one had been able to tell him what had happened on the Albenpath. Even the elves appeared unsettled. Again and again, they had asserted that the ancients' paths were safe from attack by the creatures of the darkness. *Truth wears another face,* thought Alfadas bitterly.

Ragni came hurrying toward him. "I've spoken to all of the war jarls. We've lost seventeen men. And more than twenty are . . ." He looked searchingly at Alfadas, as if unable to find words for what had happened. "More than twenty have been changed," he finally said. "And there's another problem. Do you think the elves could open that gate again?"

"Why?"

"Come with me. I've taken them into one of the tents so that no one can see what happened. Someone has joined our ranks . . ." The jarl looked at Alfadas with concern. "We are going to be in big trouble."

"Could you perhaps—"

Ragni simply took him by the arm and pulled him along. "No word of this can get out. Lambi and his cutthroats would kill him." The war jarl led Alfadas into one of the tents. Inside were Dalla, the king's healer; Veleif, Horsa's skald; and a lone warrior. The third man's face was hidden in the shadows of the hood he wore pulled far down over his head.

"What the devil is this?" asked Alfadas angrily. He understood what Ragni meant. Horsa would think that he had stolen his skald and his bedmate.

"My king told me this morning that he no longer needs my services." Dalla had sky-blue eyes, and she looked unwaveringly at Alfadas. "You know why! That talk last night changed him. And it's good that it did. I would like to offer my services to your men."

Ragni grinned lasciviously. "You could have told me that right away."

"Not those services . . . I don't care what you think of me, but I'm no whore. I loved Horsa. And I can do far more than please a man in bed! I can stop heavy bleeding, stitch deep wounds, and restore the balance of vital fluids if your soldiers take ill."

"Just the sight of you is throwing my vital fluids out of balance."

"Enough, Ragni!" Alfadas snapped at his war jarl. "No one will lay a hand on this woman. She is welcome here, now that she is with us." He turned to Veleif. "And you, skald? What led you here?"

The poet smiled apologetically. "I fear my intentions are purely selfish. I have had enough of composing lies about Horsa. This campaign is the most heroic story to happen for generations. I simply have to be part of it. You will make history, Alfadas, and I will capture your deeds in beautiful words so that future generations can learn from your courage and valiance. I have experienced more wonders in less than two hours with your army than in the forty years before. I have walked on a golden path through the darkness, stood in an elven army camp, and heard your soldiers talk about a spirit horse they encountered. I will write a saga about you, Alfadas Elvenson."

The duke recoiled inwardly at the mention of that hated epithet. He could not send Veleif back. Lyndwyn, who had opened the portal, had disappeared shortly after the army arrived in Albenmark. With her had gone most of the elves that had set up the camp. There was no turning back . . . but of course, the skald did not know that.

"I am no friend of lies and shameless exaggeration, Veleif, and I am inclined to send you back along the path of light. Maybe you will run into that spirit horse for yourself. Now go out there and look at the men that beast attacked. See what it's like to age decades in the blink of an eye. Prove yourself as a truly great skald. Sing the songs of truth."

"I always sing—"

Alfadas jerked one hand through the air harshly, cutting off Veleif. "I know what you did for Horsa. I was there when he met the elven queen, and it did not take place inside a tent on a raft."

"The king told me what I was supposed to say. I did not do it gladly. You know—"

"I know that I will send you back on the same day you spread any more lies like that. Get out there, Veleif! Look reality in the face. Give it words to match all its horror and splendor. You're dismissed."

The skald looked at him indignantly. With a sweep of his cape, he left the tent.

Alfadas now turned to the unknown soldier. "And who are you?"

"Egil Horsason." He pushed the hood back.

Alfadas looked at the young man in dismay. Horsa's son! As if he did not have enough on his mind already.

Egil's face was slim and more sharply honed than his father's. There was something febrile about his blue eyes, which were surrounded by dark rings. He wore an expensive, closely meshed chain-mail shirt and finely woven clothes. Only the cloak he wore was made of coarse wool, like those the regular soldiers of his army wore.

"Does your father know that you are here?"

Egil shook his head. "Of course not. He would never have let me go off with you. He treats me like a slave and does everything he can to humiliate me."

Alfadas did not know what to say. He did not think much of Egil and had heard only bad things about him. "Why did you come?"

"To prove myself as a warrior. One day I will rule the Fjordlands, but I am well aware that many of the jarls despise me. I was never part of one of your campaigns, Duke, and I have never had the chance to show my mettle in combat. I want to earn the respect of the men, that's why I am here."

Alfadas looked to Ragni. "He can join me and my men," said the war jarl.

"That is not a good idea." Alfadas sighed. "I will soon have Lambi and his men's shackles removed. I have no use for manacled warriors. It is clear to you, isn't it, that they will be keeping a close eye on you, Ragni? Nothing that happens to or near you will escape them. They would kill Egil just to make you fall from Horsa's favor." Alfadas turned to the king's son. "You will go with the shepherds looking after our sheep. No one there knows you, and you will be safe. Ragni, dig up some clothes for the boy that would be suitable for that work. Our shepherds don't wear chain mail or fine cloth."

"You can't just—" Egil began, but he broke off when he saw the wrathful look on Alfadas's face.

"What can't I do? Give you orders? I am the duke. My word here is law. You want to be a warrior? Then learn to obey! That is the chief virtue of any soldier. Respect has to be earned, Egil. It is not something laid in your cradle at birth. Tell no one who you are. Let your deeds speak for you, and if you are lucky and survive the weeks ahead, then you will return to the Fjordlands a respected man. And if you should rebel against me, then rest assured that I will treat you like any other rebel. I did not want any king's son here with me, and I will act as if you don't exist. From now on, your name is Ralf! And Dalla! You have heard and seen nothing of what has just happened here!"

The healer nodded silently. In a fury, Alfadas left the tent. What was the callow young fool thinking? And how would Horsa react when he realized where his son was?

"Duke?" Ollowain was coming toward him. "Count Fenryl wishes to speak with you. He would like the soldiers to break camp already."

"Why is he in such a hurry?"

"A caravan is on its way from Rosenberg to Phylangan. They have left their homeland because we are unable to defend the small settlements of the Snaiwamark. Fenryl wants us to join with the refugees because they only have a small escort traveling with them. The count does not want to interfere with your decisions, of course, but his wife and child are part of the caravan."

"How far away are they?" Alfadas asked. Now that his anger at Egil had evaporated, he began to feel the cold again. He shivered and rubbed his arms.

"We could meet them about three days' march from here. It would mean only a minor detour, because the refugees have to get to Phylangan as well. It is the only way to reach the high plateau of Carandamon."

"Good, then we will go and find them. Better for the men if we break camp soon. We should not give them too much time to think about what happened on the way through the portal." Alfadas's teeth began to chatter.

"You should not underestimate the cold, my friend. It will be the end of you. Come with me!"

Ollowain led him behind the tents to an area of the camp where the elves' cargo sleds stood side by side. More than two hundred wolfhounds sat and lay close by in the snow. They were not tethered and were unsettlingly calm, attentively eyeing anyone who came close to them.

A little farther on, Lambi's men were gathered around him. The war jarl was addressing them from atop one of the sleds.

"I hope you've got that through your thick skulls, you brainless whore-mongers. The elves have loaned us these amulets! If you lose them or—what I'd say is more likely—try to steal them, then you will be in more trouble than you can choke down! The amulets will protect you from the cold out here. It's a kind of magic. Put it on and you can go whoring in a snowdrift without freezing your ass cheeks together. You won't need a blanket or clothes to keep out the cold.

"But don't go getting carried away. The amulets protect you only from the cold, but not from anything else! Got it? Good, then come and get 'em. And don't forget that we'll be giving them back as soon as we leave Albenmark. And if a troll smashes in one of your friends' skulls, or someone throws up his guts and drops dead or gets hit by lightning while he's emptying his bowels, then make sure you take his amulet. We have to give all of them back, and I do mean all!"

The soldiers pressed around Lambi, who handed out the precious trinkets from a small silver box. The amulets looked like very thin gold coins. Alfadas was surprised at how plain they had been kept, their only decoration a few wavy lines, a sun wheel, or a small shard of ruby. They were threaded on plain red leather cords.

One of the men, a heavyset fighter with a thick red beard, marched up to Lambi. He had tied his amulet onto his fur cap.

"My magic's busted," he snorted.

"You have to wear it against bare skin," Ollowain piped up. "If the amulet doesn't touch your body, the power in it can't unfold."

Lambi glanced over at the elf. "Damn me, I'd completely forgotten that." He turned back to his men. "Did you hear that? Wear this elven gold against your bare skin or the magic won't work."

"Don't matter where?" the bearded man asked with a grin.

"Stick it wherever it makes you happy. Be my guest. But if you give it back to me and it stinks, then I'll squeeze your balls until you've licked it so clean it glistens."

The bearded man laughed. "Hear that, everyone? Our war jarl is after my balls. Let's hope he finds a willing elf girl soon who's not put off by that thing on his face that no one's supposed to mention, or the horny buck'll screw us all, one after the other."

"Do they ever talk about anything else?" asked Ollowain in his native tongue.

Alfadas smiled. "They love invented heroics almost as much. If they had a copper piece for every lie they told, they'd all be rich men."

"And you want to have their chains removed?"

"Worried they might really tread too close to an elven woman?"

Now it was Ollowain who smiled. "If they reach for any elf with those grimy fingers, then they can pick them up one at a time afterward out of the snow. What do you think Lysilla or Silwyna would do with these men if they got too close?"

"We'll have problems with some of the men if they go too long without a woman," Alfadas replied seriously. "But that should not worry us today. Are the other war jarls handing out the protective amulets to their men, too?"

"It is all going according to your plan, Alfadas," Ollowain assured him.

Alfadas went to Lambi and took one of the elven amulets out of the silver box. The moment he picked up the charmed gold piece, an agreeable warmth flowed through him. *How much power would you have to have to create something like this?* he thought. *And how much wisdom must a race have not to use that power to create weapons . . .*

All the enchanted swords that the skalds of his race so loved to ascribe to the elves in their poems could, in reality, exist if the elves so wanted. And in that moment, Alfadas wished that this is what they had done. He knew that they would need every weapon they had to battle the trolls.

Even the elves must have understood that. Why else would they have accepted the help of humans?

THE WOLFPIT

O rgrim paced back and forth among blooming bushes and trees and shook his head in incomprehension.

"Useless!" he said angrily, and Mandrag nodded. The large main cave of the Wolfpit, at one time their rock fortress, had been turned into a flower garden. And although it was the middle of winter, the cavern was overflowing with color. It was uncomfortably warm. There in the cave, it was spring. It was not right to mock the unalterable passage of the seasons like that. One could not simply revolt against the laws of nature . . . nature would always win. A smart man lived according to its rules—every troll knew that!

"Nothing is like it was," said Mandrag bitterly. "What is the king's castle going to look like if they have already ruined the order of things so much here?" He pulled his mace from his belt and stomped heavily up to the statue of an elven prince with an arrogant smile. One swing smashed the marble nose. Over and over, Mandrag hammered the stone with the heavy weapon, wiping out the elf's face, until the head of the statue broke off and rolled into a bed of roses.

Orgrim and those with him—monstrous Gran; the shaman Birga; and his artillery chief, Boltan—watched the old troll in silence. They could all feel Mandrag's wrath. When they entered the Wolfpit, they were confronted with the sobering reality: none of their mountain castles would still look as they once had. The elves had spoiled everything! They had had centuries to wipe out every memory of the trolls, and at least there in the Wolfpit, they had done their work thoroughly. The murals of soot and blood were gone, as were the rune stones and the small niches in the rocks where a man could find the pleasure of a woman while the ancients sat by the fire and talked. All gone! And in their place were wide-open caves with gardens, cave roofs magically illuminated, palaces with countless rooms, and ponds, pools, and fountains everywhere.

Boltan had pressed his cheek to one of the large stone stelae that stood everywhere in the flower gardens. "There's water flowing through this," he said in surprise. Suddenly, his face lit up and he smiled. "They're using the geysers. The rock here is very warm. That's how they've made a spring garden in winter. There's no magic to it at all!"

Birga banged her bone staff on the ground angrily. "Don't talk about things you don't understand, Boltan! There is magic everywhere here. The entire natural order of things has been warped. They have twisted everything here to serve them!" The shaman pointed up to the cave ceiling. "How do you think they could light up stone like that, like daylight? And how did they even excavate the caves? Magic, magic, magic!" She laid one hand on the damaged statue. "Even here I can feel the magic. They softened the stone until they could shape it with their bare hands, like you can form clay into a figure. The land itself will help us drive the Normirga out. It has grown tired of the elves. It will shake them off like a dog shakes off its fleas."

Orgrim thought differently, but he had no desire to contradict Birga. The pack leader knew that it was smarter if they helped get rid of the Normirga. The land had put up with them for centuries . . . Why should that suddenly change now?

Their scouts had found the Wolfpit abandoned the day before. No elves remained inside the rocky fortress, but everywhere they looked, they found signs of a hasty departure. A half-finished tapestry still in the loom. Freshly slaughtered game hung in the cool caves close to the entrance of the Wolfpit to bleed out and be skinned. All of it pointed to one conclusion: the Normirga had been warned. They knew the trolls were coming despite the fact that Orgrim had done everything possible to complete their march through the Swelm Valley in secrecy. They had moved only at night, when not even the ghostlights danced in the sky, and had stayed hidden in dense forests during the short hours of daylight. The scouts had stolen up to the fortress during a snowstorm and had found everything abandoned. It seemed almost as if the elves had somehow miraculously sensed that the trolls had returned to their homeland. The order to abandon the fortress must have been given on the same day that the *Wraithwind* anchored at the entrance to the Swelm Valley.

The pack leader made his way down a set of steps between the garden terraces and looked around for the large table he had noticed the evening before. He lost his footing and almost fell. Cursing, he grasped one of the stone stelae that lined the stairway, spaced well apart. The steps were far too narrow and small—for trolls, practically an invitation to stumble.

The strange marble table stood in the center of an arbor of climbing roses. Blood-red petals were strewn across the snow-white stone, and an uncomfortably sweet fragrance hung in the air. Orgrim screwed up his nose and swept the petals aside. The tabletop was uneven. Winding lines had been gouged into the stone, and in many places, it seemed not to have been properly smoothed at all. There was no pattern to it; on the contrary, it seemed completely random. At first, Orgrim had thought that the stone plate had not yet been finished, and he turned away from it. Then, from the stairway, he looked back at it one more time. He needed the distance to realize what he was looking at—it was a map! Every mountain had been carefully modeled, and he recognized the coastline around Whale Bay and the mountain ridges that enclosed the Swelm Valley.

Mandrag came down the stairs. "So that's the map table you told me about." The old troll braced himself against the marble plate, breathing heavily. "That's what the land must look like to a bird if it could fly high enough." Mandrag studied the map briefly and pointed to a solitary mountain. "That there is the Wolfpit." He tensed and pointed to a much larger mountain that blocked a pass. "That is the goal of all our dreams: Kingstor, the biggest and most beautiful of our strongholds. From there, our ancestors ruled over the Snaiwamark."

"Branbeard will get his old throne back this very winter," said Orgrim excitedly. "The Kingstor is much closer than I thought."

"You're mistaken, my boy." The old man ran his finger over the stone plate, following a long arc around the low foothills of a mountain range. "This is the way we have to go. From here, eight or nine days."

Orgrim slid his finger over the uneven mountains. "What's here? You could cut the distance to Kingstor in half if you went through the mountains. They don't look very high, if the map is right. What's to stop us doing that?"

"The Maurawan! These are the southern foothills of the Slanga Mountains, and their country. It is a forest of oaks as high as the sky. Even in the short summer months, the ground beneath the trees lies in permanent darkness. Hardly a ray of light can make it through the dense canopy. And the paths in that forest are enchanted. They deceive you. You can walk around in circles for days without realizing it . . ." He cleared his throat. "That is, if you're lucky. If you're unlucky, then you'll get a Maurawan arrow in the back of your neck the moment you enter the forest. They say that even the trees are the allies of the elves there and will hide them from any prying eyes. The Maurawan are always around you when you go into their forest, but you can only see them if they want to be seen."

"Aren't they the smallest of all the elvenfolk, Mandrag? How long could they resist the fury of our pack?"

"The answer to that is easy: as long as there are trees in which they can hide themselves, you presumptuous whelp. It is impossible to engage the Maurawan in open combat. If they want to fight you, they lure you into their forest, but they will never surrender in there. They run through the branches of the big trees like wind. And the minute you think you're clear of the pests, the man next to you drops dead. The miserable bastards make it a point of pride never to have to shoot more than one arrow to kill—whatever they're hunting. Going into those forests means sacrificing warriors for nothing. I hope most of all that Branbeard has the wisdom to avoid them."

The two trolls looked over the map in silence. The Slanga Mountains were like an enormous wedge driven through the heart of the Snaiwamark. On the edge of the map rose a single mountain, higher than all the rest.

"What is that?" asked Orgrim curiously.

"Albentop." Mandrag quickly made a protective gesture. "A cursed place. The top of the mountain is hidden by cloud year-round. No one who has ever tried to go there has returned."

"Pack leader!" Brud, the head scout, came running across the garden. He wore an ice-encrusted fur across his shoulders, and his face was more darkly colored from the cold. Orgrim had sent him out the day before to go after the elves that had fled the Wolfpit.

Puffing for air, Brud came to a stop at the map table. "We have spotted the refugees. There are a few hundred of them, very few fighters. Their progress is very slow; I don't think they know where we are."

Orgrim looked at the scout in surprise. Why had the elves left the Wolfpit so suddenly if they had no idea how close to them their enemies were? "Did they see your men?"

"Of course not!" Brud cried, offended.

"Where are they exactly?" He pointed to the table. "Look, this is a map. This here is the Wolfpit, and there is the bay where we left the *Wraithwind.* Can you orient yourself to this?"

The scout gazed at the table for some time, occasionally letting out a soft grunt. "This is amazing . . . it's perfect! We have to take this with us. Even the mountains are shaped just as they are." He pointed to a small hillock with a star-shaped depression on one side. "We rested three hours in this hollow last night."

"Where are the elves?" Orgrim pressed.

"Here!" Brud pointed to the center of a plain. "They're moving in this direction. There's no doubt they want to get to Kingstor."

A good opportunity for a cheap victory, thought Orgrim eagerly. Maybe there were some important elves among them that they could hold as hostages, someone they could use to put pressure on the defenders at Kingstor. "If we leave immediately, where would we intercept them? Remember that our cargo sleds will slow us down."

Brud used his fingers to measure the distance to where the elves were just then. After a moment, he pointed to an area that lay close to a low chain of hills. "We'd catch up with them here. Even with the heavy sleds, you'd be there in three days, Pack Leader."

Orgrim thought for a moment. He wanted to bring as many elves back here with him as possible. They would make good slaves and would help get the Wolfpit back to its original state, as far as that was possible. And they would be a good source of fresh meat. "What does their caravan look like?"

"A few warriors on horseback. I don't know how those vermin can stand the cold. Most of them are riding on sleds, and some of those are even fitted with sails. They've got a long convoy of yaks, too, which is what is slowing them down, and a lot of kobold servants who do most of the work for them. Many of the elves are riding in fancy sleds with silver bells; you can hear them from a mile away. I saw a few dogsleds, too. Very mixed bunch. The whole procession is more than two miles long."

"Do you think you'd be able to force them to change direction without getting involved in an open battle, Brud?"

The scout took his time answering, which Orgrim appreciated.

"I'd need at least fifty men, Pack Leader, but I think I could outwit them. They'll probably fall into a panic at the first troll they see." He grinned broadly. "The way they're behaving, they can't suspect that we're hot on their heels."

Orgrim pointed to a small incision in the chain of hills. "This looks like a wide valley that cuts through the hills. Push them through there. We'll be waiting. When they find they're caught between us and your men, the gutless imps will surrender. I'll see you in three days on the battlefield!"

THE FOUR-LEGGED FORTUNE

There was something out there! Ole reached for his bow and quiver, which were leaning against the door. His dogs were restless. Not like they had been the night the elves came, but they ran back and forth in their cages. Something was creeping around the house or was close to the edge of the forest. He would not let himself be taken by surprise this time, Ole thought angrily. And he would take more than a club with him!

Maybe it was all the magic flying around up there on the Hartungscliff that was winding up the dogs, but it was better to check before he had someone else standing at his door. He threw over the bandolier that held his whips, slung the quiver over his shoulder, and picked up the bow.

The sun had set long before, but it was not yet fully dark. The ghostly faerylight was dancing across the heavens; its green glow deepened the shadows, but in open land, one could see quite well.

He found nothing close to the house, so he went to the kennels. The dogs were pacing restlessly along the sides of the large box kennels he had crafted for them.

"Killer! Skullbiter!" he snapped. He showed the bloodhounds the whips to remind them who their master was. "Come, we'll do the rounds."

For a moment, he thought about tying them to long leather leads but then thought better of it. Everyone in the village knew that it was better not to venture anywhere near his house at night. Ole was still furious about the afternoon, about how that half-elf bastard had been given an official send-off by the king. Couldn't anyone see what a self-important do-gooder Alfadas was? If *he*, Ole, owned a magic elven sword, then he could also be a duke! All that blah, blah, blah about heroes and eternal glory made Ole want to vomit. Most of those supposed heroes would shit in their pants if they ran into one of his dogs at night.

"Skullbiter, what are you doing? Out with you!" The bloodhound was lying flat against the floor of his kennel, although the gate stood wide open. Ole took the whip and thrashed angrily at the dog until the iron spikes tore the gutless beast's hide. Blood dripped from the twisted leather knots. Reluctantly, the dog crept out of its wooden box and looked up at him, its eyes filled with hate.

"Are you looking for a real hiding, you mongrel?" Ole raised the whip threateningly.

The dog ducked its head but did not let Ole out of its sight. *That's good,* thought Ole. *Let them fear me!* It would make them better dogs. Because they couldn't do anything to him, they would take out all their pent-up rage on anyone else close by.

"Well, Killer? You've already learned that lesson, haven't you? You don't try your luck with me anymore. Clever mutt. Now go! Search!" He cracked the whip in the air. "Show me what's got you so nervous."

Skullbiter replied with a deep, throaty snarl, while Killer ran off immediately into the night. Killer wasn't quite as big as the other dogs. He had short rust-brown fur and a long snout and looked far too nice to try to sell him as a bear dog. But he was brave and obedient. It had only taken a few decent beatings to raise him.

Skullbiter was a very different beast, from the same godforsaken litter as Blood. On the outside, the whole damned litter had the makings of monsters, but the dogs were so pigheaded that they were almost impossible to manage. And then there was that whole thing with Kadlin! To this day, it made Ole ill to think of how the cur had licked the little girl's face. Blood knew exactly what he was doing. He and his brother, Skullbiter, were too clever for dogs. Even the whip hardly helped. You had to be on your guard with them the whole time. They simply would not let themselves be beaten down. *But I've come out on top of every dog I've ever raised,* Ole thought proudly. When they came back, he would beat Skullbiter until his mangy black fur hung off his bones. He would see who had the stronger will around there!

They had come within twenty paces of the forest edge. Killer was standing as if rooted to the spot, staring into the undergrowth. Ole took an arrow out of his quiver and edged forward. There was something there. Big and pale, too big for a deer. It was white! By Luth's cock! A white elk, a cow! A fortune on four legs! White elks were so rare, the kind of thing anyone saw only once a century. At least, that's what people said. It could have been an exaggeration, of course, but it was certainly true that the hide of an animal like that was worthy of a king.

Ole already pictured himself going after the king. With a little luck, he would be able to catch the king still in Honnigsvald. His onward journey to Gonthabu had been delayed. Something had happened that had put the king in a rage, and he had sent men out in every direction, as if they were looking for something. Had he perhaps heard rumors about the white elk?

Whatever the truth, a lucky star was shining down on him, Ole of Firnstayn, that night! With the money from a hide like that, he could spend a whole month in Honnigsvald drinking and whoring!

"Go, Killer, Skullbiter! Drive the cow out of there!" But their quarry had got wind of them and was moving deeper into the forest. Ole let out a curse, then thought, *You won't get away from me.*

"Luth sent you here to me," he said aloud, but in such a friendly voice that Skullbiter looked up at him suspiciously, not recognizing the tone at all. "You might as well stop! Doesn't matter where you run, I'll get you, so why not save us all a lot of running around and stop right where you are."

Killer charged off enthusiastically into the forest. Barking furiously, he tried to cut off the elk's path. Ole had a lot of difficulty following the dog through the undergrowth, but the cow elk seemed to have no trouble with it at all. And she moved so cleverly that she did not even reveal where she was with the breaking of branches. Ole stopped several times and listened. He heard Killer's excited yapping moving farther away, indeed, but he did not hear the snapping of twigs that one actually *had* to hear from an animal as heavy as an elk. Ole also found himself able to pick up its trail. It was like the beast was bewitched.

In places, he saw the imprint of Killer's paws in the muddy forest floor. Good dog! He would get a good chunk of loin. He hoped the dog did not bring the cow to bay alone and ruin the valuable hide with his attacks.

The forest had grown quiet now. The noise of Killer's pursuit had stopped. Ole cursed inwardly. With every passing moment that he did not hear the elk, the probability grew that she had escaped him.

His stalking had led him deep into the forest. Not far away, he recognized a group of stone blocks that were often used by hunters as a campsite. Ole thought about lighting a fire and spending the night there, returning first thing in the morning. The way through the dark forest was tricky and arduous when one was not caught up in the fever of the hunt.

"Skullbiter?" The pigheaded cur had disappeared into the underbrush, although he had stayed close to Ole most of the time.

The hunter blew on his fingers. They were dark with the cold. He leaned his bow against a tree and clapped his hands against his chest. He had been holding the weapon so tightly that his fingers had cramped.

"Skullbiter! To heel! Where are you, mongrel?" Nothing moved. Had the dog taken its chance and bolted? Ole stomped over to the rocks where the forest there was not as close, and one had a good view of the night sky. Here and there, stars gleamed beyond the veils of green faerylight. The rocks had a gray-green hue. The old fireplace looked like a festering wound in the forest floor. The night was deathly still, without the slightest breath of wind to rock the bare branches of the trees.

Ole looked around suspiciously. Something was off. The campsite, that night, was not welcoming at all. Uncertain about whether he should stay or turn back, he leaned down to check the niche beneath the rocks where there was always a supply of dry brushwood. It was a long hollow that had probably been carved out of the rock long ago by a now-dry spring. In heavy rain or storms, one slim man could find refuge there from the raging elements. Whoever last used the spot always restocked it with a fresh supply of firewood before moving on, so that the next wanderer could kindle himself a fire.

Ole reached into the low gap and instantly jerked his hand back. He had touched something dry and furry! He quickly drew his long hunting knife and waited. Whatever lay there in the niche did not move. Maybe a hunter had left his canteen behind or a hunting bag made of hide. It was foolish to make such a fuss about nothing!

Ole looked around uncertainly. He saw no one close by. Finally, he worked up his courage and reached into the gap again. He tugged at whatever it was until, with a jerk, it came free and slipped out onto the ground in front of him. The dried, shriveled corpse of an animal . . . its flews were pulled up, revealing long fangs that glimmered greenly in the faerylight. Then Ole saw the choke band, and he understood what he was looking at.

"Killer?" he whispered, and stroked the short fur. The dog looked smaller than ever. Something had melted away his flesh until all that remained was skin and bone.

Killer had clearly still been alive when he had looked for sanctuary in the hollow. He had pulled his legs in close to his body, and his snout poked forward defensively. But what had he been hiding from?

If Ole had not seen the dog himself just over an hour before, he would have sworn black-and-blue that the cadaver in front of him was of an animal that had been dead for many, many weeks. Killer still felt warm. Whatever had killed him must still be very close by!

Ole sensed now that he was being watched. Something was behind him—he had heard a noise, very low, like the scratch of a paw on stone. He swung around, his dagger raised to fend off any danger. Between the rocks stood Skullbiter. The large dog lifted its head, sniffing the air. Ole had never been so happy to see the stubborn beast!

"We should get out of here, my beauty. We don't want to end up like Killer!"

The big dog looked at him as if sizing him up. Its eyes were black pools, and in the dim light, Ole could clearly see the scars on its snout. Skullbiter let out a sharp snort, then turned and trotted away.

"You can't just run off, you misbegotten . . ." Ole ran after the dog.

Skullbiter had disappeared into the undergrowth. Ranks of thorns tore at Ole's clothes. What a miserable night! Fairies or goblins or some other magical creatures had probably come through the portal and were getting up to their mischief in the Fjordlands.

Uncertain what his best course of action was, Ole stopped. Just there, the forest rose along the flank of a mountain. In some places, bare rock broke through the forest floor. Behind him, the mountain dropped away steeply. Roots half covered in leaves made for treacherous snares . . . it was the height of foolishness, traipsing around there at night with no light.

Just at the edge of his vision, he noticed a dull glow. Ole turned toward it. Fairies, he was sure of it! He knew all about them; he'd heard all the stories about the malignant little cousins of the elves. Taunting lone travelers was their favorite pastime.

"You won't get me!" he murmured to himself. "Not me!"

There it was again! Something moved silently between the trees. And then he saw a massive white body behind a bush. The elk cow! It must have been moving through a depression in the ground. That was the solution. There were no fairies there, just a terrified dog breeder. Ole laughed softly at himself. The faerylight was making him see ghosts—every child knew it could do that. People were known to go insane when the green light stretched across the skies. But now his lucky star had returned. There was no reason to be afraid. He . . . Ole could have cursed aloud. His bow! He had been too startled by the husk of Killer to realize until just now that he had left it at the campsite! Luth was determined to make a fool of him! Without his bow, there was nothing he could do to the elk. It would hardly just stand there if he went over and tried to cut its throat with his dagger. But maybe he could get close enough to try a throw? If the elk was wounded, then he would be able to track it more easily.

Ole crept forward cautiously. He managed to get within ten paces of his quarry without the elk cow turning her head in his direction. A breeze had come up and was blowing toward him. It could not pick up his scent! Was Luth on his side after all?

The elk cow was standing behind a low, thorny thicket. Maybe, with a leap, he could get onto its back and stab the dagger past the backbone and directly into its brain. It would drop dead on the spot, and its hide would hardly be soiled by blood at all. Ole knew very well that that was not how one hunted elk and that an attack so daring stood little chance of success, but maybe fortune was truly smiling on him.

Five paces. Inch by inch, he moved forward. No mistakes now! A cracking twig, a stone rolling down the mountain—something small like that was all it would take to spoil the hunt.

Two paces. Ole had almost reached the patch of thorns. He tensed, ready to jump. The elk cow's head was still down. It suspected nothing of its fate.

Ole grinned. The thicket was quite low, hardly higher than his knees. The elk cow had to be standing in a ditch on the other side. Ole pushed off, leaping over it. At the same moment, the elk looked up. Its head was strange. Too slim. And its teeth . . . with a spring, the beast dodged aside. Unbelievably fast.

Ole's heart missed a beat. There was no ditch behind the thorns! Tumbling head over heels, he crashed down a steep slope covered with boulders. Unable to break his fall, he slammed into tree trunks and rocks. He felt as if a band of robbers were thrashing him with clubs. He let go of his valuable dagger and did his best to protect his head with his arms. A blow to his back knocked the air out of his lungs. He couldn't breathe. He tumbled faster and faster. His nose was bleeding. Suddenly, something snatched at his left foot, and his fall ended with a tremendous jolt. He was swung around, and his shinbone slammed against something hard. He clearly heard a dry crack, felt a searing pain shoot through his leg. He screamed out his agony in the forest; it felt as if he'd been hit with an axe. Tears poured over his cheeks, and he was washed with nausea. He tried to sit up, but his foot was still caught—he realized that it was trapped in a root. Painfully bright lights danced before his eyes. He could only vaguely see what had happened to his leg. A broken branch seemed to have bored through his calf.

Ole was panting with the pain. After some time, he managed to sit up. He had to pull the damned branch out of the wound, then bind it with his belt. But his leg was twisted in an odd way. His foot, still trapped by the root, was turned out at a strange angle. At the sight, a new wave of nausea came over him. He closed his eyes and reached for the accursed branch with both hands, pulled on it with all the strength he could muster. The pain slashed him like a whip. He bellowed like an animal, gasped, cried. It was as if someone had jammed a red-hot iron bar into his leg. Through his tears, he gaped at his blood-smeared hands and then at his leg. It was no branch protruding from the torn skin. It was his shinbone.

Suddenly, the air around him grew colder. The elk cow was standing beside him on the steep bank. No . . . now Ole saw his mistake. This thing was as big as an elk cow, but that was all it had in common with an elk. Its head reminded him of a huge dog's head. Finger-long teeth lined its jaws. And it was translucent. Pale, ghostly light emanated from it.

For a long time, the creature merely stood there and looked down on him. Ole had the impression that it was feeding on his pain. Finally, it lowered its head and approached a little closer.

Its jaws snapped at the injured leg. It felt as if an icy winter wind touched him. The creature's teeth sank into his flesh but did not injure it. Something golden shimmered between its fangs. The beast jerked its head back, tore something out of him. A snake? No. It looked more like an umbilical cord of golden light.

All his joints began to ache. Half unconscious, Ole felt for the bandolier that held his whips. The pain in his joints burned more and more. At the same time, he was overcome by a weariness as if he had not slept for days. It took all his strength of will just to pull a whip out of the leather loops of the bandolier.

"Everything that looks like a dog fears me." His voice was no more than a hoarse whisper. It sounded like an old man's voice. The creature looked up momentarily. With a weak swing, Ole flicked the whip at its snout. There was a hissing noise, as if he had thrown water onto hot coals. The thong passed straight through the creature's ghostly body. Small sparks gleamed. The creature leaped back in fright and let out a pitiful wail. Then it dashed away and vanished in seconds between the trees.

"I told you! I can get the better of any dog," Ole murmured. Then he sank back on the earth. He felt as weak as an old man, and a pounding pain tormented his leg. He tried again to sit up, but his strength failed him. He knew it was hopeless to cry for help out there. No one would hear him.

Like some spawn of the night itself, Skullbiter was suddenly standing before him. The large black dog looked at him coldly. Then it lunged forward with its misshapen head. Its jaws closed over the bone jutting from the open wound, and with a furious snarl, it shook Ole's leg back and forth.

Ole's voice broke down in shrill screaming. He heard the bone crack between the dog's monstrous teeth. Blood spattered his face. He wished he would lose consciousness, but the pain kept him awake.

Skullbiter's fangs were dug deep into Ole's flesh. Something else cracked in the wound. The huge dog pushed its front feet into the soft earth with all its considerable strength. Suddenly, there was a jolt, and Skullbiter tumbled backward. He had bitten through the leg. Without letting Ole out of its sight, the dog crouched down and tore the flesh from the bone. Blood had gathered in the deep scars on its snout, making them look like fresh wounds.

Ole's screams had lost all trace of humanity. His fingers clutched at the forest floor. He tried to drag himself away, though he knew he could not escape the hound, though he knew that the dreadful meal was very far from over.

APPENDICES

DRAMATIS PERSONAE

Aesa—Daughter of the farmer at Carnfort Farm

Aileen—Lover of Farodin; in Ollowain's parable, a legendary archer in the saga of Nazirluma and Aileen

Alathaia—Elven princess of Langollion; in a feud with Emerelle; it is said that she has walked the dark paths of magic

Alfadas Mandredson—Jarl of Firnstayn and prince of the Fjordlands in times of war; son of Mandred; grew up in Emerelle's royal household in Albenmark

Alfeid—Washerwoman in Firnstayn; mother of Halgard

Alvias—Elven chamberlain of Emerelle's court; commonly known as Master Alvias

Andorin—Elven healer in Emerelle's court

Antafes—Centaur warrior; member of Emerelle's ceremonial escort in Vahan Calyd

Asla—Wife of Alfadas

Atta Aikhjarto—Souled oak tree that saved the life of the hero Mandred

Audhild—Wife of the farmer at Carnfort Farm

Birga—Troll shaman; foster daughter of Skanga

Boltan—Troll artillery chief

Branbeard—King of the trolls

Brud—Scout in the service of Skanga

Dalla—Healer in the service of King Horsa

Dolmon—Kobold in Phylangan

Dumgar—Troll duke of Mordrock; adviser to King Branbeard

Egil—Son of King Horsa; heir to the throne of the Fjordlands

Eginhard von Daluf—Chronicler of King Horsa

Eleborn—Prince beneath the waves; ruler of the Albenkin that live in the oceans of Albenmark

Emelda—One of the names used by humans for Emerelle

Emerelle—Elven queen of Albenmark; one of the oldest beings in her world

Erek Erekson—Fisherman in Firnstayn; father of Asla

Fahlyn—Young elf woman from Phylangan; a member of the Farangel clan

Farodin—Legendary elven hero

Fenryl—Elven count of the Normirga

Finn—Oldest son of the farmer at Wehrberghof

Firn—God of winter in the pantheon of the Fjordlanders

Fredegund—Slave woman in Firnstayn

Freya—Wife of Mandred; mother of Alfadas

Galti—Fisherman in Firnstayn

Godlip—Jarl of Honnigsvald

Gondoran—Boatmaster of Queen Emerelle in Vahan Calyd; master of the waters

Gran—Exceptionally gigantic troll warrior; rival of Orgrim

Gundar—Luth priest in Firnstayn

Halgard—Blind girl from Firnstayn; daughter of Alfeid

Hallandan—Elven prince of Reilimee

Horsa Starkshield—King of the Fjordlands

Isleif—Wilderness farmer; lives on a farmstead in the vicinity of Firnstayn

Iwein—The most important livestock breeder in Firnstayn

Kadlin—Daughter of Alfadas and Asla

Kalf—Fisherman and jarl of Firnstayn

Kodran—Ferryman at Honnigsvald; oldest of three brothers

Lambi—Jarl from the Fjordlands; banished by King Horsa

Landoran—Elven prince of the Snaiwamark and Carandamon; father of Ollowain

Loki—Orphan boy in the care of Svenja

Luth—Weaver of fate; in the Fjordlands, he is the god who weaves the strands of life into a wonderful tapestry

Lyndwyn—Granddaughter of Shahondin

Lysilla—Elf woman from the Normirga race

Mag—Ferryman at Honnigsvald; younger brother of Kodran

Mahawan—Elf; once lover of Emerelle

Mandrag—Brother in arms of the troll king; interim ruler of the trolls after their diaspora

Mandred—Legendary hero among humans and elves; father of Alfadas; jarl of Firnstayn

Maruk—Pack leader of the trolls in the service of Skanga

Matha Murganleuk—Souled magnolia tree in Emerelle's palace in Vahan Calyd

Melvyn—Son of Silwyna and Alfadas

Mjölnak—Warhorse of King Horsa

Murgim—Kobold from Phylangan

Nazirluma—Legendary king of the Lamassu

Nessos—Centaur warrior; member of Emerelle's ceremonial escort in Vahan Calyd

Nomja—Elf woman; archer; once part of Emerelle's guard

Norgrimm—God of war in the pantheon of the Fjordlanders

Noroelle—Elven sorceress sent into exile by Emerelle

Nuramon—Legendary elven hero

Olav—Woodsman from Sunhill

Ole—Dog breeder in Firnstayn; uncle of Asla

Ollowain—Swordmaster to Queen Emerelle; a member of the Normirga

Orgrim—Pack leader, then prince of the Nightcrags; most competent commander of the trolls

Orimedes—Centaur prince of Windland

Osaberg—Legendary king of the Fjordlands

Oswin—Young jarl from the Fjordlands; standard-bearer of King Horsa

Ragnar—Warrior under Jarl Lambi

Ragni—A bodyguard of King Horsa; accompanied Alfadas on various military campaigns

Ralf—Name used by Egil Horsason to serve in Alfadas's army

Rolf Svertarm—Warrior under Jarl Lambi

Ronardin—Elven keeper of the Mahdan Falah

Sandowas—Elf from Phylangan; emissary in the service of Landoran

Sanhardin—Elven warrior; a bodyguard of Queen Emerelle

Sansella—Daughter of Hallandan, the elven prince of Reilimee

Senwyn—Elf; oldest of the Farangel clan

Shahondin—Elven prince of Arkadien

Shaleen—Wife of Count Fenryl

Sigvald—Wainwright from Honnigsvald

Silwyna—Elf woman; archer from the race of the Maurawan

Skanga—Important troll shaman

Slangaman—Legendary troll king

Slavak—Kobold servant; part of Shahondin's household, then in the service of King Branbeard

Snowwing—Falcon of Count Fenryl

Solveig—Woman from Firnstayn

Svanlaug—Goddess of victory; daughter of Norgrimm

Svenja—Aunt of Asla in Firnstayn

Taenor—Young elven sorcerer from Phylangan

Thorfinn—Farmer at Wehrberghof

Tofi—Youngest son of the farmer at Wehrberghof

Torad—Ferryman at Honnigsvald; younger brother of Kodran

Ulf—A bodyguard of King Horsa

Ulric—Son of Alfadas and Asla

Urk—Troll with a weakness for squirrels

Usa—Slave woman in Firnstayn

Vahelmin—Son of Shahondin; famous hunter

Veleif Silberhand—Skald in the service of King Horsa

Yilvina—Elf woman; a bodyguard of Queen Emerelle

Yngwar—Warrior under Jarl Lambi

LOCATIONS

Albenmark—Name for the entire physical world of the Albenkin

Albentop—Mysterious mountain in the north of Albenmark

Arkadien—An important principality in Albenmark

Carandamon—High plateau; permanently frozen; the original homeland of the Normirga

Drusna—Forested kingdom in the human world

Eaglescarp—A mountain fortress in Carandamon

Firnstayn—Small village in the Fjordlands

Gonthabu—Harbor in the south of the Fjordlands; residence of King Horsa Starkshield

The heartland—Province in Albenmark; location of Queen Emerelle's court

Honnigsvald—Small town about half a day's ride south of Firnstayn

Iolid Mountains—Mountain range on the edge of the heartland

Iskendria—Important trade center in the human world; famous for its library; notorious for its cruel city god

Kandastan—Legendary city/kingdom in the east of the human world

Kingdom beneath the waves—Principality on the bottom of the sea in Albenmark

Kingstor—The trolls' name for Phylangan

Langollion—Island to the southeast of Whale Bay

Mahdan Falah—The world bridge; inside the Skyhall of Phylangan

Phylangan—Also known as the stone garden; a fortress that watches over the entrance to the high plain of Carandamon

Reilimee—Important harbor city of the elves

Rosecarn—Elven settlement on the western end of the Swelm Valley; known to the trolls as the Wolfpit

Shalyn Falah—The white bridge; one of the entrances to the heartland

Slanga Mountains—Homeland of the secretive Maurawan race of elves

Snaiwamark—Original home of the trolls

Sunhill—Small mountain village on the reindeer path

Swelm Valley—Valley in the Snaiwamark that opens into Whale Bay; the troll fortress known as the Wolfpit lies at its western end

Vahan Calyd—Harbor city on the Woodmer; founded by the displaced race of the Normirga

Whale Bay—Large bay on the east of the Snaiwamark

Windland—Steppe landscape in the north of Albenmark; populated mainly by centaurs

The Wolfpit—Troll fortress on the western end of the Swelm Valley; known to the elves as Rosecarn

The Woodmer—Shallow sea in the south of Albenmark

GLOSSARY

Albenkin—Collective term for all the races created by the Alben (elves, trolls, centaurs, and so on); the humans refer to them as Albenfolk

Albenpaths—Magical paths

Albenstars—Intersection of two to seven Albenpaths; Albenstars are the entry points to the Albenpaths

Apsaras—Water nymphs

Bandag—Red-brown juice obtained from the roots of the dinko bush; used by the Albenkin to paint their bodies

Centaurs—A race in Albenmark; half horse, half elf-like

Devanthar—Half-man, half-boar creature; archenemy of the elves

Dinko bush—Bush from which the Albenkin extract bandag

Elves—The last of the races created by the Alben

Farangel—Elven clan; part of the Normirga race in Phylangan

Fauns—A goat-legged race in Albenmark

Gry-na-Lah—A cursed or enchanted arrow that flies until it kills the victim whose name is written on its shaft

Holde—One of the kobold clans of Albenmark; they live in the mangrove swamps near Vahan Calyd; their princes call them the masters of water

Ironbeards—Carved wooden figures into which one drives items made of iron as offerings to the god Luth

Jarl—Title of the leader of a village in the Fjordlands; elected anew each year

Lamassu—A race in Albenmark; body of a bull, the wings of a giant eagle, and a bearded face

Liburna—A small galley, designed to be fast and light.

Lutins—A race of fox-headed kobolds famed for their crude pranks and skill with magic

Maurawan—A race of elves that lives in the forests of the Slanga Mountains

Minotaurs—A race in Albenmark; steer-headed giants

Normirga—A race of elves that lives on the high plateau of Carandamon and the Snaiwamark

Oreaden—Shy mountain nymphs that live primarily in the Iolid Mountains

Riverbank sprites—Small, winged race of Albenkin

Shi-Handan—Soul eaters; creatures summoned by Skanga

Summoners—A subgroup of the trolls with the ability to form a spiritual connection with wild animals, to attract them and make them subservient to their will

Trolls—A warlike race in Albenmark; banished to the human world by Queen Emerelle

Warmaster—Elven title for the commander in chief of their military forces

Windsingers—A special group of elven sorcerers

Yingiz—Mysterious race driven by the Alben into the void between the worlds

ACKNOWLEDGMENTS

D espite the popular cliché of the author as a lone figure ensconced in a garret, hidden away from the world, the truth is that this book, at least, would probably never have been finished without the assistance of a great many unseen elves and kobolds. Those who helped me in my struggles with Albenmark were Menekse, who gave me my freedom when it was necessary; Elke, who knows draft horses better than I do, even though she can't stand them; Karl-Heinz, who dispensed advice freely, even at midnight; Eymard, who piloted me through the shallows of specialized nautical terminology; Gregor and Bettina, who were where I was not; and my editors Martina Vogl, who never lost faith, and Angela Kuepper, who ensured among other things that my readers were spared tapeworm sentences like this one.

Bernhard Hennen
December 2005

ABOUT THE AUTHOR

B ernhard Hennen studied archaeology, history, and German studies at Cologne University, and traveled extensively while working as a journalist. With Wolfgang Hohlbein, Hennen published his first novel, *Das Jahr des Greifen*, in 1994. Since then, his name has appeared on dozens of historical and fantasy novels, as well as numerous short stories. Hennen has also developed the story line for a computer game and has worked as a swordsman for hire in medieval shows and as a Santa Claus mercenary. *Elven Winter* is the second book in The Saga of the Elven, following *The Elven*. He currently lives with his family in Krefeld, Germany.

ABOUT THE TRANSLATOR

Born in Australia, Edwin Miles has been working as a translator, primarily in film and television, for more than twelve years. After undergraduate studies in his hometown of Perth, he received an MFA in fiction writing at the University of Oregon in 1995. While there, he spent a year working as fiction editor on the literary magazine *Northwest Review*. In 1996, he was short-listed for the prestigious Australian/ Vogel's Literary Award for young writers for a collection of short stories. After many years living and working in Australia, Japan, and the United States, he currently resides in his "second home" in Cologne, Germany, with his wife, Dagmar, and two very clever children.